HYBRID ZONE

REVELATION

C.E. GLINES

To the one who made me.

CHAPTER 1

I USED TO THINK LEAPING REQUIRED no faith at all. That the phrase, "A leap of faith," was an oxymoron. Something people said to make them feel better about dismissing their common sense. It completely ran afoul of yet another common phrase, "Look before you leap." You weren't supposed to look, decide you had no idea where you'd land, and then hurl yourself over the edge anyway. That wasn't faith. That was crazy.

Hello, Crazy. You can call me Macy.

What the heck was wrong with me? My analysis of the phrase had been seriously flawed. Now that I was the one plunging headlong into the unknown, I discovered I had neglected one very important fact. Leaping required all kinds of faith. Faith that I had apparently left on the roof, right up there next to my common sense.

Why had I never seen this before? Slicing through the air with the hard reality of the ground looming below, it was crystal clear now. It took me all of two seconds to realize I had better be rock solid in my belief that cats always landed on their feet. Either that, or they would be scraping me off the cement.

Banish that thought, I scolded myself. The fact that cats always landed on their feet was indisputable, grounded in empirical science. Didn't even require much effort on my part to believe. And since I was part feline now, it followed that I would land on my feet too. I was sure I would have taken comfort in my reasoning if not for the overwhelming panic that gripped my heart and tore my breath away. Try screaming with no air in your lungs. It sounded like I was trying to cough up a hairball.

Unexpectedly, my head snapped back as the world slowed. Panting erratically as my breath returned in a whoosh, I refocused my eyes on the ground. The upward rush had definitely stalled, and the wind in my face had disappeared. I was now floating, suspended in air that was thick, gelatinous. Balling my fist up, I felt the air squeeze through my fingers as if I had a handful of jello, but when I opened my hand, it looked just as empty as before. Then there was the weirdness of my hair drifting listlessly around me at all angles. I blew at a strand crisscrossing my face and watched it serenely float away. Somewhere in the background, I was sure the Twilight Zone theme song was playing.

Well, that's it then, I thought. I have officially rounded the corner on crazy. We had not only met, but we were now members of the same team. I had never pictured it ending this way. Not that I had pictured my end at all, but if I had, this wouldn't have been it.

Strange. I didn't feel any different, like I was one short of a six pack, but what else could it be? Some sort of panic induced delusion? An attempt by my brain to shield me from the upcoming impact? My mind raced as I grappled for understanding. And what was with this pose? My arms, stretched out wide and bent slightly at the elbows, resembled a pair of bat wings. My feet were tucked tightly beneath me as if I were preparing to launch. Which was silly, considering that stroke of genius had already happened on the roof. Couldn't my delusional mind have come up with something better? I was cat not bat. Though I would take whichever one saw me safely on the ground.

I don't know, maybe I wasn't crazy. Maybe I was just stuck—in stuff that didn't actually have any sticking power. Okay, not the best explanation, but something was going on. Something had brought me to this point. Now that I was going nowhere fast, I might want to consider what that was. Identify exactly what had caused me to determine that flinging myself from the roof of a building sounded like a good idea? I didn't even recall actually thinking about it. It just sort of happened. One minute on the roof, the next, bang! Plummeting through the air. There had to be a trigger in there somewhere.

Working my way through the last few minutes on the roof prior to blast off proved to be a painful exercise. I could still smell Adam's blood, remember the feeling of loss, and Kenny. His expression haunted my thoughts. The fierce desire for retribution painted on his face matched the belief shining in his eyes that I could give him that. He hadn't been alone in his belief either. It had radiated from all of them. That's what had ignited my heart and legs into action, their faith in me.

But I couldn't lay the blame solely on them. While their support had created strength in me, it had hurt too. A wrenching, gut twisting kind of hurt. They had looked at me like I was some kind of superhero that was going to save the day. I was no superhero—wow, that was ironic, considering my current position. But superhero pose aside, I just didn't know if I had what it would take to make everything alright again. Some things, I knew, could never be made right.

I had to try though. Not because I was responsible for what was broken. I was playing catch up just like they were. I had to try because as much as they needed me to repair the smashed pieces of their lives, I needed it too. It just wasn't in my nature to walk away. A little factoid about myself that I was forced to accept thanks to the last week of my life.

Forging relationships with the Colony hybrids had changed me in ways I was just now beginning to recognize. My old M.O. of keeping my head down and surviving, something that was normal, easy even, didn't work anymore. Surviving this last week had required something totally different, and it had awakened something in me that I couldn't turn off now. Call it some sort of maternal instinct, kick butt survival skills or label it what you will, but it was here to stay. I couldn't imagine going back now.

One week, that's all it took to rewrite the script for my entire life.

All thoughts but those of the fast rising ground fled as time caught up with me. Suddenly plummeting downward again, I could scarcely breathe as the earth rushed towards me. My stomach followed in the next beat, lodging in my throat and adding an exclamation point to the heartbeat hammering in my ears. Following some unconscious instinct, my legs stretched to meet the ground, and my arms curved upward. I tried to guesstimate the seconds until impact in my head, but I was pretty sure it translated into a squeal on the outside.

As soon as my feet made contact with the ground, I gasped loudly. The palms of my hands followed next, slapping the ground as my knees collapsed beneath me. Shaking in my semi crouch, my stomach seemed oblivious to the fact that we were no longer falling. Not helping was the taste of blood in my mouth as a result of the contact between my teeth and tongue.

Note to self…safely tuck tongue out of the way when leaping from tall buildings.

With claws dug deep into the earth, I drank in oxygen as though I hadn't breathed at all during the trip, another thing my rebellious stomach didn't appreciate. Spitting out the unsavory mixture of blood and saliva filling my mouth, I couldn't stop the combination burp and wretch that bolted from my lips. At least, I immediately felt better.

Soft thuds behind me signaled the arrival of my teammates. Dipping my head upside down to look back at them revealed Kenny a short distance behind me. Even upside down, I couldn't mistake the wide grin pasted on his face.

"Feeling okay, Doc?" he teased.

His face told me that he was never going to let me forget this, but I returned his grin anyway. What was a deeply gross burp between friends? And acquaintances, I added upon seeing the rest of the smirks greeting me. Apparently, they'd all witnessed my less than graceful landing. I could only imagine what my last few feet had looked like to them. More fodder for the blooper reel.

The sound of a door opening and closing in the clinic wiped the smiles from all our faces. As the team gathered around me, I conducted a quick headcount. Every member was accounted for, and I was certain Kenny hadn't missed any survivors. That meant whoever was in there didn't belong. Them or their flashlight.

"Do you normally carry a flashlight on your person just in case the lights go out?" Kenny asked.

No, I didn't, I thought as I shook my head. "They were tipped off," I guessed, an even worse development than someone accidentally showing up. "Let's go," I whispered.

I led us to the opposing building and waited until everyone was pressed snuggly against its side. From there, we watched the intruder's progress through the interior of the clinic. The firsthand view of the carnage didn't seem to slow them down, but they hadn't reached the worst of it yet. Still, most people would have flinched already.

Kenny caught my eye, his face pulling into a frown at the lack of response we were observing. I mirrored his expression as I nodded in agreement. The lack of reaction was concerning. It meant the intruder was seasoned or at least schooled enough not to react out of fear. I held my breath in anticipation as they reached the lobby. There was a brief pause, but no shriek of terror or erratic slash of light from a flashlight suddenly abandoned. We were definitely dealing with a professional. With long red hair?

The briefest glimpse of red hair swirled through the light reflected by the lobby doors. Uneasiness swept over me as the red hair sparked something in my memory.

"Did you see?" I whispered to Kenny who had crouched silently at my side.

He nodded while keeping his gaze trained on the clinic doors.

"Did you recognize them?"

He gave a quick jerk of his head.

Frustrated by my growing agitation, I craned my head around in search of more information that would explain this feeling. After a moment of fruitless searching, I gave up and looked at Kenny again. It had been him who had initially informed me of the intruder.

Leaning into him, I asked, "Was there just the one?"

His face remained blank as he nodded.

Sitting back on my haunches, I studied his determined attempt to avoid my eyes. Why had he been so insistent that we had to leave then? When he'd told me that someone was coming, I had assumed it was someones, plural. One person did not constitute a threat. My face went slack when the reason dawned on me. He'd been protecting me, removing me from the painful situation that had me paralyzed. If not for him, I might still be kneeling on that roof, engulfed by the loss of Adam and in no kind of shape to lead this group.

When I shifted uncomfortably, he slowly lifted his eyes to mine. Guilt clouded his normally sharp features, but he had nothing to feel guilty about. Me, on the other hand...I was in his debt. Again.

"Thank you," I mouthed silently.

He dipped his head, embarrassed by the recognition. Or rather, having been caught caring.

Gently shaking my head side to side, I was astounded and grateful to Kenny for his intervention. And I couldn't help but think that for the seventeen year old that he was, he was way too insightful.

Turning my attention back to the clinic, I grimaced at the inspection taking place. I couldn't shake the feeling that I'd seen that hair somewhere before. And the more I thought about it, the more important it seemed that I remember.

Frowning as the sensation continued to gnaw at me, I leaned into Kenny again. "I have to go back in," I whispered.

He acted like he didn't hear me.

"Kenny?"

"Why?" he asked coolly.

"Not sure," I said, which was true. I just knew that I couldn't leave here without finding out who it was and why it mattered.

"Is this one of your hunches?"

The tone of accusation in his voice surprised me. It was no secret that he'd been on the receiving end on more than one occasion. Obviously, it still rankled as further evidenced by the challenge in his raised brow.

"You know, I've saved your butt more than once due to a hunch," I reminded him sternly.

His lips pressed into a thin line. "One time you bailed me out. Beyond that, there is no way of knowing."

"Are you insane?" I hissed. "I have stopped your crazy schemes at least a dozen times."

"Exactly," he snarled. "You don't know if they would have succeeded. And they're not crazy."

"Are you two done?" Reynolds said, forcibly inserting himself between me and Kenny. "I believe we're trying to not draw attention to ourselves."

"Ow," I grumbled low, rubbing the spot on my elbow where Reynolds had inadvertently ground it against the brick.

Yeah, we were done. I knew how his plans would have ended, even if he didn't want to admit it. With his head mounted on a plaque and me out of a job. I couldn't believe some of the things he'd entertained trying to pull off. God only knew the stuff he'd managed to actually do without me knowing about it. At least I'd never been called for bail money as a result of his scheming. Not that his schemes were criminal, just dangerous.

Ignoring Reynolds' angry glare, I focused on the lobby again. I wished I had a better reason to give Kenny than just a hunch, but that didn't make one appear. Feeling of impending doom if I didn't go back in...check. Logical reason for reentering the clinic...zippo.

"A hunch is all I've got," I said quietly. "I just know that I have to." I more felt than heard his sigh.

"Have to what?" Reynolds asked.

"You shouldn't go alone," Kenny said.

"Go where?" Reynolds demanded, looking back and forth between me and Kenny.

"Just a minute," I answered Reynolds and then leaned around him to grasp Kenny's knee. "You know I wouldn't do this if I didn't think it was important. I'll be fine," I assured him. "I've learned a thing or two since you last saw me."

"I noticed," he snorted softly. Studying the ground, he began playing with the dirt as though weighing his decision, as if he had a choice.

"Kenny," I growled, my hand tightening on his knee.

"I know, Doc," he sighed. "You want me to lead everyone back into the woods?"

"Would you, please?"

He tossed aside the twig he'd been using to scribe circles in the dirt and scowled at me. "That's rhetorical, right?"

The look on my face was answer enough.

"How long will you be?"

Releasing his knee, I pulled back and shrugged. How was I supposed to know how long it would take? Any guess I made would be just that.

"Right. See you in about...whenever," he muttered angrily as he left my side to inform the others.

"Where are you going?" Reynolds asked bluntly.

Here we go again. "Look, I can't explain it, but I have to go back in."

"Inside the clinic? Where the intruder that isn't fazed by the sight of dismembered bodies is currently taking a stroll?"

The inflection on the last word let me know exactly what he thought of the idea. Just in case I didn't get the memo his face was sending.

"I know it doesn't make sense—"

"I'm supposed to shadow you," he said, cutting off my explanation.

Shadow me? I'd forgotten about his and Adam's little compact. "I'm confronting one person. I don't need a shadow."

"Adam said—"

"Adam's not here," I barked, causing heads to snap my direction.

Grinding my teeth together, I mentally slapped myself for my slip in control. The last thing I wanted was to cause more trouble. After a few anxious moments in which I determined I hadn't exposed us, I grasped Reynolds by the shoulder and forced him to look me in the eye.

"Adam's not here," I repeated quietly. "I am."

With those two words, I was declaring myself as the new leader. That I was underqualified went without saying, but this was reality. He'd either accept it or not. The stubbornness now on display led me to believe it might be the latter, not something I was prepared to allow. Meeting him stare for stare, I held his eyes without blinking until he grunted in frustration. With a slow nod of his head, he grudgingly accepted the change in command. Thank goodness, because I sure as heck wasn't going to take orders from him.

"I want you to help Kenny get everyone safely into the woods," I told him.

"Then what?"

He hadn't hesitated, but I could hear the lingering uncertainty in his voice. "Then you wait patiently for me to join you," I said confidently.

From recent experience and through no fault of my own, I knew there was a good chance it wouldn't work out that way, but I went for the sale anyway. When he looked at me like he only half believed me, I almost laughed. Add his fifty percent to my percentage, and we were almost at a hundred. At least we were on the same wavelength.

"Go on, get out of here," I said, gently shoving him with the hand still gripping his shoulder.

Kenny tilted his head questioningly at me as Reynolds jogged towards him. I gave him a double thumbs up at which he promptly rolled his eyes. Then without so much as a wave, he led the sprint for the woods. None of them looked back, but if they had, they would have seen me heaving one giant sigh of relief.

As the last of the team disappeared into the darkness, I began to make my way back to the clinic. Using the flashlight as a guide, I angled towards the door that would afford me the most protected view. Since the light was no longer moving, I guessed the intruder wasn't either. Maybe the scene had finally gotten to them. Or maybe they didn't want to step on things best not stepped on. Whatever the reason, it made it easier for me.

When I reached the door, I pressed my face against the glass and peered inside. I recognized the profile right away. It was that red haired reporter that had done the interview with the president of God's Light. My heart sank with the identification. Having witnessed her conduct the interview, I knew if she turned against hybrids, we were in trouble. She hadn't struck me as the kind of person that could be bought or silenced—short of killing her, which wasn't an option. No, I could picture her digging and digging until she exposed everything. And, she had a national audience to make her case to.

Fixing this just became number one on my list.

Pulling the door open, I stepped inside. It was only after she swung the flashlight my direction that I remembered I was still in hybrid form. Great. I'd just outed myself as a hybrid. To a national reporter no less! Crossing my arms over my chest, I sighed in frustration. I was making too many stupid mistakes.

"What brings you to this neck of the woods?" I asked while simultaneously reversing the shift.

She remained silent as she watched me. The only sign that she recognized the change was the slight widening of her eyes when I was fully human again.

"Nifty trick," she said, sweeping the light over my body before bringing it to rest on my face. "An anonymous tip that I would find something...*interesting*." Repositioning the light, she highlighted the slaughter around her. "I don't think interesting is the right word."

"Not unless you're some sort of forensic homicide expert that specializes in the supernatural," I blurted out, completely astounded at how flippant it sounded, which was not what I was going for. And regardless of what my current surroundings suggested, I was dead set on not becoming the afore mentioned expert. Well, dead set was a poor choice of words...given my current surroundings. What the heck was the matter with me? Answer the woman, Greer.

Clearing my throat, I tried again, in a more sedate tone. "Evil, monstrous, sadistic. All would be more accurate descriptions."

"Did you do this?" she asked, swinging the beam back in my direction.

I wasn't sure she'd heard my previous comments, but that was probably a good thing. I also didn't think she believed the answer was yes. But that she'd asked bothered me. A lot.

"If you believed that, wouldn't you be really scared right now?" I snapped at her.

Her eyes zeroed in on my forearms. "I did have reason to suspect," she said mockingly.

Following her eyes, I was shocked to see the amount of blood covering my hands. It extended to my elbows in some places, tails of red against my fair skin. In a rush, the memory came back to me. The pool of blood on the operating room floor and my hands grasping at it. This was Adam's blood. The room swayed as I fisted my hands and tucked them tightly to my side.

"It's not my blood," I said weaker than I intended.

"I figured," she retorted.

"No," I growled, inadvertently digging my nails into my palms. "What I mean is, I didn't do *this*. I tried to prevent it."

She regarded me coldly, not sold on my answer and clearly amused by my anger. "You failed."

Though she hadn't raised her voice, her words hit me hard. I tightened my jaw against the anger that rolled through me. I hated that she was right, hated even more the feeling of failure that her words generated.

"Is it the same throughout the building?" she asked, her tone more curious now than accusing.

"I don't know. I've only seen the first floor." And the roof, I thought silently. But Kenny had performed a sweep. He would have told me if he had found something.

Looking around the lobby again, I saw through the beam of her flashlight details that I had missed before. Some of the limbs clearly had claws on display. Various other non-human traits were also visible among the scattered remains. If her informant thought this was interesting, she had another problem on her hands.

"Could you do this?" she asked before I could tell her as much.

Exhaling the breath I'd taken, I lifted my eyes to her. "I can inflict some damage, defend myself. But not like this." At least, I didn't think I could. I hoped I never had to find out.

"Humph," she nodded, as though my answer agreed with her assessment. "Do you know who did?"

We'd come to the hard part now. I knew before I entered that she would want answers, that she'd be determined to get answers. Even now, her face betrayed her growing distrust as I delayed.

"I know you want answers," I said placatingly.

She took a menacing step forward. "I more than want answers," she hissed.

Just how much I did not like her threatening posture, I let show in my eyes. She froze, shock replacing the prior aggression.

"Threatening a hybrid is really not the right way to go," I warned softly.

Swallowing, I forced myself to calm. I tried to think how I would have reacted to me before I knew anything about hybrids, which was not a very accurate role reversal. I would have shot me on sight and ran like hell. No sir, you would not have found Macy Greer sticking around with body parts lying everywhere. The dust trail from my truck would have been all you'd have seen of me. And, I was rambling to myself again.

"Would you quit shining the light in my eyes?" I barked at her.

"Who did this?" she repeated as she lowered the beam to just below my chin.

Though her tone was firm, it was no longer threatening. It was an improvement. Now all I had to do was answer her question in a way that didn't end up with her making the call to her television crew and exploding this whole thing on national television. I suppose I could physically stop her if needed, but I didn't want to hurt her. And what would I do with her after that? I didn't think an apology would cut it. No, I just wasn't going to start down that road of no return. Not to mention, having national name recognition practically guaranteed that someone was sure to come looking for her if she went missing.

My thoughts must have been written on my face. I raised my eyebrows at her as she took an uneasy step backwards. It was a little late to be thinking about safety now.

"You shouldn't have come here alone," I muttered to myself, but loud enough that she still heard it.

This was unbelievable. It was like an idiot had taken over my tongue. I was supposed to be gaining her trust, not scaring the daylights out of her. The hand not holding the flashlight slowly slid inside the pocket of her overcoat. I was guessing she had a gun inside. Maybe not so different from me.

"I have a friend," she said, managing to keep her voice steady despite her obvious fear.

I threw my hands up in surrender. "You're not in danger. Not from me anyway. I just meant that it was stupid for you to come here at night by yourself. As you can see, the world is changing. You need to be more careful. Your little friend," I nodded towards her pocket as I lowered my hands, "is not adequate protection." I'd never tested that theory, of course, but I knew any hybrid could move faster than she would be able to get a shot off.

"What do you mean the world is changing? Are you talking about the reemergence of hybrids?"

"Maybe," I winced. "Probably. It's not clear."

My waffle of an answer was all the confirmation she needed. "The public has a right to know that hybrids still exist," she glowered at me as she channeled her fear into anger. "They've been lied to."

Well, who hasn't been, I wanted to snap. But she wasn't going to let this go. She'd been trailing this story via the extremist groups, and now Millsap had provided her with verifiable evidence. No reporter worth their salt would ignore this.

"I agree that the public has a right to know," I said reluctantly. "But this?" I swept my arms to indicate the carnage. "This represents the work of a madman."

"One might say it represented the work of a hybrid."

Her words dripped with disdain. She'd already done the calculations in her head and reached her conclusion. But she wasn't considering all the variables, like the perfectly sane hybrid standing in front of her now. I knew firsthand it was a lot to absorb. The only reason I hadn't run screaming for the hills was the fact that I was now one of things I would have been running away from.

"It is the work of a hybrid," I admitted, causing her eyebrows to rise in surprise. Really, like I could have denied it. "But he didn't do this because he is a hybrid," I continued. "He did this because he is a psychopath bent on destruction. His kind of crazy transcends hybridization."

"Isn't that all the more reason for the world to know? To expose him. They need to be warned. The authorities, the government or military, or whoever it takes to stop this guy needs to be involved."

I stared blankly at her.

Like tossing a match into a vat of kerosene, her face convulsed into a mask of anger. "They already know," she snarled. "Of course, they do. They always know." She lowered the flashlight and began to pace in a tight circle. Each carefully placed step spoke of the anger she carried until she stopped abruptly. The wave of resignation that washed over her was visible. "The extremists were right," she said dejectedly.

Once again, we were on the precipice of everything going south. I couldn't let that bigoted idiot of a man be her source. Nor could I let her think that I was part of the "authorities". Her anger had the flavor of someone who'd been burned by them before. If it got the best of her, she could react out of some misguided sense of payback. Only, her payback could tear the world apart. I had to give her enough information to wet her appetite, keep her hooked, keep her from destroying us all.

"The hybrid responsible for what you see tonight is sick and demented. And, he has plans that cannot be allowed to succeed."

Though she gave no outward indication, I knew she was listening, processing my words.

"You're the only one who can stop him?" she sneered.

"There are probably a million people who could deal with this. If they knew."

I didn't elaborate any further. What I could see of her face said she was recalling the last time people knew and the catastrophe that it was. But she was still on the edge, still undecided.

"Tonight, he took someone very important to me. What you do from here may affect whether he lives or dies."

She walked a few steps towards me, aiming the flashlight squarely at my face. "He?"

Raising my hand to shield my eyes, I said, "I'm just asking for time."

"And if I refuse?"

Though I could override the urge to attack, I couldn't suppress the shift that raced through me as a result of the threat her words posed. Following her question to its logical conclusion...if she exposed the existence of hybrids to the world? It would quite likely run counter to me finding Adam. At that moment, while my instincts wrestled with each other, I wasn't sure I had actually ruled out violence as an option.

"You make my job that much harder," I managed, barely hanging on to the sliver of control I still possessed.

She remained absolutely still as she studied me, except for the hand fingering the gun. I could clearly see the outline of the metal as she rolled it over and over while she decided whether or not she would trust me. For so many reasons, it was a stupid exercise. Guns were not toys.

She began to lower the flashlight then quickly whipped it back to my face. "I know you," she said slowly. "You look a little different, but you're that scientist. The one that isolated the gene associated with cancer." Forgetting about the gun, she pulled her hand from her pocket and repeatedly snapped her fingers as she tried to recall my name. "Dr. Greer," she said triumphantly.

Closing my eyes, I inhaled deeply. Dad gum it. All hopes of maintaining my anonymity had just vanished. You know, this being out here on a limb stuff really stunk.

"Macy Greer." I offered my hand in greeting.

She eyed it dubiously before carefully accepting it. "Your

discovery led to the development of the procedure to turn the gene off."

Since I was responsible for that too, I simply nodded.

"You saved my brother's life," she said softly.

Her ardent support of DNA research now made sense. Hope leaped within me. Maybe I had a chance of holding this thing together.

"I'm trying to save more. Reporting this now? Like this?" I looked around the room again. "I don't think I could repair the damage it would do."

Emotions played across her face. I recognized her need to inform the public and expose the government. But she wanted to trust me. I could see that, too.

"Is there any fixing this?" she asked doubtfully.

All I could do for this was get it cleaned up. But the larger picture? Without Adam? I didn't know. But I wasn't going to tell her that. "I'll do my best," I said weakly.

She surveyed the lobby again, shaking her head at the butchery. "You'll need one hell of a best." Sighing loudly, she dropped the flashlight to her side. "I'll want an exclusive," she said like she couldn't believe she was doing this.

"Of?"

"What happened here, who's responsible, why hybrids still exist." She began to pace again as she concentrated on the content of her report. When she'd reached the end of her circuit, she stopped and looked back at me. "Including how you became involved in this."

Now I sighed. "That's a long story."

"Editing will fix that," she said offhandedly, dismissing my comment with a wave of her hand. She resumed pacing, withdrawing into herself as she framed the interview in her mind. Stopping suddenly, she fixed me with her stare again. "Full disclosure. No fluff piece. I want the truth."

With each assertion, she used the flashlight like a finger, jabbing it at me to emphasize her words. I so wanted to snatch it from her and whack her with it. Instead, I mulled over the deal she was hammering out.

Did I have the authority or right to agree to such a bargain? To expose all of hybridom? Probably not. But, I wasn't really exposing anything, not when I was currently standing in the middle of done on that one. But an insider's perspective? I was barely on the inside myself. I should probably clear this with someone first. But Adam's life was at stake, and I knew she wouldn't leave here with a, "Let me get back to you on that." Asking permission had never been my way before. I sure wasn't going to start now.

"Deal," I said with a nod of my head.

She reached inside her coat, pulled out a card, and handed it to me. "I'll be waiting for your call," she said as she turned to go. She walked to the door, then with one hand gripping the frame, she paused. "Dr. Greer, don't keep me waiting too long. I'll find the answers I'm looking for. With or without you." With that declaration, she walked out of the building.

I had no doubt that she would.

The card identified her as Virginia Redding. I bet she caught grief over her red hair and last name. Maybe she used it to her advantage, like an easily recognizable trademark. Remember the hair, remember the name sort of thing. She definitely seemed like someone who could withstand the heat of the association, probably relished it. Despite the threat that she posed, I liked her.

My fingers shook as I tucked the card away, an aftereffect of the adrenaline crash and too many shifts. Balling my hands into fists, I fought to restore some kind of balance to my body. Eating would help, but I had no stomach for it right now and certainly not in this location. It had been close, I thought as the tremors progressed over my body. But I had somehow managed to delay the exposure of hybrids to the world. For a little longer. Unless she changed her mind, which I didn't think she was likely to do. The lure for more information was a strong one for her.

I didn't want to look around the lobby one more time, but I couldn't help myself. It was the last tangible connection I had to Adam, and a reminder of what Millsap was capable of. There was no doubt the world would be a much better place without Millsap in it. It wasn't like me to stand in judgment. I usually left that to people more qualified. But in this case, I was willing to make an exception and take the consequences for it, whatever they may be.

Drawing on reserves I didn't know I had, I quelled the last of the shaking. As I walked towards the lobby door, it did occur to me that even if I managed to get rid of Millsap, someone else equally as deranged would take his place. I had no interest in participating in a perpetual cycle of violence, of becoming the enforcer for hybridom. No, Ms. Redding had one thing right. This needed to be brought into the light where all the ugliness would no longer be able to hide.

CHAPTER 2

FOUND THE REST OF THE team waiting for me a short distance inside the woods. They were split into two factions, Colony hybrids on one side and Organization hybrids on the other. It wasn't fear, exactly, that I saw on their faces, more like unease. It was probably just hitting them how different their lives were going to be now, especially the Colony hybrids. As I'd witnessed many times, they had no qualms about illegally leaving the compound. But every time before, they'd always returned. This time, they wouldn't be coming back.

I knew how they felt. It wasn't but a few days ago that the definition of what I called home was forever altered. To what, was still being decided. Personally, I couldn't afford to focus on where home was now or how my life was changing minute by minute. But seeing the uncertainty on their faces, I knew I should probably say something to comfort them. What that was eluded me. Telling them everything was going to be alright was not an option, not when they were minus a home and family. Mentally cringing as I endeavored to pull something together, I eventually gave up. We'd have to weather it together and hope we survived. Yeah, pep talks weren't really my thing.

"Everyone okay?" I asked, immediately regretting the lameness of the question. Of course, they weren't okay, and of course, they would never admit it.

"What did you find?" Kenny asked, ignoring my question altogether, which was fine by me.

"Reporter."

Stillness replaced the anxiousness in their movements.

"We made a deal," I shrugged. Uncapping the water bottle Reynolds handed me, I took a sip, then lowered the bottle. "She's not going to expose us just yet."

"You believe her?" Reynolds asked carefully, trying but failing to hide that he didn't.

"I do," I nodded, half surprised by the fact myself. For certain, she was determined. Hungry? No doubt. But liar she wasn't. That was rare in the media these days. Heck, that was rare in just about everybody these days. But regardless of whether I trusted her or not, I'd been thwarted by circumstances more than once already. No need to push my luck.

"However, having someone stumble into that," I said, pointing in the general direction of the clinic. "Accidentally or otherwise, it would not be good any way you measured it. We need to get that cleaned up ASAP. Can you contact headquarters?" I asked Reynolds.

"I can," he said, looking visibly relieved to be doing something other than waiting. "I also have to update Cedars on the status of Agent Michaels." From one of his pockets, he produced a nutrition bar and offered it to me.

My lip involuntarily curled in revulsion.

"You look like you need it," he said matter-of-fact.

"Dang it," I sighed at the noticeably trembling hand that held the water bottle. I did need it. Scowling, I accepted the bar impersonating food. "You make the connection. I'll talk to Cedars."

Using my teeth, I tore the wrapper open. At least the call should distract me from the actual eating of it. Not that I was eager to tell Cedars what had happened, but the sooner I got this over with, the sooner I could start looking for Adam.

When Reynolds secured the connection, he handed the com to me.

"Alright if we walk?"

"Yes, ma'am. But we should go this way," he said and pointed in the opposite direction.

"Right," I said sheepishly. Glancing back briefly, I made sure the Colony hybrids were following. I wouldn't put it past them to decide to disappear on me, or more specifically, for Kenny to lead them away.

"Cedars here," the com barked at me.

"Cedars, it's Macy."

"Macy?" he said, surprised to hear my voice. "Is there a problem?"

Now why would he jump to that conclusion? Never mind that he was right. "We found a bloodbath at the Colony. We need a cleanup crew here. Do we do that?"

"We do. I'll take care of it. Anything else?"

"Cedars," I paused, searching for a softer way to say what needed saying, but there just wasn't one. "Adam's gone."

All the little noises associated with him dividing his attention ceased. "What do you mean gone?"

"They took him—"

"Who took him?" he demanded.

"I'm not sure. Millsap, Julia, someone else? There was a lot of blood—his blood. I traced his scent to the roof where it disappeared. I know Millsap was there. And Julia was there. But not at the same time, I think. Someone else was there, too. Cedars, some of the group wasn't taken alive. I recognized bits and pieces of them scattered about."

My report was greeted with stunned silence.

"Give me a moment," he finally said, and then put me on hold.

Absently, I bit into the bar. The taste barely registered as I gnawed on both it and what I imagined Cedars was feeling. This couldn't be easy for him, another setback in a series of setbacks. And that's all this was, because we were going to get Adam back.

"Macy, I'm going to put you on speaker," Cedars said when he came back on. "Tell everyone what you just told me."

Having said it once didn't make it any easier the second time. When I finished recounting what we had found, the room was utterly silent, unnervingly so. This happening so soon after the debacle with Olivia and Juarez had to be jarring. Remaining detached from the emotional aspect of Adam's disappearance was the only way I was still functioning. If my breakdown resulting from my previous attempt at compartmentalization was any indication, I'd pay for it later. But for now, it was all I had.

"You think Adam's alive?"

It was Olivia's voice. She sounded stronger than the last time I'd been with her.

"I know he is. He told me to find Granny. Then the bond…it's still there…but I can't reach him. I don't know if it's intentional on his part, or if they've got him incapacitated in some way. Drugged, maybe? I just know he's alive."

Relief couldn't literally travel across the air waves, but the feeling of the room breathing again was unmistakable. Juarez and Cedars began talking softly back and forth about what Adam's disappearance meant for the Organization and where to go from here. It was not a conversation I needed to hear right now.

"One more thing," I said, purposefully interrupting them. "A reporter showed up just as we were leaving." The sudden intakes of breath did carry across the line. "I managed to buy us some time," I added quickly. "Not sure how much. The reporter knew who I was." She was probably digging up everything she could on me right now. That was what I would do if I were her.

"You were in hybrid form?" Olivia asked, correctly assuming that I'd shifted.

"I was," I acknowledged. "But even if I hadn't been, the evidence of hybrid transformations was all around her."

Cedars jumped on the lead. "Her? Does she have a name?"

"Most of us do," I replied sharply. Sacrificing someone else to cover my rear end was not an option.

When no one commented any further, Miranda spoke up for the first time. "Are you coming here first?"

It wasn't me that answered her.

"Of course, she's coming here," Olivia snapped. "Where else would she go?"

The hostility in Miranda's reply was unmistakable. "To Granny's," she said, as if the two words were separated by a period.

"Just come home. We'll figure it out," Olivia said in a clear dismissal of Miranda.

I raised my eyebrows at Olivia's arrogance. First of all, I had not made a determination of where home was. Secondly, somehow, she had the mistaken idea that she was in charge of me. Where she'd gotten that notion from, I couldn't fathom. It certainly wasn't because of anything I'd ever done to encourage the idea. And thirdly, how could she even entertain the idea that I would do anything but go to Granny's?

"Macy?" Cedars asked nervously.

"Actually, Miranda is right," I drawled. "I'm not coming back just now."

"Macy," Olivia grated. "Now is not the time—"

"She's going to find Granny like Adam wanted her to," Miranda yelled in my defense.

"She's in no condition to be making decisions on her own right now. She's reeling from Adam's—"

"You don't know the first thing about Macy or how she is responding," Miranda returned. "I can guarantee you that she is nothing but business right now!"

Arguing like this was easy.

"Miranda, it might be better—" Cedars began, trying to soothe over the argument. But he didn't get to finish. Miranda rounded on him, and the discussion deteriorated from there. The debate that ensued as to the wisdom of my decision was not for my benefit, and I didn't care what their conclusion was. When it seemed like the argument was leaning towards me returning to them, I disconnected before they tried to do something stupid, like order me not to go.

Clutching the now silent com in my hand, I explored my options on my own. I was going to Granny's no matter what they said. But, I didn't see a way not to involve Reynolds. It wasn't likely that he'd let me just slip away from him. I figured I'd already pushed him as far as he would go on the shadow nonsense that Adam had charged him with. My chances at intentionally ditching him or the others were dismal at best. And, as much as I didn't like it, I knew I couldn't find my way back to Granny's on my own. I knew it was somewhere in Tennessee, but that was about the extent of my map.

"Reynolds, do you happen to know how to get to Granny's house?"

"We're talking about Agent Michaels' Granny, right?"

"That would be the one."

"Yes, ma'am," he nodded sharply. "He made sure I knew. Just in case."

Just in case? My pulse began to race. Did he know something might go wrong? And went through with the rescue anyway? "Explain just in case," I demanded.

"It was a contingency plan. One of them. He supplied me with lots of different information…just in case," he repeated.

Nodding to myself, I released the knot balled in my stomach. It hadn't been for this particular mission. Just part of an overall, far reaching attempt at evading trouble. Sadly, not far enough.

Brushing aside the encroaching feeling of loss before it could strike home, I said, "I need you to tell me how to get to Granny's."

He hesitated, twisting his head sideways a bit. "Its location doesn't really lend itself to directions," he groaned softly. Then he shook his head disagreeably and said, "No ma'am, I'll have to take you there myself."

"Then how did you learn," I said doubtfully.

"Agent Michaels taught me. I had to memorize how to get there."

"Are you serious?" I asked, studying him for any hint of joking.

"I am, and I'm not kidding about the directions. She's not on the map."

That's what I thought. The lack of identification on the dirt roads leading away from her house did point in that direction. But when had Adam taught him? It couldn't have been in the last few days, which spoke again of Adam's intent to bring me into his life. Wonder if he regretted that now.

"I will take you there," Reynolds said firmly, dispelling my thoughts of Adam.

It seemed his earlier hesitance was related to my approval of his escort and not his willingness to defy the Organization. Did that imply he wasn't blindly loyal to the Organization? Welcome to my club, exclusively for people with their eyes wide open.

"You do realize that headquarters may not sanction the trip?" I cautioned him.

"I'm aware, ma'am. But my previous orders have just been reinstated. I am once again your shadow."

And he has rebounded from the earlier push. One glance at his profile revealed the set of his jaw warning me not to try and dissuade him. Determination and gumption. I was liking this guy more and more. The prospect of actually locating Granny would certainly be higher if he was driving. How I could be a genius and be so directionally challenged was ridiculous.

So my shadow was back. I guess that was alright. Not like I was officially in charge of anything, but I was serious about finding Adam. I thought he was too. Wasn't really sure what to make of his committing to follow me so eagerly. It could be entirely due to his loyalty to Adam, but his actions would still require faith in me. That was humbling. Looking at the Colony hybrids trailing behind us was more humbling still. I knew their trust wasn't based on Adam. I couldn't understand what they saw in me that would inspire such confidence.

With the weight of so many lives dependent on what I did settling over me, I felt about two inches high when I turned around. Some leader I was. What exactly was I leading them to do? React to the hits, make it up as I go. Not exactly an inspiring mission statement. It certainly wasn't a plan I would have gotten behind prior to this whirlwind week.

But this was my life now. I had a crazy urge to grab a can of spray paint and scrawl, Hurricane Macy was here. If only I'd had time to shore up the weak areas of my life before it hit. Now, I was left dealing with the consequences of parts of my life being ripped away by the wind and the parts left standing being pummeled by the debris hurling through the air. Inevitably, it was going to be painful and hugely messy. I just hoped it didn't end up a total loss, pushed into one heaping pile of rubble bound for the fire.

Geesh, that sounded frighteningly biblical. You know, it would have been a lot easier if God had just told me the plan from the get go. I almost choked on my own thoughts. Nah, I wouldn't have believed this script, not even if a legion of angels had brought it to me. Me, a lead character, in the fight to save mankind from genetic catastrophe. Not a chance. I would never have auditioned for all this crap.

What was the saying...what doesn't kill you makes you stronger? They conveniently left out the part about being beat all to hell and the amount of rehab needed before getting stronger. Talk about fine print. You needed magical eyes just to see it, and even then, it was written in a language you couldn't read.

So here I was, left to craft my own plans. And didn't that make me feel good. You would understand if you ever saw my attempts at crafting anything. I was the classic angrily throw away the directions—which were also written in a language you couldn't understand—and build it myself person. And crafting, like arts and craft crafting, forget it. There wasn't enough ribbon in the whole world to wrap my life in and make it look good currently.

Fine. My life was a mess. Now it was time to begin the cleanup, starting with a plan for getting Adam back. It was simple. Simple because there was only one step in the plan presently, getting to Granny's. The next step depended on what happened there. I didn't know how finding Granny would lead me to Adam or what shape he'd be in when I found him.

My breath caught with my last thought. I couldn't let myself get caught up in bad what ifs. That was a road to madness. Reigning in my thoughts, I gave the com back to Reynolds and focused all my energy on strictly walking faster. My new shadow kept pace with me. Until we got Adam back, I could live with that.

We hadn't gone very far before the com began buzzing in the pouch where Reynolds had stored it. "That's probably them trying to get me back on the line," I said wearily when it started buzzing again for the third time.

"Couldn't be, ma'am. The tree coverage we've just entered is much too dense to support communications."

He'd said it with a straight face and without a single glance in my direction. I was beginning to think Reynolds was made of stiffer stuff than I'd given him credit for. Grateful didn't begin to encompass how I felt about that. Eventually, when no one picked up, they got the message. We were minus the buzzing when we stepped onto the gravel road.

"Well, that's convenient," I muttered at the cargo truck parked along the side of the road.

"I called ahead for means of transport when you were talking with the reporter," Reynolds offered with a shrug.

He must be the deluxe model shadow, fully equipped with all kinds of helpful things. I sure did appreciate his thinking ahead, especially when all my thinking was currently tangled in the here and now. Even more so because it meant we could get moving sooner.

The irony of the situation hit me like a ton of bricks. I was finally in a hurry to get moving, and Adam wasn't here to witness it. My steps faltered, causing Reynolds to send me a worried look. Since I had momentarily lost the ability to speak, I shook my head at him. He frowned but didn't ask any questions.

"You okay?" Kenny asked, placing a hand on my shoulder and squeezing gently.

"Yeah," I choked out, angrily shoving the emotion away as I forced myself to move forward again. Breaking down right now was not something I could afford. And neither could Adam.

As we reached the truck, we split with Reynolds heading to the driver's side and me to the passenger's. Kenny's voice startled me from the fog of my anger.

"Hey, Doc," he called. "You wouldn't be thinking of dropping us off and finding Adam on your own?"

With my hand still gripping the door handle, I turned slowly to face him. I hadn't been thinking about it, but now that he brought it up. His face hardened as he let go of the truck and stalked towards me. The rest of his team fanned out around him in a show of support.

"We want to help you find Adam. He has...*helped* us in the past," he said tightly.

They knew Adam?

Recognizing the confusion on my face, Wrangle explained. "He intervened, gave us nanobots...saved us from the government's research. And, he brought us you."

I was stunned. I knew there were things I still didn't know about Adam—about a lifetime's worth of things—but I was in shock over how involved he'd been in my life without me knowing about it. Also, Adam obviously cared about the Colony hybrids, however remotely. I couldn't reconcile that with his seeming unwillingness to conduct an operation to save them.

Pulling away from the truck slightly, I opened my hands in supplication. "I can't ask you to put your lives at risk to help me find Adam—"

"You didn't ask," Kenny sliced through my argument.

True. And I wasn't going to. "Kenny, all of you," I said, stepping closer to them. "You are still just kids." That was obviously the wrong thing to say. The protests that erupted caused me to all but yell to be heard over their racket. "I know that you are capable. I'm not questioning that. I just think you don't need to be exposed to any more junk."

They quieted, but not one of them so much as batted an eye at my argument.

"Haven't you been through enough already?" I pleaded, willing them to understand my desire to not see them hurt anymore.

"The man responsible for the death and torture of our family and friends is still out there, still free to continue!" Kenny growled, his eyes glowing as they sparked with leashed anger. "That is not acceptable to us."

Looking past Kenny, I surveyed the others. As one they nodded. I looked to Reynolds, who'd walked back to where we were, for help in convincing them of my rightness.

"I think they mean to go either way," he said quietly.

So much for his help, I thought in exasperation. Looking back and forth between them, all I saw was the resolve on their faces. Smiley and Flash had even joined the ranks of Kenny's team. "I suppose you want to go also?"

"Agent Michaels is our leader," Flash answered. "We don't know what's going on with the Organization right now, but we are with you if you're going after him."

Dad gum it. I was now the impromptu leader of a small rebellion against the Organization's authority. Olivia was going to love this. Hey, a plus. Throwing my hands up in the air, I grimaced as I said the words I didn't want to say. "Everyone that's with me, load up for Granny's."

"Yes, ma'am," Smiley saluted.

"Don't call me that," I griped. "Call me Macy or Doc. Supreme Overlord, even," I tossed over my shoulder as I strode to the passenger's side door and yanked it open.

"How about Boss?" Someone yelled from the back of the truck.

"That'll do," I hollered back. "And may God save us from rolling pins and hoses."

"What's that?" Reynolds asked as he climbed into the truck.

"Nothing," I muttered and slammed the door shut.

"Been on the receiving end, have you?" He chuckled. "Which one, hose or rolling pin?"

"Hose," I said glumly.

His smile widened. "There's only one thing she ever gets the hose after you for—"

"Shut up and drive," I ordered, somewhat embarrassed by his unexpected understanding.

He laughed but started the truck. The com began to vibrate as soon as we pulled away.

Without looking, I held my hand out. "Better hand it over."

"You sure, ma'am?"

Not at all, but it had to be done. Besides, if this didn't go well, I could just ignore them in the future. "I'm sure," I told him.

"Macy!" Miranda exclaimed when I answered.

They must have voted her negotiator. Obviously, they didn't

recognize how lacking she was in that arena. "Miranda," I replied calmly.

"What'cha doing?"

Her use of slang voiced in sing song fashion brought a quick smile to my lips. "Watching the trees roll by, and you?"

"Fending off the onslaught of ticked off Organization people. That's your fault by the way."

Pointing out the mistakes of the one you're negotiating with, yeah, that always generated a willingness to compromise. At least she was sticking up for me, which was another flaw in their plan. Having your designated representative on the side of the enemy never ended in your favor. And if all that failed, she'd wear them down by simply refusing to shut up. A tactic I was all too familiar with.

"I'm going after Adam regardless of what the *Organization* has decided," I said loudly enough for all to hear, causing someone in the room to swear loudly.

"That's what I told them," she said knowingly. "Cedars and Olivia don't think you should go. That you aren't qualified. They don't want to risk you, blah, blah, blah. Juarez and I, and Margaret and Lindsey, think you are the best one for the job."

Wait, doesn't that make the decision four to two in my favor? "So, I won the election?"

"Hardly seems worth mentioning, in light of your decision already being made and all."

I gave Reynolds a thumbs up. Though he'd probably never admit it, I didn't miss the brief glint of relief that flashed in his eyes. It was tied to the pang of regret that landed in the pit of my stomach.

"I presume you've been able to recruit Reynolds?" Olivia said accusingly, as though that had been my plan all along.

Anger churned within me at her accusation. I was not the one responsible for the demise of her Organization or the failing trust the cadets had in the leadership. The noise of the road fell away as I focused that anger on her. "You should be very careful what you accuse me of, Olivia."

Silence greeted my warning. After a moment, she said, "I'm not your enemy."

"Then stop acting like it," I growled softly.

"Maybe you wouldn't see me as the enemy if you stopped thinking about only yourself," she snapped.

Thinking only of myself? Was she kidding me? I wasn't even on the list of things I was thinking about. I was so angry I wanted to crush the com in my hand as a surrogate for her skinny neck.

Reynolds' hand suddenly appeared in my field of view. "Let me," he said.

Unclenching my hand, I let it drop into his.

"Reynolds, having a brain and both the capacity and willingness to use it, has determined that he will follow Adam's orders."

"Which are?" Olivia asked tightly.

"To shadow Macy in the light of unforeseen circumstances."

"What!" she bellowed. "She is nothing but one big mess of unforeseen circumstances!"

Snatching the com out of his hand, I hollered, "It comes with the territory!"

"What territory would that be?" she hissed at me.

Miranda answered before I could. "The untold power of geniusoscity."

Miranda's quip caused Cedars to chuckle and then rapidly clear his throat—probably due to Olivia's glare.

"Well the power of your *geniusocisty* better find you safe to Granny's. Call us after you've spoken to her."

The line went dead. She'd hung up on me. Worse! She'd given me an order and then hung up. I was so mad that I all but threw the com back at Reynolds.

"I am not just thinking of myself," I barked angrily.

"No, ma'am," Reynolds replied calmly.

"I'm thinking of Adam and you," I stopped as my voice cracked.

"Yes, ma'am," he said.

"And the guys in the back." I jerked my thumb backwards towards them. "And the whole dang world at large."

"Never in doubt, ma'am."

Dang straight. If I was thinking about only me, I'd get the heck out of the line of fire. To some place safe where people weren't trying to kill me or mutate me. What had I done that would give her the idea that I was only focused on me? Didn't she know that I was the one that insisted on not leaving the camp without her and Juarez?

It took some time for me to calm down enough to note the one good thing out of the conversation. I wasn't going to have to fight them to make it to Granny's. The thought of tangling with the Organization caused the anger to resurface. My thoughts seemed to have a life of their own as the rage coated me. I just knew the Organization didn't stand a chance against me. And I couldn't wait to whip Olivia's skinny butt.

"Whoa, Macy," I breathed.

"What's wrong?" Reynolds asked worriedly.

"Not sure." The depth of emotion I was feeling wasn't parallel to the situation. I didn't hate Olivia or the Organization. Being bossed around, treated like a child or insubordinate, that I couldn't stand. But even that wouldn't account for this amount of anger. It was Adam, I thought in a flash.

Closing my eyes, I laid my head against the back of the seat. *Why are you angry?* I thought at him.

A series of quick images of him being held down, immobilized, sprinted through my mind. Then it was cold. Freezing, energy sucking cold. I gasped when Reynolds' hand made contact with my arm.

"You're freezing."

"Not me," I said through chattering teeth. "Adam."

Reaching under the seat, Reynolds pulled out a blanket and tossed it at me. My breath fogged the glass as I rested my head against the window.

"How long until we get to Granny's?" I chattered.

"It's quite a ways. You should rest while you can."

That would require turning off my brain. Something I've never been very good at. Sleep for me was usually necessitated by sheer exhaustion. Living to the fullest, that was me. Miranda would argue with me, say I was a workaholic. But I liked to think of it as living with purpose. There were questions that needed answering, and I was good at finding answers. Now would be a good time to remember that.

With that thought in mind, I replayed my last moments with Adam. I guess I should have admonished him to be careful, too. He thought it was a simple search and rescue operation, not an ambush. Which led me back to the Consortium, and why they would kill the other Organization operatives but take Adam alive? If it was his nanobots they were after, they could have taken them like the others. They must want something more from him. And how did Julia fit into all of this? There were too many missing pieces for me to venture a guess.

Setting the issue of Julia aside, I focused on the one clear lead I had for getting Adam back, Granny. He must have believed that getting to her would lead me to him. He wouldn't just randomly send me there, tell her just to upset her. He loved her way too much for that. And, he would never put her in danger. No, she must have a way to find Adam. Unless he was sending me there because she was in danger. But who would want to hurt Granny? And why?

Thoughts spun in my mind, each one feeding on the next. But I was too tired to hold the threads together long enough to see the bigger picture. Each time I got close to stringing the pieces together into some semi coherent image, they turned fuzzy and crumbled like a house of cards.

Sighing at my brain's noncompliance, I swept aside the scattered thoughts and closed my eyes. I didn't expect to actually sleep, but I'd give it a shot. Lord knows I needed it. And it might make Reynolds quit looking at me every five seconds like I was going to implode or something. So, for both our sakes, I'd try.

CHAPTER 3

FOUND THAT DESPITE MY AGITATED state, I drifted in and out of sleep. Each time I awoke thinking I'd heard Adam calling me. And each time when I reached through the bond for him, only emptiness answered. It was frustrating beyond belief.

When the truck rolled to a stop, I sat up quickly in hopes that we had arrived at Granny's. But the hope evaporated as I beheld the reason for our halt, a police blockade on the next hill. In the middle of the night. On a road in the middle of nowhere.

"Wonder who they're looking for," I griped aloud.

"Yeah, I wonder," Reynolds repeated.

"How long have you been driving with the lights off?" I asked, the last bit distorted by my supersized yawn.

"Ever since I spotted the pretty swirling lights. Whoa."

I looked up to find him staring straight at me, his face blank except for the bottom jaw hanging open. There were so many things that sprang to mind that I could have thrown at him in the way of comebacks, but I didn't talk like that. Instead, I reached up and finger combed my hair down from the heights it had achieved.

Giving his head a rough shake, he scrubbed a hand across his face and added, "Long enough for them not to know we're here."

Flash appeared at Reynolds' rolled down window. "It's legit," he said, indicating the tablet device in his hands.

"That doesn't mean whoever ordered it is," Reynolds muttered as he studied the screen. "What does it list as the reason?"

"Escaped convicts."

"Humph," was all Reynolds said.

Tapping on my window drew my attention to Kenny. "Trouble?" he asked when I rolled it down.

"Roadblock," I said and pointed to it, but Kenny was looking past me to Reynolds.

"Curious thing," Flash said. "There are no reports of escaped prisoners in this area, not for hundreds of miles. No APBs. Nothing."

"Is there another way to Granny's?" I asked Reynolds.

He grimaced and bit his lower lip. "There is another way from here, but it's rough. Off road kind of rough." Turning his face to me, he lifted his eyebrows for approval.

"Will this truck make it?" I asked warily.

"Well, if it doesn't, we can always walk."

There was a vote of confidence. "Okay, let's do it before they spot us."

"Tell everyone to hang on. It's going to get a little bumpy," Reynolds warned Kenny and Flash before they headed back.

With everyone back on board, Reynolds did a u-turn and backtracked for a while. Then he made another series of turns that placed us on roads that were successively becoming less and less what I would classify as drivable.

"A little bumpy?" I shouted at him over the truck's protesting springs. "This hurts."

"Off road, remember?" he grunted as he leaned into the steering wheel.

This wasn't off road. This was stupid. If the noises of the collisions coming from the back were any indication, they weren't having an easy go of it either. At least I had ample things to hold on to, like the door panel I was currently glued to. With my face pressed against the glass, I got a clear view of our surroundings and the deep chasm I was suspended over.

"Reynolds!" I shrieked. "There is nothing underneath me."

"All I need are the wheels on the ground," he panted as he wrestled with the steering wheel

"I can't watch this," I said and put both hands over my eyes.

It wasn't any better. My imagination supplied what my eyes didn't see.

"I wouldn't do that if I was you," he warned.

"Why not?" I demanded from behind my hands.

He laughed for an answer, but it became very clear why when I was thrown into the dash. Grasping the dash with both hands, the rest of me piled onto the floorboard. I whipped my head around to stare angrily at him, but his face was the picture of joy.

"I can't believe you're enjoying this."

"Just like mudding," he beamed.

This was not like mudding. There wasn't even any mud involved. This was like going down twisting stairs in a cardboard box filled with hard things to bruise you.

"Are you going to stay down there?" he teased.

I tucked my head between my elbows and held on. "Let me know when it's safe to get up."

He never said it was safe, but a few minutes later, and I was tossed back into my seat. My hands never left the dash.

"You're back," he laughed as the truck bounced to a stop. "Just in time."

We were perched on a small hill with a river in front of us. I didn't see any signs of the previous road or a bridge, just some fallen trees. But by the smile on Reynolds' face, I knew I was missing something.

"Are you ready?" he asked, revving the engine for effect.

"For what?" I asked suspiciously.

He turned to look at me, the grin widening as he let his foot off the brake.

"That is not a bridge, Reynolds!" I shouted at him.

"It is," he said knowingly.

"I'm pretty sure it's not. It's two trees that happened to fall over the river next to each other."

"Perfect. One for each row of tires."

"You are crazy!" I screeched at him.

"A characteristic Adam said I would need."

The truck picked up speed as Reynolds punched the gas. I

held my breath as the front tires left the bank and landed hard on the parallel trunks. Reynolds punched the gas again, and the truck lurched forward, dragging the back tires onto the makeshift bridge with an equally jarring thud. The sound of extreme pruning as limbs crunched beneath the tires was deafening, but the disaster that I was anticipating did not materialize. Reynolds navigated the truck all the way across, finally pulling it to a stop on the opposite river bank.

I took a moment to just breathe and process the fact that I was on solid ground and not floating downstream. Slumped against the steering wheel, Reynolds offered me a tired smile. I laughed nervously in return as I pried my fingers from the dash. The suddenness of the door flying open startled both of us. I only caught the profile of Kenny's face as he hauled Reynolds out. That was enough.

Vaulting from the truck, I rushed to intervene before they killed each other. When I got there, Kenny had Reynolds pinned to the ground, and Reynolds had his hands locked around Kenny's throat. Without thinking, I grabbed Kenny by the collar and jerked him off Reynolds. A split second later, I caught Reynolds by the collar as he rebounded at Kenny. I now held both of them off the ground and as far apart as my arms would reach. That didn't stop their swiping at each other, not even when they accidently got me instead.

"Enough!" I roared, giving them a good shake for emphasis.

Everyone froze, including me. My voice had sounded an awful lot like Adam.

Ignoring the shiver running down my spine, I set them down hard. "If you two so much as make a move at one another, so help me—"

"He could have killed all of us!" Kenny blurted out.

"He wasn't acting on a whim—"

"Wasn't?" Kenny cried.

"Look at it!" I yelled. Now that all the periphery cover had been cleared away, the grooves cut into the trunks for tires were obvious. When he stood there staring at me, with his hands on his hips and that stubborn look in his eyes, I grabbed his shoulders, spun him around and shoved him towards it. "It's a bridge!"

Stumbling forward, he righted himself at the last moment. I couldn't see his face to know if he made the connection, but I didn't need to see his face to know that he was still angry. He wasn't the only one.

"And you!" I said, pointing an accusing finger at Reynolds. "You would do well to remember that you are working with people who don't know you and don't trust you." I didn't include the fact that I might be one of them. Jerking my head in Kenny's direction, I said, "Make it right."

"What?" Reynolds groaned when he understood that meant he had to apologize to Kenny. But I didn't care how much he hated it. He was going to do it.

"Now," I growled softly.

Squaring his shoulders, Reynolds lowered his head and walked stiffly to where Kenny was. "I wouldn't put your team in danger," he said tightly. "I apologize if you thought I was."

Kenny turned around slowly, coming eyeball to eyeball with him. "If you ever endanger my team again, I will kill you." The words were said with such quiet confidence that it left no doubt as to his willingness to do just that.

"Likewise," Reynolds answered.

It was almost like they'd forgotten I was there.

Stepping between them, I snapped my fingers in both their faces. "Just so we're clear. There is only one boss here, me. And if anybody is going to kill anyone, it will be me. This little show that you two just put on better not happen again."

Kenny glared at me, his eyes swirling with the fury he carried. "We're not in the Colony anymore, Doc," he grated.

I took in the set of his jaw, the threat in his eyes. Was he challenging me? The longer I stared at him the harder his eyes became. He was, I marveled in disbelief. What a stupid thing to do. The storm of anger that had been raging around me calmed and settled over me like a cloak. I recognized this feeling. It was what had propelled me to victory over Pike, and the same feeling that let me argue with Adam and actually believe I would win.

Smiling, I began to step methodically towards Kenny, stalking him like prey. It was unexpected enough to cause him to flinch. "No, we're not," I hissed in answer to his challenge. "There are no more rules that I am bound to follow. No more constraints. So you best decide right now if you really want to do this."

Kenny's eyes were unyielding. I wasn't certain that he would back down, not entirely certain that I could either. He tilted his head to the side as if he was listening intently to something. Then he blinked, and the fire in his eyes faded.

"You're the boss," he said without conviction.

That's it? I wanted to say. It was an entirely unsatisfying victory. All this aggression was now pent up inside of me with nowhere to go. The weight of a hand on my shoulder caused me to snap my head around. Reynolds nodded at me, urging me with his eyes to back down. But it wasn't that easy.

A quick survey of the group painted them like a bunch of whipped pups. Except for Kenny. He might be conceding to me right now, but I didn't think we were done with this. He was absorbing the shock of his team's response to my alpha act. It was for their benefit that he had backed off. But I knew Kenny. He would bide his time, use it to figure out his next move. I'd have to be on my guard, unless I dealt with this now.

Kenny was a head taller than me, but I wasn't intimidated at all as I stood with the barest layer of air separating us. There wasn't an ounce of submission in his stare, but submission wasn't what I was after. "I've never been your enemy. Would you make me one now?"

Not wanting to stir his anger any further, I had spoken the words quietly. I knew he had a lot to be angry about. And there was no denying that the portion directed at me I had earned fair and square. That was a hard pill to swallow. And that was the moment I knew I wouldn't fight Kenny for dominance. He deserved better from me. He always had.

Taking a step back, I put some distance between us. I was

determined not to fail him again, and I wasn't going to fight him. I'd let him go. Which meant they would all leave. Tears filled the corners of my eyes at the thought of losing them.

Kenny's expression softened as he read my emotions, something he seemed to have a knack for. "I do not count you as an enemy," he said haltingly.

"Good," I said, blinking back the tears. "Cause I'm not."

"Your track record as a leader is uncertain."

A nice way to say I don't trust you. But he was right. I was unproven and not entirely trustworthy where they were concerned. But I was no longer that Macy, not since Miranda and I had discussed where the HCF was heading. He didn't know any of that. I'd been abducted before I could do anything about it.

"Would it help to know that, before all this happened, I had already decided to stand against the HCF in favor of you guys?"

"Easy to say now," he said through narrowed eyes.

Okay, that stung. But again, I'd earned that one too. Placing my hands on my hips, I lowered my eyes to the ground.

"She's never lied to us before," Wrangle said quietly.

"She doesn't lie," Reynolds said.

Swinging my head his direction, I saw that he was leaning against the truck with arms and legs crossed, attempting to look relaxed. But his eyes gave him away. There was nothing relaxed about the way he was watching Kenny.

"Honest," he smirked indifferently. "Adam said it was one of the things he loved…" His voice trailed off as his bravado waned under the heat of my gaze. "Sorry," he mumbled quietly.

Dragging my eyes from Reynolds, I turned and marched away from the group. "Everybody take five," I called over my shoulder. I needed a break from all the testosterone polluting the air. Kenny… well…I hoped he was still here when I got back.

Waiting until I was safely out of sight, I began to run. There were an inordinate amount of fallen trees in this forest. I jumped over the ones I could and slid under the rest. This wasn't going to end well for my pants, but I was growing accustomed to that. When I reached a log jam I couldn't leap or slide under, I used it like monkey bars, propelling myself from one to the other until I reached the top. It wasn't as high as the living trees, but it didn't need to be. I'd been running uphill. As a result, the valley was laid out before me.

Inhaling deeply, I let the scent of pine fill my nostrils. What was I going to do with these boys? Young men, really. The cadets might even be my age, not counting my hibernation periods, which gave me no standing as far as age went. But they weren't the ones giving me trouble. It was Kenny. Knowing now that I would never fight him, I wished I could snap my fingers and have him obey. But truth be told, he never really obeyed me before. And I was too new to being a hybrid to fully understand how the whole alpha thing worked. It kept showing up, shocking even me at the power of it, but I wasn't consciously operating it. It just sort of leaked out. And it sounded like Adam.

Closing my eyes, I reached out to him again and came up empty. It was like we'd never been linked.

Pressing the heels of my hands into my eyes, I considered my next move. Did Millsap have the connections to set up a roadblock? I guess it wouldn't be that hard. You'd probably only have to know one person around here to get that done. My breath caught as I lifted my head from my hands. The roadblock also meant that he knew where we were headed. "Granny."

Urgency to get to Granny overwhelmed me. Leaping from the mountain of broken logs, I hightailed it back to the truck. Anxious faces greeted me as I skidded to a stop just short of colliding with Reynolds.

"What is it?" he asked worriedly.

"Did you file a travel plan with anyone other than the Organization?"

His eyes widened in understanding.

"Time to go," I nodded.

The air was still thick with tension, but I ignored it as they climbed back into the truck. All of them. Kenny hadn't left during my absence, and despite their body language, both he and Reynolds were still in one piece. So, yay for me. It was quite possible that the only thing quelling the brewing civil war was my prior performance as alpha. I didn't know if I could do it again, summon it at will. With any luck, it would continue to happen naturally, because like everything else on my list right now, there wasn't any time to devote to it.

"How much longer?" I asked Reynolds as he slid behind the wheel.

"Hard to figure. Two, maybe three hours."

Too dad gum long. I needed to be there now, not sitting in this truck with each minute that passed eating away at my patience. And Reynolds wasn't helping either with those worried looks he kept casting my direction. Ignoring them was almost as annoying as not. But saying the things that popped into my head would have been mean. I wasn't mean. Like Reynolds, I was worried. All signs now indicated that Adam had sent me to protect Granny. If I failed at that…I just needed to get to Granny and make sure she was okay.

One hour passed, then two before I began to recognize the roads I'd travelled with Adam when we'd left Granny's house. The truck couldn't move fast enough now, and I glared at Reynolds each time he braked through a turn or the truck slowed as it climbed a hill. Logically, I knew he wasn't purposefully delaying our arrival, but after thirty minutes of slow going, I told him if he didn't put his foot down, I'd chunk him out the window and drive myself. We made a little better time after that.

Our final turn brought a clear view of Granny's house. I greedily absorbed every detail of the scene. Nothing seemed out of the ordinary, no obvious signs of a struggle. In fact, it looked a little creepy in the predawn light. Had that whole abandoned cabin in the woods vibe down pat. Scanning the grass for signs of tire tracks didn't yield anything either, just where Adam had parked a few days before.

The knot in my stomach uncoiled a little. I didn't think Granny was prone to going quietly, especially if she was within reach of something she could swing. The way things were tacked to the walls in there, she had a lot of ammunition to work with.

Maybe she was okay. And if she was okay, then she might know how to find Adam.

A brief flare of hope lit within me as Reynolds brought the truck to a stop. Trying not to betray the desperation I felt to the rest of the team, I managed to wait until the truck came to a complete stop before hopping out. But I couldn't stop myself from running to the porch, leaping up the steps and pounding loudly on Granny's door.

"Granny!" I yelled. "It's Macy."

When I stepped back to wait for her to come to the door, I noticed that I was alone on the porch. The cadets were waiting respectfully at the bottom of the stairs while the Colony hybrids had barely exited the truck.

"Have y'all ever met Granny?" I asked.

"Once," Reynolds answered. The Colony hybrids shook their heads no.

"Well," I said, cringing as something crashed inside. "Try to remain calm."

Smiley chuckled dryly at my advice. Yeah, it wasn't that great. She was something you had to see to believe.

The door suddenly wrenched open, and there stood Granny in her underwear.

Granny panties, they do exist.

Oh, Lord. I was not prepared to see this. Were those really foam curlers piled high atop her head? Didn't they stop making those, like in the 70s? At a loss for words, I blinked repeatedly at the specter before me.

"Come all this way to gawk at me in my underwear, did ya?" she snapped angrily.

Nope. Never even occurred to me as a possibility. Seizing upon the rolling pin clenched in one hand, the one piece of evidence that identified her as truly Granny, I apologized. "Sorry, Granny. I forgot what time it was."

"Forget the sorrys. Whatcha want?" she demanded gruffly.

This was not exactly the reunion I had pictured. I mean,

Granny could be cranky, but this was over the top. "Adam sent me to find you," I said carefully.

"Why would he do that?" she sniffed disbelievingly.

I flat out wasn't prepared for the way Granny was treating me. It was like she hated me, like my time here hadn't happened.

"Adam's in trouble, Granny," I pleaded softly.

Slowly, she lowered the rolling pin. "That accounts for it," she muttered. Then she looked up and seemed to recognize me for the first time. "Wait here," she said and closed the door.

My one and only lead just slammed the door in my face. I was flabbergasted. I didn't come all this way to wait. And what did it account for? If she knew something, why didn't she just tell me now? The temptation to get angry, to pound on the door as my frustration mounted was great. But I knew acting from a place of anger wouldn't accomplish what I needed, and it would probably get me a good smack of the rolling pin. So instead, I backed away from the door, admittedly less hopeful than I was only a few seconds ago.

Nine pairs of eyes bored into me when I turned around. Nothing like a little pressure to get the juices flowing.

Wearily, I crossed the porch and dropped into the swing. The slight tang of fear swirled in the air around me. After the earlier incident, I didn't know if it was me they were afraid of, the tension between Kenny and Reynolds, or Granny. I hated to think they were afraid of me. I only wanted my enemies to fear me. Look at that, I had real life enemies now. The whole team did. Three cadets, six Colony hybrids and me. I'd bet not a one of us was over thirty, except for one crotchety old lady who may or may not join the bunch. Oh yeah, we were a winning team.

Kenny came to sit beside me on the swing.

Recognizing it for the peace offering that it was, I nonchalantly asked, "So, how was the trip?"

He barked out a laugh, causing me to snicker too.

"Painful," he grimaced, rubbing a spot on his right arm. "But enlightening."

"Really? What'd you learn?"

He stretched back, lengthening his body and clasping his hands behind his head. "That our...*leader*...has potential."

Reaching up, I flattened a mosquito bouncing around my face. Potential for what I'd like to know, I thought as I wiped my hand on my pants.

"I'd say, there's a fifty fifty chance," he added as he crossed his ankles.

"Of what?" I asked warily.

"Screwing up or saving the day. It could go either way."

He was messing with me. Trouble was, he wasn't far off in his assessment. "I'm thinking bigger," I said knowingly.

"Oh, yeah?"

"Yeah. Success plus all the fireworks of disaster."

"Is that even possible?"

"It's a uniquely Macy talent," I conceded.

"Macy special," he mused out loud. "I think I've looked down that barrel a time or two. Now that I think about it, sort of common, aren't they?"

More so than I'd like. "They are hard to miss," I agreed.

"Harder to live through."

"You should see it from my end."

"No, thank you," he laughed. "I couldn't live with the humiliation. The disappointment—"

His litany of classifications of things he couldn't live with was momentarily suspended when I shoved him off the swing. He rolled with the push, laughing all the way. And with that, the prevailing tension began to dissolve, much to my relief or embarrassment.

"So, Granny," he said mockingly when he regained his composure enough to rejoin me on the swing.

"Adam told me to find her. There has to be a reason."

"I'm not doubting Adam," he said quickly. "I just pictured a more...gentle Granny."

Snorting as I remembered the more ladylike Granny I had expected, I said, "Gentle is not a word I would ascribe to Granny."

"We don't have much personal experience with Grannies or old folks in general."

No, I guess they didn't. The only people they were allowed to get up close and personal with were me and Miranda, and that had more to do with us than the government's orders. The doctors treating their parents were mostly middle aged. But they were forced to maintain a formal distance. The presence of the guards ensured that. No telling how old the guards were. They were covered head to toe. Not that it mattered. They were there to maintain order, not buddy up with the hybrids.

Their parents should have been middle aged.

Sighing at the guilt I still carried over that, I felt like I should formerly apologize for whatever part my presence had played in it. I knew their premature deaths weren't my doing, but I probably could have done more to save them. I was working on it, but not fast enough. There is nothing like hindsight to point out where you should have gone and the chances you should have taken.

"I'm not looking for an apology, Doc," Kenny said quietly, correctly reading me yet again. "We all make choices that we don't know the outcomes of."

"I just wish that I would have done more. Regardless of what the government wanted. I was working on a cure for your parents. If I had known—"

"But you didn't," he interrupted. "There's a lot I didn't know either. I would have done a lot of things different if I knew then what I know now."

"Me, too," I whispered. I would have chunked being afraid of the government and worked harder on a remedy for his parent's generation. I would have done…like he said…a lot of things.

"We can't go back," he said. Shuffling his feet uncomfortably, he pulled them underneath the swing and sighed heavily. "I know it's not all your fault. You're just an easy target." He smiled softly, not an expression I'd seen often on him. "Well, not so easy anymore."

"Forward then?" I offered.

"Onward and upward," he nodded. "You do know how to operate a parachute, right?"

"Don't even joke about that," I warned him. That was really where I drew the line.

As we waited in the silence that descended, I noticed that all of the Colony hybrids were on one side and the cadets on the other. It dawned on me that they'd all sort of been thrown together in the chaos that happened after Adam went missing.

"Have you guys been introduced to one another?" I asked them as a group.

"I don't think so," Reynolds said as he climbed the steps to the porch. "I'm Elijah Reynolds or ER." He pointed at Flash who stepped forward. "That's Flash, for obvious reasons I'm sure you'll see sooner or later."

Flash gave a quick wave to the group.

Pointing at the last cadet, Reynolds said, "That there is Smiley." He waited until a huge smile spread across Smiley's lips, transforming his entire face. "Also, for obvious reasons," he chuckled.

Kenny didn't get up when he started his introductions. I had the feeling it was intentional, though I didn't understand the meaning behind it.

"Kenny," he tipped his head.

A loud crash sounded from inside, causing all of us to stare at the door. What was she doing in there that was causing so much racket? Better yet, why wasn't she opening the dang door and letting me in?

"Should we check on her?" Wrangle asked.

"I don't think so," I answered. "Unless you want a good walloping with whatever she happens to be holding in her hand. Wait until you hear her cooking."

"Shouldn't it be taste her cooking?" Kenny asked.

"Yeah, that too," I agreed.

Taking his cue from Kenny, Wrangle stood up. "I'm Wrangle. Mom sort of had a thing for cowboys." He shrugged and sat back down.

She did, too. Her apartment was like entering a country western store.

The next to introduce himself was Linc. "I'm Lincoln Cabrera. My friends call me Linc. Especially my *lady* friends," he said, waggling his eyebrows suggestively.

Oh, brother. "Keep it PG, please," I complained softly.

Van leaned over and high fived Linc. "Van," he said and then walked to stand next to the guy seated on the steps with his back to us. Gripping him roughly by the shoulder, Van jostled him as he spoke. "This here is the thinker of the bunch. He does so much thinking that we don't even know what he's talking about most of the time."

"Shut up, Van," Charlie huffed. Shaking off Van's hand, he stood and faced the group. "Charlie," he said and waved awkwardly.

"We're missing one," I said as I recounted the group.

"Here," called a voice from behind me. He jogged around to the front of the porch and up the first few steps. "Name's Jake, but people call me Scout." He looked at Kenny and nodded.

"What's that about?" I whispered to Kenny.

Before he could answer, Granny swung the door open. She had on the familiar apron and had lost the rolling pin. The curlers, however, were still in her hair. I stood and approached her cautiously.

"They with you?" she asked, tossing her head in the general direction of the others.

"Yes, ma'am," I nodded.

"Come on in," she said and left me standing there holding the door.

Looking back at everyone, I rolled my shoulders uneasily. "Welcome to Granny's, boys."

CHAPTER 4

GRANNY HAD POSITIONED HERSELF AT the fireplace with her back to me. The picture she presented was in stark contrast to the firebrand I remembered. Her whole frame seemed smaller, like the problem she was nursing had sucked all the life out of her.

Making sure to keep my steps light, I joined her by the fire.

"I know'd something was wrong," she said so softly that I almost missed it. Raising one hand to grip the mantle, she buried her face against her arm. "I been having the worst dreams."

My heart skipped a beat at the mention of dreams. "About Adam?"

"He's the only male leopard I know," she nodded into her arm. "I'm not sure they's only dreams. They seem so real." Her eyes closed, squeezing so tightly shut that the pain she felt radiated across the lines it drew in her face.

"Granny—" I breathed, my voice trembling at the unspoken images her pain conjured. I closed my eyes and took a moment to steady myself before speaking again. For both our sakes, I thought it best to skip any further discussion of dreams. "Adam told me to find you. Do you know why he would do that?"

"What happened?" she asked bluntly.

Her question triggered the replay in my mind of following Adam's scent and then finding what was left of him at the clinic. This was the truth, not some scene featured in a dream. I did not want to paint that picture for her.

"Macy girl," she huffed at me with a glimpse of her former strength returning.

I had to tell her. She deserved to know. But I didn't have to tell her everything.

Taking a deep breath, I plowed over the knot in my stomach and told her what I knew without adding the grizzly details. "He's alive." That's the first thing she needed to know. "But he's been taken. He's hurt. Angry. I don't know much more than that, other than he said to find you."

She remained utterly still, so long in fact that I started to worry. Gently, I touched the arm hanging loosely at her side. "Granny?"

Her chest rose sharply as she breathed in, then fell as she exhaled in slow motion. And just like that the hesitant, uncertain—unrecognizable—Granny was gone.

"Adam made provision for all sorts of things." Grunting loudly, she slapped the mantle with the hand that had previously gripped it. "I don't remember the particulars," she said as she straightened. "But I know'd where to find'em." In one motion, she pushed off the mantle, whirled around, and began marching towards the back door.

The strength permeating each step as she moved away from me was something to be admired, a testament to the power of purpose. While I didn't feel like a bastion of strength currently, I did have the same reason to move. Using that, I could match her stride for stride.

My pursuit of Granny was halted when Scout stepped in front of me. "The house is being watched," he whispered.

"It is?" I baulked in surprise, then immediately felt like an idiot. Hadn't I already suspected as much?

"I counted five in all," he nodded.

"We got bugs, too," Flash whispered. Holding his tablet up, he indicated the areas flashing red.

My gut twisted with the information they supplied. Had my rush to get to Granny led all of us into another ambush? I brought my hands slowly to my hips as I mulled the situation. We should have done recon. We—I should have approached this like a real operation. Like a real team leader would have done.

The slam of the screen door stunned me back into the present. Granny had gone on without me.

"Granny!" I called as I plowed into the door. I wasn't about to let anything happen to her. Adam would be furious with me. I would be furious with me. And Granny would probably become a member of the undead just so she could beat me with the rolling pin for letting something happen to her. "Can we get something to eat?" I shouted at her. It was the first thing that came to mind.

She stopped mid stride, her shoulders bunching up around her ears. Slowly, she swiveled to face me. "You want to eat?" she asked, incredulous at my sudden and utterly unimportant demand.

I was a little confused myself, but I went with it. "Absolutely, we do," I said while shaking my head no.

She stared hard at me as she tried to decipher the meaning behind my behavior. The only clue I offered her was the raising of my eyebrows in supplication. It didn't even come close to me yelling, "Get your butt back in here before you get killed!" like I wanted to.

Exasperated, Granny gave up her attempt to read me and stubbornly crossed her arms over her chest. "Your arms broke?" she barked at me.

My face fell flat. Couldn't she tell this wasn't about cooking? And seriously, I was here one time, and now I was responsible for fixing my own meals? "Obviously, my arms are not broke," I snapped back while waving them wildly at her. I could only imagine how this weird exchange was being interpreted by our unwanted viewers. "Unbelievable," I muttered under my breath. Even from this distance, I could clearly make out the single eyebrow raised in defiance. It reminded me of Adam so much it hurt.

Granny froze. Dropping her hands to her hips, she lifted her nose and sniffed. "About how many need to eat, would ya say?"

What difference did that make—Oh. "Five?" I said hesitantly.

She pursed her lips and scanned the surrounding woods. Frowning, she sniffed the air again.

"Granny?" I called nervously.

The huff she issued sounded more like a challenge than

acquiescence, but at least she was moving this way. Throwing her hands down, she stomped towards the house. The porch steps rattled with each foot she hammered into it.

"I smelled more," she grunted as she drew even with me. "More and soon to be dead," she added with a slow blooming smile that looked downright wicked.

"Oh, boy," I breathed while easing the screen door shut behind us. Grasping the door knob, I closed the back door too. I knew it wouldn't make any real difference, but it felt safer that way.

Flash and Smiley had already set to work on the electronic surveillance. Using Flash's tablet and the laser pointer thing that Smiley held, they were methodically scanning the cabin. I did wonder where they were getting all these devices from, but not enough to ask.

"Are you sure about the number?" I asked Scout.

"Yeah, I's sure," Granny hollered at me, wrongly assuming that I was talking to her. "What are they doing?" she demanded, jerking a thumb in Flash's direction.

"I think they're getting rid of the bugs you've acquired," I whispered.

"That what that buzzing is?" she barked at Flash.

"Yes, ma'am?" he replied timidly.

Granny rolled her eyes and heaved a sigh. "For a while, I thought my nanos were going bad." For emphasis, she stuck both fingers in her ears and wiggled them roughly.

Her behavior drew strange looks from the guys. At least she wasn't making that hacking noise to scratch the back of her throat—oh wait, there it is.

"Flash, are we good in here?" I laughed.

"Living room's clear," he nodded. "Just don't holler."

"I'll try to contain myself," I smirked at him. "Granny, how long have your...uh...ears been buzzing?"

She made a show of wiping her hands on her apron, then screwed her face up as she thought about it. "A week ago Sunday. And, I'll tell ya, Macy girl, I don't like it none. Between the buzzing and the dreams last night, I was beginning to think I done gone plum crazy." Suddenly, she fisted both hands in her apron and skewered me with her emerald gaze. "You mean to tell me, that someone's been spying on me this whole time?"

"Probably," I nodded.

The fabric caught in her grasp twisted as she wrung her hands on the apron. "Ain't nobody got the right to invade my privacy."

No argument from me. The violation I felt due to the Organization's spying was still fresh.

"I ain't smelled'em til now."

They moved into position today. I guessed it had something to do with our presence or Adam's capture.

"Now that y'all are here, I expect we'll take care of'em?"

She had phrased it as a question, but her finishing glare daring me to contradict her left no room for argument. "Yes, ma'am," I answered.

Satisfied with my response, she adjusted her apron, smoothing out the wrinkles her fists had caused. "Gonna take some fueling up to get ready." Eyeing Flash and Smiley as they worked, she said, "Reckon cooking will disturb'em?"

From their position near the kitchen and without interrupting their work, they gave a simultaneous thumbs up.

"Yeah, I know'd I'd remembered those two," she muttered. Then she clomped towards the kitchen, uttering, "Ain't never full," and, "Bottomless pits," and other such comments regaling the eating habits of young men. Almost immediately, her unique symphony of banging pots and swearing began to fill the house. I suppose it shouldn't have been comforting, but it was.

With Granny fully occupied, I approached Scout again. "Didn't you tell me there were five?"

He nodded. "Two in a deer blind about ninety yards behind the house. Two hidden in a gulley ninety degrees from the deer blind, and one in a vehicle opposite him. We passed it as we came in."

"You mean the camo painted van without a hint of dirt?" Reynolds asked.

"That'd be the one," Scout snickered.

"Granny said there were more," I told them.

"When I checked, there was only five," Scout said. "Unless they've found a way to camouflage their smell..." He shook his head uncertainly.

Maybe Granny had miscounted. Either way, there were at least five people that shouldn't be here. "Is there any reason to think these aren't bad guys?"

"They smell funny," Scout said and then shrugged. "Like at the Colony."

Reynolds was already moving towards the front door when he said, "I'll verify."

"What are you thinking?" Kenny asked.

"How would the Consortium know about this place?" I didn't think Granny's existence was common knowledge, even at the Organization.

"What is the Consortium?" Kenny asked.

"The Consortium is responsible for what happened at the Colony. Or, most of it, anyway."

"Why?" Kenny demanded. "What reason did they have for butchering us?"

"If I'm correct, they were after the nanobots. They want to introduce hybridom to the whole world in a forced participation sort of way."

"What they did was not necessary for that," he snarled in anger. "They didn't have..." his words cut off abruptly. Swinging around, he laced his fingers behind his head and paced away from me as he struggled to gain control over his anger.

"I know," I answered quietly. "I cannot account for the savagery."

"Wait," Wrangle said. "They want everyone to become hybrids?" The disbelief was evident on his face and in his voice.

"They might have succeeded," I confessed.

Startled faces spun my direction, but before I could explain, Reynolds returned. "I think it's them," he said.

"You think?"

"It smells like them, and it doesn't. But, mostly like them."

A mutation maybe? Or some newly concocted breed. I could smell for myself, but it didn't really matter. Anything that remotely smelled like the Consortium, I was designating as an enemy.

"What are we talking about?" Smiley asked as he rejoined the group.

"Furries," Reynolds said.

"Furries," Smiley repeated loudly. "Couldn't have a party without them, could we?"

Looking from one cadet to the other, none of them seemed rattled by the identification. But the Colony hybrids were visibly nervous, excluding Kenny, of course. He looked ready to tear into someone. But that was nothing unusual.

"Furries?" Wrangle asked.

How much Adam had told the cadets before the start of this mission or what they were allowed to know by virtue of being part of the Organization, I didn't know. It was clear the Colony hybrids knew nothing. As I was now the leader of this group, that was about to change.

"Okay, here's the deal. You guys," I said, looking at the cadets, "probably know most of this already, so bear with me." Turning to face the Colony hybrids, I said, "You know Adam was part of the Organization."

They all nodded.

"Do you know what the Organization does?"

"Defends the nation," Wrangle answered quickly. "Adam said they defended the nation."

"That's only the Expeditionary Force part of it," Linc corrected.

"The rest of it is research and development," Charlie said. "Everything related to hybridization." Then, motioning to the device Flash held in his hand, he added, "And the toys they play with."

"Right. Well, currently, the Consortium—the bad guys—have managed to launch a plan that has released mutagen bacteria capable of inducing hybridization into the general public. We may or may not have that contained." Frowning, I made a mental note to get an update from Juarez. "There's more," I continued.

"I discovered another plan they have. It's more along the lines of what we saw at the Colony. I'm not sure who all the players are yet." Finding Reynolds' eyes, I said, "But Julia is one of them."

He looked like I had just shot his dog. Walking slowly to the fireplace, he sat down on one of the stools there.

"She's the leader of the Organization, right?" Van asked cautiously.

"Was," I corrected.

"What about Renard?" Reynolds asked quietly.

Man I hated to do this to him. "He was shot in the heart and neck."

"So he couldn't heal before he bled out," Flash said in understanding. Shaking his head, he pulled up a stool next to Reynolds.

Smiley crossed the floor to stand next to them. It was like they were unconsciously closing ranks. "Did Julia do it?" he asked.

"We don't know. In fact, there's a lot we don't know."

"What's going to happen with the Organization?" Reynolds asked.

"I am not entirely certain. Adam was going to take over. They're still working on stopping the mutated bacteria. I'm working on finding Adam." I sat down on the couch and clasped my hands together. "Look, I know things are screwed up right now. The Organization has been betrayed at the highest level. Chains of command are sketchy at best." Looking down at my hands, I said, "If you want to back out…try to lead a normal life…I won't hold it against you. I won't even try and stop you."

"Get while the getting is good?" Flash asked sadly.

"I'm not telling you to go. I'd like you to stay. But I cannot make these decisions for you. I think some bad stuff is going to go down. Very powerful people are involved, and I don't know whose side they're on. I'm not sure who'll be left standing when this is over. In fact, right now, there's more that I don't know than I do."

Heaviness enveloped the room as they processed my words. It left a lot to be desired in the way of explanations. It certainly wasn't inspirational. Maybe one of the worst speeches I'd ever given. It was like saying, "Hey, I don't know where I'm going, or exactly what's going on, but follow me anyway. And by the way, there's a pretty good chance you'll be killed or otherwise harmed along the way." This was so messed up.

Unable to remain seated any longer, I stood and angrily strode across the room until I reached the far wall. Swinging around to face them, I told them the one thing I did know. "I will figure it out. I don't know how or when or what it will cost me, but I will figure it out." Looking at the three huddled by the fire, I added, "With or without the support of the Organization."

"Going rogue?" Kenny scoffed.

I met his eyes. I'd never looked at it like that, but I guess by definition that's what I was doing. I'd rather not go it alone, but I was prepared to. In that way, it wouldn't be much different from my normal life.

"Well," Wrangle said, "quitting's never really been my style."

"Leaves a bad taste in your mouth," Smiley agreed.

"Like burping broccoli," Van added, shoving Linc's shoulder as they shared some inside joke.

Linc clapped Van on the back in return. "It's like you're a poet," he answered.

Regardless of the seriousness of the moment, I couldn't help but smile at the interplay between them. It reminded me of easier times.

In the wake of their joking and excluding Granny's ruckus, silence descended on the room. I waited in the silence. Not everyone had made a decision yet.

"If anyone can figure it out, you can," Kenny said, nodding in affirmation of his vote.

Ha. If he only knew the truth in that.

There was one more response I needed. Reynolds hadn't said a thing or even moved since my pledge to uncover the truth. I wasn't sure how to interpret that, but next to Kenny, he was the one I most wanted to stay. Really, the one that I most needed to stay. I held my breath as he slowly lifted his eyes to mine.

"I never really knew Julia," he said. "But I trust Adam with my life. I'm going to help you find him. Beyond that…" He shrugged his shoulders. "That will depend on Adam. Or you. I'm not going back to the way things were."

Exhaling slowly, I nodded in relief. I didn't tell him, but he wasn't going to have to worry about things being the same. I was pretty sure that train had already jumped tracks. Ending in a big fireball? That he should worry about. But I didn't tell him that either.

"I know one thing," Scout said. "We have to deal with the spies surrounding us."

Yes, we did. I heaved a sigh at the unwanted complication.

"I think we have to assume they're hostile," Reynolds said.

"I agree," I nodded. It was strange, though, that they hadn't made a move when their surveillance equipment was killed. "You would think they would have attacked by now." I mused aloud. "Wouldn't the surveillance suddenly vanishing have clued them in?"

"It might have, if it had vanished and not simply malfunctioned," Flash answered.

"They think it's a problem with their equipment?" Charlie asked.

"Should take them ten minutes or so to realize there's a problem and then another twenty minutes to repair what they think is wrong," Smiley nodded.

"If they have the replacement parts readily available," Flash said, then exchanged a fist bump with Smiley.

"You said what they think is wrong. Their repair won't fix the problem?" I guessed.

"Bingo," Smiley sang. "And I'm betting they will have no idea why."

Nice. So, how was I going to do this? I didn't want to send any of them out to fight. I didn't know enough about the cadets to know what their strengths and weaknesses were. And the Colony hybrids I knew as teenagers, not soldiers.

"We have roughly thirty minutes or less?" I asked Smiley.

"Give or take."

"Then I think the first thing we need to take care of is the surveillance van. We need to make sure they don't relay any more info than they already have to whoever they are reporting to. Maybe even figure out who that is. Can any of you take care of that?"

"I can," Flash said as he stood up.

"I'm in," Charlie said eagerly.

"I'll go with them," Smiley offered. "Wouldn't want them to be offed when their eyes glaze over at the sight of the digital landscape."

"Please don't talk like that," I moaned as they bounded down the porch steps. "I do not want any of you hurt," I yelled after their retreating forms. Facing the rest of the group, I asked, "Can you guys actually fight?"

Kenny looked at me like I had seriously insulted him.

"Look," I chuckled involuntarily. "I know you can avoid capture. I've just never seen you fight. Furries may not be pretty, but they are fighters. And they're ridiculously fast."

His glare softened a little. "We," he said, gesturing to his team, "have been hybrids since birth. And, we've had the nanobots for years. We know how to fight."

"We were trained by Adam," Wrangle explained.

They were? I was going to have to stop being surprised by the extent that Adam was an unknown part of my life. Before I could ask when or how, Scout entered through the front door, which was impossible given the fact that he hadn't left.

"They're on the move," he warned.

"I thought we had more time," I protested. "And how would you know?"

"They're closing in," Reynolds confirmed, studying the tablet he held in his hand. "Probably adjusting the perimeter for visual surveillance. If we're going to do this..."

He left the statement open-ended, but I got the implication.

"Linc and Van can take the blind," Kenny suggested.

"I wanted the gulley," Van whined as they headed for the door.

I did not like this at all. Sending them out there by themselves felt wrong. I wanted to protect them, not watch as they marched into danger. And they didn't have to act like this was some kind of joke. They could be seriously hurt or worse. I didn't find that funny.

"They'll be fine," Kenny said, answering my unspoken thoughts. Then to Reynolds, "How are your stealth skills?"

"Near perfection, but I'm staying with Macy," he said.

What? "Reynolds, I'll be fine," I said in surprise. He might be taking this shadowing thing a little too seriously.

"Sorry, Macy, but I have Adam to answer to. And, he thoroughly filled me in on your ability, without any prior notification, to suddenly find yourself in trouble."

I narrowed my eyes at him, but, dang it, I couldn't argue the point.

"Looks like it's you and me, Wrangle," Kenny said as he jogged for the back door. "Try to stay out of trouble until we get back," he called through the screen.

Yeah, yeah.

My stomach rumbled audibly as the smell of Granny's cooking began to fill the house. But I guessed it would be bad form to eat while everyone else was fighting. Rubbing my stomach, I sat down next to Reynolds on the recently vacated stool. We didn't know each other very well, but I still felt bad for him and the way his life had turned upside down.

"Where are you from originally?" I asked him.

"Lafayette," he answered.

"Louisiana?" I asked in surprise. "I don't hear a trace of Cajun."

"I work real hard for dat," he joked, allowing the accent to show for the first time. "People sometimes don't think you're too smart when they hear the accent."

I knew all about that. "Try adding female with blond hair and blue eyes to the mix," I challenged.

"Are you seriously trying to one up my handicap?" he shot back.

Taking a breath to respond, I replaced it with a smile. "No." We all had our handicaps to overcome.

"Besides," Reynolds said. "Your handicap looks good on you."

Was he flirting with me? This just got awkward. I cleared my throat and tried to think of something, anything to fill the silence. But I came up empty. Even Granny was quiet, which absolutely was not right.

"Scout," I breathed, "Did you check the house?"

His eyes widened at the same moment my wrong-o-meter suddenly flared to life. Crap.

"Reynolds," I whispered as I stood up.

"Trouble's arrived?"

"Right on schedule," I confirmed. "I don't smell Furries. Do you?"

"No," he said, mirroring me as I edged slowly towards the kitchen. "I don't smell anything other than breakfast."

Together, we reached either side of the door frame.

"Where's Scout?" I mouthed to Reynolds after I turned to spot him and discovered that he was gone.

Reynolds looked over his shoulder, then back at me and shrugged.

Great. This was a fine time for hide and seek.

Peeking inside the kitchen, my eyes were immediately drawn to the spot in front of the stove. No, I didn't see Granny, but it was hard not to notice the gigantic grizzly standing on what was left of her apron. Made me wonder if this was Granny or what ate her.

Whipping my head back to Reynolds, I said, "Granny's a bear?"

He was speechless as he shrugged again.

Then I saw the curlers. "Reynolds, is that bear wearing curlers?"

"Uh, I do believe so," he half laughed.

"Granny," I called softly to the bear.

It swung its head towards me and grunted. The motion dislodged one of the curlers which did a slow slide down Granny's ample head before plopping noiselessly to the floor. The whole scene was so bizarre it struck me like some kind of cartoon episode. Chuckling in relief, I leaned heavily against the door frame. Now that I thought about it, it wasn't hard at all to picture Granny as an ornery old bear.

The sudden roar caught me off guard.

Snapping my attention back to Granny, my heart raced as I saw her. She was now an easy six feet tall as she stood upright. My, what big teeth you have Granny and those claws. Thankfully, she was staring intently at a corner of the ceiling across the room from her and not at me. For a moment, I thought I'd made that ornery old bear comment out loud.

Leaning around the door frame, I saw what she was staring at. The corner of the roof was being slowly peeled back. Nails began to whine, piercing the silence as they were forced to give way. I winced at the shriek the corner made when it was torn free. Whatever was coming through was really strong.

"Easy, Granny," I crooned in an attempt to soothe her, but she was having none of it. Curlers flew every direction as she slapped the floor with her paws, then rose again to shake her maw in warning. I strongly identified with her desire to attack, but I wanted to know what I was dealing with before I made a move. Granny had no such compulsion.

Tired of having her warnings ignored, she charged towards the corner. Standing on her hind legs, she was tall enough to swat at the intruder. I managed to see one large taloned hand before it was batted away. It was replaced by the toothy snout of the creature that began to eat its way through the wood, or more accurately, dissolve its way through. The wood was literally melting in its mouth, the leftover drooling to the floor below and onto Granny.

"Acid," Reynolds hissed softly in recognition, getting a nod of agreement from me.

Granny howled upon contact. Angrily, she swiped her paws across her face and muzzle where most of the acid had landed. But her efforts to try and rid herself of the corroding mix only managed to spread it around. Dropping to all fours, she began a side to side shake. I watched in horror as whole clumps of fur flew from her.

"Look at the floor," Reynolds said.

Tearing my eyes from the raw patches of skin on Granny, I looked at the floor. Small plumes of smoke rose from where ever the acid drool made contact. The walls near Granny were in a similar state. This stuff ate through everything. Fur, wood, whatever shingles were made of. I was betting it wouldn't have a problem with flesh either.

Granny made a sound deep in her throat and rose on her hind legs again. Now spurred on by her pain, she began to furiously swing at the intruder. Most of her attempts missed the creature, landing her claws on the ceiling instead. She was actually widening the opening, but I wasn't going to correct an angry bear.

Scout startled me by unexpectedly tapping me on the shoulder. "Don't scare me like that," I snapped at him as I rubbed the spot on my head that had connected with the door frame.

"There's a lot of them," he said. "I've never seen hybrids like this before."

Well that made two of us. Truly, I hadn't even seen this one fully. Granny's bulk blocked most of the view.

"Granny, look out!" I shouted when the creature retreated from the hole in preparation for a tail strike.

Granny posed in anticipation, not what I meant by look out. As the lizard swung, she caught the tail with her claws and began to pull the lizard inside. More bits of the roof showered to the floor as the hole was forced to widen again. The lizard's claws screamed against the wood as Granny, with one last haul, yanked the lizard completely through the opening. It landed heavily on its back, its clawed limbs flailing wildly and catching Granny repeatedly. But she kept a firm hold on its tail, intentionally preventing the lizard from righting itself. They danced around the floor in this manner with Granny only letting go in brief spurts to assail its unprotected belly. She made the most of it, ripping and shredding until I had to turn my head away.

"There's another one," Reynolds warned.

I got a better look at this one through the now larger opening. It was humanoid, but scaly like nothing I'd ever seen. Its mouth looked similar to a crocodile's.

"What are they?" Reynolds wondered aloud.

"Lizard? Dragon?" I guessed.

"Dragons have wings," he said dismissively.

"Since when are you a dragon expert?" I jeered at him.

Dragon or not, we had to help Granny. Along with the large swathes of missing fur on her muzzle, there were now smoldering patches on her back, and the fur on her paws was almost nonexistent. She had to be in pain or would be when her anger was sated.

Having learned from its companion, this next creature came in headfirst. It gripped the roof with its talons and began to move across the ceiling while Granny was occupied with the other one. The vacancy in the opening was immediately filled by yet another lizard.

"How many of these things are there?" Reynolds grumbled.

Remembering what Scout had said, I turned to ask him for an estimate, but he wasn't there. Again. "I don't know," I said uneasily. "But we have to do something." And fast. Granny was almost done with the first creature.

Looking quickly around the kitchen, my eyes came to rest on her collection of cast iron. I would have preferred a gun, but it was better than nothing. Lunging for the makeshift weapons brought me right in front of the stove, right in front of the plates piled high with pancakes and bacon. Aw, man.

"Macy," Reynolds hissed in a strangled whisper.

Right. Focus. I threw a piece of bacon in my mouth and picked up the Dutch oven in one hand and the lid in the other. When I turned around, I was skewered by Reynolds look of disbelief.

"I really don't think this is the time for breakfast," he said angrily.

"Didn't your mama ever teach you that breakfast was the most important meal of the day?" I joked, banging the two pieces of cast iron together for emphasis.

"I'd like to stay alive long enough to eat breakfast," he retorted as he sidestepped the slashing tail of the lizard who'd maneuvered from the ceiling to the floor when I was distracted.

"Catch," I called and tossed him the cookware.

He caught them smoothly and clocked the advancing lizard in the head. "Huh, not bad," he mused, spinning the lid to adjust his hold.

The stunned lizard lurched backwards, just as Granny finished her kill. Realizing there was another one in her kitchen added new life to her. She raced towards the lizard, shifting her heading at the last moment in order to use her front paws like battering rams.

"Granny, no!" I yelled, but it was too late.

Howling at the pain the acid inflicted on her tender paws, she clamped her jaws around the lizard's neck and threw it against the wall. A wide spray of acid flew from the lizard's body. Some of it landed on my arm before I could pull it back. I wiped it on my pants immediately, but that didn't stop the burning that erupted. It felt like my skin was melting off. Venturing a quick look at Reynolds, I saw that he was furiously scrubbing across the side of his neck.

"It's their whole bodies," he said through gritted teeth. "They're covered in it."

Before I could deal with the dilemma of how to fight acid covered lizards, several rounds of what sounded like gunfire reverberated through the kitchen, followed by one singular howl. Reynolds and I exchanged looks, but it would have been pointless to consider sending him to find out what that was about. He wouldn't leave me, and I wasn't leaving Granny. Granny, who, though it obviously hurt her, smacked the lizard back into the wall every time it stood up.

"Heads up," I shouted when the third lizard cleared the hole. "Look who wants to join the party." Removing a large skillet from the nail it hung on, I swung it back and forth a couple of times to test its weight.

"I think this one is bigger than the other two," Reynolds said as he angled towards me.

"You know what they say. The bigger they are…"

"The more acid they have?" he finished.

Not the answer I was looking for.

Scout limped into the kitchen, a blood soaked towel wrapped tightly around one thigh. "Don't shoot them," he panted. "The bullets just ricochet."

A cast iron skillet and back up griddle it was.

"Look how the ceiling's bowing," Reynolds said. "It's going to pull the whole thing down on top of us if it doesn't get down from there."

Adjusting his hold, he hefted the iron into position to take a swing at the lizard, but Granny decided she wanted first dibs. Abandoning the lizard she was using as a play toy, she rose on her hind legs and roared at the new lizard. It was impressive, made even more so by the saliva dripping from her teeth.

The lizard answered by slashing its tail around the length of its body. The light fixture exploded in a hail of glass and sparks, causing the lizard, formerly known as Granny's play toy, to burst into flames. The inferno that molded to its body snapped it back to life. It thrashed wildly about the kitchen, colliding with the curtains at one point and setting them on fire.

It was too much for Granny. She dove at the blazing lizard. The force of their collision sent them slamming into the far wall. A loud snap echoed through the room, and Granny and the lizard disappeared as they fell through the wall.

"Granny!" I yelled, quickly rushing forward. But my chase was cut off by the lizard clinging to the ceiling suddenly dropping to the floor in front of me. I jumped back out of pure instinct, causing the ring of acid launched into the air to mostly hit my pants. Not a shock, considering the universe seemed to have it in for my pants.

Reynolds joined me on the opposite side of the stove. His pants were polka dotted with little plumes of smoke. It would have been funny if I didn't know how much it burned.

"Oh, look. Another guest," I said sarcastically of the one crawling up through the newly created hole in the floor.

"We've got to stop creating doorways," Reynolds said, eyeing several other holes in the floor where only plumes of smoke had been previously. "It's like they see it as an invitation."

Yeah. I'd like to speak to the person responsible for the guest list. "Oh look, they're talking." The two lizards huddled in the corner opposite us were exchanging a steady stream of hissing and gurgling. Reminded me of Harry Potter. "It's always good to have someone you know at a party."

The lizards stopped making noises and looked at us.

"You know," Reynolds drawled. "I don't think I like your parties." Then he leaped towards the lizard that charged at me, driving the handle of the Dutch oven into the lizard's side. It curled in on itself, modeling the letter C as it barreled over into the burning curtains and burst into flames—barely missing Scout, who'd materialized out of thin air—what the heck? Hadn't he just been on the other side of the kitchen? And where'd he get the fire extinguisher?

Whirling in panic, the newest recruit to the flaming lizard brigade careened into the next lizard emerging from the floor and produced yet another burning lizard in Granny's kitchen.

"If any more show up, they're gonna have to start wearing name tags," I hollered in aggravation.

Scout hefted the fire extinguisher he was holding and aimed it at the lizards. One bolted for Reynolds, the other for me.

"Batter up," I hollered, raising the skillet into position. The sickening thud of Reynolds' hit sounded the second before mine. The lizards arched away from us, colliding in a tangle of movement and fire.

"Man, that stinks," Reynolds coughed. "Like burnt beans and sulfur."

I stood up to take a breath and nearly gagged when the smell hit me. "Oh, that is rotten." Wrapping a hand over my mouth, I tried to protect the air I was breathing. "Scout, you're the closest. Push them through the hole in the floor."

He couldn't answer given that he was currently bent over, retching.

"Macy, watch out!" Reynolds shouted.

The window next to me exploded. In my attempt to avoid the

flying debris, I rammed into Reynolds, sending both of us to the ground.

"Cast iron is not meant for landing on," I moaned as I fished the Dutch oven lid out from under my hip and handed it back to Reynolds. Rubbing the quickly forming bruise, I tentatively pushed to a stand, only to be arrested by the sight of Granny. Her front paws rested on the floor of the new opening where the window used to be. Her muzzle was caked with blood and there was a disgusting piece of lizard tail hanging out of her mouth.

"That is gross, Granny," I said flatly.

With much exaggeration, she sucked the lizard tail in and swallowed, and if it was possible for a bear to smile, smiled at me. Again, the bacon threatened to make a reappearance.

Reaching behind me, I offered Reynolds a hand up. He had good reason to move slower than me. He'd landed half in and half out of the Dutch oven, dissecting his most intimate parts. Youch.

"Be careful of the floor," I called to Granny as she climbed back into the kitchen.

She was careful alright. In one movement, she leaped over the holes, snatched a lizard from the ceiling and dove into the jumble of lizard on the floor.

"That was impressive," Reynolds whistled in amazement.

"I didn't know bears were that nimble," I marveled. I almost felt sorry for the lizards as I watched Granny work. She was so fast and powerful. Her paws were practically on fire when she came up for air.

"Seriously, Granny," I said in exasperation. "It's like you want to burn up." Retrieving the skillet from the floor, I moved away from Reynolds, who wasn't quite able to stand upright yet, and hefted it into position. "Stop hogging the lizards. Herd them over here. And whatever you do, do not breathe deeply." They might have been scentless before, but man howdy did they stink when they were on fire.

She did send one my way, and I swung the skillet with all my might. It caught the lizard right underneath its jaw, like an uppercut. But instead of sending the lizard hurtling away, it spun in place, slinging acid and fire, and one very wicked tail.

"Crap," I yelled and dropped the skillet. Diving under the table, I balled up behind the griddle I snatched from the wall. The majority of the acid and fire missed me, but I still felt the smack of the tail as it shoved me out from under the table and into the wall. When the drapes crashed to the floor on top of me, I used the griddle like an umbrella. Scout fished me out, liberally dousing me with the extinguisher as he did.

"It doesn't work," he said, shaking the extinguisher in frustration.

As I was clearly soaked, I knew it did.

Using the back of my fingers, I slung the frothy mess from my face. "I wasn't on fire," I snarled him.

"You could have been," he shrugged. "The griddle is." He discharged the extinguisher on the griddle. The flames merely flickered in the draft created by the spray.

"Yikes," I shrieked and dropped it. "Watch out!" I grabbed Scout and spun him out of the way.

The lizards were charging at will now, like it was their last ditch attempt, which it might be. The kitchen was a mess. There were numerous gashes in the walls, and large portions of the floor and ceiling had also disappeared during the fray.

Granny tried to fling the lizards out of the openings she'd created, but her aim wasn't that great. The house rattled each time she hurled a lizard into the already fractured walls. Reynolds, Scout and I took turns at the lizards with the cast iron, but so far we'd only managed to kill one of them.

"At this rate, the house will burn down around us before they're dead," Reynolds said.

Nervously eyeing what was left of the kitchen, I thought he was right. Granny must have, too. She abandoned her attempts at tossing the lizards from the kitchen. Falling heavily on the nearest lizard, she used her weight to trap it while she dug her nails deep into the scales around its neck. Loud bellows of pain echoed through the kitchen as the fur on Granny's belly melted away.

Scout took a step forward to help her and fell through the floor up to his waist. Sensing an opening, the remaining lizard charged towards Scout. Reynolds and I simultaneously dove for it, catching the lizard's head in a cast iron pancake. It was disgusting, but effective. The lizard sank to its belly and didn't move again.

Tossing the skillet aside, I rolled onto my back. The flames had licked a path covering half the ceiling already. We needed to get out of here before it caved in. "Reynolds."

"Yep," he answered.

Working together, we freed Scout from the floor boards entrapping him and began to carefully pick our way across the pockmarked surface. Granny had finished the remaining lizard and was almost to the living room. Her gait was decidedly painful as she lumbered out of the kitchen, but considering the state her paws were in, I was grateful she could walk at all.

"So, that's trouble?" Reynolds murmured, gingerly fingering the burns on his neck as we crossed the threshold into the living room. "Adam wasn't kidding."

Scout winced and pulled a spike size wood splinter from his abdomen. "And, how," he nodded in agreement as he tossed it to the floor.

"You got a little something," Reynolds said. He waved his hand, motioning towards my back.

I turned in a semicircle, looking over my shoulder at my back, trying to see what he was talking about. "Ow!" I cried involuntarily as a sharp pain laced down my back.

"Got it," Scout said and added the glass shard to the rubble in the kitchen.

"A little warning next time!" I yelled at him.

He shook his head no. "Creates too much drama."

"I don't know," observed Reynolds. "That was pretty dramatic."

Glaring at them did nothing to wipe the smiles from their faces. Knuckle heads. Turning from them, I went in search of Granny. I found her. Back in human form and buck naked. Closing my eyes, I roughly shook my head. I guess we were even now.

From what I could see, which was everything, Granny was a

good deal worse off than us. She had very little skin that hadn't been eaten away by the acid. Her hands concerned me the most. They didn't look like they were scabbing over like the rest of the burns. By the way she was cradling them, I knew they hurt her the most.

"I'm so sorry, Granny," I said softly. I wanted to reach out to her, but due to the extent of her injuries, I didn't dare.

"Water's a no go," Scout yelled.

That meant the house was going to be a total loss. The look on Granny's face told me she understood that too.

Reynolds gently wrapped a blanket around Granny's shoulders. "Is there anything you want to save?" he asked.

Heaving a sigh, she grasped the blanket firmly about her and headed for the back bedroom.

"Come on," I whispered to the guys and started after Granny.

CHAPTER 5

"WRANGLE, DID I SAY START trouble or stay out of trouble?" Kenny asked as I came down the front steps towards them.

"I'm relatively certain that it was the latter," Wrangle answered sagely.

"You know, I could smell something burning. But I thought, nah. Surely Doc—"

"Shut up and help," I snapped at them. Shoving the load I was carrying into Wrangle's arms, I pointed him in the direction of the drop off point. "I did not do this."

"So, the others started the fire?" Kenny asked doubtfully.

Wrangle paused and turned sideways to wait for my answer.

"No," I said, avoiding their eyes and picking at the flaking bits of my semi burnt shirt so I wouldn't think about how lame what I was about to say sounded. "It was the lizard people."

"Lizard people. Of course," Kenny deadpanned. "My mistake." Hanging his head, he shook it gently. "Only you," he muttered in disbelief.

"Yeah, well, at least Granny found some clothes," I griped as I stomped up the stairs after him. "At least, you're spared from that shock."

Kenny suddenly paused in front of me. "Company," he said, shielding his eyes as he turned.

Squinting, I could just make out Smiley behind the wheel of the camo van. But he wasn't smiling as he pulled it into Granny's front yard.

"I got it. Keep helping Granny," I told Kenny.

"What happened?" Smiley asked when I jogged over and hopped onto the running board.

"Giant flaming lizards."

Charlie's face appeared behind Smiley. "Seriously?" he asked.

"Seriously," I nodded.

"That is...uh...I got nothing."

I've got the burns to prove it. And witnesses. "Any sign of Linc and Van?"

"They're in the back," Smiley answered carefully. Too carefully. I didn't like the way that Charlie slunk back into the interior either.

Opening the door, I climbed in and made my way past Smiley to the rear of the vehicle. The back door was open, but Van wasn't there. Linc, however, was on the floor. I froze when I saw the reason why.

"Linc? Are you okay?"

He popped his head up. "Right as rain," he quipped, then let his head fall heavily back to the floor.

"Maybe, if you're talking about a torrential, gut piercing rain. You do know there's a small tree limb sticking out of your stomach?"

"Yeah," he groaned. "I know it."

"I told him not to jump," Van growled angrily as he climbed back in. Over his shoulder was a large duffle bag with the words first aid stamped across it.

"Van won't let me forget," Linc whined dolefully.

I was thinking it was more the stick's fault than Van's.

Setting the bag aside, Van kneeled over Linc to closely study the wound. "This wouldn't happen if you'd listen to me. But you never listen, and this always happens."

"He always impales himself on tree limbs?" I asked, only half joking.

Van reached forward and grasped the limb with both hands. "Among other things."

Linc grunted loudly when Van ripped the limb from him. I

couldn't help but gasp at the same time. It hadn't been a gentle tug.

Holding the stick with one hand, Van pulled his shirt over his head and used it to wrap the bloody end of the stick. "Toss that in the fire, would ya?" he asked, handing it to Charlie.

I nodded at Charlie when he made eye contact with me.

"This time it's a tree limb," Van continued. "Last time it was an antenna. You don't even want to know where that one went in. I'm still having nightmares about it."

"Me, too," Linc moaned softly.

"Maybe one of these times you'll listen to me, you idiot," Van snapped at him.

"And break the cycle?" Linc wheezed.

"I think this might be a cycle you want to seriously consider breaking," I told him. Really, what was there even to consider? Limbs in the gut or out? Seemed like an easy choice to me.

Van laid three suture kits on Linc's chest, then after studying the wound again, reached in and grabbed one more. "I've got this, Doc," he assured me. "Believe me, it's not the first time I've had to patch him up."

"So you've said," I mumbled. And that was the problem. Just what the heck had they been doing that would have resulted in repeated impalements? Enough so that Van had to learn how to do stitches by himself? Frowning, I watched Van work for a minute. He did look like he knew what he was doing. "You're sure you've got this?"

"Yeah. Lucky for him."

"He'll have me put back together in no time," Linc panted, wincing as the needle pierced his skin.

"Shut up. How many times have I told you no talking when I'm sewing?" Van demanded.

"Every time," Linc said dejectedly, his words slightly slurred.

Narrowing my eyes at the two, I opted for not pursuing the issue right now. But it was going on the list, somewhere between survive this day and save the world.

Shaking my head to dispel images of Linc spearing himself in various ways, I switched my focus to finding something that might help Granny. "Do you have anything in there for acid burns?"

"What kind?"

"The kind oozing from lizard, humanoid, thingies."

He looked sidelong at me.

"Yeah, I don't know," I sighed. Which meant anything we did could potentially make it worse. "Let me know if you need me."

"Will do," he said absently. The majority of his attention was now focused on closing the gaping wound in Linc.

Reynolds was waiting for me when I exited the van.

"Simple impaling," I explained. "Apparently, it's a common occurrence." Though how I'd never known this before was a mystery.

The kitchen, or what had been the kitchen, suddenly separated from the rest of the house and crashed to the ground. It was no longer in flames. The fire had moved on to greener pastures, eating its way through the rest of the house. A surge of guilt washed over me when I thought of Granny homeless.

Speaking of Granny, where was she?

Leaving Reynolds, I circled around the house until I found her. She was standing with a long stick extended over the fire. On the end of it, I could have sworn I saw wienies.

"Decided to have a wienie roast?" I asked as I tentatively approached.

She sighed heavily at the intrusion. "It's just a house. The only thing I care about in this world ain't in it."

Then why the heck did we have to carry out all that stuff, I thought as I rubbed the back of my stiff neck.

Oblivious to my thoughts, she pulled the stick back and began to blow on the dogs. "No sense in letting 'em go to waste. Anyways, I didn't get to eat breakfast."

How could she be so calm? Roasting wienies over her burning house like it was nothing? We just fought giant flaming lizards for goodness sake. She was practically a walking scab!

I stopped rubbing my neck and placed my hands on my hips. If she wasn't going to make a big deal out of it, I certainly wasn't. I really hoped this wasn't going to be one of those delayed reaction kind of things. "Got any more?" I asked.

She threw the pack at me. Hard. I caught them with my stomach.

There was a taste of delayed reaction. Who knew a pack of hot dogs could fit so snugly in a stomach cavity from the outside as well as it did from the inside? Maintaining my grasp on the package, I slowly stood back up. So, that's how it was going to be, paid for a little at a time. It took me a minute before I could get enough breath to say thanks.

By the time I'd fully recovered, Wrangle had found us. He got permission from Granny and gathered sticks for everyone. As a result, we were all grouped around the far edge of what was left of Granny's house, roasting wienies. I could only eat one, and I had to force it down. They had a twang to them, and not one that I normally associated with hot dogs. It wasn't exactly like burnt beans, but given what the fire was made of, the association was already there in my mind.

Tossing my stick into the fire, I walked a few paces away. It was hard not to stare at the group. We were a rag tag looking bunch. Clothing was ripped and torn or missing altogether. Hair was plastered to foreheads by sweat, and we were covered in black smudges and now hot dog grease. Granny, Reynolds and I also had gross looking scabby blisters covering most of our exposed skin. We needed showers, and fresh clothing. And time to heal.

Turning my attention to the multiple piles of Granny's belongings, I wondered what we were going to do with it all. Better yet, what was I going to do with Granny?

"You done?" Granny asked, startling me by her sudden appearance.

"Yes, ma'am," I answered.

"You asked me why Adam would send you to me."

I perked up immediately. "I did." I hadn't for even a moment forgotten why I was here. But considering all that had just happened, I wasn't sure when I should bring it up again.

"Follow me."

My following stopped when she opened the door to a dilapidated outhouse and went inside. The door slammed shut behind her, presenting me with the classic crescent moon. Was she making a detour?

"Macy, get yourself in here," she hollered. Irritation radiated through her voice.

"You could have told me beforehand," I mumbled as I carefully opened the door and peered inside.

She looked up from the hole in the ground that she was kneeling beside. "What's that?"

"Nothing."

"That's what I thought," she said, fixing me with her steely eyes. "Well, are you coming in or not?"

I stepped inside and let the door hit me in the backside.

"We've got to go down there." She looked up at me, then pointed to the hole, like I couldn't figure out where down was.

Down the deep, dark hole in the ground. Of course we did.

Heaving an exasperated sigh, she gingerly lowered herself into the hole. I leaned over and examined the darkness that swallowed up Granny. I'd really like to have a word with the one who tied my destiny to dark tunnels. And if there was something fouler than dark air at the bottom of this, I wanted more than words.

Grasping the sides of the hole, I lowered myself until my feet touched a ladder rung. At least it came equipped with a real ladder this time. That was a solid improvement.

"You can jump, if ya want to," Granny yelled up at me.

I knew she had. I had heard her landing. "How far?" I yelled back.

"Twenty, thirty feet."

It was doable. I'd already jumped way more than that. But not in absolute darkness. "Cats always land on their feet," I whispered to myself.

"Do something!" Granny hollered. "Either let go or climb. Time's a wasting."

Pressing my lips together to keep from smarting off to her, I let go and dropped. Granny cocked her eyebrow at me as I rose slowly from the superhero worthy pose I'd struck when I landed.

"What?" I said defensively. There wasn't a law against looking good when I performed daring feats of daring and such. People got paid a lot of money for it in Hollywood.

She rolled her eyes at me and flipped on the light switch.

"You couldn't have done that before I dropped?" I said accusingly. I mean, hybrids could see in the dark pretty well, but not this dark.

She didn't even try to hide her patronizing smile. Payback. Coming to a Macy near you.

Walking a few steps forward and away from Granny, I placed my hands on my hips and inspected the room. It appeared to be a much larger version of what Juarez had in the SubV. Except, maybe not as updated. Or clean, I thought as I ran my finger through the thick layer of dust coating a row of terminals. Either way, I was never again going to enter a shabby dilapidated out building and expect it to be a shabby dilapidated out building.

"Macy?" Reynolds yelled from above.

"Down here," I called. "There's a ladder or you can drop. It's about *fifty* feet down." I looked pointedly at Granny, but it only served to widen her smile. Sooner or later, I was going to have to point out the fact that I was not the one who torched her house. Given the size of her smile, I had better make that sooner.

Reynolds landed lightly. It wasn't as pretty as my landing, but he hadn't even hesitated with the decision to drop. There was something to be said about knowing your abilities.

"Whew," Reynolds whistled. "Looks like we hit the jackpot." He studied the controls a minute and then walked back over to the ladder. "Flash," he yelled. "Get down here."

Two thuds later, Flash and Charlie dropped in.

"Home away from home," Flash said, rubbing his hands together in anticipation. But his enthusiasm hit a snag when he examined the equipment more closely. "Geesh, a bit old, isn't it?"

"Ancient," Charlie agreed. "It's like we've fallen into some 1980s bomb shelter."

"Kind a cool, actually," Flash said. "Very retro."

"I feel ya," Charlie said, nodding to some groove that only he heard.

Then they looked at each other with big goofy grins on their faces.

I was definitely on the outside of this circle, and more than a little weirded out by their enthusiasm.

Charlie wheeled a couple of chairs over to the row of terminals and shoved one Flash's direction. "Hope you haven't forgotten the basics," he teased.

"Even if that were possible," Flash said as he caught the chair and pulled it beneath him. "I'd still know more than you, Co-boy."

Then the conversation got even stranger, dissolving into successive insults too obtuse for me to follow. What was fortran anyway? I was glad they were enjoying themselves, but I didn't know how any of this was going to help us find Adam.

"Granny, Did Adam ever give you any instructions if he should come up missing?"

"Just to bring whoever showed up here."

It was frustrating doing nothing but watching Flash and Charlie. But where computers were concerned, that was all I could do. We were not the best of friends. It was all well and good until it didn't obey my commands. Then it was all rage and nearly irrepressible urges aimed at destruction. And that was before I had claws to actually rip the computer apart.

I walked up behind Flash and Charlie and placed a hand on the back of each of their chairs. "Adam told Granny to bring us here if he went missing. So there has to be a way of locating him down here."

"Like a tracking mechanism?" Charlie asked.

"That'd be my guess," I said, nodding to Kenny and the rest of the guys as they dropped in. Except for Scout, who I guessed was somewhere scouting. "Flash, did the Organization microchip you or something like that?"

"Not that I'm aware of," he answered. "But, if I was going to create a way to track myself, should I ever need to be tracked, I know how I would do it."

Charlie leaned over and watched what Flash was doing on his screen. "That's what I was thinking," he nodded. "Almost impossible to trace."

"Unless you know what you're looking for," Flash said.

Then they both looked at me.

"What?" I said warily.

"You and Adam have the same nanobots, right?" Flash asked.

"Yes," I answered, backing up in order to make room for him as he stood. Then my stomach sunk. "And, no," I added slowly.

Pausing in his scouring of the cabinets, Flash said, "What do you mean, no?"

"It is true that I have Adam's nanobots."

"But?" Charlie asked with upraised eyebrows.

"But, I also have other nanobots. At least, I did a long time ago."

Kenny took a few steps in my direction. "Long time ago?"

It felt like I was on trial. I couldn't miss Granny's amused look at my discomfort either. Truth was freedom, right? Right.

"In the midst of discovering Julia's betrayal, we also discovered my origins. It seems that I was created via DNA manipulation with repeated nanobot integration," I said quickly.

My words seemed to echo in the awkward silence that developed. No one repeated it out loud, but I could see them working it out in their minds.

"You mean you were genetically engineered? A test tube baby?" Reynolds finally said.

"Yep," I nodded. "If it's true. It could just be a piece of planted information," I shrugged.

"I guess we're about to find out," Charlie whispered.

"If you say so," I said uncertainly.

Flash found what he was looking for and walked back towards us. In his hands, he carried a large silver ring. Placing it on the floor, he pushed a series of buttons and said, "Initializing."

"I've got it on screen," Charlie said. "Calibrating in three, two, one."

Everyone was silent while a blue light travelled in circles around the silver ring.

"It'll take a minute to set the parameters," Flash said. "When it's ready, you'll need to stand here." He pointed inside the ring then looked back at me for my response.

Stand in the ring? I could do that. "No problem," I said more confidently than I felt.

Flash rejoined Charlie at the computer and repeatedly looked back at me and offered suggestions to Charlie that I didn't understand. The only thing I did surmise was that it was a scanner focused in on my nanobot signatures. Living science fiction, that's what I was now.

"Okay, we're ready," Flash said as he backed away from Charlie and knelt down in front of the ring again.

"This better not be taking nudey pictures of me," I warned as I stepped inside the ring.

Flash rolled his eyes up to me. "Though I may not find that to be totally unpleasant, let me say one word. Adam would kick my—"

"That's more than one word," Charlie interrupted.

"Still true," Flash muttered.

"You got that right," more than one person repeated.

It seemed Adam's reach was a great one. In this instance, I didn't mind.

"Macy, I'm going to need you to stand perfectly still. Nobody else move," Flash directed. "I'm only half certain that this will work, and I don't want it keying in on someone else."

Flash fiddled with the device a few more times before he said, "When you're ready."

My heart rate picked up. I was about to be confronted with physical evidence one way or the other about my origins. I hoped how nervous I was didn't show.

"We're live," Charlie said as the ring began to glow. Pulsing blue waves rose from its surface, one after the other until they formed a curtain of sorts that stopped somewhere above my head. "I've got two distinct signatures."

"Locked?" Flash asked.

"Locked," Charlie confirmed. "You can disengage."

Disengaging caused the shimmering curtain of blue to collapse back into the ring.

"Okay, Macy, you can step out now," Flash said. He waited until I was clear, then picked the ring up and headed to the back of the room.

"I'll take one, you take the other?" Charlie called to Flash.

"Roger that," he answered as he secured the ring back in its original box.

Now it was all over but the waiting. For me, anyway. Trying to give them space to work, I took a few steps back and bumped into Granny. "Sorry," I whispered.

"Don't mention it. It ain't the worst thing that happened to me today," she grumbled.

She was angry. I was angry too. "This is not my fault," I snarled at her. "I had nothing to do with Adam's disappearance, and I certainly didn't order lizard men to attack your house."

Her eyes softened a little, as if she just realized that her anger existed. She looked down and away, heaving the sigh I was familiar with. "What is going on, Macy?" she asked quietly. "What happened to Adam?"

"Has Adam ever mentioned the Consortium to you?"

"Briefly."

"After we left here, I found out that my hybrids—the ones from the Colony—were in trouble."

"What Colony?" Granny asked suspiciously.

"In New Orleans."

She narrowed her eyes at me. "You got ta be kidding. New Orleans?"

I shrugged. It wasn't my choice.

"There's a colony of hybrids in New Orleans?" she chuckled.

"Was. There was a colony of hybrids in New Orleans," I said sadly. "It's been decimated by the Consortium."

"Are there other colonies?" she asked.

I started to say no, but then I thought about it. There was no reason the government couldn't have planted hybrid colonies all over the country. That might be worth looking into. You know, should I need to raise an army and all.

"I don't know. A lot of things exist that I didn't think possible before."

"And Adam?"

Her question stopped the pacing I had unconsciously started. What about Adam? I reached through our bond again and felt the nothingness, like an ache where he should be. I sighed and crossed my arms over my chest.

"Macy," Granny said softly.

Opening my eyes, I took a moment to blink away the tears poised to spill over. "When we went to rescue the hybrids at the Colony, we separated. Adam was leading the team that went to the Colony, and I was in the woods. We were almost finished with transferring the hybrids to safety when he disappeared."

"If you weren't with him, how do you know he disappeared?" Granny asked.

"We have a bond. I hear him, feel him. Inside." I thumped my chest with my hand, my eyes inadvertently meeting Kenny's. I hadn't been sure that he had a bond with Crystal until that moment.

"The connection was cut?" Granny asked.

"Not entirely. It's been shut off or blocked somehow. He's still there. I just can't reach him. I led this team to the Colony grounds." I had to stop and take a few deep breaths. Talking about it made it feel like I was there again.

Reynolds stepped forward, providing the words that I was having difficulty uttering. "The Consortium had left quite a visual. Very graphic, ma'am. A lot of body parts, blood, including Adam's."

Granny shut her eyes tight against Reynolds words. I lightly touched his arm, stopping him before he could continue.

"He's alive, Granny."

She opened her eyes and looked at me.

"I was able to restore our connection long enough for Adam to tell me to find you. Since then, I've had dreams, sort of." At the mention of dreams, her face collapsed. I didn't' know what she had seen in her dreams, and I didn't want to know. He was alive. I had to believe that, and so did she.

"He wouldn't have sent me here without a reason," I told her.

After a moment, she nodded. "No, he wouldn't," she agreed.

There was a moment of furious whispering between Flash and Charlie, causing me to turn away from Granny to watch them. Frowning at their behavior, I began to move towards them.

"I think we've got it," Charlie said.

He leaned away from the screen, giving me a clear view as I approached. "Is that D.C.?" I asked.

"Looks like it," Reynolds said from beside me.

"It fits," mumbled Wrangle. "Remember, the smell on the roof?"

The capital smell. But why take him to Washington? They could experiment on him anywhere.

"We forgot to tell you, but the surveillance…it originated from D.C. too," Charlie said.

This was about more than just Consortium experimentation. I had yet to question the rest of the gang on their encounters, but this whole thing had a different feel than the Consortium. The added confirmation of the link to D.C. more or less established this as something else. Yet the lizards had a similar smell to the Furries. A collaboration, maybe?

"We should let Cedars know," Reynolds said. "There should be a sat phone around here somewhere."

I nodded absently. Dad gum it, I wish this would quit getting more and more complicated. What was the point of observing Granny? Leverage on Adam? But they already had him incapacitated, and they'd tried to kill Granny. A dead Granny was the opposite of leverage. It didn't make any sense.

Letting go of the chair, I scrubbed my hands across my face. "Has anyone checked on Linc recently?"

"He's fine," Van assured me. "I'll check on him in a minute."

Though his words didn't indicate it, he looked worried. I watched him walk over to the cabinets and began randomly searching for the sat phone. Catching Kenny's eye, I raised my eyebrows.

He closed the distance between us before whispering, "Cousins."

Cousins? My eyebrows shot even higher when I worked through the family tree. I'd have hated to attend that family reunion. Kenny nodded at the look on my face. But still, he had family. That was something not many of us here had left. Not by blood, anyway. My family was Miranda. And, I guess now I had to add Cedars. And, the Colony hybrids. The cadets, I suppose. Granny felt like family too. And, Adam. What could I say? I had a big heart. Annoyingly, unpredictably big.

"Is Scout okay? He had a small impaling of his own. Oh, and he sort of shot himself."

Kenny smiled. "He's sore, but he'll live. How bout yourself?"

"Me? Stellar." I let my gaze drift to the ceiling as I exhaled. "It's been a stellar morning."

Our eyes met, then we both laughed at my answer.

"Hey, I haven't talked to you about this, but are you cool with going back to the Organization? As in, making it your home."

He regarded me a moment, his face bearing the old cockiness that I'd grown accustomed to. "For now," he nodded.

Oh, there was a boatload of non submission in those two words, and I was right there with him. I was done playing by rules set for me by others, be they friend or foe.

His slow grin let me know he knew exactly what I was thinking. "Going rogue," he snickered knowingly.

I narrowed my eyes at him. That was the second time he'd accused me of going rogue. How did he read me so well? And, I wasn't so much going rogue as I was doing whatever the hell I wanted from now on. Wait, wasn't that the definition of going rogue?

"Maybe," I shrugged. I felt lighter almost immediately. Macy unleashed. It felt good. "Probably," I nodded and lifted my eyes back to his. "If you change your mind between now and then, you'll let me know?" I asked.

He just stood there looking at me.

"Kenny," I whispered. "If you just disappeared without any notice—"

"Like you did?" he cut in.

"I was kidnapped," I shot back in surprise. "I didn't leave by choice."

He crossed his arms over his chest and scowled at me. "By the Organization?" he said skeptically.

"I didn't know there was an Organization at that time," I snapped. "Or a Consortium, which also kidnapped me."

"You were kidnapped twice?" Scout asked as he suddenly appeared next to me.

"Yes and where the heck did you come from?" I demanded.

"Behind you," he said, looking at me like I was crazy.

"You were kidnapped by the Consortium?" Kenny asked, prodding me to continue. Though now, he wasn't so much angry as he was concerned.

"Yes," I said, still eyeing Scout. We were going to discuss his magical disappearing and reappearing act at some point.

"Why?" Kenny asked.

Sighing at the conversation I knew was coming, I shifted my gaze back to Kenny. "They wanted to use my DNA to create a hybrid army."

"Why would they want your DNA?" asked Charlie, who had swiveled his chair to face us.

Here we go again. Bombshell number three. I sat down in the chair nearest to me and cleared my throat. "It seems that, when I was engineered, I was part of a project called Mindbenders. Whether it was government sponsored or wholly Organization, I don't know."

"Just a minute," Flash and Charlie said together.

"Race ya," Charlie challenged as his fingers flew across the keyboard.

"You're on, monkey breath," Flash laughed.

Monkey breath?

"What are you racing for?" Van asked, having abandoned his search for the phone.

Kenny walked up and laid his hand on Van's shoulder. "If that file has at anytime, anywhere graced the depths of a computer, Charlie will find it."

"Not before me," Flash said triumphantly.

"You found it?" I asked surprised.

"Dang it," Charlie crowed.

Rolling my chair between their two consoles, I looked at their screens. They were looking at two different files. "This is the one that we found," I said, pointing to the familiar abstract. The other, I'd never seen before. I pointed to it. "Can you print this one out?"

"Yep," Flash said.

"Does this indicate you?" Charlie asked.

I looked where he was pointing. "Yeah, that's me," I said blandly.

"Wow," he breathed, quickly scrolling through the file. "You're like a mega genius."

"Didn't you know that already?" Wrangle said sarcastically as he leaned in to read over Charlie's shoulder.

Leaving them to their discovery, I went to the printer and collected the report. Briefly skimming the first few pages left me unsure if it was the same project. It had eggs dividing which wasn't mentioned in the original report. I started to throw it away, but then caught myself. Considering the pace at which everything kept changing around here, I should probably keep it. I folded it and put it alongside the list that Kenny had given me of the missing and dead.

"You're old," Kenny cried just as I slapped the pocket closed. Lifting my head in his direction allowed me to see the back of their heads all clustered around the terminal as they read the report.

"Real old," Van whistled. "Like over a hundred or something."

"I am not!" I yelled. "It's sixty seven…or so," I finished lamely.

Every one of them turned to stare at me. Then they broke down in hysterical laughter, leaning against each other for support.

"That's real mature guys." Who was I kidding? I was talking to a bunch of young men. Maturity wasn't even in the room. "I wasn't even conscious for most of it, which you'll see if you shut up and keep reading," I said loudly enough to be heard over their laughter. "I give up." Walking to the far wall, I turned and braced my back against it.

"You okay with all this?" Granny asked as she joined me.

"I'm okay with it," I shrugged. Not much I could do about it anyway. Placing one foot flat against the wall, I crossed my arms and watched the boys cracking jokes with each other about me. At least they were starting to become comfortable with one another.

"Granny, what are you going to do?"

"About the house?" she asked.

"Yeah," I nodded. "I don't know if the Consortium will send anyone else here. You might ought to come with us."

She looked up at the ceiling. "Oh, I don't know about that. I'm pretty good in the woods."

"Yeah, about that. A bear?" I said, looking at her sideways.

"Sort of fits my personality, don't it?" she chuckled.

She said it, not me. Out loud anyway. "Wait a minute, Adam made you a bear?"

"He wanted something that would fit in. Not cause trouble, ya see. Remember this was a long time ago. Before Adam know'd everything he does now."

"You mean he couldn't separate the repair function of the nanobots from the animal DNA?"

Granny cocked an eyebrow and looked at me blankly.

"Never mind, I got it. He made you a bear."

"That he did," she nodded.

"But what are you going to do now? Without the house? And your injuries..." I trailed off at her sharp look.

"I'll be alright," she said dismissively. "I got friends, ya know?"

"Where?" I asked, turning to face her. I didn't think there was anyone for miles.

"In the woods," she repeated. "In town."

The caginess of her response alarmed me. "Do you mean hybrid friends?" I asked suspiciously, my eyebrows rising at her tight smile. Hold up. Where had these other hybrids come from? I was almost certain Adam wouldn't have created a whole bunch of hybrids outside of the Organization. My eyes widened further as the answer struck home. "Granny!"

Her hard as steel glare caused me to snap my mouth shut before I could voice what I was thinking. I might not say it, but Granny, you got some splaining to do. She wouldn't let me near Adam, while she had frolicked with the mountain folk? Propagating hybrids everywhere?

"Don't ya look at me like that, young'un," she said, wagging her finger at me. "I had forty years of faithful marriage." Casting her eyes around the room, she cleared her throat and whispered, "I was lonely."

I looked away from Granny then, mostly to allow her to hide her embarrassment. I didn't care if she had sought companionship with someone or more than one someone. It probably was very lonely up here. And she had sort of told me before when she'd threatened to tell me about her hybrid love experience. I just hadn't thought she was serious, nor had I thought of it since then. On purpose.

"Granny, you do know that you seeking...kinky hybrid—"I started laughing.

"Watch yourself, girlie," Granny growled.

"I'm trying to say that I don't think less of you, for...for..." I was trying to think of how Miranda would phrase it as I bent over with both hands on my thighs, my whole frame shaking in laughter.

"You ain't too old for me to take over my knee," she threatened.

When my behavior began to draw the attention of the boys, I knew I had to stop. Forcing myself, I managed to quit laughing, but I half strangled myself in the process. "Whew," I breathed as I stood up and wiped the tears from my eyes. "I am not judging you, Granny. Believe me, I don't have that right or want to."

"You bet your britches you don't," she snarled, her face red with embarrassment.

Laying one hand on her arm, I faced her. "Granny, I'm serious." I hoped she could read the sincerity in my eyes.

"Humph," she grunted in response. Shrugging my hand off, she turned her back to the wall again as if the discussion was over, which I guess it was.

"If you're determined to stay here, then I'm giving you my cell number. Just in case." I would at some point be reunited with my cell.

"I won't need it," she said, annoyed by the mere suggestion.

"Just in case," I repeated again.

"Suit yourself," she mumbled.

Granny could be so ornery. Like a big craggy mountain. But there was gold inside. I'd been treated to it last visit. This visit? Pretty much all crag. If she didn't rein it in, I was going to start calling her the Kraken. Visions of rolling pins raised high in Granny's hand overtook the newly developed nickname. Maybe not.

Leaving her to her cantankerousness, I walked back over to the console and pulled up a chair. "This Adam?" I asked, pointing to the blinking light on the screen.

"That's him," Flash answered.

"That's him," I repeated to myself. I so wished I could reach through the computer screen and pull him back. Then a thought occurred to me. "The other nanobot signature, did you get a read on it?"

Flash and Charlie looked at each other. "We were going to get to that," Flash said reluctantly.

Crud. I braced myself for more complications. "What?" I drawled, not really wanting to know the answer.

"There are two identical signatures—" Flash began.

"Identical to the other one you carry," Charlie finished.

"Right," Flash nodded. "In Montana."

I blinked repeatedly as I processed the information. "You're telling me that two other individuals are carrying the same nanobots that I was created with and are currently located at Organization headquarters?"

"It appears that way," Flash said hesitantly.

The room grew unnaturally still as they waited for me to respond. I wished I had some brilliant conclusion to give them, but I didn't even have a brilliant comment. All I had was this nagging urge to look more fully at the other report. Prying the velcro apart, I reached in and pulled it out of my pocket.

The first and second pages only indicated an experiment in genetically engineering an embryo but gave no identification of the origin of the component DNA. On the third page, I found what I suspected. The egg had divided twice. One of the embryos from the first division was labeled 1945MG001, my label. The others weren't given any designations at all. That was not something that would have happened in a lab setting. The omission here was intentional. Why, I didn't know, but either way, there should have been a total of four signatures.

"You guys are sure there are only two other signatures?" I asked them.

"That's all that shows up," Flash nodded. "Why?"

"There should be four. Unless someone is dead." I folded the report and put it back in my pocket.

"It could be," Charlie began, "that the potential other signature is too far out of range. We could boost the signal?"

I started to tell them not to bother, but then thought about it again. Knowledge was power and right now, I needed all the power I could get. "Do it," I nodded and walked towards Reynolds. "Did we locate a phone?" I asked him.

He handed me a dinosaur of a phone. "It's old, but it will work," he assured me.

Not willing to risk another confrontation with Olivia, I dialed Miranda's cell. Then careful to avoid the monstrous antenna, I lifted the phone to my ear.

"Hello?" Miranda said uncertainly.

"Miranda, it's me."

"I was hoping it was. Did you find him?"

"We know his location."

"Hang on. I'm putting you on speaker. Cedars and Juarez are here."

No Olivia. Thank goodness. Muffling the end of the phone, I turned to Flash. "Can you send them the coordinates?"

He thought about it, then nodded. "These babies are hard wired. I should be able to send it anywhere."

"Flash can transmit Adam's location when you're ready," I told them.

"Tell Juarez it's a fixed transmission," Flash said.

"I heard," Juarez said before I could. "Give me a minute."

"Is everyone okay?" Cedars asked.

"Uh? Mostly."

"We're fine," Reynolds interjected. "Minor casualties. Down a house."

"Alright, show me what you got," Juarez said. "Hmm," he moaned softly.

"What's wrong?" I asked.

"If the coordinates fall where I think they do, he will be in one of the tightest security facilities the United States government has to offer."

My heart dropped at the news.

"I'm going to need some time to look at this," he added.

Great. Let's hope Adam had time.

Switching gears, Juarez said, "Hey MK. Don't take Olivia's anger as directed at you personally. After the loss of Renard and Pike and Julia's betrayal, and now Adam…she can't stand the thought of losing anyone else."

I didn't know how to answer him without insulting Olivia. So, I didn't.

"Macy, we really do need you to come back now," Cedars said cautiously. "We need time to find a way in—"

"Won't be easy," Juarez commented.

"Additionally," Cedars continued, "before you left, Adam set up a contingency plan should the existence of hybrids be exposed."

"Great. What does that have to do with me?"

"You are the face of that contingency."

"What?"

"President O'Conner has called demanding an answer for New Orleans. I need you here now."

"You want me to represent the Organization to the President?" I squeaked.

"Adam does," he said firmly.

"Of the United States?" My voice kept rising higher and higher with each word.

"You can do this, Macy," Miranda said encouragingly.

I didn't want to do this. I didn't sign up for this junk. I just wanted to find Adam, not talk to the President of the United States about the massacre in New Orleans. How did he even know about what happened in New Orleans?

"Who better to represent all of hybridom but the super brain herself?" Miranda said.

"We have already maneuvered transport close to your area. I want you back here before noon."

Did he? Not if he thought speaking to me like that was okay. I was not going to be ordered around anymore, by anyone.

Realizing his mistake, with a little help from Miranda, he quickly amended his prior statement. "Please, Macy. We'll figure out the organizational details later. Just get your butt back here. Please."

That sounded like something Adam would say, except for the please, which he'd said twice. There wasn't anything I could do here anyway, and maybe I'd light a fire under him if I was there.

"Okay," I agreed. "Tell Reynolds the details." I handed the phone off to Reynolds and went to stand by Granny. "You're sure you're going to be okay here by yourself?" I asked her.

"I lived most of my life by myself," she said sarcastically. "And, like I said, I ain't exactly alone."

"You could still come with us?"

"And leave all this?" She looked around lovingly. "Nah, I'll stay here and let ya focus on finding Adam."

"And what if the Consortium comes back?"

She cut her eyes to me. "I think I've demonstrated my abilities there."

"But we were here too."

She shrugged unworriedly. "My people will help."

"I don't want to hear about an animal led massacre on the evening news."

She chuckled dryly. "Oh, we won't leave no evidence."

"You're really going to stay?"

"I am. Ya know'd how to find me if ya need to."

She had obviously forgotten who she was talking to.

CHAPTER 6

I T WAS NEARLY THREE IN the morning when I stepped into the Organization's kitchen. Except for the light over the large wedge island, the kitchen was mostly dark. Miranda was seated there, nursing a cup of something hot. She looked up when I walked in.

"You're up late or is it early?"

"Couldn't sleep." She blew on the cup she held in her hands. "Want some? It's some sort of sleep inducing, tension nullifying tea. Margaret made it."

"Margaret's up?"

"Not anymore."

I walked over and slid into the stool across from her. I was so tired. Not that I could sleep. All my attempts on the plane had been a very successful string of failures. Bone weary was probably the more appropriate term anyway. Could bones get tired?

"Got anything stronger?" I asked.

"You don't drink," she said without looking up from her cup.

"I'm reconsidering."

She snorted softly, causing her tea to slosh over onto the countertop. "I'm not sure now's the time for you to start sewing wild oats and all."

"You're one to judge after all the crap I've had to put up with from you over the years."

"Not judging," she shook her head. "Advising. I think we are going to need every available brain cell you have to get out of this one."

And then some. Grabbing a cup from the stand, I drug it

across the granite and waited while she filled it with tea. I brought it to my nose and sniffed. It didn't smell too bad.

"You okay?" she asked cautiously.

It was the same question I'd asked myself the whole plane trip back. "I don't know," I sighed. "Everything's different. Now, everything's changed again. I keep trying to take a step back and just breathe. But every time I think I'm headed in the right direction, something new gets added to the mix."

"Well, I hate to be the bearer of unwanted news, but more changes are on the way."

I took a long sip of my tea and followed with a roll of my shoulders. "What am I in for now?" I asked reluctantly.

"President, Joint Chiefs, and other such notables."

Shoot. "When?"

"In the morning."

"It is the morning."

"Well, at least you won't have the agonizing wait to contend with."

I eyed her over my cup as I drained it. Not enough tension tamer in the world.

"Any word from Adam?" she asked

"None," I said, setting the cup down hard. I hadn't heard from him since before the whole debacle at Granny's.

"You're doing better than I would. If something happened to Jamie..." She set her cup down and wrapped her arms around herself like it physically hurt her to consider the possibility. Lashing out unexpectedly, she gripped my hand tightly. "I'll do anything you need me to do," she whispered fiercely. "Whether the other inhabitants of this house approve of it or not. Legal, illegal, I don't care. You hear me?"

I gave her a small smile. It seemed I had a knack for inspiring rebellion against authority. I didn't know if that was a good thing or a bad thing.

"Easy, Wolfie," I teased, patting her hand before wriggling free. "I don't even have a plan yet."

"Are we making plans?" Juarez asked as he passed us. Making

a beeline for the fridge, he opened it and started pulling out stuff and tossing it on the counter.

I caught the tomato as it rolled off the island. "I'm always planning," I quipped and set the tomato back on the counter.

"Not that they're always good plans," Miranda muttered into her tea.

"They'd work if I didn't always have someone messing them up," I said tightly.

"It's called improvising," she retorted while glaring at me.

Holding her stare was easy, especially when her improvising was more like pain in the butt or whatever other body part took the hit because of her meddling. "Your improvisation skills leave much to be desired."

Pressing her lips together and narrowing her eyes, she bowed her head slightly. "Granted," she grudgingly acknowledged.

Juarez reached for the bread on the counter. "I heard about the lizard situation," he said. "What these people come up with is downright weird. Instead of learning how to integrate the animal DNA with the human, they overwrite it. And why, of all things, a lizard?"

"I don't know. Why choose to make a furry?" I countered.

"Furries may be ugly, but they can fight. From what Reynolds said, these lizards weren't very effective fighters." He looked to me for confirmation.

"They had a mean tail whip. But generally, they were slow and not very coordinated. The only thing they used their mouth full of teeth for was to chew through the roof."

"Yeah, I saw his burns." He looked me up and down. "You seem to be healing well."

"Well enough to commence rescuing Adam?" I asked hopefully.

He popped the top on his soda without answering the question. Opening the bread, he pulled out four slices and haphazardly tossed them onto the paper plates he'd gotten. With his hands resting on the countertop, he paused. "Getting to Adam is going to be tough," he said. "Near as I can tell, he's in a CIA black site."

"What's that?" Miranda asked.

"It's a prison on steroids," he answered. Sliding the cutting board over, he laid a knife on top of it. "Slice that, will ya?" he nodded toward the tomato.

Picking up the knife as directed, I started on the tomato. "But you can find a way in?" I asked.

"Depends."

"On?"

He didn't answer me immediately. His whole attention seemed to be focused on the construction of his sandwiches, but I recognized it for the stalling that it was. The longer he delayed the more nervous I got. Finally, he looked up and said, "You."

"Me?" I said in surprise. "Why me?"

He pulled the cutting board with the newly sliced tomato towards him. "Tell me about the episode in the hangar, when you stopped the attack on Adam."

What? I thought back to when it happened. "I remember my normal senses falling away. I saw colors around everyone—"

"Like auras?" Miranda interrupted.

"I guess," I shrugged. "Everyone was sort of shimmery." I rubbed my hands over my eyes as I tried to recall the incident. "Most of the colors were blue or green, but hers was black with red streaks running through it. Nobody else seemed to see her. I started moving towards her—"

"Did anyone see you coming?" Juarez interrupted.

Replaying the memory again, I frowned. "They didn't seem to. Except for one guy. I shoved him out of the way, and he looked angrily at me, but then just looked away."

"Is it possible he looked away because he didn't see you?"

I thought about it a moment. "I guess. What are you getting at?"

"Did time slow down?"

Taking a breath to say no, I stopped. "I don't remember time slowing down, but I distinctly remember snapping back into real time." I looked up at Juarez. "It might have slowed down."

"Has it happened before?"

I looked at Miranda. She raised her eyebrows at me.

"Maybe once…with Adam. Right before we had to go scuba diving. But he didn't seem to notice anything."

"It will take some practice," he said, still nodding, "but you might just be our ticket in. Avoid a whole lot of trouble."

"What will take practice?" I demanded.

"She's a possible TS?" Cedars said from behind me.

I'd been so focused on Juarez that I hadn't heard Cedars come in.

"Time Shifter," Juarez supplied to mine and Miranda's confused faces.

Cedars walked around and laid his hand on Miranda's shoulder. He leaned in and gently kissed her forehead. "How are you feeling?" he asked her softly.

"Better," she smiled at him.

"What is a time shifter?" I asked, while still examining the exchange between Miranda and Cedars.

"We've just recently discovered that some of us are able to shift through time. Like fazing in and out," Juarez answered.

I stared at him blank faced.

"Honest," Juarez laughed.

"That is messed up," I sighed in disgust.

"Yep," he nodded and took a bite of sandwich. He slid the other sandwich he'd made over to me.

Not feeling the slightest bit like eating, I stared vacantly at it.

"Eat it anyway," Miranda encouraged. "You need to eat," she said pointedly when I looked at her.

I picked it up and took a bite. It tasted like wax in my mouth. Ordinarily, I loved a good sandwich. But nothing was ordinary anymore. I put the sandwich back down.

"Are you saying that I can jump through time?"

"Not jump. Shift. You can travel through normal time at different speeds." He took another bite of his sandwich. "Maybe."

"How is that possible?"

"Physics. It has something to do with the nanobots opening a small tunnel in space? I'd have to get the techs in here to explain it to you properly."

"Don't bother," I sighed and picked up the sandwich again. Physics. Worse, physics with tunnels. It was one big cosmic joke on Macy. Putting two and two together, I said, "You think I can get inside by using this."

"Maybe."

"How do you know that's what I'm doing at all?"

"I don't. Like I said, it's new. We'll have to play with it."

"I can do it," Olivia said, coming to stand beside Juarez. She wrapped her arm around his waist and gave him a quick hug.

Doesn't anybody ever sleep around here? "Wow, you look better than the last time I saw you," I told her.

"All better," she acknowledged with a smile. Then the smile faded. "Are you attempting to make plans without my input?" she asked accusingly.

Intentionally moving slowly, I put the sandwich back down and stared hard at her. Perhaps she was a force to be reckoned with for her students, but I was not her student, and I was dang tired of being treated like one.

"Olivia, we should get one thing clear right now. I will do what I will do, and I don't need your permission or even your blessing."

"Well, someone's a grouch this morning," she said, meeting my gaze without flinching. Then she turned her attention back to Juarez.

Not a grouch. Tired of being pushed around and having to fight everyone all the time. Tired of being shoved into containers that were not Macy shaped.

"I'm going to bed," I said and slapped my hand on the counter as I pushed away. Striding out of the kitchen, I was determined to put some space between me and them. I walked until I found a set of stairs. At the top of the stairs, I ran into Margaret.

"Where are you headed?" she asked softly.

"I have no freaking idea," I said, throwing my hands up in the air.

"If you are looking for Adam's suite, go up one more flight and turn right. The hallway dead ends into it."

I nodded, halfway to tears. "Will I need a key?"

"Adam already coded you in. I think the password had something to do with a nickname he gave you?" She shrugged helplessly.

"Thanks, Margaret."

"Anytime, Macy."

She was a nice lady. I wondered if she was a hybrid.

Following her directions did indeed lead me to Adam's door and the keypad. I tried to figure out what nickname he had given me, entering them as I thought of them. Mace? Nope. MK? MacyKat? The red light on the lock was laughing at me, I just knew it. What would he have tagged me? Leaning my head against the door, I stifled a yawn. I was too tired for all this trouble.

"Oh." I keyed in the corresponding numbers. The lock turned over and the door slid open. Trouble. That's how Adam thought of me.

The door closed behind me automatically when I entered the suite. It seemed bigger than I remembered. Funny how one person could take up so much space. Silently crossing the floor, I sat down at Adam's desk.

I could hardly believe it. Time travel. Was this really my world now? Juarez said I travelled at a different speed...within a time bubble? This was Theory of Relativity stuff. My head was starting to hurt just thinking about thinking about it. How could I have Einstein's DNA and not rock at physics? I guess that part didn't take.

Could Adam slide through time too? Of course not. If he could, he would be out by now. But why could I do it and he couldn't? I had his nanobots. But, not just his nanobots. I began to knead my forehead with my fingers. I wasn't thinking clearly anymore. I needed sleep. I picked up the phone and called Miranda instead.

"I'm tired of cleaning up the mess you leave when you exit a situation," she snapped at me.

In the background, I could hear all the commotion. "What are they arguing about now?" I sighed.

"Pushing you too hard, too much info, so on and so forth."

"I don't much care for being handled or spoken to like I was an underling."

"I've tried to warn them. I've—" Whatever she was going to say was interrupted by her squeak of surprise. "That is it. Y'all are a bunch of morons!" she shouted. "I'm coming up," she told me and hung up.

I placed the phone back in the cradle. What were they getting so worked up about? I mean, I was a shape shifting, soon to be time travelling guru. I could handle anything. Then I started to giggle. I could sprout claws and slip through time. See auras and stuff. By the time Miranda made it to the room, I had tears streaming down my face from laughing so hard.

"Come in," I panted when she rang.

"You have to open the door," she called back.

Doubling over in laughter, I screeched, "I don't know how."

"Push the top of the keypad on your side. The one with the word "open" written on it!" she yelled through the door.

Staggering to the door, I pushed the prescribed button. The door whooshed open to reveal an irritated Miranda, which only made me laugh more.

She looked me up and down as I tried to remain standing. "It's worse than I thought," she grumbled, shaking her head in consternation. "Meeting the big boys in the state of silly tired will not go over well."

She led me over to the couch and shoved me into the cushions. Taking a seat opposite me, she remained quiet while I tried to regain control. After a long few minutes, I drew in a ragged breath. Miranda regarded me warily as I calmed, like I might revert at any moment, which, granted, was a possibility.

"Laughter's good for the soul," I told her knowingly.

"And stomach muscles," she sighed, looking longingly at her stomach, which was completely hidden by the layers of cotton she wore.

"What are you wearing?" I asked her.

"I believe they are called warm ups. Duh."

"I know what they're called," I said, rolling my eyes. "Why are *you* wearing them? You never wear sweats."

"I do now." She huffed and looked down again. "I think I'm pregnant," she blurted out.

Oh. That was not funny. I pushed myself upright. "Think as in possibility or certainty?"

"I'm late. I'm never late." She smoothed down her top. "Jamie says it's certain."

"How does he know?"

"Apparently, I smell different."

Without thinking, I leaned over to sniff her.

"Don't you dare," she hissed at me.

Geesh. I see the mood swings had already set in. "Okay," I drawled and moved away. What was the big deal? She was barely, maybe, one week pregnant. How different could she smell? By the look on her face, different enough. "Are you okay with being pregnant? Cause you don't look okay."

She pinched her mouth, drawing her whole face to one side. "I don't know. Timing kind of sucks. And, I'm not really the motherly type."

"Nonsense. You take great care of me. You'll be an awesome mom."

She folded her hands in her lap, not looking the least bit reassured.

"Are you worried about the unwed mother thing? I know you have always railed against that. But Miranda, seriously, none of us are going to judge you for that."

She wouldn't look at me, and I knew her hands were not that interesting.

"Miranda, c'mon—"

"I'm not worried about that," she spit out quickly.

I held the breath I'd taken. Why wasn't she worried about that? In the past, contrary to the rest of her morals, she had taken a very dim view of unwed mothers. I could never quite wrap my head around the contradiction. Now the one eighty?

"Actually—" she said, wringing her hands together and doing her best to avoid my eyes.

"What!" I yelled in sudden understanding.

"I was going to tell you, but then you went and got all kidnapped—"

"You got married!" I yelled as I stood up.

"At the house in New Orleans," she nodded, her voice almost a whisper.

"Without me!" I could not believe she would leave me out of this. I thought we were family. I considered her a sister.

"Look!" she yelled back. "For once in my life, I wanted to do something right. Jamie is right—"

"How could you possibly know that Jamie is right? You just met him!"

"Do you know that Adam is right?" she charged.

I swallowed my next comment. "That's not fair," I choked, pointing my finger at her. I'd at least taken what? Five, six days? Was that all it really was? But I wasn't married to him. But if he asked? I pressed my hands to my eyes.

"I wasn't trying to hurt you," she said gruffly.

Spinning away from her, I swiped angrily at the tears on my face. Then the realization of what she'd said hit me. Turning back to her, I crossed my arms over my chest. "Are you telling me that you married him before close encounters of the blue satin sheets?" I waited for her answer with upraised eyebrows and doubt clearly written on my face.

"That's what I'm telling you," she replied through clenched teeth.

"You just went off and married him on that first night?"

"No, the second or third, I don't know which one it was," she said in frustration. "The morning you called me after you were kidnapped, that was the morning after we got married. You know our neighbors, Ezra and Hazel? They're priests."

"Of what church?" I asked, flinging my arms wide in disbelief. "And when did you even find time to do this?"

"It doesn't take long to say I do," she snapped angrily. "I don't know what church. Universal something or another. Anyway, the point is we are married now, and that's all there is to it." She crossed her arms tightly over her chest and stared straight ahead. "And, I'm going to have a baby."

Oh, is that all, I wanted to reply. I was so mad and hurt. How could she go and get married when she didn't even know where I was? Did I matter so little to her? I didn't understand how she could do this to me?

"I know what you're thinking," she said quietly. "But this is not something I did against you. It's something I did for me. There's a difference."

I rolled the words over in my head. Putting herself first was allowed, I guess. But it still hurt. To exclude me from the wedding meant she wanted to be with him more than she wanted to wait for me. Now, a baby? Someone else who would come before me. In the back of my mind, I always knew this day was coming. And I was prepared to step aside, eventually, one day. But I didn't expect it to be today, and I certainly didn't expect it to be like this. It was like she was slipping away right in front of my eyes, the end of M&M.

She remained silent while I stewed in my emotions, and she hadn't changed positions either. The way she was holding herself looked like she was trying to shield herself from me. My stomach rolled over in regret. Sisters shouldn't have to protect themselves from one another. So she got married without me. It wasn't like she cut me out of her life. She was allowed to love other people. I wasn't that selfish.

Forcing my hands to my sides, I walked back to the couch and plopped down. After a moment, I said, "Did you know that I am a shape shifting, time travelling mutant?"

From the corner of my eye, I saw her relax into the couch.

"That's a mouthful," she said. "You should shorten it to S H T T."

"I'm a shtt?" I said, cutting my eyes her direction. "Really?"

"That's what I'm thinking," she exhaled.

"Well," I sighed. "I suppose I've been called worse."

A good five minutes passed before I spoke again. "I notice you're not wearing a ring," I told her.

"We haven't had time to get any. And, I haven't much felt like looking for any."

"Queasy?"

"Unbelievably so."

"And you are wearing the sweats because...?"

"I can't fit into my other clothes."

I looked at her stomach and then her eyes. I wasn't sure what she was seeing because I couldn't tell any difference. "Estimated gestation?"

"We're not sure. Human is nine months, wolf is a little over two. We figure somewhere in between. Leaning more towards human though."

"Has no one ever had hybrid babies around here?" I asked.

"No. We will be the first."

I looked at her doubtfully.

"It's true," she said, nodding her head emphatically. "M&M has caused a wave of rebellion to sweep over the Organization."

My heart softened at her reference to M&M. Maybe it wasn't totally dissolved, only evolved. Yeah, I liked that a lot better. A wave of rebellion, she said. Huh?

"I am prone to wild and unruly behavior," I said knowingly.

"Well, who isn't?" she agreed.

"Organizational people with an affinity for rules." I curled my lip as I said it. She met my eyes with the same disgusted look. I knew who we were both thinking of.

"At the Colony, gestation varied wildly. But none of them encompassed nanobots. It was only after birth they were given them, right?" I looked at her for confirmation.

"I really don't know. I'll check with Jamie."

"Having the nanobots could really speed up the process," I mused. Having nausea in the first week seemed extreme to me. But, then again, I'd never been pregnant.

"That's what I'm afraid of. Even less time to prepare."

I scooted over next to her and laid my head on her shoulder.

"Everything's going to be okay. You're not alone. You have me and Cedars. Margaret, too. Does she know?"

"Not yet. We haven't told anyone. Jamie doesn't think I'll be able to camouflage the smell much longer. Or the stomach."

"I don't know what you're going on about. You look as skinny as ever." Bringing both hands up, I covered the yawn that engulfed me. "There's really never been any other hybrid kids?"

"Nope."

"Then there is more at work here than nature."

"That's what Jamie said."

Rolling away from her, I stretched out on the couch. "Does he have any proof?" I asked as I pulled a throw pillow under my head.

"His nanobots had built in birth control," she nodded. "Unbeknownst to him, I might add. Jamie reversed it."

"Without telling you?"

"This was before me. He found out by accident…it's a long story."

"What about Adam?"

"You've slept with Adam?" she cried in surprise.

"No," I corrected her quickly. "Just wondering. For the future. If Cedars was…blocked…then the rest of the guys probably are too."

"Well, I cannot attest to Adam's virility. You'll have to ask him yourself."

Closing my eyes, I imagined how that conversation might go. A smile ghosted on my lips when I pictured his response. Now, I was definitely going to ask him about his fertility, if for no other reason than to see the look on his face when I did.

CHAPTER 7

ARS DISSECTED MY VIEW. THEY belonged to the cell surrounding me. I had a blanket, but it wasn't protection against the cold that seemed to come from within. Everything in me wanted to fight, to escape from this place, but the cold wouldn't allow it. It was as if my body didn't belong to me. Suddenly, I realized, in that detached dream sort of way, that it wasn't my body. What I perceived as a blanket was actually fur. I was seeing through Adam's eyes, and he was entirely a leopard.

"Good, Kitty," the man in the surgical mask sneered, drawing my attention past the confines of the cell. "You're right on schedule."

Panic overwhelmed me as the man picked up a syringe. I wanted to lunge at the bars, to grasp the tender flesh at his neck between my teeth, but I was paralyzed by the cold. Or rather, Adam was. The stark realization that Adam wasn't going to be able to stop what was about to happen to him drove fear into my heart. It was followed by an anger deeper than anything I'd ever felt before. Welling up inside me, it crashed in a wave of despair as the man turned towards the cell.

Adam, I moaned, trying to shut out the image before me.

Macy?

Adam sounded so disconnected from himself, like he'd already given up.

You can't give up. I'm going to find you.

Macy?

His voice was stronger this time. *Hold on,* I urged, pouring all the strength I could into him.

"Macy."

Adam was fading.

"Macy."

"Go away," I whimpered. I was with Adam.

"I'm sorry, Macy, but it's time to go."

Opening one eye, I squinted spitefully at Miranda.

"Don't look at me like that. I let you sleep as long as I could."

I rolled onto my back and stared helplessly at the ceiling. "I was with Adam."

She sat down on the couch near my feet. "How's he doing?" she asked, gently wrapping one ankle with her hand.

"He's completely shifted."

"Full-fledged leopard?"

"He's in a cell," I nodded. "And he's so cold. He can't function." I sat up and pressed the heels of my hands into my eyes. Crying wasn't going to save Adam.

"We're gonna get him back," she said, gently squeezing my ankle.

"When?" I demanded angrily. "Why do I have to waste my time meeting with the president? What does talking to the stupid president have anything to do with finding Adam?"

Quirking her eyebrow at me, she repeated, "Stupid president?"

"Well, I don't know," I snapped. Shoving my hair behind my ears in frustration, I crossed my arms over my chest. "I haven't really been paying that much attention the last few years. And that doesn't answer my question."

She removed the hand on my foot, and clasping both her hands together, set them in her lap. "Would Adam meet with the president to explain the situation?" she asked quietly.

He probably would. I couldn't picture him shying away from anything. But that was not an answer either.

"If you ignore the president and what Adam wanted in appointing you to speak to him, and then the relationship with the government sours, how are you going to justify that to Adam? Because, correct me if I'm wrong, but you are planning on retrieving Adam, right?"

Refusing to answer the ridiculousness that was that question, I skewered her with my scowl instead.

"And maybe you can find Adam on your own," she continued, completely unaffected by my glare. "Maybe, you don't need the Organization at all, but I'm betting Adam does."

Crap, I thought as my scowl faded. She was right. He actually might need it now more than ever. "When do I leave?" I asked weakly.

"Half an hour. I tried to leave you enough time to at least shower." Then she reared back and looked at me. "And to do something with that hair. Why don't you get it cut?"

This was about the thousandth time she'd said that to me since we'd known each other. And this was the thousandth time I'd answered her the same way. "I don't do short hair."

"Maybe not, but your *long* hair is doing a number on you," she replied sarcastically.

Again, I chose not to respond to her.

"Do I have any clothes," I asked as I scooted from the couch and headed for the shower.

"I'll get you some," she called. "You need to hurry. You're down to twenty-six minutes."

"Right, what are they going to do? Leave without me?" I muttered. I'd actually welcome that.

The relaxation normally included with a hot shower was lost on me. I barely felt the water as I wondered what the heck I was going to say to the president. I tried to imagine what questions he might ask. What I would ask if I were the president. How was I going to explain New Orleans? If I told him there was a rogue hybrid on the loose with the plan that Millsap had, he might round all of us up. If I feigned ignorance, he might conclude that the Organization was no longer useful. Either way was littered with pitfalls. In the end, I was too tired and too rattled by my time as Adam or in Adam to think clearly. I would just have to hope that my brain would come up with something when it was time.

I found the clothes that Miranda left for me on the bed. They were not my usual jeans and t-shirt, but it was the president I was meeting. I pulled on the skirt and slipped the blouse over my head. When I leaned back to pick up the jacket, the smell of Adam arrested me. Forgetting about the jacket, I moved on all fours, tracking his scent across the bed to his pillow. Sitting back on my knees, I picked up the pillow and buried my nose in it. Adam flooded all of my senses.

Miranda's cough alerted me to her return. Not ready to let go of Adam just yet, I turned my face sideways against the pillow to look at her. Her eyes were brimming with tears.

She hurriedly laid my rescued black leather boots on the bed next to me. "Sorry," she apologized while fanning her face with her hands. "Hormones."

As she retreated a few paces, I pressed my face into the pillow again and breathed in. Though the scent was strong, it was no substitute for the real thing. Adam wasn't here. I placed the pillow back on the bed, my fingers trailing across its face as I pulled my hand away. Then intentionally shifting my focus to the boots, I picked them up.

"They look pretty good," I said through clenched teeth.

"Juarez fixed them."

"Juarez?" I sniffed.

"Apparently, leather working is a hobby of his."

Out of the corner of my eye, I saw her frown in worry, but she didn't comment on the source. We were both doing our best to ignore the tears streaming down my face.

Swinging my legs over the edge of the bed, I leaned over and pulled on the boots. Not wanting a repeat of what happened the first time, I stood and walked around the bed to collect the jacket.

"Do you have any idea of what you're going to say?" Miranda asked as she followed me out of the room.

"Not particularly." I slipped the jacket on, then plucked a tissue from the desk and wiped my face free of tears. "Any suggestions?"

"A couple," she said, waiting until I faced her to continue. "I would suggest that you call him President O'Conner or Mr. President rather than stupid president. And please, do not use the angry voice on the president."

"Angry voice?"

"Yeah. Like the one you use on Olivia. Maybe you don't notice, but she's ducking and covering. I feel it too, and it isn't even directed at me."

Really? Another possible incarnation of the alpha thing. That might come in handy down the road, assuming I learn to control it.

"Okay," I agreed as I sat down at Adam's desk. "No angry voice when addressing the president. How do you think he knows about New Orleans?"

She sat down in the chair opposite me. "I have wondered that."

"Did Jamie tell him?"

She was quiet a moment. "No," she shook her head.

"Someone called the reporter, too. Told her she would find something interesting."

"We could find out who called her." She looked at me expectantly. "Aw, c'mon, Macy. Jamie's not going to have her killed."

"Maybe. But I don't know, other than you, who isn't a traitor around here."

"Jamie's not. I'd know it if he was."

Would I know if Adam was a traitor? I wasn't so sure. Adam was very good at shielding.

"Still no success with the shielding?"

"None," she said, rolling her eyes dramatically. "And apparently, pregnancy smells really good, if you know what I mean."

Wow. Even in her delicate state, she was not chaste.

"It's not funny," she wailed when I started giggling. "I really do need my sleep and have headaches and stuff."

The giggles turned into full on howls of laughter. I couldn't help it. Her outraged face was hilarious, especially when compared to her prior life. Man had she reversed roles. From huntress to "Not tonight, honey." I laughed until I cried. But this time, the tears were not due to pain.

"Just wait until it happens to you," she snarled, angrily pointing her finger at me.

I had no immediate response to her pronouncement, and Cedars rang the bell before I could craft one. It wasn't the first time that I left Miranda stewing in her chair about something.

"Ready?" Cedars asked when I opened the door.

"Not even a little."

I was surprised when that admission didn't bother me. Maybe I was too tired to care. Kind of ironic that the one designed to know the answers didn't care if she currently had them. Maybe I was just tired of having plans blow up in my face. Life as a hybrid didn't seem to be meshing with planning very well. I was going to have to do something to change that. But for now, it was life on the fly. From the bruises to the exhaustion and stomach gripping hunger, something told me it wasn't all it was cracked up to be.

"Macy?" Cedars asked.

"Present," I blinked up at him. "Give me a minute."

Smiling at his furrowed brow, I backed away and went to the bathroom where my dirty clothes were. I fished the reporter's card out of the pocket and tucked it inside my jacket. Then I pulled out the mindbender report and the list of the missing and dead that Kenny had given me. There were a lot of names on this list. How was I going to account for this?

Walking slowly as I read over the names again, I found myself standing next to Miranda. She didn't need to see this right now. Folding it in half, I laid it on Adam's desk. "See what you can find out about this," I told her as I handed her the new report.

She took the papers and scanned the first page.

"Two of them, not including me, are here. Remember that."

"Okay," she agreed hesitantly.

"You'll understand what I mean when you read it," I assured her. "Ask Charlie or Flash about isolating the signatures."

"We need to go," Cedars said.

Miranda pulled me into a hug, wrapping her arms tightly around me. Felt more like being restrained than a loving embrace. "Make sure you come back this time," she commanded. "And please try not to become imprisoned for slugging the wrong person. Oh, I don't know, like the president."

"Yes, Mom," I drawled, returning the hug by awkwardly patting her sides with the only portion of my arms free to move.

When she let go, it was Cedars' turn. I didn't miss the way she melted into him. Guess she didn't need a nap right now or have a headache or stuff.

"Try to get some sleep," Cedars said, gently touching Miranda's cheek.

The concern in his voice worried me. I moved to get an unobstructed view of Miranda's face. Like the rest of us, she was tired. Beyond that, there was something.

She caught me studying her and quickly turned her face away. Now I knew for sure she was hiding something. Sort of like she'd been hiding the pregnancy before.

Cedars took her movement as a sign that she wanted a more lengthy goodbye. Uugh. That was my cue. I walked out the door to wait in the hallway.

When the door whooshed open, they emerged hand in hand.

"Don't forget." I nodded to the papers in her other hand.

She saluted me with them and sauntered off down the hallway.

Headache my swaying backside.

As soon as she was out of earshot, I cornered Cedars. "Is she alright?" I asked. It really rankled that I had to ask him about the wellbeing of my best friend, but, circumstances being what they were, for better or worse, he was the one most likely to know.

"She's fine. It's normal, I guess," he shrugged. "The uncertainty, I mean."

They had a little more to be uncertain about than most expecting couples, but pointing that out would just be mean. If uncertainty was all that she was concealing, well, I guess that was normal for all new mothers to be.

"So, who's going with me?" I asked in a definite change of subject.

"Reynolds," he said. "Since you've taken such a liking to him."

I ignored the dig. "Reynolds is good. I want Kenny, too. I don't care if he's not Organization trained. I trust him, and I want him with me."

"He said you'd say that," he muttered under his breath.

He did? Why was I surprised? Kenny knew me. That was another reason I wanted him with me. I liked Reynolds, even trusted him a little. But I was sure he'd gotten an earful from Olivia about loyalty and such. I just wasn't a hundred percent sure about him. Kenny, I'd stake my life on. Already had a few times.

"They're both going with you," he acknowledged. "I might add that I have approved this despite Olivia's objections."

He didn't appreciate the disdain expressed in my eye roll. Sure, I was grateful that he made the right call. But Olivia was being a control freak. He wasn't doing me any favors by overriding her. He was doing what he should do.

"Cedars?" I called, spinning around when I realized he was no longer with me. He'd stopped about five paces back and now stood with his head bowed and his hands planted on either hip.

"Macy, I'm not against you," he said quietly. "It's just...I..."

"Don't know me," I finished for him. I felt the same way about him.

"I don't know you," he agreed. "But, I know Adam. And, I know Miranda." He lifted his head to look at me. "If anything ever happened to you...I don't know if she'd recover."

I wanted to argue with just how well he knew Miranda, but as I watched the myriad emotions play across his face, they finally settled on one that I couldn't mistake. It was the first time I'd seen real love, not just lust, coming from him. In that moment, I realized he would do anything to protect her.

Closing the distance between us, I walked back towards him. "I love her, too."

Something like relief passed over his face. Geesh. I hadn't realized it was so important to him that I acknowledge his feelings for her. Kind of felt bad about it now.

"In the interest of family relations," he sighed. "Please come back in one piece and without having created a situation where I have to whisk us off into hiding."

"You have a plan for that?" I balked in surprise.

"Macy, until you showed up, I thought I had a plan for

everything." With a shake of his head, he started down the hall again.

He was a planner? Finally, something I could like about him, besides the fact that he had excellent taste in women. "Were you watching Miranda while Adam was watching me?" I asked when I caught up to him.

"Maybe," he said, his lip curling into a half smile.

"Didn't have enough excitement in your own lives?"

"We kept ourselves amused."

"I'll bet. So, what was it about Miranda that caught your eye?"

His smile widened to include the other half of his lips. "Her gusto for life. The way she totally immersed herself into whatever she was doing. I mean, she could be partying at the NOLA Blue and have every guy there doing her bidding. Or even if she was tackling calcium buildup in the bathroom, she totally owned it."

"You caught that episode, did ya?" I chuckled.

"It still makes me laugh when I think about it. And her smile. She has the most amazing smile," he said dreamily.

"She's pretty amazing. That makes me pretty smart for having her as a best friend."

"As long as you don't screw it up. It's kind of a miracle that you two are friends. I'm not sure you could be more different."

"I'll do my best," I smirked.

"You say that a lot."

That's because people kept demanding impossible things from me where I could not even entertain the idea of guaranteeing success. Like I had any business meeting with the president and speaking for all of hybridom. Me, the newest kid on the block.

"Are you sure about this?" I asked, stopping him with a hand on his arm.

Rolling his shoulders, he sighed in resignation. "Adam believes in you. Miranda unequivocally believes in you. I'm starting to." Tilting his head to the side, he lifted his eyes to the ceiling. "There's something about you that makes people want to trust you. I don't know what it is, but you're highly believable. Maybe because you believe the things you say." At a loss for words, he shrugged and began walking again.

Well, at least it was good to know that I could inspire something other than rebellion. That wasn't exactly what he said, but that was how I was interpreting it.

"Hey," I said as I jogged to catch up again. "What did you find out when you questioned Langston?"

"Not much. She can't remember anything. Juarez thinks she's being controlled somehow. He's working on finding the source."

That was scary. "And the rescue plan for Adam?"

"We're working on that too. When you get back, we are going to find out for sure if you're a TS."

"That's not what Miranda calls it," I grumbled. Faintly, I heard Cedars' confused reply, but we had entered the kitchen, and for the first time in a while, I was hungry.

"Macy, we really don't have time for this," Cedars complained as I opened the fridge door. "You can get something—"

"How about you take this with you, huh?" Margaret said. Using both hands, she held out a large tote to me. "There's brisket sandwiches, chips, beans and potato salad. It might not be as good as what you're used to, being from Texas and all," she winked at me. "But I think it will do."

I was so grateful I could cry. Again. "Thanks, Margaret," I crooned as I relieved her of the tote.

"You're welcome, dear," she replied cheerily, then walked out of the kitchen.

"Is she for real?" I asked, staring wistfully after her.

"Yep, she's the real deal. Now let's go. We don't want to keep President O'Conner waiting."

Now that depended entirely on how good these sandwiches were.

CHAPTER 8

W E TOOK A SMALLER JET this time, but there was still plenty of room for the three of us. Reynolds had been tapped to pilot us to our destination. That both did and did not surprise me. He was young, but as I was slowly discovering, he had a lot of hidden talents. Kenny kept me on my toes too. Besides being in my face about everything, he ran his group like a well-oiled machine. Something I needed when you considered my lack of leadership experience. Most of my talents had been utilized on a singular level. No one even knew what I was talking about most of the time, except for Miranda.

That was before the Organization where everyone was a genius. Now, I had a whole crew of people depending on me that got to witness every grueling, awkward step I made. It wasn't the way I liked to operate, and back when life was normal—normal for me, anyway—just the thought of living under that microscope might have killed my appetite.

I hugged the tote to me and smiled. Good thing those days were gone.

Reaching inside, I pulled out one of the cellophane wrapped sandwiches and held it up. Here's to the new chapter in my life, I mused silently. One where I was learning to loosen up, to be more lenient with myself, to forgive myself—and others—and move on. No more time for cradling offenses and holding grudges. Things were moving way too fast to be able to keep up with all that baggage. And truth be told, it was a freer way to live. Scarier, but freer.

After assurances that they'd already eaten, I plowed into the meal Margaret prepared for me. Barbeque for breakfast. It was pure genius. I wasn't sure how she kept mysteriously appearing during my time of need, but I was thankful for it. I'd have to make that abundantly clear the next time I saw her. This sandwich was delicious. It'd be nice if everyone on the team was as helpful as her.

Leaning forward, I tried to catch a glimpse of Reynolds. The wall between the cabin and the cockpit prevented me from seeing anything other than his profile. "Hey, Reynolds, did you get the lecture about loyalty?" I just knew Olivia had laid into him regarding his *traitorous* behavior.

Across the plane from me, Kenny echoed my opinion by snorting irreverently.

"Yes, ma'am," Reynolds drawled. "I told *her* that my loyalty was perfectly intact. To which she replied that she couldn't sense any loyalty to the Organization at all. That's when I informed her that my loyalty wasn't to the Organization. It was to Adam and by extension, you."

Oooh, I bet she loved that. "How'd she take it?" I asked as I popped the lid off the potato salad.

"Not well, ma'am," he replied stoically. "Not well at all. And I don't think she was too keen on you speaking to the president either."

Oh, I'm quite sure she wasn't. For all the reasons I myself could list. "Well anyway, I appreciate your loyalty to Adam and by extension, me."

"I thought you might, ma'am."

"Reynolds, I thought we were past the ma'am already. Call me Macy."

"Yes, ma—I will do that."

Chuckling softly, I cleared away some of the empty containers crowding my lap. "So, no feelings of being torn between the Organization and Adam?"

There was a brief pause as he contemplated the question. "For me, Adam is the Organization. If he doesn't return, I don't see me staying."

Me either. Without Adam, I'd be stuck with rules, rules and

more rules. And, as my prior behavior had demonstrated, I wasn't very good at following rules.

"You missed some," Kenny said, pointing to his cheek.

I grabbed a napkin and swiped it across my face, then looked at him for approval.

A single eyebrow darted up in challenge.

And that's why I always felt like he was concocting some plan sure to cause me trouble. Like right now, that devious, calculating look in his eyes. He was planning something. He gave nothing away as he matched my stare, but I knew it was there, and it had something to do with the future.

Balling the napkin up, I squeezed it tightly in an effort to purge my unease. It was probably some crazy scheme like a Greer home for wayward hybrids with me as the headmistress, forcing me into a lifetime of servitude filled with teenage drama and no sleep!

I inhaled and exhaled slowly. On second thought, that wasn't much different from right now. But there was barbeque. It wasn't all bad.

Determined to ignore Kenny's treacherous plotting lest he ruin my breakfast, I concentrated solely on finishing my meal. By the time I had emptied the last container, I could feel sleep pulling at me. That was the last thing I wanted to do. My reaction to what I'd see or not see in my dreams was too much of a risk. I had to keep it together for this meeting, play the part of the polished professional. At the very least, I had to make it look like the Organization wasn't falling apart.

"How long until we arrive?" I asked Reynolds while I gathered up the remains of the meal.

"About forty-five minutes."

"Do you have a plan?" Kenny asked.

As much as I ever did these days. "Don't die, don't harm hybrids everywhere." I paused, then added, "Don't insult the president?"

"We're in trouble," Kenny groaned.

I nodded at him. Trouble was a hallmark of my administration. Speaking of which, "Hey Kenny, do you have any idea how the president found out about New Orleans or who might have informed the reporter?"

His eyes drifted to the left, focusing on nothing in particular as he thought about it. "The new guards that showed up…it was obvious they weren't HCF material. It wasn't just that I didn't recognize any of them. They acted different. Too focused." He paused, his eyes darkening as he sank deeper into the memory. "I had a feeling things were going to get bad. That's when I started moving people out. Crystal's Mom was dying. She wouldn't leave until it was over. Over was too late." He clamped his jaw shut while he worked his way through the emotions. When he spoke again, there was no trace of the turmoil he'd just relived. "My last sweep, before you arrived, I heard, or rather felt, someone talking. It was a man, a late arrival to the action. He was speaking to someone on a cell phone." He hesitated, frowning in earnest. "He had a sense of authority about him, like he was someone you didn't want to mess with. He stuck out so much that I almost approached him. In the end, I didn't." The memory having run its course, he looked back at me. "Mid-forties, slightly graying, built well. And his eyes…they were the most peculiar ice gray color."

Garrison?

"He spoke very softly. I had to strain to hear what he said. I only caught a few words before he left. He said that GM had gone too far and that he would deal with it now."

Garrison was alive? And he knew who or what GM was, as did the person on the other end. "Could you hear the person he was talking to?"

"It was a woman. I didn't recognize her voice. She told him to be careful."

He could have been talking to the reporter, but the woman on the other end had advised him to be careful. Like she knew what he was facing. Red clearly hadn't been expecting what she witnessed. The pieces didn't fit. They were yet more random fragments of information.

Leaning my head back against the seat, I sighed in frustration. I needed a super-sized white board.

"Do you know who he is?" Kenny asked.

Allowing my gaze to shift to Kenny, I said, "Maybe. But he was presumed dead."

"Dead people don't talk," he quipped. "Unless of course, zombies are real, and they look way better than they do in the movies."

Zombies. That's all I needed. "Let's don't even entertain the thought of creating trouble where there isn't any—"

"No trouble. I like it!" Reynolds belted.

Pausing long enough to roll my eyes at his interruption, I continued with my answer to Kenny's question. "When the Organization people first kidnapped me, they took me to another agency. Garrison was the director of that agency. But I'm not sure it exists anymore. There was an attempt on my life, explosion, big fire. Garrison was presumed dead."

Kenny stared at me in stunned silence. "You just can't help yourself, can you?" he said bluntly.

"Makes me nervous to be in the same plane as her," Reynolds agreed.

"Listen you yahoos—" The comeback was cut short when the plane dipped sharply. My arms flew out, death gripping either armrest. "Reynolds!" I gasped as the plane plunged again. "Talk to me!"

"The controls aren't responding," he barked.

Pushing my feet into the floor against the stomach sucking feeling, I did my best not to scream like a little girl. Seeing Kenny helped, almost enough to make me forget we were falling. His eyes were a flaming dark red, and his face almost matched the white of his knuckles gripping the seat. I couldn't tear my eyes away from him. He looked like a makeup artist's version of a whacked out ghost. Any second now, I just knew the creature from Alien was going to erupt from his stomach.

The plane hopped several times, like a rock skipping across a lake, then mercifully leveled out. In my peripheral vision, I saw Reynolds lunge to the floor and began ripping open the front panel.

"What are you doing?" I asked as I scrambled to his side.

"Manual override," he shot at me. "I have to regain control."

"You're not in control now?"

"Nope," he said, not bothering to look away from what he was doing.

"Take this," Kenny insisted, shoving a medium canvas covered pack into my hands.

I stared blankly at the large print label. PARACHUTE. USE IN CASE OF EMERGENCY.

"You're supposed to put it on," he said slowly, like my mind had been addled by the aerial gymnastics.

"Only if I plan on jumping out of this plane," I clarified. Staring at the parachute like it was the plague, I added, "Which I don't."

"You're being ridiculous," he snapped as he fastened a chute across his own chest. "You'd rather die than put it on?"

"Put it on," Reynolds ordered, reaching deeper into the panel to wrench more wires free.

Crud. That couldn't be good. Reluctantly, I slipped the parachute over my shoulders and fastened it. But I refused to actually consider it an option.

Reynolds tried the controls again and grimaced. "I have to set us down. Now." His frown deepened as he surveyed the landscape for possible landing sites. "With all the trees, it's going to be rough."

Rough, I could do. I could not do falling through the air outside of this plane. At least, not without having a heart attack, which would kind of defeat the purpose of jumping.

Shrugging out of the chute, I handed it back to Kenny. "Not today, not ever."

"You guys should strap in," Reynolds said.

Returning to my seat, I secured the restraints with the metal clasp. Across from me, Kenny did the same.

"We're going down," Reynolds called. His voice strained with uncertainty, full of all the ways this could go wrong.

"You'll do great, Reynolds," I tried to reassure him. "Think of happy landings."

"I don't know about great," he returned. "I'm trying to do alive."

Alive worked.

The plane jerked hard to the left, and then tilted my way, like someone was pushing up on the right wing. The storage compartment above Kenny's head popped open and dumped its contents in my direction. "Oomph," I grunted as a canister of something hit me solidly in the stomach.

"Sorry," Reynolds yelled as he righted the plane.

"You okay?" Kenny asked.

Picking up one of the discarded parachutes which had found me again, I threw it at him.

"Listen, this bird is pretty tough. But there are a lot of trees. If this doesn't work—"

"It's going to work, Reynolds," I said, cutting him off before he could voice anything bad happening to us.

That was the last thing said before the jet broke the tree line. After that, it was too loud for casual conversation. The sounds of screeching metal and rat-a-tat of the plane hammering the trees covered everything but the loudest of shouts, and most of those weren't meant as communication anyway.

"Brace yourself!" Reynolds yelled.

We hit the ground hard. The initial impact reverberated through my tailbone into my gut. Likewise, I felt the plane groan and rattle as it dug into the earth. The window next to Kenny shattered, filling the air with a sudden burst of pine needles. Before they had reached the floor, the plane struck an obstacle that didn't yield and flipped end over nose. The top of the plane slammed heavily to the ground, causing the restraints holding me in place to dig sharply into my skin. Both mine and Kenny's eyes widened at the tree trunk that now stood as a centerpiece in the plane.

The whole prior acrobatic maneuver hadn't been too bad, but

when the next collision started us spinning, it was too much. I lost my sandwiches.

The spinning also served to congregate every loose item flying around the plane and plaster them securely to the sides, right where Kenny and I were seated. I couldn't see anything beyond the orange life vest glued to my face, nor could I move for the same force pinning me in place.

My head was reeling so much that it took me a minute to realize the plane was no longer moving. The sudden quiet was more confirmation. Though welcomed, the silence was eerie. It had the distinct feel of that moment on a carnival ride when you weren't quite sure the ride was over, and you didn't want to let go, just in case.

I peeled the life vest off, clearing a small area in front of my face. "Is everybody okay?" I yelled, cringing at how loud my voice sounded. Untangling the blanket that had somehow wrapped itself around my neck, I tried again. "Guys?"

There was still no response.

My movements became more hurried as worry crept in. Using my feet, I toppled the pile of debris between me and Kenny. His eyes were wide open and staring straight at me. "Kenny!" I screamed, near panicked with fear.

He slowly lifted one arm and pushed aside a cushion concealing his lower half. A tree branch protruded from his gut, just below his sternum. Just like Linc, only so much worse. My joy in the fact that he was alive quickly faded with the image he now presented.

"You puked on me," he said raggedly.

As claimed, a splash of vomit decorated his torso, stretching diagonally from his neck to his waist.

"Hang on. I'll get you out of there."

With my eyes still fastened on him, I undid my restraints. I forgot that we were upside down. The hit I took on the landing created an immediate stab of pain across the ribs on my left side. Wrapping a protective arm around my midsection, I pushed myself up and began to pick my way to Kenny.

"Reynolds," I called breathily as I stumbled over the debris pile. "Reynolds," I repeated more sharply when I realized the wall separating the cabin from the cockpit had been cut in half.

"I'm here," he answered groggily.

"Are you hurt?" I asked, shoving aside the last bit of wreckage between me and Kenny.

"Just banged up, I think." He stumbled into what used to be the doorway, his hand cradling his head. "Dang," he whispered when he saw Kenny.

Grasping the edge of Kenny's seat, I peered behind it for a point of entry. From this angle, it looked like the branch had missed his spine.

"Y'all act like you ain't never seen a guy with a tree in his gut," Kenny joked, his words slurring a bit as he spoke.

Actually, it was the second time I'd seen it, and that was two times too many. "I can undo his restraints," I said to Reynolds. "Can you help me catch him?"

He lowered the hand supporting his head and nodded at me, then began to make his way through the wreckage towards Kenny. When he was in position, I pulled myself up until I could reach the straps holding Kenny in his seat.

"I'm pretty sure this is going to hurt."

"I'm pretty sure you're right," he grated.

"Ready?"

"We should have jumped," he mumbled as he closed his eyes.

Taking that as a yes, I undid the clasp. He fell forward so fast that I was barely able to catch him under one arm. The gasp of pain he made when his stomach connected with Reynolds' shoulder was lost among the noise of the debris shifting under the sudden increase in weight. Reynolds had to shuffle awkwardly in his effort to remain upright. Gingerly, so as not to start another landslide, I stepped into the space their movement had cleared.

"Kenny, you really stink," Reynolds complained.

"Doc puked on me," he stuttered.

Reynolds looked at me reproachfully.

"I didn't mean to," I snapped at him as I helped lower Kenny to the ground. "You're the one that spun the plane like a top."

Reynolds' face turned ashen. Pressing his hand over his mouth, he said, "Get that off of him. Please." Then he staggered out of the plane through the opening where the tail used to be.

Seriously? It was just a little vomit. It even still smelled like barbeque. Mostly.

"Oh my god, that hurt," Kenny moaned. "I can't believe Linc goes through this so much."

"Well, I'd thank you not to do it again," I fussed at him. "I've seen more sticks in guts than I ever wanted to see."

In one quick movement, I ripped his shirt off and balled it up, tossing it in the opposite direction of Reynolds. Searching through the mess, I found a water bottle and emptied its contents onto a piece of cloth that might have been part of a shirt at one time. Kenny jumped when the wet cloth touched his skin.

"I'm sorry I puked on you," I whispered guiltily as I continued wiping away the vomit. "But, to be fair, you have done way worse to me."

A smile ghosted on his lips in reference to the incident. "Your fault," he croaked.

It was Miranda's actually, but I wasn't going to argue with him in his current state. I looked up at Reynolds as he came back inside. "Better?" I asked him.

He nodded then took two more steps into the plane and wrestled free a first aid kit. Joining me at Kenny's side, we worked together at cleaning and bandaging the wound. I was aware of the hisses Kenny made at our touch, but I had to mainly tune it out. Otherwise, I wouldn't have been able to touch him at all. As it was, Reynolds did most of the work. Another thing to add to the list, how to render first aid to a hybrid.

When we were finished, I shoved away from Kenny and sat with my back against the plane. Bringing my arms up to rest on my knees, I noted that my hands were coated in blood. Again.

"Use this," Reynolds said, tossing me a towel he'd found somewhere in the mess.

I worked my way methodically over my hands to clear away

the worst of it, but without water, anything more was pointless. "Reynolds, what happened?"

"Someone tried to remotely commandeer the plane." He pulled the first aid kit into his lap and began rifling through it.

"I didn't sense much steering going on. They wanted us to crash?"

"Seems like it," he nodded. "I destroyed the tracking devices I found and my com, in case they were keying in on that too."

"If you missed one, they'll know exactly where we are."

"Yes," he said tightly.

Dang it. "We need to move." Breathing out heavily, I gathered my legs underneath me.

"We need to take care of that first," he said, absently gesturing at me.

"Take care of what?" I asked in confusion as I stood.

He flipped the lid shut on the kit and looked up at me. "That gash on your forehead." Gripping the supplies he'd collected, he crawled towards me. "Don't touch it," he said testily.

I lowered the hand I had instinctively brought to my forehead.

"Take a seat," he said. "We don't have time for stitches. Hopefully, the nanobots will work quickly." Looking over at Kenny, he added, "For both of you."

Clenching my jaw against the pain, I remained motionless under Reynolds' studious cleaning. As we had used all the gauze on Kenny, I assumed cleaning was all he was doing, and I breathed a sigh of relief when he let up. But then he leaned way back and pinched something out of the first aid kit that looked like superglue.

"What is that?" I asked while doggedly avoiding his outstretched hand holding the giant swab applicator.

"Instant skin." Sighing in irritation at my efforts, he lowered his extended arm. "You need this. Hold still."

Huffing in protest, I stopped avoiding him and let him glue me back together. Until I felt the stinging fireball of penetration that it packed. "That burns," I snapped at him and swatted his hand away.

"It does," he scoffed knowingly. But his smile disappeared when he looked at Kenny. "You'll need to hold him down."

Blanching at the thought of what Kenny was about to endure, I crept over to him. He had bled through the gauze already. More movement was only going to make it worse. But we didn't have a choice. We had to get out of here.

Gently grasping Kenny by the shoulders, I leaned over him. "Kenny—"

"I was listening," he breathed. "You won't need to hold me down. But I might punch Reynolds, just for the fun of it."

Smiling at his bravado, I reached forward and peeled away the soaked bandages.

"Put them in here," Reynolds said, holding open a trash bag. "I'll burn it before we leave."

After disposing of the bandages, I repositioned myself by Kenny's head. Once again, I grasped him by the shoulders, and then nodded at Reynolds to go ahead.

"On three," Reynolds said. He counted, "One, two," then began pouring straight from the bottle before reaching three.

"You SOB," Kenny hissed, his whole body going taut with pain.

"I'll thank you not to bring my mama into this," Reynolds mocked. "She raised eight boys, and I'd bet on her whipping your ugly butt any day of the week."

Veins began to crisscross Kenny's torso under the strain of remaining still, which he did for the most part, except for the involuntary quivers that shook him. At the same time that I noticed the edges of the wound starting to bubble angrily, the distinct smell of burnt flesh wafted in the air.

"Chemical cauterization?" I guessed aloud. No wonder it had burned so much.

"Sort of. But because of the nanobots, this is more specialized. It forms a cellular barrier they won't cross. But you can't put it on too early. Too early, and the nanobots think there isn't a problem."

"And they don't show up?"

"And they don't show up," he repeated. "Not in the numbers

you need to recover from something like this. That's why I did you first. To make sure I wasn't rushing it." Leaning over Kenny, he studied the newly formed seam. "I think it's ready. Time to roll him over."

When I got my first look at the entry point of the wound, I was thankful that I didn't have anything more in my stomach to lose. The hole was fist sized. If he'd have stood up, I could have seen daylight on the other side. How were the nanobots going to fix this? The plane swayed as I suddenly felt woozy.

"Macy, you still with me?" Reynolds asked.

I couldn't answer him, only watch as he poured the contents of the bottle into the wound. Kenny's arms snaked through mine, and I leaned into them, adding my weight to help him remain still. Reynolds did the same, pressing the entire weight of his body into Kenny's legs. I closed my eyes as the smell of burning flesh rose once more. I wished I could have closed my ears to the sound of Kenny's pain. He didn't deserve this.

"Macy?"

Reynolds sounded worried. "I'm here," I managed to say. Opening my eyes, I took a deep breath. Everything smelled like blood and pain.

"I'll have you out of here soon," he nodded at me.

I nodded in return.

Reynolds waited until the worst of Kenny's pain had subsided, then sloughed off his jacket. He pulled his shirt over his head and ripped it down the middle. Using it in lieu of bandages, he wrapped it tightly around Kenny's midsection.

"Think you can stand?"

I didn't know if he was talking to me or Kenny, but after unwinding our arms, I stood up.

"Get his legs," Reynolds directed.

Moving mechanically, I traded places with Reynolds. The yelp Kenny uttered as Reynolds lifted him almost stopped me. But I quickly remembered we didn't have any other option. Settling myself to the fact that this was going to hurt him, I began to move. More rapidly than I should have maybe, but I figured it was like a bandage, rip it off quick.

Between the two of us, we were able to get Kenny clear of the wreckage. One thing was for certain, Kenny wasn't the only one hurting. I was starting to think my ribs were more than bruised, and though he didn't complain, the whole side of Reynolds' face was now purple.

"That's not going to help," I grumbled when I saw the path the plane had carved out as it went down. It was like a giant arrow pointing directly to us.

"Roger that," Reynolds said, echoing my worries of discovery.

"Do you know the location of our meeting with the president?"

"A decommissioned ammunitions plant. I reckon we are still a few good miles away from it."

Being that the miles were through densely populated woods, ripe with a hundred different things to slow us down, I wouldn't have called them good. "How many is a few?"

"Ten, plus or minus."

"I think we are going to be late," I said ruefully.

Reynolds snorted at my assessment. "By the coordinates given to me, we need to head southeast."

"Southeast it is." I swiveled my head back and forth, trying to locate the intended direction. "Uh, which way is southeast?"

"That way," he pointed.

"How'd you know that so quick?"

"The sun rises in the east, sets in the west. It's late morning." He pointed at the sun and shrugged. "There's the sun."

In other words, work it out. I guess he didn't read the sign my brain had posted: Sorry for the inconvenience, but we are temporarily unavailable. I didn't miss the smile he hid while pretending to wipe his face.

Kneeling beside Kenny, I mouthed, "Ready?" to him.

He stared blankly at me, unable or unwilling to respond.

Right. Stupid question.

With Kenny draped between us, we struggled through the woods in the direction that Reynolds had indicated. Kenny tried to help us, but he was in a lot of pain, and everything we were making him do wasn't diminishing that. I had no idea where to find help for him or if he even needed it. It wasn't like we could just show up at an emergency room. Then there was the environment of the woods which did not lend itself to travel three abreast. As a result, we weren't making good time at all.

"You know," Reynolds said when we stopped to rest. "This would go a lot faster if I could just carry him by myself."

Using my shirt sleeve, I mopped up the sweat on my forehead. "Are you able to do that?" The bruise on his face that was still spreading made me wonder. And now it had begun swelling as well. He was barely able to keep that left eye open. And yet, it did not hinder the look he gave me.

"Yes, I am able," he said coolly.

"Well, why didn't you offer an hour ago?" I griped.

He inclined his head toward Kenny. "He was still conscious."

"What?" Snapping my head back to Kenny, I saw that he had indeed passed out. "I hope that's a good sign," I said as I knelt to check on him.

"I think it is. I think I remember something about a coma like sleep being related to nanobot repair of severe injuries." He shrugged when I looked at him. "It wasn't my thing."

"Are you sure the nanobots can repair this?" I asked quietly.

"He didn't bleed out. Didn't cut his spine in two…given enough time…he'll be okay."

That did not sound like the definite yes I wanted. Lifting my hands, I concealed the surprise yawn that overwhelmed me.

"No you don't," Reynolds drawled. "I can't carry two of you through these woods." He walked over and scooped up Kenny, laying him gently over his shoulder. As he stood, he grabbed my elbow and forced me up with him. "That way," he nodded, indicating for me to go first.

"What are you? Like a living compass or something?" I said grumpily.

"Not everyone struggles with directions, Macy," he chuckled.

Maybe not, but I certainly, inexplicably, did. "So why am I in front exactly?"

"So I can make sure you don't go to sleep on the job," he huffed as he readjusted Kenny's weight.

Yeah, like that was going to happen.

"Wake up covered in poison ivy or God knows what. Maybe caught in a hunter's trap." He snorted loudly. "Could be cornered by skunks. That would be hilarious."

"Hilarious for you. We know what a strong stomach you have."

That shut him up. For a minute. Then he started in again, nothing as grandiose as before, but I let him talk freely. I had a feeling he was trying to keep both of us awake. We continued this way, poking fun at each other, until we reached a break in the trees at the top of a small ridge. Reynolds stepped from behind me to get a better view of the valley.

"What are you smiling at?" he asked as he blew at the sweat dripping into his eyes.

"How long have you been with the Organization?"

"Three years. Why?"

"And how long with the Expeditionary Team?"

He shifted uncomfortably. "That'd be about two days."

"Two days? Really?" He seemed more experienced than that.

"Yes. Again, why are you smiling?"

"Reynolds," I said, pointing at the house across the valley from us. "I know that house."

"You know that house," he said skeptically.

"I know that house and any other house that looks like that house." Wow. Say that five times fast.

"Wait," he objected, grabbing my elbow to stop me when I started down the ridge. "How do you know this house?"

"I've stayed in one before. It's the Organization's universal safe house. Adam said they had them all over the world. He didn't tell you this?"

"He mentioned it, but I don't have the house memorized."

"Oh, ho. Look who's coming up short this time." I patted his hand latched onto my elbow. "Don't worry, Reynolds," I chided him. "I'll scout it out."

"I'm not sure that's the best idea," he mumbled.

Placing my hands on my hips, I turned around to watch him hurriedly deposit Kenny on the ground.

"At least, I've had some training," he argued.

"Fine." I extended my hand in invitation. "Be my guest." Crossing my arms over my chest, I said, "And what is the signal for all clear?"

He pulled up short, bringing a hand to his chin as he considered it. "How about, if you don't bring trouble, there won't be none?"

Narrowing my eyes, I glared at him. "How long have you been waiting to use that one?"

He stopped trying to hide his smile and started forward again. "If I don't come back, you'll know something's wrong," he said as he passed.

"That's not funny, Reynolds."

"Would you prefer ice cream sundae with a cherry on top if it's clear?" he called over his shoulder.

No. I would prefer to eat the ice cream sundae with the cherry on top. "Just be careful."

"Yes, ma'am," he replied, saluting the air as he went.

Several retorts accurately describing his current behavior sprang to the tip of my tongue. They were poised, just right there, but I clamped my mouth shut as I headed back to stand guard over Kenny. He would have only taken it as a compliment anyway.

Kneeling down next to Kenny, I felt for his pulse. It was slow, but it was there. I guessed the nanobots were doing what they were supposed to. When I turned back around, Reynolds was slinking in and out of the shadows surrounding the house. It was nerve wracking watching him, but I couldn't look away, not until he disappeared from sight. Every second after that seemed like an eternity.

Oh, crap, I thought as I sunk to the ground. Miranda was going to hit the roof if she found out that I was off the radar again. Maybe Cedars wouldn't tell her right away. Dad gum it. He would never be able to shield something like this from her. That's it. She was going to ground me. There wasn't a baked good decadent enough to get me out of this one. I blew out through my lips as I considered the wrath that would be awaiting my return. But there was nothing to be done about it now. No use even thinking about it.

Refusing to dwell on it any longer let my thoughts drift to Adam. I remembered him telling me that he wasn't able to make a full conversion yet. Something had obviously changed that. Since the nanobots were the catalyst for the shift, it stood to reason that they had been altered in some way. Or, the human side of Adam had been suppressed to allow the nanobots to surge into the shift. But if Adam wasn't the one initiating the change, could he shift back by himself?

Reynolds' appearance on the porch interrupted my thoughts. He lifted his hand and waved. Was that the signal? Throwing his hands up in a show of frustration, he disappeared inside. He came back out carrying a roll of paper towels which he bent over as he wrote. Then he ripped off a strip and held it up.

"Hot fudge sundae with a cherry on top," I read quietly. There were those words again, right on the tip of my tongue. All of them consistent with the backside of a donkey.

Smirking at Reynolds, I turned my back to him as I knelt by Kenny and prepared to lift him to my shoulder. I got one arm under his back when I heard the distant pop of gunfire. I didn't have to turn around to know what I would find. The sinking feeling in my gut told me plain enough.

My knees dropped slowly to the ground, even as my heart rate sped up. I gave in to the urge to shift and let it race through me. Then careful not to make any sudden movements, I lowered Kenny back down and turned around.

Reynolds was lying face down on the porch. I couldn't tell from this distance if he was still breathing, but I refused to believe that he was dead. I wasn't sure where the shot had come from, and any possible culprits still weren't visible. Voices were starting to filter through, but they were faint. That could have meant they were still far away or they were shielded by the house. Before I did anything, I needed to know for sure.

Hooking Kenny under the arms, I moved him into the underbrush and covered him up as much as possible. Since I knew for sure that the gunshot didn't originate in this area, the woods directly behind us seemed the safest place to do surveillance. I found a tree whose branches would afford me some cover and quickly scaled it. From there, I looked over the area again.

The house was still quiet, but the sight of the camouflaged van hidden in the distance confirmed the suspicion that these guys were not working alone. I hadn't mentioned it to Reynolds earlier, but someone at the Organization had to be in on it. Who else had access to plant the trackers? The bugs could have been leftovers from Pike's time there I supposed. It would be nice to believe we didn't have an active traitor in our midst. And without certainty, foolish.

I transferred my gaze to the house again. It couldn't be coincidence that they had shown up here, not even if they were parlaying off the tracking data. Only Organization people knew about the safe houses, another bullet point to support my suspicion.

Closing my eyes, I concentrated on listening. There were two distinct sets of voices, one in the woods and one near the house. The pair in the woods was moving away from the house, towards me, the one that Reynolds had held the sign up for. Tuning out the pair near the house, I concentrated on the duo headed towards me until I could see them. They were dressed in fatigues, but had no insignias identifying them. Inhaling deeply, I determined that they didn't smell like furries or any other hybrid. Hybrids smelled like a mix of human and their animal with a distinct earthy undertone. I wasn't sure when I had learned to distinguish between the smells, but there it was.

Two human beings against me might be a fair fight. Having only been in one fight so far, I really didn't know. And, I wasn't positive, but I was betting those guns holstered at their sides weren't loaded with blanks. I liked my odds better with them separated.

One of the guy's radios buzzed. I couldn't make out what was being said, but by the way they changed directions, I knew they were being called back to the house. With my odds diminishing with every step they took together, I tossed a couple of pine cones to the ground in an attempt to gain their attention. Human hearing, Macy, I scolded myself when they didn't stop. Slapping my pockets in search of something heavier, I located the flashlight. It thumped loudly as it struck the ground.

Stopping in unison, they both looked behind them. "I'll check it out," one of them said. "Probably just a squirrel." The other one laughed and continued on to the house.

Yeah, come and get your squirrel, I thought as he backtracked towards me. I waited until he passed me and then eased down from the tree. He walked right by the flashlight lying on the ground in plain sight. Clearly, not the most astute hunter. Shrugging, I picked it up and hefted it to strike. When he stopped suddenly, I swung and caught him on the back of the head. He crumpled like a rag doll. Never even knew I was there.

I tucked the flashlight back in my pocket and drug him over to a nearby tree. I used the rope hanging from his belt to secure him. Rifling through his pockets produced a snickers bar, keys and a phone. I crushed the phone and added the keys to my pocket. I started to eat the snickers bar, but thought Kenny or Reynolds probably had more need of it.

The radio hanging from his belt crackled. I wasn't going to even pretend to answer. Instead, I sprinted a short distance away and climbed a tree to wait for his partner to come out looking for him. It didn't take long until his buddy was crashing through the woods. I was so focused on him that I almost missed the one that had stepped onto the porch.

I froze as I stared into the barrel of the gun sighted in my direction. Fear and anger washed over me at the same time. Fear due to the extent of my exposure in my current location, and anger at the realization of the threat he posed. Part of me wanted to pull back to the trunk of the tree, to hide from the one holding the gun. The other part of me wanted to attack both of them. My muscles became rigid in response, locking my limbs in place. If I didn't make a decision soon, I wasn't going to be able to help anyone.

Closing my eyes, I sank lower onto the branch. Reynolds and Kenny needed me. Running away and abandoning them wasn't an option. I had to get the leopard part of me to understand that, to not obey its natural instinct to flee to safety. We, the leopard and I, were no longer solitary creatures. We had each other. And we had a family to protect.

The release was immediate. With the decision to fight, all of my senses kicked into overdrive. It took me a moment to adjust to the increased levels of sound and smell, and now my muscles shook with pent up energy. But it was better than paralyzed any day.

I focused intently on the man heading my way, blinking when his appearance shifted to a water color image. But no matter how many times I blinked, the image only grew. A halo developed around him, the color of which I found hard to describe. I flicked my eyes to the man on the porch. The colors radiating from him were more intense, darker. These were bad men. I could smell it now, too. It reminded me of an infected wound, a sort of cloying, rotting stench. The closer he came, the stronger it got. Once again, I was thankful that my stomach was empty.

Verifying that the man on the porch was still in position, I prepared myself to leap. Right as he passed under the branch I was crouched on, I sprang at him. I landed on his upper back and snapped his neck before he hit the ground.

Jumping aside quickly, I looked down at him, then at my hands. I didn't think I had planned to do that. I didn't even know I could do that.

A shot rang out, splintering the tree next to me. These are very bad men, I reminded myself as I tossed my uncertain feelings aside and ran. I could hear the footfalls of the other man as he charged into the woods after me. Veering left, I sprinted in a wide arc away from my current location before leaping into the trees.

From my new vantage point, I could tell he was a very large man. Something instinctively told me that he would win in a hand to hand fight. Trusting that instinct, I quietly dropped to the ground and cut a path towards the house. As I drew level with the back porch, I strained to hear the sound of Reynolds' breathing. To my immense relief, he still was.

Using the woods as cover, I circled around to the back of the house and approached the porch. The main door was open, leaving only the screen door to get through. I stole up the steps and knelt off to the side of the door. Every sound became magnified as I concentrated on listening to what was happening inside the house. I nearly blew my cover when I was startled by the loud swearing of the one who'd just found his dead partner.

Bringing a hand to my chest, I willed my racing heart to calm. When I could hear something other than my heart pounding in my ears, I leaned forward to listen again. The house was silent. Seizing the handle of the screen door, I eased it open a few inches and leaned forward on one knee. The interior was dark, like the power was out. Forgetting about the unwritten rule that all screen doors must creak, I stiffened at the whine that sounded as I inched the screen open further.

"Dang it," I swore silently. Wrenching it open far enough to allow me to enter, I dashed inside and hunkered down beside a bookshelf.

The fourth guy rounded the corner with a pudding cup in his hand. "Nettles, that you?"

Wow. Even I knew that you did not announce your position to the unidentified entrant when you had two guys missing. Not to mention, his attention was focused on the pudding in his hand and not the door.

He reached the door and pushed the screen open slightly, holding it steady as he conducted his inspection. "Must have been the wind," he muttered and let the screen door slam shut. He turned to leave and then paused. Reaching for the main door, he closed and locked it. That was where his caution ended. His attention was already focused on the pudding cup before he had fully turned around.

The radio tucked into the pocket of his trousers popped, and the guy in the woods more or less began a litany of undecipherable growling through the speaker. But I understood the instruction to contact headquarters. When he reached to set his pudding cup down, I stepped up behind him and tapped him on the shoulder. He spun around, and I hit him with the barometer that had been attached to the wall above my hiding place.

"I don't think you should make that call," I said as he fell.

If he'd had a gun, I would have picked it up. But all he had was a pudding cup, which I may or may not come back for later. Stepping over him on my way to Reynolds, I spied the familiar hutch. I hoped it had a separate power source from the house. Reynolds would probably know.

I opened the front door and stopped cold. The one I'd left free in the woods, the one too big to fight, was standing with one foot on the stairs and one foot on the porch next to Reynolds' shoulder. The gun he held was pointed squarely at my chest.

Prying my fingers free of the door knob, I pushed the screen door open and stepped onto the porch. "You made good time," I said casually, sparing a brief glance at Reynolds.

"I knew which way you were headed," he rasped. "Though, I didn't think a little thing like you would be the source of trouble." He lifted his head away from the scope. "You're the first hybrid I've actually seen. Gotta tell you," he sneered. "Looks real good." His eyes slid greedily over me. "Real good," he repeated.

Revolting. But my salvation was at hand. Tilting my head to the side, I made sure the assailant's eyes stayed locked with mine as Reynolds' hand snaked towards his ankle. "You think?" I flirted as I smiled. "I've only ever seen myself in hybrid form one time."

"Oh, yeah," he drawled. "Like right out of a fantasy movie."

If Reynolds didn't finish this soon, I was going to attack out of sheer disgust.

"You know, we might—"

Reynolds grabbed his ankle and jerked him off his feet before he could complete the thought. The clattering of the rifle to the porch was followed by the thud of his head striking the steps. When the attacker remained still, I stepped forward and leaned over him. He was out cold.

"No we won't," I breathed in relief.

The explosion of gunfire and the sudden eruption of blood from the guy's chest startled me. I stumbled down a couple steps before spinning around with wide eyes. Reynolds held the attacker's rifle pressed to his shoulder.

"Reynolds," I gulped, pressing both hands against my face while my heart rate settled back down.

"He shot first," he said without emotion.

"Yes, he did," I agreed, carefully watching until Reynolds lowered the rifle. "Are you okay?"

He set the rifle aside and stood to his feet. "I've been better," he groaned. Pulling his jacket to one side, he reached a hand to his chest and freed the bullet forcing its way out through his skin.

"Want to trade?" I asked, holding out a slightly melted snickers bar.

He snorted and then winced, gently massaging the fast healing wound. "I believe I would."

I took the bullet from his outstretched hand and gave him the snickers bar. The bullet was torn up pretty badly, but I thought the distorted letters were DTP.

"Any idea what DTP stamped on this bullet might mean?" I asked Reynolds.

"Disturbing the peace?" he said quickly.

I looked back up at him with raised eyebrows.

"Not like I would have experience in that…it's common knowledge." His face hardened at my look of disbelief.

"Have a wild side, do ya? A taste for creating disturbances?"

"Now that's the pot calling the kettle black," he answered flatly.

I started to respond, then let it go. I did look good in black.

CHAPTER 9

ANOTHER LINK, I THOUGHT, ROLLING what was left of the
bullet between my fingers. The woods in New Orleans,
probably Granny's and now here. Was the common thread
me or the hybrids? I tossed the mangled casing onto the porch. It
wasn't going to tell me anything further, and there were still two
men hanging around who wanted to see us dead.

"We still have two guys left to deal with," I told Reynolds,
trying not to look envious as he shoved the remaining bit of
snickers into his mouth. "I left one guy tied up in the woods, and
the other one I clocked inside. Or more accurately, barometered."

Reynolds snorted softly in understanding as he sucked the
chocolate from his fingers.

"And we have to retrieve Kenny."

"Maybe not," Reynolds said, shifting his gaze to focus over my
shoulder.

"You don't have to worry about the one you gift wrapped."

My head swiveled in the direction of Kenny's voice. He stood
a few feet in front of the porch, a cord of rope held loosely in
one hand. The only visible traces of the wound were the bloody
remains of Reynolds' makeshift bandage still clinging to him.
There was one huge worry gone.

"You might want to change," I suggested wryly. "We are
supposed to be meeting the president."

"Have you looked at yourself?" he replied tersely.

I could have guessed well enough, but I took an inventory
anyway. My boots were all muddy. The blouse…beyond saving,
unless bloody handprints were the newest rage. I'd also given new

definition to the slit that had originally stopped somewhere mid-calf. To say the fashion ground I was standing on was thin was an understatement.

"Any left?" I asked Reynolds, who was examining the rifle's chamber.

"Are you asking about the snickers or the rounds?"

"There's snickers?" Kenny asked hopefully.

"Not anymore," Reynolds said.

Smiling sadly at Kenny's dashed hopes of a quick sugar fix, I said, "I was referring to the bullets."

"Two," he nodded.

"Let me see one."

He slid the bullet free and tossed it to me. "I only need one anyway."

"Wait," I said sharply, reaching for him as he turned to go. "You can't just kill him."

"Keeping him alive is not worth the risk. I have to ensure that you stay alive. That's my number one priority."

"He was a techie, not like these other guys."

"Techie or not, he came here as part of a team to complete a mission. Do I need to remind you what that mission was?"

"I know, but—"

Two shots splintered the front door cutting off my objection. Reynolds hit the deck, taking me with him.

"Can I shoot him now?" he sneered.

"Shoot him!" Kenny encouraged from beneath the porch.

I tried to hand Reynolds the bullet I was holding, but another shot piercing the floor between us caused Reynolds to roll away from me. I'd been wrong about him not having a gun, and in too big of a hurry to get to Reynolds to do a proper sweep of the place.

"Still waiting on that permission," Reynolds gritted as he lifted the rifle in place.

"Do it," I squeaked, hugging the railing as the biggest volley of shots yet peppered the porch. I cringed when I heard Kenny yelp.

"Shoot! Him!" Kenny roared in pain tinted anger.

Reynolds fitted the tip of the rifle into one of the holes the shooter had created in the door and pulled the trigger. I didn't flinch this time when the gun fired. After Reynolds entered the house, I melted from my knees tucked position and lowered my face to the porch floor. Through the gaps between the boards, I found Kenny.

"You okay?" I whispered.

"Just great," he snapped. "I was planning on getting a butt piercing anyway."

"A butt piercing…Oh, Kenny—"

"All clear," Reynolds yelled.

Kenny crawled out from under the porch and hobbled towards the steps. My eyes were naturally drawn to his rear end. The blood stain wasn't large, nothing like what happened earlier.

"It's just a scratch," he said, clearly annoyed by my attention. "Don't even think about taking a closer look. These sweet cheeks are someone else's territory."

Smiling at him, I said, "Ah, come on. I'm a doctor."

"Nice try," he muttered. "Did you search him?" He tilted his head in the direction of the guy prostrate on the steps.

"No."

"I'll do it."

The only sign that Kenny was in pain were his deliberately slow movements. Whether that was in relation to the previous impalement or the new wound, I couldn't tell. Taking a breath, I held it a moment before expelling it. What a crappy day this had been so far.

Glancing at the unused bullet clasped in my hand, I verified the pristine GM and DTP stamped on its head. No way to misread that. I slid the bullet into the pocket of my skirt, and after one last look at Kenny, went inside to search the other one.

Reynolds glanced at me as I knelt down by the body. But as soon as I started rifling through the pockets, he turned his attention back to the screens inside the hutch. Kenny came in just as I finished, a pair of handcuffs dangling from one finger. Opening my hand, I revealed the lighter in my palm.

"Think of the trouble we could get into with these," he grinned wickedly.

"I'd rather not," I chuckled and handed him the lighter.

"We're not going to be able to do much here," Reynolds said, frowning at the still black screens. "I can't even turn them on."

I stood up and joined Reynolds at the hutch. "I was hoping it ran on a separate power source."

He reached a hand and clasped the back of his neck. "It can. Only the battery is so old that I can't get it going. The ions are probably depleted. There's one more thing I can try, but it's even less likely to work."

"No water, either," Kenny said while repetitively working the faucets at the sink.

"I guess it's official then. No clean-up for us." I left Reynolds and began to walk the row of cabinets. Each door I opened revealed a bare cup board. "These cabinets are as empty as my stomach," I griped. What kind of safe house was this? No food, no water or power, but fully stocked with lethal enemies. I closed the last door and turned to face Reynolds. "Do we at least know the time?"

Reynolds glanced at his watch then out the window to his left. "Roughly ten o'clock."

"Why roughly?"

He held up his watch to show me the shattered face.

Great. Now I wished the barometer really had been a clock. "What time were we supposed to meet the president?"

"Ten to forty-five minutes ago?" he shrugged.

"That's what I thought," I mumbled. So much for a good first impression. You know, if our appearance didn't preclude that already. Remembering the keys I found earlier, I pulled them out of my pocket. "I'm going to look for some wheels."

Reynolds looked away from the hutch, worry clouding his features. "There could be others."

"I got it," Kenny said, gingerly sliding from the counter he'd claimed for a seat.

Like I needed a bodyguard. Hadn't I just demonstrated that I could take care of myself? I mean, technically, I took out three of the guys by myself. True, I only killed one. The hand reaching for the door paused. I had killed again.

"Doc?" Kenny questioned, reaching around me to pull the door open.

Actually, we all had killed. Reynolds twice.

Realizing Kenny was staring at me, I smiled at him. "I'm fine." It wasn't a lie. I was fine. A little thrown by my actions, by the world of violence I now inhabited. But I would adjust. I had to. They weren't leaving me any other choice.

Gripping the keys tightly, I crossed the porch and jogged down the steps. At the edge of what was loosely the yard sat what had to be a custom painted truck. I couldn't be blamed for not spotting it earlier. It was like someone had photographed a picture of the woods and transferred it onto the truck. I pointed the key and pushed the unlock button. The alarm trumped in acknowledgement.

"Mission accomplished," I remarked dryly. Now on to the juicier task of locating the gadget, gizmo, and all things too technical for Macy to understand hideaway. Returning the keys to my pocket, I ventured deeper onto the property surrounding the house. After making a complete circuit, I stood where I started. "Come on," I complained softly at the lack of potential candidates.

"What are we looking for?" Kenny asked as he joined me. He'd been following from a respectable distance, close enough for me to know that he was there, but far enough away that it didn't annoy.

"An old decrepit shed or outhouse. Any kind of structure that could house the wonder lab."

He grunted in understanding.

"It has to be here," I said, my eyes still raking the property for suspects. Spotting a large tree partially concealing a broken down tree fort, I started in that direction. "What do you think?" I asked Kenny as I stared up at it.

He looked at the tree house, and then back at the truck. "I think I'd rather take the truck."

"Wimp," I teased and leapt onto the branch supporting the structure. Upon closer inspection, my belief that this was my target waned a little. The tree house was in shambles. Pieces were literally falling off.

"This is what we're looking for?" Kenny asked skeptically after he'd completed a more leisurely path to the branch opposite me.

"Maybe," I shrugged.

"The door looks like it will fall off the hinges if you open it."

"It does," I nodded and reached to open it anyway. The hinges screamed in protest, but the door didn't fall off. It didn't reveal any secret hideaway, either.

"This looks even worse," Kenny grumbled, pressing against me to get a better look inside.

I didn't disagree. The floor was covered in dust and leaves, like it had seen a hundred seasons of summer and winter. I lightly ran a hand through the accumulation. Bits of the floor broke free and crumbled into the litter.

Kenny leaned past me and thumped the floor with his fist. The tree house reverberated ominously. As his hand retreated, he pulled his face to one side. "Let me guess, we're going in anyway."

"Yep," I nodded and crab walked across the threshold. The moan the tree house uttered was almost comical.

"Oh yeah, this is going to end well," Kenny muttered.

Hoping that was true despite the sentiment motivating the comment, I took another step, then another, until I made it all the way across. Kenny waited until I stopped moving, then stuck to the periphery as he slunk in after me.

"This doesn't resemble the bunker at Granny's house at all," he complained.

"That's because this isn't a bunker. It's the cover for it." At least, that was the assumption I was operating under.

"What are y'all doing?" Reynolds asked, poking only his head through the door.

"Me and that ray of sunshine over there," I said, looking pointedly at Kenny, "are looking for a secret hidey hole."

Reynolds' gaze swept the interior, his face contorting into a mixture of surprise and confusion. "Oh," he whispered.

"What?" Kenny and I said together.

"I might know this one." Eyeing the floor warily, he crouched down and crept forward. The floorboards strongly objected to the added weight, cracking loudly when he was only a few feet in.

"I think it's time to scrap the tree house," Kenny recommended.

"Let's hope that's after we're not in it," Reynolds said. "Macy, we need to trade places."

Slowly, I began to retrace my steps.

"Does anyone else feel like we're swaying?" Kenny asked nervously.

I paused and focused on the horizon beyond the tree. We were swaying a little. "It's just the wind. We'll be fine."

"Isn't that what you said right before a tree limb dissected my internal organs?" he argued.

"No," I huffed as I continued to move. "I said Reynolds would do great."

"And that included the tree—"

"I am trying to concentrate," I spoke over him.

"Yeah, you do that," he mumbled to himself.

Geesh. Cranky much? What was his problem anyway? I glanced briefly at him. One hand was gently massaging his stomach, the other his backside. Ah, pain. I supposed having a limb rammed through your midsection and being shot in the butt for real might tend to make one a little cranky. And mad.

The floor tilted too far to the right, and I froze.

"Hang on," Reynolds said louder than was necessary. He backed his way out of the tree house, then motioned for me to continue. The floor leveled out when I started moving again.

I shot Kenny another look and couldn't conceal the smile that blossomed on my face. He was fighting mad, ready to chew someone up and spit them out. I knew it wasn't something I should be laughing about, but still I struggled to contain it. It was even funnier to think that I might be the one he wanted to take a bite of.

Seeking the source of my sudden joy, Reynolds followed my sporadic peeks at Kenny. At first, he looked confused, then fought to contain his smile as well. Kenny finally figured out that we were laughing at him, and growled his annoyance, which was the last straw. The tree house shook as the silent laughter found its voice.

"Laugh, why don't ya?" Kenny barked. "Go ahead, bring the house down. See how many branches you can impale me with this time. I'll be your living dart board. Will that make you happy?" he demanded.

I laughed until I thought I was going to pee on myself.

"No one is going to knock the tree house down," I insisted once I'd gotten my breath back. "Or use you as a human dart board. Just shut up and let me get across."

Kenny was beyond replying now. With arms crossed over his chest, he stared daggers at the branches visible in the interior, like he was daring each one to even think about it.

After Reynolds and I had safely traded spots, I asked him, "What is it that you think you know about this place?" I cocked my head to the side. "Did I say that right?"

"Little heavy on the wording perhaps," Reynolds chuckled. "What I know," he said, stressing the last word, "is that early on in my first year at the Organization, they taught us about places like this." He reached the other side and stood to inspect the section of trunk invading the fort. "They're pretty much considered obsolete now. Used mostly for storage. I'm not sure what we'll find that's going to help us much. But here goes." He began pushing on the knots in the tree and the planks of the tree house, alternating in some unspecified pattern.

"This going to take much longer?" I asked after he'd been at it for a while.

"Longer now, since you just made me lose count."

"Sor-ry," I cracked, but we could have cut the tree down faster. Seriously, this was akin to watching paint dry. "I'm going to wait outside. Holler when you get it." Reynolds' sigh of frustration caused me to cringe. Crud. Now he had to start over again.

Outside the air was better, not crowded with cobwebs and leaf litter, and I could breathe without wanting to sneeze. Climbing as far out as the limb would support, I sat down and straddled the branch. It probably wasn't very ladylike, but I did it anyway. If

Olivia could see me now. Giggling to myself, I tucked the edges of my skirt in around me. I could at least maintain the pretense of modesty.

Allowing my gaze to sweep over the property, I had one singular thought. Man I wished I had a soda. Then I could properly lift my mug to make a toast. Here's to another day not going the way I envisioned it. Leaning forward, I propped my elbows on the limb and dropped my head into my hands. Yet another delay in the rescue of Adam. I'd fire myself if it was possible.

The door creaked as it opened. "Well, that's attractive," Kenny sneered.

I so wanted to say something equally as unladylike as my skirt tucked around my legs like a baggy pair of shorts. But I couldn't think of anything and was forced to hold my response to a simple scowl.

"Also, not attractive." The tree house moaned as he shifted his weight off the structure and onto the tree itself.

"You are so expelled from Macy's home for wayward hybrids," I bit at him.

"You have a home for wayward hybrids?" he scoffed.

"No," I drawled. Obviously, I didn't. Why would I subject myself to that?

We were quiet a minute before he said, "You sort of been working towards it."

"No I haven't," I vehemently disagreed.

"You have," he argued. "The moment you crossed the line between the scientist they wanted and the one you wanted to be, you started down that path."

My mind raced as I examined his words. Miranda and I hadn't made any concrete plans, other than to refuse to surrender my report. I hadn't gotten the chance to work out what it meant for the hybrids.

"You might not have a choice, you know?"

"I'm probably not the ideal candidate for headmistress," I sighed. "I'm not the best mother figure in the world."

"No," he agreed. Then quietly, he added, "But you're not the worst either."

Oh, that was encouraging.

"Annoying big sister who thinks she's always right?" he proposed.

I liked it better than the title, Not the Worst Mother in the World.

"Do you remember what Granny said...about there being more colonies? Do you think there are?"

"I truly don't know," I shrugged.

"If there are, and there are others like us, same condition... under attack..." his voice trailed off, allowing me to fill in the gaps.

I knew what he was trying to get me to commit to, but I didn't have the resources to conduct some large scale rescue operation. Contrary to what everyone thought, I wasn't actually running anything.

He cleared his throat, then began speaking in a blatant impersonation of an infomercial announcer. "With great power comes—"

"I will knock you off this tree limb," I threatened.

His abrupt silence confirmed he'd gotten the message. He didn't attempt to sway me again, but I still felt the pressure of his expectation. I supposed that was my fault. Even though our relationship at the Colony had been somewhat adversarial, an unavoidable complication of the job, I'd still been there for him—for all of them. I guess I had acted like some weird mixture of scientist and overseer. Was it strange that he expected no less now? Albeit, he was presently advocating on a much larger scale. For hybrids he didn't know and whose existence hadn't been established yet. Despite all of the walls Kenny used to shield himself, sometimes his heart refused to remain hidden.

With neither of us speaking, the silence grew in reprimand until it pressed unmercifully against my heart. "I'll do what I can, Kenny," I finally consented. "That's all I can promise."

"I know you will."

When our eyes met, I was treated to his cocky smirk. He'd known all along that's what I'd say. Secretly, as soon as he'd presented the possibility of more hybrids in need of rescue, I knew it too.

A dull scraping sounded from inside the tree house. "I got it," Reynolds called.

Unwrapping myself from the branch, I followed Kenny back inside. A large square shaped opening stood where the trunk had been. The hand Kenny used to feel inside the opening came back covered in cobwebs.

"It's a slide," Reynolds announced excitedly.

"A slide? It looks like a spider cave." I pointed to Kenny's hand as evidence.

"It's a standard entry." He reached inside and pulled out two headlamps swamped in spider webs and offered one to me. Shrugging when I refused, he gave it to Kenny and climbed into position. "Let's go meet Spiderman. To the Bat Cave!" he yelled as he let go.

"Mixing up your comics," I shouted halfheartedly after him. The sound of his slide and the rising pitch of his "Woohoo" ended with a crash and a sudden burst of laughter. "Reynolds?" I leaned in and called.

"Sorry," he answered breathily. "Really long slide."

"My turn," Kenny said, rubbing his hand together expectantly.

"You sure you're up for it?" I asked, looking pointedly at his tush.

"Just a scratch, Doc," he whined in annoyance and shook off the hand I had used to stay him. Securing his place at the start, he rolled his eyes to me. Then in one motion he snapped his legs together and crossed his arms over his chest.

And he's off, I said to myself. The hushed sound of his descent ended the same way as Reynolds'. The laughter that pealed from both of them let me know they were okay. No one left but me. I climbed into position and tried to determine the length of the slide.

"Hey, shine some light on this, will ya?"

Two mismatched lights bobbed over the galvanized surface of an insanely long, steep slide. Dad gum it.

"What did y'all crash into?"

I heard "boxes" and "stuff" spoken simultaneously.

"Boxes of stuff," Reynolds clarified. "You'll be fine," he yelled encouragingly.

"Yeah, you'll be fine," Kenny repeated in a tone that suggested otherwise.

"We made it," Reynolds said placatingly.

"But y'all are idiots," I muttered softly.

"Hybrids, remember?" Kenny growled. "Whispering really doesn't help."

"Still true," I muttered again.

"Well, you're our leader. What does that make you?" Kenny challenged.

Dipping my head in defeat, I said, "Queen of the idiots," and let go.

For someone who hated the dropping sensation where your stomach tries to claw its way up your throat, I sure kept subjecting myself to it a lot. And, as I had discovered, falling was not analogous to the Band-Aid example. Faster did not make it any better.

I couldn't help myself. My hands went out in sheer instinct. Accompanying me now was the screeching sound of my claws cutting channels into the steel. Determined for that to be the only screeching coming from me, I clamped my jaw shut tight. I made sure to keep the heels of my boots away from the metal too. There was no way I was going down this slide headfirst like what had happened to me in the airshaft.

"We'll catch you," Reynolds bellowed as he came into view.

"Assuming she doesn't bring the slide down with her," Kenny joked.

Both of them had huge smiles plastered on their faces.

The moment of collision nearly upon me, I tensed in anticipation. As a result, I barreled into them like a bowling ball. Not only did they not catch me, I drug them with me. All three of us careened wildly into the boxes of stuff, producing one heaping mess of limbs and crushed cardboard, with them laughing hysterically the whole time.

"You're a lot heavier than you look," Reynolds howled.

Wrangling myself free of the wreckage, I sank to my knees. "I do not see what is the slightest bit funny about this."

"You should have seen your face," Kenny hooted as he rolled to his side. "I wished I'd had a camera."

"Do you have any claws left?" Reynolds shrieked.

Resisting the urge to look at them, I snatched the headlamp from Reynolds and looked for a light switch. I found one next to the slide's exit and flipped it on. Reynolds had been right. This wasn't a normal Organization hideaway. There weren't any souped up ATVs or wall of weapons. Just a row of computers older than the ones at Granny's. All my irritation with them evaporated along with the hope I'd been holding onto.

"Not what you were expecting?" Kenny guessed, all traces of humor gone from his voice.

"Not exactly," I shook my head.

Having pulled himself together, Reynolds sat down at the nearest terminal and turned it on.

"Will you be able to contact the Organization using these?" I asked him.

"We've got power back. All things are possible. It might take a minute though," he cautioned. "And, I need Juarez to be watching for us, which he likely is due to the loss of contact."

I left him to it and started perusing the boxes we'd scattered everywhere. Some of the stuff I recognized as medical supplies. Other items I had no clue about. Opening one box, I pulled out a very dated pair of night vision goggles.

"How old is this stuff?" I wondered aloud, pausing to snicker at the sight of Kenny in some kind of ancient gas mask.

"We're in luck," Reynolds declared.

"Juarez was watching?" I asked as I put the goggles back in the box.

"No. But Flash and Charlie were. They're getting him."

"Can we talk to them?"

"Yeah," he nodded. Then he slid an old camera device over and positioned it on top of the monitor, which was not a flat screen. "Just look straight into the camera."

"Flash, Charlie, can you hear me?"

"And see you too. Pay up," Charlie said.

"For what?" I said indignantly.

"Not you. I bet Flash that your clothes wouldn't make it five hours."

"So glad you found something to amuse yourselves with in my absence," I griped. "Is everything alright there?" There was a long silence filled pause. "Guys? Are you still there?"

"Right here," Reynolds said, pointing at the monitor.

In front of me appeared a very grainy picture of Flash and Charlie.

"We're here. Things are…interesting," Charlie said.

"No they're not," Flash argued. "Things are tense. There seems to be some kind of power struggle going on between Olivia and Miranda and by extension, Olivia and Cedars."

"Juarez is trying to smooth everything over, but…" Charlie quieted as Juarez's face replaced theirs.

"MK," Juarez sighed. "You are making my life very difficult. I don't like difficult."

"You know, neither do I, but it seems to like me plenty."

"Humph," Juarez huffed. "What have you gotten yourself into this time?"

"If you don't know, I'm sure I don't. Reynolds said someone tried to commandeer the jet. Do you know who was trying to take over the jet or who was waiting for us here?"

"No and not knowing where you are makes it a little difficult to find people waiting for you. You were ambushed?"

"Pretty much. Four guys. At the safe house."

Juarez's face hardened. He'd gotten the implication.

"When we lost you," he began, quickly glossing over the realization he'd just had. "I was able to trace the interference to a location in Florida. But after studying it, I'm almost certain that is a bogus tie. I've got them on it," he said, hooking a thumb at

Flash and Charlie. "But it will take time to isolate the one thread that is real, and by the time we do, they'll probably be long gone."

Dang it. "What about the meeting with the president?"

"It's still on. President O'Conner was delayed by some crisis with Syria. From what I understand, you've got another couple of hours. Okay, I got you." The salt and pepper image of Juarez appeared startled on the screen. "I didn't think we had sites like this still active. How'd you even find it?" he laughed.

"We stumbled upon it," I said testily. He didn't need to know that we literally stumbled upon it. "Hey Juarez, are things alright there?"

There was a short pause as he looked away from the camera. "They will be just as soon as they settle who's in charge," he said quietly.

"Adam left Cedars in charge."

"I know," he agreed.

"Does she?" If she couldn't accept Adam's choice, then we had a problem. Because I, in no way, trusted her to be in charge. I just didn't.

"She knows. But I don't think she trusts anybody else to run things right now."

Wanting to hold on tighter after everything around her had fallen apart was understandable. Betrayal did have a way of arousing suspicion, especially about people you didn't know.

"Juarez, I can understand her reluctance to let go of the strings. But, as I understand it, she wasn't the one ever in charge, and I don't think she's in any condition to objectively rule the roost."

He pursed his lips and then grinned like it hurt him. "She'll come around, Macy. She doesn't have a choice."

Yeah, a lot of that going around. I wanted to tell him that cornered wouldn't necessarily produce the reaction he was hoping for, but I didn't.

"In other news," Juarez said, simultaneously slapping the desk as he pushed away. "Find an old com, and we'll try to establish mobile communications again. Signal the Bobbsey Twins when you find one." The screen went black as he exited the picture.

Standing up from where I'd bent over Reynolds' chair, I was immediately met with their concerned faces. "You heard the man," I charged. "Find a com."

We scattered about the room, each of us randomly searching through the boxes and cabinets for a usable com. I grimaced loudly when I opened a box filled to the brim with so called nutrition bars. Everything was exactly the same on the packaging. These things hadn't been updated in decades.

"That's it," I said. "When I get a spare moment, we are deep sixing these things and coming up with something better."

Reynolds and Kenny stared at me like I was crazy.

"What?" I demanded, waving an offending bar at them. "I bet these things haven't been redesigned in over a hundred years."

"I don't think the Organization's that old," Reynolds said.

"You know what I mean. Taste has come a long way since these things were thought of." I made a disgusted face and tossed it back into the box.

"We need to get her fed before she turns feral on us," Reynolds joked.

"Soon," Kenny agreed.

Whatever, though I did agree with the feeding part. Since I'd lost my previous meal, technically, I hadn't eaten in a very long time. But not long enough to make me even consider eating one of these yuck bars.

"Here we go," Reynolds said, locating our prize in an overhead cabinet. He offered me a genuine crank, side roll switch, walkie talkie from the contents of the box he set on the counter.

"This is what we've been reduced to?" I griped, accepting the relic he held out to me. I blew at the dust covering the surface, right into Kenny's face. "Sorry," I cringed when he coughed loudly.

Reynolds wound the crank, then flipped the switch on the side uncertainly. He flipped it again to silence the static. "We'll figure this out as we go. Right now, we should start heading to the meeting."

"Leaving, yes, that sounds great," Kenny chimed in. "How do we do that? Leave, exactly? That slide is way too steep and slippery to climb back out. Probably not structurally sound either after what Doc did to it."

He didn't have to add that last part, but my glower was lost on the back of his head. Turning my attention to something useful, I looked for what should have been a given for any room, a way out. But my survey only revealed what Kenny had already noted, a conspicuous lack of obvious exits. After only a few seconds, I found myself staring at Reynolds. His expression was as blank as mine.

Ah, crud. "Get Juarez back on the line," I hollered.

CHAPTER 10

WE MADE IT OUT OF the hideaway, but not before Juarez had a good laugh. Since there were no nifty escape vehicles to be had, we were left with the bad guy's truck. Seemed kind of stupid to me to bring your personal vehicle to the type of assignment they had, but it attested to the fact that at least one of them was local. And prideful enough to think it wouldn't matter. The pistol stowed openly on the dash was further evidence.

"Is that safe?" Kenny asked as I scooped out honey from a jar I'd pilfered from the case sitting in the truck bed.

"I figure my nanos can handle it," I shrugged.

"No identification," Reynolds said, rounding the tailgate we were sitting on, his eyes fixed on the honey in my hand.

Leaning back, I freed another jar from the case and tossed it to him. Then I handed one to Kenny. Reynolds didn't hesitate, but Kenny was a little more cautious. He took his time just opening the lid.

"I've had bad experiences with honey," he whispered cryptically. Lifting the jar to his nose, he inhaled deeply.

I started to ask what kind of bad experiences you could have with honey, then stopped. There were only a couple of directions I thought that answer might go, and I really didn't want to know about either one.

"I didn't figure there would be any id," I said as I turned back to Reynolds. Country boys used trucks like these for running the back roads. They built them, they fixed them, and they didn't apologize to nobody for it. Something in me reflexively liked people like this. I wished I could have gotten to him before GM and DTP twisted his mind.

Reynolds upended the jar he was working on, his tongue working furiously to try and capture every last drizzle. When he was done, he licked his lips with vigor and then wiped his arm across his mouth.

"We've got a whole case over here," I said, using my thumb to point at the box.

"Maybe later," he smiled and wiped his mouth again. "I don't like it, but this truck is the only transportation available." Screwing the lid on the jar, he fitted it back in the case. "Whole county probably knows who this truck belongs to."

"Yep," I drawled.

"There's a good chance we'll never even make it to the meeting."

"Who are you kidding? They'll never even see us coming." I waved my hands wildly at the custom camo.

"It is a nice paint job," he laughed. "Ready to load up?"

"Oh, yeah," I nodded. I couldn't wait for the air conditioning to begin drying my sweat drenched clothes. We were going to smell so good when we finally made it to the meeting. "How long do you think it will take us to get there?"

"A couple hours."

"Shotgun," Kenny yelled, jumping off the tailgate and darting for the passenger door. He had a jar of honey in each hand.

"That didn't last long," Reynolds said, speaking of Kenny's resistance to the honey.

"Nope," I agreed.

Reynolds held the keys out to me with a questioning look on his face.

"You'd better drive," I said as I replaced my empty jar inside the case. "You're the only one who knows where we're going."

He clasped the keys in his fist, staring at it with a face that was not the picture of confidence.

"You do know where we're going, right?"

"Mostly." He looked up at me and grinned. "We'll be there on time."

"Reynolds, we're already late."

"I figure they can't start without you."

I pointed a finger at him. "I like the way you think."

Sliding off the tailgate, I headed for the passenger side. Since the front seat was fully occupied, I opened the back door and climbed in. We had barely gained any distance from the house when my eyes started drooping. The reasons for not wanting to sleep before the meeting were fuzzy to me now. I glanced at the rest of the seat to my left. Not counting all the empty slim jim wrappers, it was completely empty. One sweep of the hand sent them fluttering to the floor board like a herd of jerky butterflies. For his sake, I hoped he had made a point of drinking a lot of water.

Scooting over, I stretched out in the newly cleared seat. The smell of jerky was overwhelming and heavenly, and I didn't even like jerky. It took me a minute to find a position that didn't have the seatbelts digging into my bruised ribs, but as soon as I did, my whole body relaxed. A flash of Adam's face reminded me of why I had objected to sleeping, but it was moot now. The darkness had already closed in, and I'd just have to hope for the best.

"It's kind of hilarious, you know?" Kenny said.

What was hilarious?

"I don't know that hilarious is the right word," Reynolds disagreed. "More like inexplicable."

"The trouble that shows up when she's involved is unique," Kenny allowed.

"You mean like getting shot and crashing a plane?"

"Yeah, like that. And being speared by tree branches."

"Don't forget the flaming lizards and house fires," Reynolds added.

"That's what I mean," Kenny laughed. "Who else do you know that has this sort of stuff happen to them?"

Now halfway awake, I was aware that I was the subject of their conversation, but I didn't comment. What could I say in my defense, anyway? I didn't know anybody else this stuff happened to either.

"She is the common denominator," Reynolds agreed. "Never a dull moment, that's for sure."

Kenny was laughing so hard now that he was making those little squeaking noises that happened when you were laughing too hard to actually form words. This was the second time I'd witnessed Kenny in a fit of laughter. It was so opposite his normal personality, but Lord knows he deserved a good laugh. Even if it was me he was laughing at.

"You never know what's going to happen next," he finally managed to get out.

Reynolds chuckled in agreement. "Giant buzzards—"

"Dragons!" Kenny blurted out. "It has to be dragons."

Over the back of the seat, I could see Reynolds' shoulders beginning to shake as his composure dissolved.

"Got it," he gasped. "Giant dragons…could swoop down from the sky…and burn us all up." The last three words were slurred together in one loud shriek.

Unable to resist any longer, I sat up quickly, draping my arms over the front seat. The way they jumped to the sides, I knew I had startled them both.

"First of all," I stated firmly, "dragons do not exist. Furthermore, if they did, they would certainly not be interested in me. Not to mention the fact that I am much too cute to be burned to a crisp or in any other fashion fried."

My sudden appearance had momentarily stunned them into silence, but after my objection, they burst out laughing again. Sighing in disgust, I gave up and laid back down with my arm flung over my eyes. I didn't care what they said. I was not being barbequed by a dragon.

When they had gained enough breath to speak again, they spent it concocting increasingly elaborate ways in which we could be attacked. As far as I was concerned, it was indisputable evidence of too many video games in their spare time.

"What's wrong?" I asked groggily when the truck unexpectedly rolled to a stop.

"We're out of gas," Reynolds answered.

"You have got to be kidding me," I moaned.

"Not kidding. But good news. We're here." He pointed to a rusty gate about half a mile up a heavily tree lined road. We'd have never seen it if not for the bend in the road.

"Alabama Munitions," I read aloud. "Has it been two hours?"

"There about," Reynolds affirmed.

I must have fallen asleep again. And, again not dreamed of Adam. I didn't know what that meant, but I didn't like it.

As Kenny and Reynolds had already left the truck, I opened the door and got out. The gravel under my feet crunched loudly as I walked the short distance to where they waited.

"Anybody else's back feel like it has a target painted on it?" Kenny asked, his eyes nervously scanning the woods that surrounded us.

The spot between my shoulder blades itched in agreement.

"We could move into cover," Reynolds said, motioning to the trees. "But anyone with ears already knows we're here, and then there's those." He pointed to a nearby camera hidden in the trees, then again at another one. There were cameras spaced evenly all the way to the gate.

"They look new," Kenny said, squinting as he looked at them.

"Probably part of the security package for the president. Though why they wanted to have the meeting way out here and not at a more secure location is a mystery."

"I think that was the point," Reynolds commented. "To be in the middle of nowhere."

"Maybe they anticipated the Organization sending you," Kenny smirked. "When it explodes out here, it won't endanger an entire town."

Reynolds swiftly clapped a hand over his mouth in an effort to smother the surprise bolt of laughter that shot from him.

I stared daggers at Kenny, to no avail. He was impervious to my attempt to cow his attitude. Too much evidence to the contrary already supported his position, as I well knew from the verbal documentary he'd performed during the trip here. Ignoring him and his condescending stare, I turned on my heel and started for the gate. And that wasn't easy with my heels digging into the gravel with every step I took. My poor boots. If their condition was any kind of reflection on the state of my life...well, that was just sad.

By the time I made it to the gate, Kenny and Reynolds had caught up. It was a wonder that we'd been able to read the sign before. Up close, the paint was so faded that the name merged into one giant blur. No telling how long the plant had been abandoned.

"They certainly weren't trying to keep anyone out," Reynolds said. Stepping forward, he pushed the gate open with his foot. It swung wide, colliding with the opposite fence and showering rust onto the ground.

"Their defenses may not be here, but they're out there," Kenny said as he gripped the fence and pressed his face through the bars. "I can feel it," he whispered.

Turning from Kenny, I considered the setting on the other side of the gate we were about to enter. The gravel road had given way to asphalt that had definitely seen better days. The amount of trees was different too. They were so thick that they hid anything else that might be out there.

"Make sure you don't display any special talents you might have," I whispered low. "I don't want to give anything away for free." I also didn't want to strut down the middle of the road like a deer into a clearing. But remembering the cameras hidden in the trees, I knew the woods weren't any safer. "Well, I, for one, have had enough adventure today. Let's get this meeting over with and get out of here." Gritting my teeth against the feeling of unease, I set off down the road.

We walked maybe ten, fifteen minutes before the road deposited us in front of a grouping of buildings. The best looking one had a row of black SUVs parked in front of it.

"Looks like they beat us here," Kenny said.

"Yeah," I agreed nervously, my prior resolve to get this over with diminishing a little in the face of the task awaiting me.

"Still not sure what you're going to say?" Kenny guessed.

"Not particularly, no. But I'll think of something." I knew the words would be there when I needed them. Freezing in high pressure situations generally wasn't part of my character. If anything, I became more bold, more targeted as the tension pressed against me. Not sure if that was going to be a good thing in this situation.

The door to the warehouse opened, and a suit waved us over. No getting out of it now.

"Reynolds," I whispered. "How do I look?"

The expression on his face was priceless. I laughed all the way to the door.

The hum of conversation stopped as soon as we stepped inside. I counted five men grouped around what had been a table used in the packaging of the ammo product. Reels of labels bearing the Alabama Munitions name still hung loosely from various attachments. A few of the men faced us in preparation for greeting, but the disapproving looks they aimed our way as they appraised our attire telegraphed their displeasure. They should try being the ones wearing our clothes, or lack thereof in this case. Live through a plane crash and a God awful hot trek in the woods. Then try fighting some guys intent on taking you out, and see if you didn't rip your skirt a little.

"You're mumbling," Reynolds whispered in my ear.

Was I? They were lucky that was all I was doing. Pulling my shoulders back, I lifted my chin and strode confidently toward the group. I couldn't deny a certain sense of satisfaction from ruffling their unsullied feathers when I stuck my grime covered hand out.

"Good afternoon, gentlemen. I'm Dr. Greer."

The man to my immediate left hesitated only briefly before accepting my hand. "Mallet. General Mallet," he said.

Though he was smiling, his eyes told a different story. He was less than pleased that we were here, maybe even a little surprised. That was interesting. More interesting was the fact that I recognized his name.

"Mallet of Rust, Texas?"

"I'm from Enid, Oklahoma, ma'am," he stated tightly.

Maybe he was, but that's not where I knew him from. He was the one responsible for pulling the plug on a research project I was part of around five years ago. He was paranoid then, and by the look of him, he was paranoid now.

"Where's the president?" I asked after a quick survey didn't identify the president among them.

"He'll be here momentarily," Mallet answered.

"Well then, General Mallet, how about you introduce the rest of the crew."

He stared at me for a moment, like he didn't fancy the role I'd thrust upon him. Or maybe it was the fact that I'd given it to him. The smile he displayed as he acquiesced in no way hid the venom growing in his eyes.

Pointing to a really tall man on his left, he said, "This is Admiral Murdock."

Admiral Murdock was the picture of a grandpa, right down to the receding hairline and kind eyes. Shaking his hand was easy.

"Rafael Trace," Mallet said, waving to the next man in line.

I shook his hand.

Foregoing Mallet, the next gentlemen introduced himself. "Max Lender," he said.

"Mr. Lender," I nodded, accepting the hand he offered. When he withdrew it, he wiped it on his trousers, almost like an afterthought. I didn't quite know what to make of it.

The man with his back to me, who'd been involved with a phone call, hung up and turned around. The hand I was extending towards him froze.

"General Garrison," he said, deftly capturing my hand which hung limply in the air.

"Dr. Greer," I repeated, squeezing his hand tightly after recovering from the brief shock.

The president picked that moment to make his appearance.

Closely following him was the Chairman of the Joint Chiefs, General Hurser. I'd heard he'd been selected to fill the post. He was a good man for the job. I'd never worked with him directly, but those under his command had always been fair to me.

The Secretary of Homeland Security was a step behind General Hurser. I couldn't recall his name, but I remembered him from news reports. I didn't have an opinion on him one way or the other.

President O'Conner paused as he judged the appearance of our group, his eyes widening as he lingered on the blood stains. "Dr. Greer?" he said uncertainly.

Forcing a smile, I nodded. "That's me." Briefly, I regretted the condition of my clothing, but that vanished as soon as I thought about informing Olivia in what state I had greeted the president.

"Looks like you had a bit of trouble," he said as he shook my hand, his eyes darting to Kenny when he snorted in agreement.

"Some," I acknowledged.

"You're not what I expected." He didn't even try to conceal the disappointment in his voice.

"I get that a lot," I admitted.

Withdrawing his hand, he used it to signal the secret service agents that accompanied him. Everyone stepped back to allow them to arrange the chairs they retrieved from a nearby pallet. When they finished, the president nodded and the agents left the room.

"Shall we?" the president asked, indicating for everyone to sit.

Kenny nudged my elbow as I grabbed the back of my chair, tilting his head in Garrison's direction.

"I know," I whispered. Dead man walking. I sat and then turned to verify where Reynolds was. He'd chosen to remain standing and though his posture suggested he was at ease, his face was anything but. I waited until I caught his eye, then gave my head a gentle shake. We did not need him unleashing his inner hybrid. At least not until the meeting had officially gone to hell.

"Dr. Greer," the president said, recapturing my attention. "I've called this meeting to find out what happened in New Orleans and to determine a course of action. I'm hoping that you have the answers I need."

All heads turned to me expectantly, putting me squarely in the spotlight. And for one brief second, I had the distinct feeling that this was rigged. Like I was supposed to give some grand performance. There was just something in the president's eyes that was too certain of the outcome, too confident. It didn't identify him as an enemy, but it made me wary of playing along. Not that I had a choice. But if he already knew what had happened in New Orleans, then what did he want me to say?

The question of what happened in New Orleans beat against me while my mind sprinted through the memories of my time there. I knew the president was referring only to the recent incident, but that was the result of something larger, not a singular event. The tragedy that had unfolded at the Colony was ultimately the culmination of a government turning its back on the hybrids. That power vacuum had been filled by someone intent on creating made to order hybrids. Maybe someone else found out about it and stepped in. Maybe they issued an order to clean house. That wouldn't account for Millsap, unless they used him in their cleanup effort. It would account for the HCF's subsequent absence during the cull. Someone had given the order for HCF personnel to bug out.

"Dr. Greer," the president prodded.

"Betrayal," I said. "It's a tale of betrayal and murder."

"I knew it," Mallet barked, slapping the table for emphasis. "Hybrids cannot be trusted."

The president's eyes never left mine as he made quieting motions with his hands towards Mallet. "Dr. Greer, you were saying."

The note of approval in the president's voice rang loud to me. Guess I was on script. "I was speaking of the government's betrayal of the hybrids," I clarified.

"How do you mean?" Admiral Murdock asked.

"The government confiscated the hybrids, all the associated technology, created the HCF and then ignored them. You did nothing for the first generation hybrids, other than let them die. And then based on the success of the second generation, which you knew nothing about, started concocting plans for designer hybrids."

"Oh great, we've got a pansy liberal on our hands," General Mallet muttered loudly.

Ignoring Mallet's comment, Mr. Trace said, "Dr. Greer, no one at the HCF had any plans to create designer hybrids."

"That you were aware of," I corrected. "Someone did and had started instituting policy decisions based on that goal."

Mr. Trace shook his head. "There were no policy changes approved in the general operation of the HCF. I am the one who would have had to grant any such approval."

"Like I said, betrayal. I believe the cornerstone of betrayal is not knowing."

The room shifted uncomfortably at my assertion. Apparently, none of them had considered the possibility.

"Dr. Greer, how do these purported changes in policy relate to the massacre? Are you implying that they were the cause? An inside job?" the president asked.

Very good, maestro. It was an inside job in the respect that someone at the HCF allowed it to happen. I knew firsthand that the acting head of the HCF, Norris Cain, had been mixed up with the Consortium. He had confirmed to me personally that Millsap knew about the Colony. But Cain was weak, just a bureaucrat in search of power. He didn't have the wherewithal to accomplish this. Someone else had been the impetus for the policy changes. Judging from his responses, the operation of the HCF fell under Mr. Trace's purview. But he was ignorant of what was going on, which meant he wasn't my guy.

"The HCF may not have personally carried out the attack," I said. "But they allowed it."

"I cannot believe what you are saying," Trace blurted out. "The HCF was attacked, not just the hybrids. Mr. Cain is still missing."

"Mr. Cain is dead," I said bluntly. "And not as a result of the attack, though he bears some responsibility for it."

"This is ludicrous," Trace protested.

"Are you saying that Cain was the traitor?" Admiral Murdock asked.

"One of them," I nodded.

The Chairman of the Joint Chiefs leaned forward. "Excuse me, Dr. Greer, General Hurser," he said, indicating himself. "I'm curious to know how you deduced that Mr. Cain is dead."

"I was there when he died."

"You were there?" he repeated doubtfully.

"I was. I also know that he revealed the location of the Colony to some very bad people."

The Secretary of Homeland Security scooted his chair forward, as if he'd just decided to join the conversation. "If I understand correctly," he drawled. "Are you not just a scientist under the employ of the HCF? I find it incredible that you would be in possession of any such knowledge."

Just a scientist? I smiled indulgently at him. "What I find incredible is that you are not. It is inconceivable that a conspiracy regarding a highly secret—must stay secret for the good of the country—program is conducted right under your nose, and you haven't the slightest inclination that anything improper is happening."

The Secretary sat back in his chair, glaring at me through calculating eyes. He was furious that I had spoken to him like that. I was furious that he'd called me a liar.

"I believe we are getting off track," President O'Conner said quickly. "Dr. Greer is a member of the Organization," he said as an aside to the secretary, but it didn't lesson the secretary's anger.

"Allowing that what you are saying is true," General Hurser continued, as though the secretary hadn't spoken. "Then this problem extends beyond the confines of the HCF." He paused and looked at me, waiting for confirmation.

"Dr. Greer," the president said, drawing my eyes to him. "How far does this reach?"

Crap. I didn't know for sure. More and more the evidence pointed to the fact that the Consortium wasn't acting alone. Who at the HCF was working with them, I didn't know yet. But the potential reach? It was big.

"It's pretty far, Mr. President."

That was the opening Mallet had been waiting for. His voice was soft, insistent as he leaned forward to plead his case. "This is the possibility I've been warning you about, Mr. President. We have got to rid ourselves of this threat once and for all before they all go rogue." He twisted in his chair, looking back and forth between the other men as he gauged support for his position. "Once this gets out of control, there will be no stopping it. Our lives—the lives of the American people will be a horror movie."

The room was silent as they digested Mallet's words. It was evident they hadn't fallen on entirely deaf ears.

"Dr. Greer," General Hurser spoke again. "The brutality of the attack would suggest that it was executed by hybrids. Is that what we're dealing with? Rogue hybrids?"

That was a fair assessment. "Yes, sir," I nodded.

"Then this should be easy enough to deal with," The Homeland Security Secretary said confidently. "We treat it like any other thug war that needs to be quashed."

I shook my head in amazement. "I don't think you grasp how far hybrids have evolved," I said.

"What do you mean by evolved?" Mr. Lender asked, his eyes rife with unmistakable curiosity. That was when I understood that Mr. Lender was a scientist.

"Why does it even matter," the Homeland Secretary answered. "We shoot, we kill. End of story." Sitting back in his chair, he smugly crossed his arms over his chest. "We're talking about hybrids, not superheroes," he dismissed. "What? Are they faster than a speeding bullet? Able to leap tall buildings? Vampires, maybe?" He laughed loudly so as to emphasize the ridiculousness of the idea. He stopped when he saw my face.

I was beginning to think that the whole apparatus for the security of the nation had been left out of the loop on hybrid advancement. Not Garrison, of course, but he hadn't said one word in this meeting so far.

"Mr. Trace."

He looked up at me.

"How much do you know about hybrid capabilities?"

"We were waiting on your report," he said helplessly.

Just another bureaucrat then. "Mr. President?"

"Likely more than you do," he answered flatly.

I raised my eyebrows at him. I really doubted that was the truth, especially considering the lack of knowledge his advisors had. Except for Garrison. Garrison could have kept the president informed if he chose to. Still, the president's response did not directly admit to knowing about the existence of nanobots. With all the other people present, I wasn't going to take the chance of them learning something they didn't need to know.

"A military exercise aimed at ridding the world of hybrids is very ill advised," I cautioned them.

"It worked well enough at the Colony," Mallet muttered under his breath.

Strange that he would classify what happened at the Colony as a military exercise. I fixed my gaze on him. "Did it? Seems to me that it managed to capture the attention of the one force capable of dealing with this."

"You are speaking of the Organization?" Admiral Murdock asked.

"I am," I nodded at him. And that was all the information I was going to give them. "Mr. President, you're just going to have to trust that the Organization is handling it."

The brief respite of silence quickly dissolved into chaos as the various attendees felt the need to voice their objections to my assertion. The spit flew as Mallet engaged Trace in a shouting match. Not to be outdone by them, the president's advisors argued equally as loud. Even Mr. Lender became animated. The only ones not engaged were President O'Conner and Garrison. Behind his hands, I could just make out the smile that Garrison was hiding. In contrast, the president's face was dark with anger. This was not going the way he wanted, which made me think he was in favor of hybrids. I couldn't help but wonder why that would be.

Camouflaged by the arguing, I caught the president's attention. Just below a whisper, I said, "Mr. President?"

He tilted his head slightly, lifting his eyebrows at me in invitation to continue.

"There is a very real chance of hybrid exposure to the world," I whispered softly.

Clasping his hands together in front of his mouth, he asked, "Can the Organization handle it?"

My heart skipped a beat. He had really heard me. The president was a hybrid. Blinking rapidly, I scrambled to process the startling revelation. I wanted to turn to Reynolds and Kenny and say, "Can you believe this?" But the souring expression the president wore as I stared blankly at him nixed that idea. Quickly, I scanned the rest of those assembled, but everyone except for Garrison was oblivious to our interaction.

Raising my shoulders in a shrug, I let them drop. "Working on it."

He lowered his hands, revealing the hard set of his jaw. He wasn't pleased with my response.

"Gentlemen," the president said loudly. "If we could all please retake our seats."

It took a minute, but everyone finally conceded to sit.

"I'd like to know if the Organization considers what happened in New Orleans as handling it?" the president asked, hurling my words back at me.

I fumbled the catch. His switch in tactics had caught me off guard. Anger bubbled inside me, forcing me to take a few seconds before I could answer calmly. "We were caught by surprise, as were you," I reminded him. "That won't happen again." I could hardly believe I had just promised that.

"Mr. President, we cannot entrust the safety of this nation to the Organization," Mallet growled. "Hasn't that already been proved by the massacre? I say…"

Mallet's voice faded into the background. Why did the president have this idiot here? Nothing useful was going to come out of this meeting if he didn't shut up. All he was doing was exposing himself as a problem. I looked up at the president who was staring at me. Maybe that was the purpose.

"Shut up," Trace ground at Mallet. "The last time I checked, we needed answers, and you didn't have them."

Giving up all pretense of persuasion, Mallet turned on Trace. "If we don't put a stop to this," he snarled, his finger pounding the table, "the whole world is going to find out."

"Find out that you lied?" I asked abruptly.

Mallet looked like I'd punched him in the face. Studying his response, I had a thought. He looked to be around sixty. He could have been around when this all went down the first time. He might have even been in on the decision to hide the hybrid program.

"I don't know what you're talking about," he snapped at me.

But I was on to something. Then I recalled his first name, Gene. GM, just like the initials stamped on the bullet. The anger that had cooled to a simmer roiled to the surface. I ground my teeth together even as I fought the urge to shift.

"Breathe, Greer," I heard Garrison whisper faintly.

I was breathing, intentionally taking deep breaths in an attempt to maintain control. But too little sleep and too many frayed nerves wasn't making that task easy. I knew that letting loose on Mallet right now would only strengthen his position. It might even incite the others to join the charge against hybrids. I couldn't let that happen, no matter how much I longed to grab those Alabama Munition tape reels and wrap him like a mummy.

"Dr. Greer," Garrison said. "In your opinion, how does the president need to prepare his administration to handle this?"

The sound of Garrison's voice penetrated the vision I was creating. Slowly, I repeated the question to myself. He was leading me in the direction he wanted the discussion to go. I had a ridiculous urge to yell, "Objection, leading the witness."

Kenny walked up and grasped my shoulder, just firm enough for me to notice. I was grateful for the support.

"Being prepared for the worst and not having that happen is always better than being caught unaware," I managed to say calmly.

"The worst being?" the president questioned.

"The worst being the revelation of the government's role in maintaining the hybrid program."

"The 1940s all over again?" General Hurser concluded.

I nodded, but then stopped. It didn't have to end the same way. "That is not necessarily true," I amended. "Hybrid research has uncovered some truly remarkable things. Benefits to humanity that cannot be overstated. If the government were to position itself in that light, there could be a whole different outcome."

The Homeland Security Secretary cleared his throat. "What benefits are we talking about?"

"Cures to diseases, regrowth of limbs. Soldiers with remarkable capabilities. The possibilities are virtually endless."

"I thought you were against designer hybrids," Mallet jeered.

"You thought wrong. I'm against slavery, and I have never been against a superior military."

General Hurser leaned back in his chair and clasped his hands behind his head. Hunger radiated from every fiber of his being. I'd seen it often enough in military commanders. They wanted the world's supreme military, and here I was, dangling it in front of them.

"We would require proof of such claims," he said carefully.

"What do you think the hybrid program has been doing all these years?" I challenged.

"I'm really not sure," he said, clearly flummoxed by his lack of knowledge.

Mr. Trace leaned forward and looked at me intently. "You've seen this? The regrowth of limbs?"

I hadn't, but I'd seen the formation of appendages that should never have been there. "I've witnessed unbelievable things," I nodded at him.

"Come on," Mallet whined. "We cannot really be talking about considering even the possibility of intentionally revealing the existence of hybrids to the public?"

"You cannot possibly believe that you can keep this hidden forever?" I shot back. "With all the new technology…cell phones, google glass for goodness sake. This particular event may not be the one that exposes hybrids, but it's going to come out eventually, one way or another."

"Most secrets do have a way of coming out," Admiral Murdock observed quietly.

The room took a collective breath as each one of them contemplated the possible future before them.

"We're not necessarily talking about revealing the continued existence of human animal hybrids," General Hurser said. "This is strictly a medicinal application we're examining."

Medicinal? I didn't think anyone was buying that from him, not with all those visions of super soldiers dancing in his eyes.

"We could stand as heroes to the world," Trace mused aloud.

Or the worst villains mankind had ever seen, but no one mentioned that. They didn't have to.

"Well," the president said. "I think we know what we have to do." He pushed his chair back and stood up. "Dr. Greer, I'll be in touch." He winked at me as he turned to leave.

Garrison stood up and reached to shake my hand. He was smiling like he'd gotten what he came for. "Dr. Greer," he nodded his goodbye.

General Hurser and Admiral Murdock wanted to talk specifics, but both of them were pressed for time. They left with a promise that I'd meet with them soon. In the end, the only man not to shake my hand was Mallet. He left immediately after the president and never looked back. A perfect imitation of a coward if I ever saw one.

Exhausted by the tense meeting, I collapsed back into my chair. "What just happened?" I asked as I stared absently at the rafters framing the ceiling.

"You promised to handle the rogue situation, create the baddest military the world has ever seen, and orchestrate the revelation of hybrids in a manner that's all sparkles and fluff," Reynolds answered glibly.

"Did I do that?" I wondered aloud.

Kenny snorted at me. "One thing's for sure," he said. "Mallet hates you."

Oh yeah, Mallet. Fishing around in my pocket, I found the bullet I was looking for and tossed it to Kenny. "Check out the initials."

"GM and DTP?" he read. "So?"

"Mallet's first name is Gene."

"This from the shooting earlier?" Reynolds asked as he took the bullet from Kenny and examined it.

"Yep." Turning my head that lay against the back of the chair, I looked at Reynolds and wiggled my eyebrows at him. "Ready to go hunting?"

A slow smile spread across his face. "Oh, yeah," he drawled.

CHAPTER 11

"GARRISON HAS A LOOK ABOUT him," Kenny said as we bumped along.

We were squished into the front seat—the only seat—of an old pickup truck that had definitely seen better days and shocks. I didn't see why we couldn't borrow some gas for the other truck, but Reynolds had insisted that we leave it where it was and find a safer mode of transportation. Just how this qualified, I wasn't sure, but I'd let him do all the talking at Wild Bill's Auto Depot. Translation, you better have tools cause you'll need 'em to make it home. Wild Bill himself was laughing at us as we drove off the lot.

"Do you mean how he acts like he's watching things unfold as they happen, when he's actually the one orchestrating the whole thing?" I suggested.

"Yeah," Kenny exhaled. "Sneaky, that one is."

"Garrison was the guy who remained mum through most of the meeting?" Reynolds asked.

"Until he wasn't," I answered sourly. I couldn't put my finger on why his presence bothered me so much. The outcome of the meeting had been okay, thanks to his redirection. Better than what could have happened.

"I'd say Garrison wasn't the only sneak in the room," Reynolds said. "Some of the questions that President O'Conner asked were clearly leading, like he already knew the score. And what's up with him being a hybrid?"

"I don't know," I confessed. "I'm beginning to wonder who isn't a hybrid." And Reynolds was right. The president had manipulated me too. But he didn't bother me as much as Garrison. Maybe because he was supposed to be the leader.

"Thought you were the one who was supposed to know," Kenny spoke into the silence that had settled around us.

"I'm working up to it," I griped. "I will be anyway, once we finally get…back." I almost said home. If my brain was now registering Organization headquarters as home, things really had shifted. No pun intended. Just wished it didn't come stocked with so much drama. Speaking of drama. "Hey guys," I said as I pulled the reporter's card from my pocket. "I need to make a phone call."

Kenny glanced down at the card in my hand. "Who is Virginia Redding?"

"The reporter that was at the Colony."

"You are actually going through with it?" Kenny asked.

"We made a deal."

"You think that's wise?" Reynolds asked, looking at me sideways as he drove.

"Wise?" I took a deep breath and exhaled it slowly. "It seems inevitable that the existence of hybrids is going to become common knowledge." I looked down at the card, recalling her interview with Randall and the knowledge of her brother's recovery. "She has reason to be on our side, and we are going to need people on our side. In any case, I gave my word."

"You want to contact her without the Organization knowing about it?" Reynolds guessed.

"I'd prefer it that way," I nodded. "What's the best way to accomplish that?"

"Disposable phone," they answered together.

"You can buy them at Walmart easily enough," Kenny added.

Why he knew that, I wasn't going to question. But I did have a question for Reynolds. "Do you have any money?" I asked him, because I certainly didn't. Yet another thing I had to add to my emergency bag.

"How do you think I bought this truck?" he scoffed.

"Oh, I'm sorry," I said, putting a hand to my chest in mock

surprise. "I assumed the price of this mighty fine piece of truck might have wiped you out."

"I've got all we need," he growled in irritation, as if the possibility of him being low on money was somehow an attack on his character.

"By all means then, good sir, carry me thither to Walmart post haste."

His eyes cut to me, then back to the road in front of him. "I don't know what you said, but I'll get you to the nearest Walmart."

"That's all I'm asking."

"Hmm," he rumbled deep in his throat.

"At this moment," I added quickly.

"Now that I can believe."

Me too.

We used old school methods to locate a Walmart. Reynolds stopped at a convenience store and made Kenny go in and ask. I busted out laughing when he came out of the store wearing a pink "Bama Lover" t-shirt.

"Shut up," he scowled. "They only had three." He tossed Reynolds an "I Bleed Red and Cream" t-shirt, and I got "Roll This" with a very rude gesture for illustration.

Pulling the t-shirt on over what was left of my blouse, I fished some safety pins out of the ashtray and pinned my skirt together. From there, it was on to Walmart.

They had a surprisingly large stock of disposable phones. Reynolds bought one to contact Cedars, and I bought a few, including one to add to the emergency backpack, which I also bought. Reynolds carried an awful large amount of cash.

While still in the parking lot, I made the call to set up the interview. She was pleased to hear from me, but hesitant about another face to face encounter. After many assurances and my threatening to forget the whole thing, she finally agreed to a meeting one week from today at a location yet to be determined. I told her I'd email her with the location, and after we hung up, I tossed the phone into the dumpster.

With nothing left to slow us down—not counting the two pee

breaks Kenny demanded after inhaling the super sized soda despite my warnings—we were homeward bound. Reynolds drove us to a small airport where Cedars had arranged for transportation in the form of another jet. I couldn't say we were thrilled by Cedars' choice, but the plane ride back was surprisingly terror free. I thought the boys would have been pleased by this turn of events, but it just made them more nervous. I tried to persuade them that my life did not entirely consist of one catastrophe after another, but they were not convinced. As a result, the apprehension in that little cabin space we shared was as oppressive as a hundred degree day in Houston right before a thunderstorm broke.

Landing was an immense relief.

We nearly ran each other over trying to exit the plane. After that, we were shuttled from one vehicle to another until I found myself standing alone in the kitchen of Organization headquarters. The clock said it was dinnertime. Well that and the rumbling in my stomach.

Where is everybody, I wondered?

"I believe Miranda is waiting for you in your suite," Margaret said as she entered the kitchen and saw my puzzled face. "Cedars is working in his, and Juarez is consoling Olivia." She rounded the island, stopping directly in front of me. Her eyes got real big in preparation for her next statement. "You missed one heck of a row. Yelling and screaming. They almost came to blows." She shook her head and bit her bottom lip. "I wasn't sure there would be an Organization left when they were through."

More drama. Great. I pulled out one of the stools at the island and sat down, letting my chin flop into my hands. "I take it Olivia didn't win?"

"Not as far as I could tell."

Margaret seemed relieved by the outcome. I knew I was.

"Hungry?" she asked, her voice strangely muffled.

Lifting my head from my hands, I found her half-hidden by the fridge door. I hadn't realized she'd moved. "I could eat," I answered.

"How does beef stew sound?" She poked her head around the door to see my response.

"That'd be great," I smiled. She was so helpful. As I watched her busy herself fixing me a bowl, I realized, other than that, I didn't really know too much about her. "Margaret, what is your position around here?"

"Oh," she giggled embarrassedly. "I'm like caulking. I fill in the cracks."

Wow. She must be working a lot of overtime lately. "How did you come to be here? At the Organization, I mean."

She pulled the bowl out of the microwave and set it in front of me. "It all started when Adam rescued me. I was just a little girl. About two or three they tell me."

She placed the salt and pepper in front of me as I chewed the first bite. Whoa. I never knew stew could taste this good. "What did he rescue you from?" I asked between mouthfuls.

"Apparently, my father piloted a plane which crashed into the nearby mountains. Everyone on board, all of my family, was killed. Adam saved me, gave me nanobots. Without prior approval, I think. Anyway, for some reason, they didn't take."

I paused with the spoon halfway to my mouth. "They didn't take?" I repeated.

"I think Adam referred to it as a natural kill switch. But, they helped long enough to save my life. After that, I never left. Adam sort of adopted me, and the rest is history."

My mouth gaped in amazement. I couldn't get the picture of Adam as a father out of my mind. "Adam was your dad?"

"The only one I remember," she nodded.

"And, you grew up here?"

She nodded again. "It was a great place to grow up. There was never a shortage of playmates. Or food," she sighed and patted her round stomach. "Now that I'm grown up, there's not much to do out here but eat. Not that I'm complaining, but I'm not a genius like the rest of you. My options are limited."

"You're wrong," I disagreed, using my spoon to point at her.

"You are one of the best cooks I've ever met. That's a genius all on its own."

"You're a hybrid. You're practically starving all the time. Anything tastes good to you," she said, waiving away my critique.

"That's not true," I argued. "Well, the being a hungry hybrid part is, but that's not it. The way you can switch between genres. And nail each one." I shook my head in admiration of her skills. "It's impressive."

She chuckled in appreciation. "I've got a lot of time on my hands to practice."

"Well, anytime you need a guinea pig, I'm at your disposal." This was one task I didn't mind signing up for. "You know you're options are only limited if you stay here. You could leave."

"That's what Adam always says. I know I could. But my family is here." She lifted her arms and shrugged.

"Tell you what," I said as I laid the spoon on the edge of my empty bowl. "The next time I go to New Orleans, you come with me. You could open a restaurant in a snap."

"Guinea Pigs?" she suggested for a name.

"Absolutely," I nodded. "You'll have people wrapped around the building waiting to get in." Picking up the bowl, I scooted from the stool and walked it over to the sink. "Seriously, you should think about what you would like to do. Even if it's not opening a restaurant." Turning my back to the sink, I leaned against the counter. "Margaret, did anyone ever follow up on your natural kill switch?"

"I don't think so," she said. "Adam's never said, but I think he broke a lot of rules keeping me here. I'm not sure what the Organization knows as far as nanobots and me goes." She let go of the towel she'd been picking at. "You're the only person I've ever told. I'd like to keep it that way."

I nodded at her. "Is there anything I should know about the confrontation that happened earlier?"

She grimaced and looked away. "Tread carefully around Olivia," she said. "I'm not sure how much more she can take. It's understandable what with all she's been through." She shrugged her shoulders again. "I think you can guess whose side I'm on."

Same as me, I hoped. Pushing off the counter, I aimed to leave the room, but hesitated as I drew even with her. "I'm sorry about your family."

"Not your fault," she smiled. "Anyway, I don't remember them."

Nothing much to say to that. Maybe it was better that way and maybe it wasn't. But I knew from experience that the lack of memories wasn't a comfort. "Thanks for the stew," I smiled and began walking again. Her voice stopped me in the doorway.

"Macy," she whispered, her voice quivering with unspent emotion. "You are going to find him?"

"I am," I breathed and hurried out of the kitchen before all the doubt in her voice got to me.

I didn't realize that I had made it to the suite until I was standing in front of the door. Startled that I had found my way on my own, I entered the code and braced for the smell of Adam. It was in the rest of headquarters too, but faint. Nothing like what awaited me here.

"About time," Miranda complained and switched the television off as I walked in. "Nice t-shirt."

"Hey," I greeted her. "How'd you get in here?"

She rolled her eyes at me as I joined her on the couch. "Like the password was hard to figure out."

Right. I plopped down next to her and stared at the blank television. "I didn't know we had a television in here."

"It slides down from the ceiling. The button's on the remote." She held it out to me.

We both watched as the screen noiselessly ascended into the ceiling.

"Cool," I muttered. The absence of the television gave a clear view of the surrounding mountains. Night was quickly replacing the daylight, but I could still make out the white tops. They reminded me of Adam's teeth.

"What are you thinking?" Miranda asked me.

"That the white mountain tops remind me of Adam's teeth."

"They are freakishly white," she agreed.

"How are you feeling?" I asked, half turning to face her.

"Same old, same old. You?"

"Tired. Numb. Like I'm in a dream."

We stared at the mountains as the night grew darker. "Cedars is working on the plan right now," Miranda said in an effort to comfort me.

"Margaret told me there was some big argument earlier."

"Yes, there was. I think…I hope we finally settled who's in charge around here."

"It's me, isn't it?" I said glumly.

She snorted at me. "What was your first clue?"

"The state of things."

"Well, things do have a certain Macy flair to them," she teased. "But, the gist of it is, that Cedars, supported by Juarez, maintains control, and he has clearly indicated that he is going to follow your lead."

"I bet Olivia loved that."

"Oh, no. No, she did not. I've never seen her so mad. I thought she was going to punch Cedars and Juarez both."

I might liked to have seen that.

"So how did the meeting with the president go?"

"Spectacularly," I deadpanned.

"That bad, huh?"

"No, seriously. They loved me. They've hired me to do everything."

"Everything meaning…?"

"Usual stuff. Save the world, heal humanity, blah, blah."

"It's great that we have all this time on our hands."

I laughed deeply, ending in a long drawn out breath. "Did you look into the papers I gave you?"

"I did, and I found some stuff on Garrison too, I think." She looked at me and frowned, but didn't say anymore.

"Well, tell me." Since he was no longer dead, I would really like to know what he's been up to.

"Macy, you're dead on your feet. Take a shower, get some sleep. It will keep till morning."

A shower sounded great. Sleep even better. "You're sure it can wait until tomorrow?" I asked, failing to disguise my hope.

"Yes," she laughed and pulled me from the couch. "Wash, girl. You stink. Again. And, I'm relatively certain that the skirt I gave you did not offer a preview of your underpants before you left this morning."

"Well," I said, looking down at my skirt. "You know how I love to show off my underwear."

She shoved me in the direction of the bathroom. "At least you had some on this time," she snorted.

"Hey," I protested. "When have I ever been without—oh, never mind." You lost your underwear one time and suddenly it was a way of life. Granted, it was all of my underwear at one time. But, it wasn't my fault. Oh, forget it. I couldn't even justify it to myself.

"I'll let myself out," she called after me.

"It happened one time," I yelled weakly.

"That was enough, believe you me," she mumbled as she stepped through the door.

I turned and watched the door close behind her. We'd been through a lot together. Re-outfitting my underwear drawer was just one among many of the M&M files. It hadn't helped that my choices were limited by time and budget, primarily budget. I found out real quick what designs were on every woman's, *Not if it was the last pair of underwear left in this world* list. Ah, good times.

Who would have ever thought that I'd be rifling through a man's underwear drawer looking for something to put on. Was I about to answer the age old question of boxers or briefs? This was just plain weird, but not weirder than streaking around his suite naked would have been, hence the rifling. In the end, I bypassed the undies and opted for a t-shirt, which, fortunately for me, hung to my knees. True, I was underwearless at the moment, but it wasn't my fault.

Dad gum it. I had to remember to add underwear to the emergency pack.

Rather than preparing me for bed, the shower had the opposite effect. It left me feeling invigorated, ready to tackle the puzzle manipulating my life. Sitting down in Adam's desk chair, I tucked one leg underneath me and used the other to slowly spin the chair. When I faced the whiteboard, I dropped my heel to the floor. The notes I'd made earlier in the week no longer accurately represented the situation.

Sliding from the chair, I picked up the eraser and wiped the board clean. Then I wrote Garrison in all caps right in the middle. I just had a feeling that he was at the center of it all, the one gear around which everything else was rotating.

Out to the side, I wrote GM and DTP on separate branches. I thought I knew what the GM stood for, but I was still fuzzy on the DTP. I looked back to the computer on the desk. It seemed to be up and running. That didn't mean I could access it, of course, but I wouldn't know until I tried.

Retaking my seat, I moved the mouse to see if it was password protected.

"Please state your name," the computer requested.

Oh, Lord, I groaned inwardly. My experience with talking equipment since I'd encountered the Organization had not ended in my favor. "Macy Greer?" I said hesitantly.

"Was that a statement or a question?"

Say what? "It's an answer," I sneered.

"To what question?"

"What do you mean what question? My name."

"Macy Greer is not your name."

"Yes it is," I vehemently disagreed.

"Is defines a state of being. Please state your name."

We'd come full circle. "Listen you expensive piece of metal with a bad attitude, my name is Macy Greer."

"Should you wish to be granted access, please state your name."

"I am going to grant your access if you don't stop," I growled, staring evilly at the screen as though that would intimidate the pretend male computer voice. This was ridiculous. I was arguing with a computer. I didn't remember Adam going through this.

"Hostility is a prevalent sign of stress. Please state your name?"

I straightened in sudden understanding. It was a riddle. In order to gain access, I had to give the correct answer which was not my name. After thinking about it a minute, I did just as instructed. "Your name," I repeated back to the computer.

"Excellent. What is my name?"

Aw, c'mon. How the heck was I supposed to know his name? Quickly, I searched the edges of the monitor for any indication. Wait. I said your name to him, and he responded with excellent. Frowning slightly, I guessed, "Excellent?"

"Define excellent."

Are you serious? "Superb. Perfect," I threw out, neither of which solicited a response. "Fantastic. Great. Outstanding." Each attempt was met with silence. "What? No obtuse comebacks?" I ground angrily at the monitor.

Sitting back, I crossed my arms over my chest and stared at the screen. I was stumped. How many words in the English language could define excellent? But this was Adam's computer I reminded myself. I had to pick an answer he would choose. Lifting my eyes to the ceiling, I tried to imagine where Adam was going with this. Then I remembered that the entry code to the suite was based on me. I had a thought, but surely it was wrong.

"Macy," I whispered.

"Macy is excellent," the computer agreed. "Access granted." The search engine appeared in place of the black screen.

"Dad gum it, Adam," I whispered as I squeezed back tears. One might get the impression that he was serious about me. All the more reason to figure this thing out and get him back.

"No crying tonight, Macy Greer," I scolded myself. I had much more important things to do, like nail Gene Mallet's hind quarters to the wall.

Searching for Mallet in the cyber world might be like the proverbial needle in the haystack, but I did have a pretty good idea which haystack to search. Extremist groups. I figured with his hatred of hybrids, he'd need a safe place, a supportive place to air his grievances. That's how most tyrants worked. They found people willing to stroke their egos and applaud them when they took action. It was sickening.

The results of my search for extremist groups related to hybrids in the last five years were mostly dominated by God's Light and their very vocal leader. Too vocal. Mallet would never stand for sharing the spotlight like that. After twenty more minutes and an equal amount of pages, I identified a blog belonging to a group called Born to Rule that seemed to have a similar agenda. Their website had hundreds, if not thousands of entries.

Not fancying searching through each one, I scrolled back up to the top and read over the tabs. The events section would probably give me a good idea of the real pulse of the group. I clicked on the tab. They were certainly a busy group, I'd give them that. God's Light might have had all the publicity, but these guys knew how to party. And there was ample documentation to prove it.

I selected the most recent rally summary. Along with the text, there were loads of pictures with each set organized into specific categories. Little bit on the OCD side, if you asked me. After viewing a few subsets, I knew I would have picked better titles too. Like, Numbskulls Holding Posters, Idiots Guzzling Beer... oh, you're kidding me. A barfing contest? Who takes pictures of that? No, who does that? Moving on to guest speaker—hold up.

I zoomed in on the page. "Well, I declare. I do believe that is one Mr. Gene Mallet." I should have checked top billing first. "And what's that on your shirt, General?" Zooming in again, I read the logo, Department of the President. "So that's what that stands for. I bet that's a department the president's never heard of," I joked as I opened another window and typed it in the search field.

Instead of whisking me to a list of corresponding possibilities, the computer froze. Jiggling the mouse rapidly didn't help release it from the freeze frame either. Frustrated by the delay, I reached out to restart the computer. Just as my hand made contact with the power button, the computer started hissing and gurgling.

No longer a stranger to the danger concealed within innocuous looking items, I wasted no time in reacting.

Snatching my hand back, I vaulted from the chair and grabbed the most dangerous weapon in the near vicinity. I now stood poised with Adam's umbrella held high should the computer actually go all transformer on me. But after a few seconds, the noises stopped and the screen displayed the homepage of the Department of the President.

Feeling like an idiot, I sheepishly lowered my make-do weapon. The pop the umbrella made as it unexpectedly opened caught me completely off guard. I screeched an expletive even as my startled release slung the umbrella across the room. With both hands clamped over my mouth in shock, I watched the umbrella bounce off the wall and roll to a leisurely stop in front of the door.

Everything was silent until I caught a glimpse of my shifted self in the mirror hanging next to the door. "Really," I mumbled into my hands as I reversed the shift. Once I looked normal again, I lowered my hands to my sides like nothing had happened. "Sincerely hoping this whole episode doesn't show up in a blooper reel somewhere," I muttered, recalling the NOLA footage that had done precisely that. "And for the record, I meant shoot."

Huffing in aggravation at myself, I ignored the umbrella for the time being and returned to the computer to resume searching. The DTP website was a no frills, just the facts experience. Of the three headings listed, Personnel looked the most promising. I wasn't surprised by the size of the picture that popped up to go along with the title of Acting Director. It matched the ego of the man it belonged to.

I went to the board and wrote Gene Mallet next to GM and moved DTP to the same branch. There was no question now where the bullets were coming from. It must have really irritated him to see me still very much alive. It probably made his skin crawl to have to interact with me, the one he was hunting. Well, the tables were turned now. We'd see how much he liked being hunted.

Chunking the marker on the desk, I sat back down to study the website in depth. The mission statement of the department was listed as the protection of the purity of the human race. As such, it had determined that the most effective way to achieve this was the elimination of all mutant humans whether created by nature or man. Wasn't that a glaring example of prejudice.

Clicking on the Operations heading pulled up a list of targets. Not surprisingly, I didn't recognize hardly any of them, but if this list was accurate, there were way more hybrids than anyone here knew about. Page after page scrolled by. Most of the targets seemed to be merely proposed at this point in time, with no strike team or date assigned. And there was no indication of success or failure until the Colony's name appeared.

My hand stilled on the keyboard. There was a big red "Mission Complete" stamped across the Colony's name. Slowly, I read it again. I knew Mallet was responsible for the shooting incident in the woods near New Orleans, but this put him at the Colony too. Neither Trace nor Mallet had indicated that Mallet had any authority over the HCF. But for Mallet to move on the Colony, he had to pull the HCF guys out. He had to have someone on the inside.

I got up and began to pace as I worked it over in my mind. Given Mallet's attitude towards hybrids, it wasn't likely that he would have worked with Millsap. But I knew Millsap had been there. His scent had been just as strong as Adam's. And the brutality with which the hybrids were killed was all Millsap. But not everyone had been killed. Kenny had said they had been disappearing for days, coinciding with the arrival of the new guards. Assuming that Millsap was responsible for the murders, the disappearances were left to Mallet. But why go through the trouble of taking over the place and not dispose of them there. Why take them somewhere else?

Standing back from the board, I scanned the notes again. My eyes settled on Garrison. He had been there too. Kenny said that Garrison had told someone, a female, that it had gone too far and that he would deal with it now. Sighing in frustration, I turned and started back for the desk. Any of the three could have taken Adam. My steps faltered, leaving me standing in front of the desk as I realized why it could have been any of them. Because we had shown up at the exact wrong moment.

Gripping the desk with both hands, I leaned over the top. I had been the one to push Adam to go. I was the reason that Adam was missing, and that the other Organization cadets had died. It was my fault.

Releasing my hold on the desk, I turned and perched on the edge. How did Adam do this all the time? Make these kinds of life and death decisions? Drawing in a ragged breath, I scrubbed my hands across my eyes. Guilt could not be allowed to master me this time. Everyone, including the president I'd made promises to, was counting on me to solve this mess. I had no time to waste on unproductive feelings of guilt.

Breathing deeply, I pushed away from the desk and began pacing again. Whoever had Adam, it wasn't their intent to kill him. At least not right away. They seemed to be trying to control the shift, to induce the more base animal instincts. That seemed more up Millsap's alley. Then another thought struck me. Had Millsap known we were going to be there or had it been a coincidence? Because if he knew, it confirmed that we still had a traitor in our midst.

I went back to the board and added Millsap back in along with an arrow pointing to nothing. Could Julia have told him? She'd been there. Did she still have a hand in the Organization? I added her to the board.

The image the notes made resembled a hurricane logo used by meteorologists. It was a pretty good synopsis, I thought. Everything spinning and spinning. Someone was bound to be thrown out. I'd have to make sure to have my catcher's mitt handy when it happened.

Leaving the notes behind, I collected the print out I'd made of the DTP's operations. Folding it in half, I wrote Cedars name across it. I'd give it to him first thing in the morning. I was certain he'd want to lead the charge in eliminating their operations. And the hybrids we located because of it, well, it looked like Kenny might get his wish after all. Because that's what we needed around here, more hybrids. I should find out from Margaret how many this facility would accommodate.

The unexpected ringing of the phone startled me. Rubbing my knee where it had collided with the desk, I looked at the caller id. It was blank. I shrugged and picked up the phone.

"Hello?"

"Dr. Greer?"

It was the president. "Yes, sir."

"I need you to handle something for me."

More? Were you kidding me? Out loud, I said, "What would that be?"

"I need you to be the face of the rebirth of hybrid research into the public conscience."

I was sure my heart stopped beating. "You want me to what?"

"I need you to handle presenting this to the public in the terms you painted earlier today."

"Mr. President," I began, not even trying to hide the exasperation I felt. "I don't know if I'm the best person for the job."

"Sure you are," he interrupted. "You already have a good public persona. The military likes you. Not Mallet, of course. But Hurser and Murdock like you well enough. And, what's more important than all of that, is that I trust you. I know you have just as much riding on this as I do."

I heaved a deep sigh. Those were decent arguments. "Mr. President, I feel compelled to issue a warning. Lately, everything that I attempt to clean up gets a whole lot messier first."

"Yes," he said, clearing his throat in a failed attempt to stop his laugh. "I did notice the rather peculiar nature of your attire."

"Mr. President—" I stopped. How was I supposed to explain to the president why my skirt was ripped to my hip?

"Don't worry, Dr. Greer," the president chuckled. "I thought the bunnies were cute. I'll be in touch," he choked out as he hung up.

Dad gum it. The president really had seen my underwear. Correction. Every man in that room had seen my underwear. And why'd it have to be bunnies? That's it. From now on, nothing but fierce underwear. Like wolverines or spiders. Oh yeah, that'll work. They'll really respect me when they get a look at my Marvel underoos.

"Uugh," I groaned loudly. I didn't even get to ask him about the DTP.

CHAPTER 12

THE CLOCK SAID IT WAS ten. I didn't think I could sleep, but I knew I needed to. Leaving the desk, I climbed into bed and held my breath as Adam's scent settled around me. After a moment, I grasped his pillow and pulled it to my chest. If I saw Adam tonight, I was going to get something I could use to solve this mess. That was going to be harder than it sounded. Each dream I'd had of him didn't last very long and had mainly consisted of making sure he was alive. Tonight needed to be different.

"I'm coming, Adam," I whispered as I hugged the pillow. That was the last thing I remembered until I woke up inside of him.

It was dark where he was. Looking out through his eyes and being able to see well let me know that he was still in leopard form. And given the bars surrounding him, still in the cage. The relative quiet within him led me to believe that he was sleeping. But then, how could I see through his eyes? This nanobot metaphysics stuff was just plain weird.

From the little probing that I did, he didn't seem to be physically injured. And his mind had lost that thick molasses feeling. Hopefully, that meant he was finding a way to cope with what they were doing to him. Feeling him stir, I tried to tamp down on my presence. It was that effort that found me suddenly standing outside of Adam, like I was a ghost or something.

Macy? Adam said sleepily.

It's me. I think. Frowning at my new waif like form, I pinched myself. Ow. Definitely me. *I'm here, but not here. Can you see me?*

Can't open my eyes.

The effort it had taken for him to say those four words scared me. Abandoning my self-examination, I focused on him and my pledge to get useful information.

Adam, do you know who's holding you captive?

My stomach turned uneasily as I waited for him to answer. I wanted to rush to him, to tell him everything was going to be alright, but that felt wrong. So did standing here while his struggle broke all kinds of things in me.

Adam? I tried again, wrapping my arms tightly around myself to keep from moving.

Before he was able to form an answer, the door to the lab opened, and Julia walked in. Unsure of whether she'd see me, I remained silent as she stole across the floor and stopped in front of Adam's cell. Adam recognized her scent immediately, but he refused to open his eyes in acknowledgment.

"Adam," she whispered. "I'm sorry it has to be this way. I'm trying to help." She grasped the bars in front of her, lowering her head to stare intently at Adam. "You must believe me," she pleaded.

Adam didn't offer any outward response, but inside he recoiled from her entreaty. Had he been able to move, her assumption of safety would have been a deadly mistake. My safety, however, was intact. She had eyes only for him. And wow, her eyes and everything else looked like it did forty years ago.

"I know it's difficult for you to respond, but just listen, okay? It's not like you think. When I founded Biometrics, my only goal was to further the advancement of genetics. To push boundaries, for sure, but not to endanger the human race. I wanted to amplify our abilities, to incorporate the best of other species into our own genetic makeup. Yes, I did want to craft the perfect human. Still do. But Renard…" She swallowed, her hands gripping the bars tighter. "You may find this hard to believe, but the rush to production, the unorthodox experiments, it was all him." She paused to wipe a single tear from her cheek. "We were linked, you know? But Renard was very good at shutting me out. I didn't realize what was happening until it was too late. He refused the shifting. Not at first. But when it was clear that we would eventually be able to shift completely into the animal who's DNA we carried, he rebelled. Said it was unnatural. He started doing things. Things meant to ultimately destroy the Organization."

Letting go of the bars, her gaze dropped to the floor. She lifted hands that were shaking to smooth her hair, then took the time to straighten her jacket. It made her appear strangely vulnerable.

"You can't know how it feels to be shut out by someone that you have a bond with."

I did. I knew what it felt like.

She looked back up, straight at Adam. "We had been linked for nearly sixty years. I almost went insane. If not for," she shut her mouth quickly, like she'd caught herself about to say something she hadn't intended. "I found help. It may not have been appropriate, but I needed it. When Renard no longer had anything to do with me, I was beside myself with grief."

By the look on her face, I could tell that she hated herself for whatever help she had accepted.

"Renard's dead," she whispered. "I felt it when it happened."

She turned quickly towards the sound of voices just outside the lab. When they had passed, she turned once again to Adam. "Everyone thinks I'm a traitor. I'm not. If you can hear me, Adam, please help me clear my name. My work is all I have left." She hesitated, like she wanted to say more, then pressed her lips together and vanished.

I stared at the spot where she'd been. So, that's what time travel looked like. And her story? It was very...what? Enlightening, confusing. But there was no flavor of lying to her words.

Truth, Adam said, agreeing with my assessment.

Do you trust her?

There was a pause as he considered it. *Many Questions,* he finally said.

I agreed. There were too many gaps in the information she'd given. Frowning at Adam still prone on the floor, I reached over and ran my hand across his back. *You're so silky,* I marveled.

Biased, he grunted.

I laughed at his comment. At least his words were coming

more easily now, though they still sounded guttural. Stretching out on the floor next to him, I trailed my fingers through the fur on his back. *I need any information you can give me on who is holding you captive.*

Turmoil engulfed his mind when he began to concentrate. I felt it as a deep throbbing in my own head.

Bio...bio... He growled in frustration.

It's okay, Adam, I said soothingly. I had been wrong about the molasses being gone. Only now, it felt more like some kind of concrete sludge. *Just work your way through it,* I encouraged.

Genetics.

Biogenetics?

Shorter.

Biogen?

Yes, he answered quickly, relief mingling with the angst of the effort.

Biogen didn't ring any bells, but there were thousands of firms related to research that had similar names. *Juarez said that you were somewhere near D.C. I'll search for a Biogen in D.C. when I wake up.*

Dreaming?

I think so.

Granny?

She helped us find you. Why didn't you tell me that Granny was a bear? I chided him.

Adam made a hacking sound that I could only interpret as laughter.

Adam, you know that you are entirely shifted. There was no response, but I could feel his anger rising. *Adam—*

Hurts.

My hand stilled on his back. *Being shifted?*

Fighting it, he panted. *Need to change back.*

Did he mean fighting the shift or fighting the need to change back? *You don't want to change back?* I asked, trying to mask the sudden fear I felt.

Not strong enough.

Maybe I could help with that. Closing my eyes, I sank back into Adam and pushed as much of my strength into him as I could. I felt it when he breached some predetermined threshold and took a relief filled breath. But the moment of peace quickly gave way to the struggle between the desire to return to human and the need to remain a leopard. It felt like electricity circulating through his body, not blindingly painful but not comfortable either. I wanted to help him with that too, but I didn't know what to do.

You have helped, he said, his voice sounding more like himself.

Needing to do more, my mind worked furiously for a solution. *Adam, push the electricity into me,* I demanded on impulse.

No.

Just do it, Adam.

No, he said more firmly.

Fine. I didn't need his permission. Zeroing in on the current of electricity, I reached for it and began pulling it inside of me.

Macy, no! Adam yelled.

I continued to siphon the discomfort despite Adam's protest. It no longer required much effort. All I did was absorb the surge as it rushed towards me.

Stay strong, I told Adam as I felt him fading. My name as a tortured growl was his reply.

The next instant Adam was gone, and I was back in the suite. Opening my eyes, I saw Miranda standing in the doorway. Both of her arms were frozen midair, like she'd been freeze framed while running. And her mouth was wide open. But something else was different besides her bizarre body posture. It was me I realized suddenly. I was hunched over on the bed, my paws awkwardly tucked beneath me. Wait, paws?

"Nice kitty?" Miranda stuttered.

I growled at her through my rising panic as I struggled to stand. Oh my god, that was a real growl. From the throat of a leopard. What was I going to do? This did not bode well for my hybrid revelation publicity tour.

"Macy, I have—" Her voice faltered as her body began to shake with laughter. "I have put up with a lot of things from you. Less than good housekeeping." She swiped her hand sideways, pausing to let the laughter consume her. "Tex-mex out the wazoo," she exclaimed when she caught her breath. "But I am not...under any circumstances...going to put up with hairballs...the size of small rodents," she screeched with tears rolling down her face. Then she flung herself down on the bed, giving herself fully to the laughter and not the least bit intimidated by my new form.

Ignoring her momentary loss of sanity, I took a careful step forward, and then proceeded to roll head first off the bed when my paw caught in Adam's t-shirt. The sound of ripping fabric was quickly followed by another peal of laughter from Miranda. Hissing in her direction, I gathered my legs underneath me and wriggled free of the t-shirt remnants.

"Man I needed that," Miranda moaned from the bed where she'd propped herself on her elbows in order to better observe me. "Move the opposite front and back legs at the same time," she suggested.

Right, I knew that. I'd seen animals move before. Leading with the right front leg, I coasted into the living area. Miranda followed close behind, if leaning against everything upright between the bedroom and couch in order to stabilize herself as she laughed counted.

"You look like you're cross country skiing," she said in a strangled voice. Then she proceeded to do a poor imitation of the Nordic track.

Seriously, some people succeeded in spite of their friends.

Huffing at her abundantly clear lack of empathy for my condition, I decided to ignore her entirely. Maybe I did look like that, but I'd like to see her try it. Going from two legs to four was not as easy as you might think. Not even with a tail that swished all by itself.

Forget walking, I thought angrily. I should concentrate on shifting back. Lowering myself to the floor, which was more or less a controlled collapse, I turned my focus inside. The electricity that had coursed through Adam wasn't present in me, but it had to be just like normal shifting. Right. As if shifting was ever normal.

Hunkering down, I strained to pull the leopard back inside. The first tendrils of fear started pooling at the base of my neck as the transition delayed. I was on the verge of giving up when I felt it. Like the ripple that forms when you gently blow across the surface of water, the change was smooth. Beginning slowly, it flowed from my head and traveled down the length of my body until it consumed my feet. Goose bumps raced over my skin in its wake. Exhausted by the process, I didn't even open my eyes to verify that I was human again.

"Macy Greer," Miranda said reprovingly. "Where is your underwear?"

I lifted my head to see her peering at me over the couch where she'd taken a seat. Twisting my head over my shoulder gave a clear view of my completely exposed backside. "I don't know," I groaned, laying my head back down on my arms as a wave of dizziness washed over me. "What are you doing here, anyway?"

"Clearly, to gain material for the next chapter in Macy's most embarrassing moments."

The room suddenly went dark as the throw blanket Miranda launched at me landed on my head. "Ha, ha," I said, pulling the blanket off my head.

"It's nine in the morning. You never sleep late. I was worried."

I turned my face towards her. "You said it was nine?"

She nodded and then looked pointedly at my bottom. "I see I was right to be worried."

Unfolding the blanket, I wrapped it around me as I stood. "So, it's not the turning into a full blown leopard that has you concerned," I teased.

"Granted, it was a shock. But if anyone could figure out how to get their nanobots to graduate ahead of schedule, you could."

"I took it from Adam."

"What do you mean you took it?" she asked, eyeing me uncertainly as I moved around the couch.

"I don't know," I shrugged. "I grabbed this electric rope thing and pulled it from him."

"Maybe you uploaded the programming?" she said thoughtfully. "Through the bond."

Yes, the bond. An actual physical connection between Adam and myself. It's what he had used to find me once. Maybe these "out of body" experiences I'd been having with him were my nanobots attempting to do the same thing.

"Maybe," I shrugged again, not liking how much that word had become a part of my every day vocabulary. But the bond was as good an explanation as any, even if I couldn't examine it on a piece of paper. If I truly had downloaded the programming, then I ought to be able to shift back and forth at will. "I'm too tired and hungry to figure it out right now."

"I asked Margaret if she could bring up breakfast for us. Which reminds me. You might want to get dressed. Cedars and Juarez should be here any minute to discuss the plan to rescue Adam."

She had barely finished speaking when the doorbell sounded. "I'll get it," she smiled.

"Thanks for the warning," I muttered and dashed off to the bedroom in search of clothing.

"Look on the floor by the chair," she shouted after me. "I brought in your duffle from the truck."

I poked my head back out. "My truck is here?"

"Cedars had it brought up."

I was starting to like that man more and more.

"Morning, MacyKat," Juarez called cheerfully. "No one told me we were going toga style this morning."

"I like to keep it fresh," I joked before closing the door.

"Do us all a favor and just keep it covered," Miranda hollered through the door. "Seriously, is that too much to ask?" she begged of Juarez.

Not an entirely unfair question. With everything that had befallen my clothes lately, I was beginning to wonder myself. Maybe growing a natural fur coat wasn't such a bad idea. "Umm," I grumbled. There was that word again.

By the time I came back out, Cedars had arrived. He was

seated next to Miranda on the couch, and Juarez was opposite them. Judging by his face, he was all about business this morning.

"Macy," he nodded in greeting, then trained his gaze on Juarez.

Sensing eyes on him, Juarez lowered his coffee mug like he'd been caught doing something wrong.

"Let's get started," Cedars said.

He saluted Cedars with his mug, then had one more swig before setting it down and angling himself to face me. "The first thing we need to know, is if you can travel through time. Or more importantly, if you can control it. To that end, we have set up a series of tests. Pending those results, we can go from there."

"Okay," I said. With what I had witnessed with Julia and the strange appearances and disappearances with Scout—even though he had admitted nothing—I now had too much evidence to believe that it didn't exist.

"Let me tell you a little bit about how the nanobots normally work," Juarez continued. "They respond to the directives your brain gives the rest of your body. They are programmed to read the signals, in some cases intercept them entirely, and carry out the prescribed functions. Everything nice and tidy."

I nodded to let him know I was with him so far.

"That's not how they work in time shifting."

Miranda and I huffed simultaneously in annoyance.

"I'm not sure what programming they are following," he admitted. Oblivious to our show of frustration, he reached up and scratched the stubble of his soon to be goatee. "We've managed to isolate only the beginning of an episode. Near as we can tell, they are not involuntary. Well, they are and they aren't. There has to be a catalyst. Once that catalyst is engaged, the nanobots are proceeding at their own discretion. The pathways are too convoluted for me to dissect." He stopped and retrieved his coffee mug.

"I just need to determine my catalyst?" I guessed.

"Right," he nodded as he lowered the mug. "From what you've told me, each time it happened to you before, you were under duress. That means it was interpreting your fight or flight signals as the catalyst. The need to protect Adam and get to Langston, fear of scuba and delaying it."

"Preparing to leap at an attacker," I added, recalling the weird halo effect during the fight after the plane crash.

"Precisely. Once we isolate that, we should be able to refine it so that you don't actually have to be in danger to initiate it. You can simply will it to happen."

"I have to learn to will my body through time," I repeated dully.

"Right," he nodded again.

This seemed like it was going to be a lot more difficult than I anticipated.

"Don't worry," Juarez chuckled. "That's what the tests are for. To learn to intentionally send the right signals."

"If you say so," I answered weakly.

Miranda reached over and squeezed my shoulder, smiling encouragingly at me until I returned her smile.

"Moving on," Cedars said. "Adam's location—"

"I know where he is," I interrupted. "The name of the place."

"You had another dream?" Cedars asked.

I looked at Miranda, who grinned guiltily. Of course she would have told him, and truthfully, I wanted him to know. "I did. Biogen is the name."

"Biogen? Hold on," Miranda said. Flipping through some papers on the ottoman, she found the one she wanted and held it out to me. "Is this Garrison?"

"No," I said, reaching for the page. "It's Mallet."

"Gene Mallet?" Cedars asked.

"Uh huh," I answered as I scanned the paragraph below the picture. "Do you know him?"

"I've heard of him. Nothing good."

"Is he involved with Biogen?" I looked back at Miranda.

"I'm not sure. I haven't found a direct connection yet, but there are a lot of mutual interests between the two. Biogen itself seems like any other standard genetic research firm. But there are loads of layers and double talk. You know how much can be hidden in plain sight."

"Keep digging," I told her and handed the paper back. "One more thing." I went to the desk and retrieved DTP's operation list for Cedars.

"What's this?" he asked as I handed it to him.

"This is a list of current operations from a group called the Department of the President. The group's mission is to maintain the purity of the human race and thus to eliminate hybrids everywhere. Acting Director, Gene Mallet."

He unfolded the pages and skimmed through them, stopping short when he found the Colony. "They were at the Colony? How did you discover this?"

I didn't miss the suspicion creeping into his voice. "I'm a researcher, remember?" I said, meeting his eyes squarely. "Before I ever encountered any member of the Organization, I had a little run in where I collected a shell casing. Stamped on the outside were the initials GM and DTP. At the meeting with the president, I met General Gene Mallet, GM. And a little research last night tied him into the Department of the President."

"DTP," Cedars said thoughtfully.

"Too bad he likes to stamp his initials on his bullets," Miranda said.

"Yeah, you can never find a madman who just wants to remain anonymous anymore."

Cedars handed the list to Juarez, who briefly looked it over. "I didn't realize there were this many colonies. The government's been holding out on us," Juarez said.

"I don't think it's the government," I countered. "I think it's Mallet. I think he's been in on this from the beginning. I think hiding the hybrid program may have been his doing."

"He does seem to have his hand in a lot of pots," Miranda said, jiggling her page for emphasis.

"That would imply that he has access to every hybrid ever created," Cedars said.

"Including here?" Miranda asked in sudden alarm.

My breath caught at her question. I hadn't considered that possibility. "He did know where the safe house was. And Granny's. Assuming that was him."

All eyes turned to Juarez. But he was deep in thought, almost like he was somewhere else.

"Juarez?" Cedars prodded.

Juarez held his hand up, signaling him to wait. After a moment, he said, "The security at this location has not been breached." The glaze left his eyes as he lowered his hand and focused on Cedars. "I'm sort of hardwired to this place now," he said sheepishly.

"What do you mean hardwired?" Cedars demanded. "Through your nanobots?" His voice was incredulous at Juarez's claim.

"Not quite sure how. It started as just a feeling, something niggling at me." He shook his head and shrugged. "I began to recognize that it would start every time something security related was going down. Little by little—mostly by trial and error—I've been learning to identify what the feelings mean."

"Your nanobots have hooked into the security measures for the complex?" I asked, shocked by the mere idea of that happening.

"That's where it started," he nodded. "Now, it's more like every security protocol we have."

"What happens if someone fries the system?" Cedars asked. "Will it fry you too?"

Juarez shrugged his shoulders. "Don't know."

Well this was just crazy. Juarez was a living breathing wifi cyber device. "Why didn't you ever tell Adam?"

"It just started," he shrugged. "I'm still working out the kinks."

Miranda looked at me and widened her eyes, mouthing the word "wow" as she did. "Does it hurt?" she asked Juarez.

"Nah," he said. "Like scrolling through a schematic on the computer."

"Juarez, did you ask them to do this?"

"Who? The nanobots?" He shook his head in bewilderment. "I don't talk to them. I just want stuff and it happens."

That's what I thought. Filing that bit of info away for another time, I tried to focus on the reason for the meeting. But man, where did you go from this?

"Any who," I drawled. "Since we are not under the threat of imminent attack, we need to put a stop to DTP's operations. Cedars, can you handle that?"

"We don't have a choice, do we?" Miranda asked, looking back and forth between me and Cedars.

Cedars shook his head. "We don't," he agreed. "I don't know what we're going to do with all the influx. It's not like we can turn them loose on the public. Not yet anyway."

Miranda leaned into Cedars. "We'll manage," she said. "Just think how happy Olivia will be with all the new students in her steely grasp."

Next to her, Juarez chuckled.

The mention of Olivia made me wonder why she wasn't here, but Juarez seemed happy enough. There was probably nothing to worry about.

"Okay, next item on the agenda," I said. "Where are we with the original situation involving Millsap? Mutated bacteria set to hybridize humankind, anyone remember that?"

"How could we forget," Miranda muttered.

Juarez reached forward and picked up his tablet. "We did the original kill," he said. "But we are still having random occurrences outside of the initial range. Before you say anything, I'm already working on boosting the signal for the kill code."

"And Langston?"

Cedars and Juarez exchanged a look.

"What?" I asked both of them.

"Langston is dead," Cedars answered.

"It's my fault," Juarez sighed. "She had a microchip embedded in her central cortex that was, from what I can tell, being used to control her. My efforts to remove it ended with her death. There was code within code and then some. I shouldn't have rushed."

"We're all rushing, Juarez, not just you. You weren't trying to kill her." I waited with upraised eyebrows for his reaction.

"No," he slowly acknowledged.

I knew his admission wouldn't lesson the guilt he felt, but there wasn't much I could do about that. "Do you have a way to test the rest of us for it?" I asked him.

"The control chip?" He thought a moment. "Yeah, that should be easy enough."

"We need to do a sweep pronto," Cedars added.

The sound of the door chime interrupted Cedars' next comment. I walked over and opened it, my face falling when it was Olivia who stood before me.

"Good morning to you too," she smirked, sidestepping me into the suite.

"Sorry. I was hoping you were breakfast."

Following her back to the couch, I watched her plop down next to Juarez. "What'd I miss?" she asked.

"All the adoptions about to occur," Miranda answered. "Oh, and Juarez is a Borg."

"You told them about the security link?" she laughed.

"Yep," Juarez said, handing her the DTP operations list. "Check out all your potential students."

She viewed the list, her eyes widening as she turned the page. "Is this what I think it is?"

"It is if you mean previously unidentified hybrids," Miranda said.

"And we're going to bring them here?" She paused and looked to Cedars for confirmation. "We have no way of knowing the intelligence of these hybrids," she said as she resumed scanning the list. "I'll have to make adjustments in the curriculum. Not to mention incorporating the fact that they are already hybrids. I assume this DTP—"

"Department of the President," I supplied.

"Department of the President has something to do with Adam?" She finished the list and looked up at me.

"Maybe," I shrugged.

She nodded and handed the paper back to Cedars. "While you were away, I've been going through Julia's office." She opened the file she brought in with her. "I don't know how to be diplomatic about saying this, so I'll just say it." She paused, shifting her focus from Miranda to me. "You two are sisters."

I looked over at Miranda. She gave me what we called the big eye wink.

"I take it that's what you found," I giggled.

"Yep," she nodded.

"You two knew about this already?" Olivia asked, disappointed her revelation didn't pack more of a punch.

"I didn't know who it was," I shrugged. "I, actually, Flash and Charlie found an additional report about mindbenders that included the division of two separate eggs."

"Right," Olivia nodded. "There should be two more, but so far, I haven't found any indication of who that is. I found a genetic profile in Julia's lab that matched the one we have of Miranda. That's how I knew she was one of the eggs. I'm still looking for the other two."

"Wait—" Miranda objected. "You have my genetic profile on hand?"

"We have everyone's genetic profile on hand. In case of emergencies…" she said exaggeratedly slow.

"I'm sure that's the only reason," Miranda said tightly.

"So, you know the details about the makeup of Miranda's DNA?" I quickly redirected.

"It's in here," Olivia said, tapping the file with her finger. "According to the report, she's got genes from half the scientists that you do, and the rest is a combination of famous inventors, artists, etc."

That explained the wildly creative side she so often displayed.

"However, there is one major distinction between you and the other eggs," she continued. "They were not subjected to the repeated nanobot injections that you were. The result being, they didn't experience the hibernation periods that you did. They were birthed later."

"So, I'm the oldest?"

"You would go there," Miranda muttered under her breath.

"Technically, I suppose you are, but not really," Olivia added.

"The eggs are the same age, but you they birthed immediately, and the others they froze and started much later."

Did she know how many cases were won on technicalities? It was good enough for me.

"I haven't had a chance to talk to them since I got back, but you might want to talk to Flash and Charlie. They identified a signature of some sort related to the nanobots given to me during my development. It might help you find the others."

"Will do," she said and wrote something on her tablet.

"Getting back to Adam," I said, prompting Juarez for a response.

"Tests first and then we can finalize the plan to rescue Adam," he answered.

He wasn't actually saying it, but his insistence on these tests gave me the impression that the rescue mission might be riding on my success. I guess that made it a darn good thing that I usually aced my tests.

CHAPTER 13

"HEY GUYS," I SAID TO my team as I trailed Miranda into the room set up for monitoring the testing. That's what I considered the Colony hybrids plus the few cadets that had stuck with me. Mine. "Come to watch the big show?"

"And eat," Wrangle added.

"So this is where breakfast went." I walked over and picked up some bacon, stuffed it in a biscuit and began to eat. I managed to eat three of them and a handful of grapes before Juarez set his coffee mug down.

"So what we've got here is an Indiana Jones style obstacle course laid out for you," he said as he flipped on the lights to an adjoining gym.

"Did you have this on hand already?" I asked, pressing my nose against the glass of the windows lining the walls. The contraption they'd rigged for me was kind of amazing. Depending on the ages of all the hybrids we had penciled in to rescue, it might come in handy as a play fort.

"Not in this particular configuration, but yeah. See the flag?" He pointed to the far end of the gym. "The objective is to get the flag first."

"First?" I looked around the gym. "Who am I racing against?"

Olivia suddenly appeared at my side, wearing gym clothes and an impish smile.

"We thought a little competition might help you learn faster," Juarez shrugged.

That's great. Pit me against the one that could already do it.

Indicating the red tape stretched across the floor, he said, "Starting line's over there."

"See you inside," Olivia said sweetly and stepped into the gym.

Miranda gripped me by the shoulders and massaged them like she was a boxing coach. "Don't let her get to you," she groused.

Oy. Now I was really dreading this. My potential failure had witnesses. I hadn't been nervous until now.

"Here we go," I breathed and stepped out to follow Olivia.

"Get'em, Doc," Kenny yelled, then followed with a loud whistle.

That primed the whole group for hooting and hollering. Seriously, it was like they were at a sporting event. I was more embarrassed than ever when I reached Olivia's side.

"You've got some fans," she said sarcastically.

I had something alright. "Any pointers?"

"You just have to focus on what you want. See it."

"Like regular shifting?"

"I don't know. This is the only shifting I do."

"The rules," Juarez said, "are as follows. Olivia, no time bubbles for you. Two minutes on the clock." He pointed to the large digital clock on the wall just above the flag. "Stay on the course. No shortcuts. And time starts on my mark. Any questions?"

Olivia was suddenly standing at the opposite end of the gym, one hand holding the flag. "Oh, I'm sorry," she said innocently. "I thought you said go."

Rolling my eyes, I waited for her to reappear. Quicker than the next heartbeat, she was standing next to me again, a single eyebrow lifted in challenge.

"Olivia," Cedars called in warning. "Follow the rules."

"I'll do it too," Scout offered. Stepping from behind Juarez, he trotted out to the gym floor where he inserted himself between me and Olivia. "It's not that hard," he said reassuringly. "Just focus only on where you want to be. Otherwise, you'll end up somewhere you don't want to be."

Wasn't that always true?

"Everyone ready?" Juarez asked.

I plastered a fake smile on my face and gave the yeehaw double thumbs up for good measure. The cheering section went wild.

"Go," Juarez said, through stuttered laughter.

The gym went dark, except for the red numbers counting down on the clock. Figuring I would need every advantage, I shifted. The other two were already moving when I cautiously ventured forward. I didn't think Juarez believed a simple ropes course would be enough to spur the catalyst. Alert for any hidden surprises, my skin was crawling with nerves as I stepped onto the first bridge. I paused when Olivia cried out. Eh, eh, surprise number one. A few seconds later, Scout cursed and appeared right in front of me.

"Ah, sorry, Doc," he breathed, falling heavily against the ropes and causing the bridge to swing wildly.

"Everything okay?" I asked as I hung on.

He exhaled a laugh. "Seems Juarez has a few surprises."

"Scout, you're disqualified," Cedars announced.

"Yeah, yeah. It was a defense mechanism," he complained. "Good luck," he said and swung off the bridge.

I didn't like this. Not the dark, not trying to anticipate Juarez's surprises. Wasn't there a less stressful way to get the time juices flowing?

When the bridge had stopped swinging enough to safely move, I continued along the ropes until I reached the first intersection. Not having studied the course previously, I didn't know what each direction held. Looking at them now, they both seemed to follow a long convoluted route to the flag. Directly in front of me was an open space about ten feet across. I could easily jump it to the platform on the other side and forgo the longer routes. I would still be on the course. Time in the air didn't count as off the course, did it?

Bending my knees, I launched myself forward. I had almost reached the platform when something barreled into me from my right. I hit the ground hard and skidded into the underbelly of the course.

"I guess that did count as a shortcut," I grumbled, gently massaging the hip that had connected with the floor. "Can't say he didn't warn me." Rolling to my knees, I got a good look at what had plowed into me, which, contrary to the way it felt, was not a swinging log on a rope. It was a hybrid, but it looked more like the werewolf of legend than any hybrid I had ever seen. In other words, scary as hell. "Okay, that he did not warn me about."

Catching my scent, the thing howled and whirled in my direction. "Shoot!" I hollered and ducked behind the nearest wooden support when it lunged at me. The entire course shook when the wolf hit the pillar sidelong. Disoriented by the collision, the creature stumbled over itself trying to stand. I used the opening to skirt around behind it and dart underneath the other side of the course where the beams were shorter and my chances of survival seemed greater.

By the time I turned around, the werewolf was back on its feet. It rose on its hind legs and lifted its nose into the air. Stretched to its full height, it towered over me. Just one of its claws looked as big as my hand. It didn't take a single genius gene to know I was seriously outmatched.

With its nose still in the air, it turned slowly, an effective distraction from the swiftness of its attack. I narrowly missed the jaws as they snapped shut. But I got a full whiff of its breath. It reeked like something had crawled in there and died.

"Uugh, I think you missed some of your last victim," I groaned in disgust.

The creature turned and lunged again, forcing me further underneath the course. I knew with its size that it would have a hard time following me into the congested foundation. So as fast as I could, I wound my way deeper into the maze. The only drawback was the restriction in my own freedom of movement. I glanced over my shoulder at the wolf. And the fact that the wolf was still following despite its size.

"Come on," I moaned, glancing back at the wolf again. Why hadn't Juarez turned on the lights yet? Couldn't he tell I wasn't on the course? Clearly, I should be disqualified. Me and my inability to follow rules.

Studying the path before me, its size was decreasing by the inch.

If I went in much further, I'd be on my stomach, and something told me the wolf had a better military crawl than I did. I gasped as my boot suddenly jerked backwards. Scrambling frantically when the rest of me began to slide, I wrapped the nearest pillar in a hug. The wolf's claws clacked repeatedly against the floor as it fought for leverage in the tug of war. If it realized it would be easier to let go and spring at me again, I might be done for. Thank God it had only buried its teeth in the heel of the boot, or I'd be missing a foot right now.

The wolf began to shake its muzzle, and my leg, and my whole body attached to my leg. Gritting my teeth, I let everything go loose, including my arms glued to the pillar. Otherwise, the tension could start causing parts of me to tear off or bend at weird angles, and I kind of liked everything where it was.

Sensing it had accomplished its objective, the wolf stopped whipping its muzzle back and forth and tried to wrench me free, but not before I'd latched onto the pole again. The creature howled its fury at being thwarted, coating my boot in a layer of saliva so warm I could feel it through the leather.

Okay. This was extreme, even for Juarez. Enough of this waiting to be rescued.

Using my free leg, I brought the heel down soundly on its snout. The wolf reared back, consumed by the sneezing fit the contact had caused, but it was still too close for comfort. And way too close to turn my back on. As it continued sneezing, I pried one of the smaller studs free and waited for it to attack again. When it did, I swung the stud and caught it under the chin. The blow had enough force to drive the wolf clear of the underbelly. Seizing the opportunity, I dropped the stud and pushed deeper into the maze. At some point, the wolf would not be able to follow. I hoped that was before I had to stop.

My stomach clenched as the space in front of me narrowed quite a bit. I could see that it went all the way across, but I really would have to do the military crawl to make it through. I was toying with the idea of backtracking when a loud crack sounded behind me as a pole gave way. Forward it was.

Lowering to my stomach, I used my arms to pull myself into the new section. I hadn't gotten very far in when I heard whimpering off to my right.

"Olivia?" I whispered.

The sobbing grew louder.

Aiming towards the sound, I crawled forward until I found her. She was lying on her side, and her eyes were glassy and unfocused.

"Olivia, can you hear me?" I asked, brushing aside the hair that trailed across her face. Blood coated her cheek in three parallel stripes. "Olivia," I said more forcefully. I would have slapped her, but I didn't have that much room to maneuver. Besides that, the wolf had found us. We needed to move now.

Spinning myself around, I shoved my head into her gut and heaved both of us forward. I didn't stop pushing until we surged free of the course's underpinning. Scrambling to my feet, I scooped up Olivia and dashed for the door.

The door opened before I reached it. Gathered in the doorway was a confused set of spectators.

"What?" I exclaimed as I studied my empty arms.

"What are you doing?" Miranda asked worriedly.

Ignoring her question, I asked, "Where's Olivia?"

"Olivia's still on the course," Cedars answered and pointed towards the gym.

Juarez flipped the lights on, revealing an undamaged and werewolf free course.

"Did she do it?" Olivia asked, stumbling from the maze with a disgruntled look on her face.

"And Scout?"

"Here," Scout answered and waived at me from behind Cedars.

Miranda touched my arm. "What's going on?" she asked.

"Are you sure Langston is dead?" I asked them.

"Yeah," Juarez answered. "Why?"

"Did you know she had the ability to make you see things that were not there?"

"Astral projection?" Olivia said, now standing in the doorway of the gym next to me.

Cedars crossed his arms and looked around, like he was taking stock of everyone in the room. "Is that what happened?" He asked.

"Being that there is no werewolf on the loose, I think so," I nodded.

"Langston could do this?" Cedars asked.

"She did when she attacked Adam. That's why no one else, even Adam, didn't make a move to stop her."

"Why didn't you mention this before?" Cedars demanded, clearly aggravated with yet another problem to deal with.

"I don't know, Cedars. Maybe I assumed you knew the abilities of your own people. Maybe, I assumed you actually knew what you were doing."

"Macy," Miranda whispered.

Recognizing the pleading tone in her voice, I clamped my mouth shut.

"Who knew about the test, other than us?" Reynolds asked.

"Margaret knew," Cedars said.

"It's not Margaret," Miranda, Olivia and I said together.

"Lindsey," Juarez said quietly. "I needed her to round up the supplies. Lindsey knew."

"Find her," Cedars growled.

"On it," Juarez said, wheeling around to tap away on his keyboard. "She's moving away from us." We all watched the red dot that was presumably Lindsey retreating fast.

"Exactly how are you tracking her?" Miranda asked suspiciously.

"I tagged her," Olivia spoke up. She shrugged at the many narrowed eyes aimed her way. "I didn't trust her. Too many coincidences to actually be coincidences. And after what you implied to Juarez." She shrugged again. "I was suspicious."

Regardless of how grateful I was for Olivia's foresight right now, I was going to make sure that Flash and Charlie figured out a way to scan me for trackers. Also, I was going to write Lindsey's name in my traitor spot on the whiteboard.

Miranda pulled me to the side when Cedars began issuing commands. "What did you imply to Juarez?" she asked.

"That we still had an active traitor in our midst."

"And you didn't tell me this because…"

"I knew it wasn't you, and I didn't want you going all Nancy Drew and spooking the mole."

She pursed her lips, desperately seeking a way to argue. Wasn't going to happen this time. I was there when she bought the overcoat.

"That was a long time ago," she protested.

"Tell me," I said, turning and looking squarely at her. "Did the coat manage to make its way here?"

The passion behind her argument deflated. "It's cold up here," she said wanly.

"Um hum," I hummed, crossing my arms over my chest to signal my victory.

"It's just a coat," she muttered.

"You asked," I reminded her.

Kenny caught my eye, waiting for approval to carry out Cedars' orders.

"Your call," I told him.

Cedars noticed the exchange, but he didn't comment. Kenny had never even pretended to be loyal to the Organization.

Stepping closer to get my attention, Olivia said, "We should keep working on you. They can handle this."

"Fine. But can we forget about all the competition stuff and just try jumping?"

"Whatever you think will work," Olivia nodded.

"I look good in the coat," Miranda said as she followed us out.

"Let it go, Miranda," I chided her. And seriously, who didn't look good in London Fog?

Olivia stopped walking and turned to face me. "Let's start small. Say, from here to the first post." She pointed at the one she was indicating.

"Remember, it's like shifting," Scout reminded me as he walked up.

I nodded and focused on the post. My mind was a total blank. Dropping my head dejectedly, I let out a troubled breath.

"You can do this, Mace," Miranda said encouragingly.

I needed to do this. I knew that much. Focusing on the pole again, I tried to see myself next to it, but all I saw was Adam. Adam, lost and unbearably cold. Adam as a leopard.

"Adam?" I whispered uncertainly.

The next instant, I was pulled down to the floor by my legs sudden inability to support my weight. I didn't even have the strength to catch myself as I fell. When I finally got my head turned around, I saw for myself what the interior of his cell looked like.

Oh, crap. Scout had warned me not to focus on anything but where I wanted to be.

Breathing became a chore as my lungs turned to ice. The crushing weight of the cold forced me to focus all my energy on just rolling over. "Adam," I called, but my voice lacked the strength to wake him. The side of my face against the floor started to ache. With some confusion, I realized the floor was grated. Hooking my claws in the grate, I used it to creep over to where Adam lay.

"Adam," I repeated, putting more effort into speaking this time.

A low growl rumbled in his chest as he lifted his head. But then he laid his head back down, as if that effort had exhausted him.

"I have to go back," I whispered.

Adam didn't respond to me. I didn't want to go back and leave him here. I wasn't even sure I could get myself back, and I certainly wasn't going to risk Adam. But staying here wasn't safe for either of us. I wanted to explain this to him, but what little strength I had was failing, and there was no guarantee that he'd understand.

With my head pressed against Adam, I pictured Miranda in the gym. The look of worry that would be on her face, and the pole that I was supposed to be at. I knew without opening my eyes that I was back in the gym. I fell forward from my kneeling position, gasping raggedly for air.

"Macy!" Miranda yelled.

Following that were the footfalls of multiple runners. Both of my arms were suddenly gripped, and I was hauled upright. I wanted to answer, to tell them I was okay, but all I could do was breathe as my lungs thawed out.

"Give her some room," Reynolds snapped. He had pulled me in front of him, my head now supported by his chest. "She's cold," he said, and I felt someone grasp my hands and begin rubbing them.

"Macy. Look at me, chica."

I focused on Miranda kneeling in front of me. The worry was just as I had pictured it. "You're gonna get wrinkles," I rasped.

Her breath caught as she laughed. "Well, I'd have you to thank, wouldn't I?"

"We need to get you to the infirmary," Olivia said. She reached for me, but Reynolds tightened his arms protectively.

"No," I said, leaning more heavily against him and away from Olivia. "I'm okay. Just zapped."

"Where did you go?" Miranda asked.

My answer was delayed as I maneuvered myself into sitting without Reynolds help.

Understanding flooded Olivia's eyes. "You were with Adam," she said softly.

I nodded.

"I told you to only focus on where you wanted to go," Scout said, frowning at me from above.

"I was and then I wasn't."

"Then you were with Adam," Miranda finished.

"I guess that answers the question of whether you can get in."

I looked up to see Juarez standing in front of me, a smug look on his face.

"We've got Lindsey," he said, bumping my leg with the toe of his shoe. "You want to be in on the interrogation?"

Hell yeah, I did.

CHAPTER 14

I WAS STILL A LITTLE SHAKY when we left the gym, but I was determined not to be excluded from the questioning. "How are we preventing her from projecting?" I asked Olivia as we walked.

"Right now, proximity. I'm working on a cortical injection that will disable that part of the brain without dire consequences."

"Right now, you're working on it?"

"Up here," she said, tapping her temple. "You're not the only genius in the bunch."

Thank goodness, because this genius was tired. "You better work quick before she expands the range."

"How in the world would she do that?" Olivia asked doubtfully. "Her ability is what it is."

I cut my eyes to her and back.

"It is fixed," she said with less confidence. "Macy?"

Here was where I risked looking like an idiot to everyone. If I told them about what I'd been kicking around in my thoughts, they would argue with me. Tell me all the reasons why it couldn't be. None of the reasons would matter to me, of course, but did I want to subject myself to a lecture? Nope.

"It'll keep 'til later. Tell me about Lindsey and Adam."

Olivia frowned at the change in subject. I could see her trying to work out what I had hinted at. Good luck trying to catch that train of thought. I was barely on it myself.

"You know about them?" she asked dully.

"Adam told me. But that was from a man's perspective."

"Humph," she grunted. "It was a long time ago, but they

were very close. I think she wanted more from Adam than he was willing to give. It seemed like they were getting close again." She hesitated.

"What happened?" I pressed.

"You," she sighed. "You happened. About five or six years ago, Adam discovered you. From the first time he saw you he was enthralled. He didn't pay her much attention after that. They were amicable enough. I thought she was okay with it."

"You never smelled anything suspicious?"

She shrugged, her face echoing the uncertainty. "Every now and then, but I just thought it was normal. Nothing to indicate she could or would do this."

"Wait a minute," Miranda said. "What do you mean by smell anything suspicious?"

"Yeah, tell her what I mean, Olivia," I said with a smile.

"Thank you so much, Macy," Olivia drawled without the slightest bit of gratitude.

"What? You were hoping to keep it a secret?"

"It would have been nice," she spat back.

"This from the queen of spying. You know everything about me."

"People, focus," Miranda interrupted with a clap of her hands. "Smell," she prodded.

Through my peripheral vision, I saw Olivia take a deep breath at the same time that I did. I didn't know how we kept ending up fighting with each other, but I didn't like it. The clash of two strong personalities, I guess. Two very different strong personalities.

"I can essentially smell emotions," Olivia admitted.

"That's a new one," Miranda said thoughtfully. "Bet that gets overwhelming sometimes."

"It does," Olivia confirmed while looking pointedly at Miranda.

"What? I'm a deeply emotional person," she said defensively.

Olivia didn't say anything further, but she had to be thinking it. Being no stranger to Miranda's dramatics, I could only imagine what Olivia had to go through around her. Or any of us for that matter.

"You can't shut it off or mute it?" I asked Olivia.

"Not even a little," she said as she reached for the door.

I felt a sudden surge of sympathy for Olivia. I didn't know she couldn't turn it off. Sure it was an asset to be able to identify what people were truly feeling. But what about the times when you didn't want to know. Like right now. Was she smelling my concern?

As if she'd read my mind, she smiled sadly at me.

"Sorry," I told her. "Wish I could design an off switch for you."

"I'm working on that too." She tapped her temple again, then opened the door for us. "Maybe you can help if things ever return to normal."

Maybe. And maybe she could teach me to identify emotions too.

"Macy," Olivia said as I moved to enter. "If there is something I should know..."

"There's lots of things you should know," I said sarcastically, but relented when the expression on her face soured. "I'm still ruminating on this one."

"Maybe you should work more quickly so we don't get blindsided again."

Miranda wrapped one arm around each of our necks and began to pull us through the door. "Maybe you both should shut up and enter the room," she hissed at us. "We're here," she announced loudly as she drug us through the door.

The worried faces that greeted us turned into confusion. I wriggled free of Miranda's hold to find Olivia already staring daggers at her.

"You okay?" Kenny asked as he approached cautiously. "I heard about the disappearing." His eyes flicked nervously between the three of us. "Almost thought you'd been taken again."

"Sorry, not taken," I said, shifting my stare away from Miranda.

"I'm okay," I shrugged weakly. Somehow, the words didn't feel right in my mouth.

"Adam's okay as well?" Kenny asked.

"He's alive. Okay? I don't know." I wrapped my arms around myself as I walked further into the room. "The cold is unlike anything I've ever felt before. It seeps into your bones, paralyzes you."

"Could be some sort of stasis field," Cedars commented. "Could he communicate?"

"No," I shook my head. "He could barely move his head. The last time, he'd made it seem like that was by choice. Like he didn't want to be discovered. Now? I don't know."

He nodded, turning his attention to the large screen facing us. Lindsey was center stage. "Anyone who comes within a hundred feet of her is subject to the projection."

"That's quite a distance," Olivia observed as she stared at the screen.

"Too close for a simple shot," Cedars agreed. "The only reason we were able to catch her was because we were too quick for her to project on all of us at the same time."

"Who was the one that got close enough to knock her out?" I asked.

He hesitated, a frown creasing the space between his eyes. "Kenny," he admitted grudgingly.

I could have called that one from any distance. You wanted someone skilled at evading attacks, Kenny was your guy.

"Okay then," Olivia said, breaking the tense silence. "We'll make it a long shot." She backed towards the door, pushing it open with her backside. "I'm going to the lab to finish working out the details. Any volunteers?"

"Are we talking 3D modeling of projectable inhibitors?" Charlie asked.

Flash's eyes lit up. "Including programming biometric parameters?"

"And shooting," Olivia teased.

"I'm in," Wrangle said, sliding from the desktop he'd used as a seat.

Kenny watched them go, a look of concentration on his face. "I'd better keep watch. Be the voice of reason."

"If you're going to start being our voice of reason, we really are in trouble," Miranda griped.

"I thought that was already a given," Kenny retorted as he pushed the door open.

Shaking my head at the both of them, I walked over and sat down on the small couch against the back wall. What I wouldn't give for a three day nap.

"Is the plan for Macy to teleport to Adam, and then bring him back with her?" Miranda asked.

"It would help tremendously if that were possible," Juarez said. "The security involved with this place…it's not impossible. For me," he clarified. "But, I'd rather not have to go that route. As she's the only one with a connection to Adam, she's our girl."

Opening my eyes, I focused on Juarez. "I've barely teleported myself. I don't even know if I can repeat it yet. And bringing someone with me?"

"You have time to practice still. We need you to be a fast learner on this," he said, his voice conveying the urgency.

"Juarez—"

"We know you can do it. You know you can do it. Adam needs you to do it. So just do it," he barked angrily.

I snapped my mouth shut. Fine. I would do it. Apparently, I didn't have a choice in the matter.

Miranda crossed the room and sat down next to me on the couch.

"Macy, look," Cedars said, positioning himself to break the eye contact between Juarez and myself. "I think what Juarez is trying to communicate to you is the danger involved with mounting our normal response to this. Countering the security in this place would leave us vulnerable at a time when we really cannot afford to be. The state of the Organization is unstable enough as it is."

Miranda reached over and grasped my hand. Her gentle

squeeze told me everything I needed to know. Things were about to hit the crap pile again unless I did this. Super Macy to the rescue. Again.

"I think I'm going to want an official super suit. Something in red."

"I like red," Miranda nodded.

"And black," I added.

"Ooh, we should make it like one of those paso doble costumes. Leather with silver studs."

"Do I get thigh high boots?"

"Definitely," Miranda said enthusiastically.

"Finally. I'll take it," I sang out.

We looked up from our conspiring to find Juarez and Cedars staring at us through narrowed eyes.

"What?" I frowned at them.

"There's no rule about not looking bad ass when you're being bad ass," Miranda argued.

"Exactly," I agreed, crossing my arms over my chest.

"You two," Cedars groaned, gently massaging the bridge of his nose.

"Juarez," I said seriously. "You're going to have to give me a way to disrupt the stasis field. I could barely move the last time. Just getting myself back took everything I had." I shook my head as I recalled the difficulty. "Will it matter that he is entirely a leopard?"

Juarez and Cedars exchanged several glances in that language that seemed to be all their own.

"It might," Juarez said. "I'll get Olivia on it."

Sighing, I settled back into the couch. "It seems to me that we have too many things and not enough people to get on it. Where are all the other people in this Organization?"

"We've sent most everyone on vacation," Cedars answered.

"Whether they wanted to or not," Juarez added. "Getting some of these people to take a few days off is downright impossible."

"When was your last vacation?" Miranda asked Juarez.

Realizing he'd just convicted himself, he scowled out at her. "Whatever," he grumbled as he returned to his work.

"It will be really nice to have Adam back and have everything get back to normal," Cedars said, but his voice lacked conviction, like he wasn't sure what normal was supposed to look like anymore.

"If you're looking for normal, you better find yourself another hero," Miranda countered, earning her another look from Cedars.

Piercing look aside, let me say a hardy Amen to that.

From that point on, Cedars directed his full attention to prepping for the interrogation. I stayed on the sidelines mostly, passing the time by talking softly with Miranda. That was mainly to give myself a chance to identify what was bothering me. I followed their progress, the phone ringing and the communication back and forth between Olivia and Juarez regarding the new inhibitor they were designing for Lindsey. But it wasn't until half an hour of waiting had passed that I pinpointed the problem.

"None of you were aware of Lindsey's ability?" I asked.

Cedars looked up from the notepad he was writing on. "No," he answered. "It was my understanding that she was designed for spying. Enhanced hearing, vision and camouflage…" his voice trailed off as he reached the same conclusion I did.

"As in, she was perfectly designed to get next to Langston without anyone knowing," I finished.

"Damn it," Cedars swore, slamming the notepad against the desk where Juarez was working. "She walked right in. Right under our noses." He laced his hands behind his head and lifted his eyes to the ceiling. "I am so tired of playing catch up."

The room sort of froze after his outburst. I could totally relate to his disgust of being one step behind. It was like trying to put together a jigsaw puzzle where the picture kept changing as you were assembling it.

"You want confirmation she stole her new found ability from Langston?" Miranda asked gently.

Cedars put his hands on his hips and looked at Miranda without really seeing her. "Yes," he nodded. "Too many things are slipping through the cracks as it is. I don't want to find out the hard way that somebody else has this ability."

"Off we go then," Miranda said, taking my hand and pulling me to my feet.

"I have the strongest urge to sing something from Snow White," I said.

"Thank you ever so much for the refrain that is now punctuating every step I make," Miranda said while outpacing me down the hall.

Well, Hi Ho to you too. "Do you know where you're going?" I yelled to her retreating form.

"I'm following the yellow brick road," she bellowed at me as she turned the corner and vanished.

"Wrong movie," I muttered. "And there is no yellow anywhere. Hey, slow down. I'm still recuperating." Increasing my pace, I rounded the corner. "Miranda?" The space where she should have been was completely empty. "Miranda!"

"Stop yelling," she said as she popped her head through the doorway on my right. "I'm right here."

"Miranda," I sighed. "This is not a good time to play hide and seek."

"Who's playing hide and seek? The morgue is right next to the infirmary, which is right next to the holding cell, which we were right next to."

She lost me at infirmary, and I had to work my way backwards. "You said all that to say that we were already next to the morgue?"

"Exactly," she smiled.

I eyeballed her all the way through the door.

Over the years, I had been in plenty of morgues. They all seemed to have two things in common, poor lighting and a distinctly disturbing smell. They never failed to give me the creeps.

Miranda walked to the counter holding the box of gloves and fished out a pair for herself and one for me. "She should be right here," she said, approaching the wall of stainless containers and fingering one of the handles. "I was there when she died, so I sort of helped with the storage. But we didn't do an autopsy. We didn't think we needed to."

"We don't need to do an autopsy now," I said as I slid the last glove on.

She pulled out the drawer and folded the sheet back. "We're looking for puncture marks, right?"

"Right." Positioning myself near Langston's head, I began to examine her upper torso.

"Do you think she'd bother with concealing it?" Miranda asked.

"Probably. She wouldn't want it to be obvious, but she'd want a clear shot at it. Somewhere that didn't clog the needle with debris." I moved Langston's hair to better see the skin on her neck.

"You think she was going for a straight transfer?"

"Wouldn't you? Taking time to process it might draw attention, which reminds me. We need to get Juarez to reprogram all nanobots to die after leaving the body."

"You might not be alive if that were the case now," she said meaningfully.

Pausing my inspection, I thought about what she'd said. "Okay, how about a shelf life. Something like...if they are not replanted inside of another compatible biochemistry inside of ten minutes they die."

"I think that's long enough," she nodded. "I mean, the only good reason that you would transfuse them would be in a life or death situation. It doesn't take that long to do that."

"That's a lot better than what it is now. If I forget, please tell him."

"Will do. I think I got something."

Joining her on the other side of the table, I took Langston's hand from her and looked where she indicated. Between the middle and ring finger there was a definite puncture mark.

"It's kind of small," she said.

"Yeah. I don't think this is it, but it might be what killed her. Was a tox screen done?"

"None that I know of."

"Let's roll her over." I picked up the edge of the sheet and wrapped it around Langston.

"I hate this part," Miranda groaned.

The moment we flipped her over, we found what we were looking for.

"So much for trying to hide her tracks," I said, recoiling at the stain discoloring the sheet.

"That's a dead giveaway if ever I saw one," Miranda agreed. She reached out and eased the sheet down. Thick greenish fluid oozed from a wound on Langston's lower back. "Post mortem?" Miranda cringed.

"That is seriously creepy."

"She's got zombie nanobots in her. We should warn somebody."

"I think we're the somebodies," I whispered.

"She used a rather large needle," Miranda pointed out.

"And they worked."

Our heads whipped to each other. Simultaneously, we stepped away from the body with our hands raised in the air.

"We have to burn that," Miranda hissed, her breathing now heavy with fear.

I threw the sheet back over the body and went straightaway to wash my hands. Miranda backed all the way to the sink.

"I'll watch for you, and then you watch for me. I am not going to be one of those dumb girls that stupidly talks away while the zombie rises in the background."

It was ridiculous, but I felt exactly the same way. "Tell Cedars what's going on."

"Already did. He's on his way."

"Your turn," I said and stepped to the side to make room for her at the sink. "What do you think Lindsey was thinking when she did the injection?"

She waited until she had finished drying her hands and turned around before answering. "I assume she was thinking about the nanobots she wanted."

"I don't think I could do it," I shuddered.

"Not unless I was dying," Miranda agreed. "Maybe not even

then. Not with everything else I'd be injecting with it. I mean, she didn't even go for a blood vessel. She went through skin, muscle… everything."

Eww-wah. "That is disgusting," I moaned, trying hard to look everywhere but at the body of Langston.

Cedars arrived at that moment and punched the door open, causing Miranda and I to jump together. The look on his face when he saw us huddled by the sink said everything.

"He thinks we're being silly," Miranda said icily.

"No," Cedars said, struggling to contain his laughter. "Really, it's perfectly normal."

All right, time to behave like a professional. I let go of Miranda and bravely stepped forward. "I don't think Juarez killed her. Not directly. There's evidence that she was injected between her middle and ring finger on her right hand."

That was enough to quell his laughing. He started toward the body to make his own examination.

"Don't touch it," Miranda said, rushing to intercept him.

He caught the pair of gloves I tossed him and slipped them on despite Miranda's glare. "I'm not doing anything that you didn't already do," he said as he lifted the sheet.

"That was before I knew she had zombie nanobots."

"They're just tiny robots," he replied. "Metal and plastic and stuff." Finished with her hand, he moved on to the puncture on her back. "She really wanted those nanobots," he grimaced. After studying it a moment longer, he replaced the sheet. "We'll run a tox screen, but I think you're probably right."

"Kind of strange that Lindsey would kill her before obtaining the nanobots," I said.

"Spur of the moment?" Miranda guessed.

"How many hypodermic needles filled with enough poison to kill a hybrid do you usually carry around?" I asked with raised eyebrows. "No," I shook my head. "She planned it."

"Langston knew something Lindsey didn't want revealed," Cedars said.

"And why the projection nanobots?" Miranda asked.

We grew silent as we each tried to fathom the reason for that. The only thing she'd done with them so far was to punk me.

"Maybe—"

The phone on the wall rang loudly, startling all of us.

"Geez," Miranda exhaled with a hand to her chest.

Cedars snapped the gloves off and tossed them in the trash before picking up the receiver. "Cedars." He listened for a moment, then said, "I think that's best. I don't want another screw up." Still holding the phone, he placed it back in the cradle, his head bowed deep in thought.

"Can we get out of here?" Miranda shivered.

Waking from his trance like state, Cedars looked at her. "Yes, ma'am," he said and exchanged his grip on the phone for an arm around her waist. "Macy, the drawer?"

I turned and slid the drawer housing Langston back in place, then followed Cedars as he led Miranda out of the room.

"That was Juarez on the line," Cedars said. "We're going to hardwire for the interrogation. With Juarez being plugged in like he is, he doesn't want to risk being subjected to projection if something goes wrong."

"I do not like this projection ability," I said forcefully.

"I'm with you on that one," he agreed. "Camouflage is one thing. This…this is something else."

"Dangerous is what it is," Miranda said. "The ability to manipulate what someone else is seeing? That's not something that should exist."

"Agreed," I nodded.

"Do not tell General Hurser about this," she ordered.

"I'm not planning on it."

"Your plans don't always go as planned."

"I'm not going to tell the military or anyone else about this," I insisted. I couldn't imagine a scenario where it would be necessary for me to reveal this particular trait. Just as soon as I could, I was going to eliminate it from the gene pool permanently.

"Where are we going?" I asked as we passed the room we'd been in previously.

"Juarez said he needed more ports," Cedars said. "It's right around the corner."

"Someone remember to tell Juarez about the new theory on Langston's death. He'll be relieved."

"Until it turns to anger," Cedars said.

Juarez angry. Hadn't seen that too much. Knee deep in hardware like he was now? All the time. "Your favorite student has arrived," I announced as I stepped through the door that Cedars held open.

"Hand me that cord," Juarez told Reynolds. "No, the other one."

"Lie detection," Reynolds explained. "Apparently, we're not currently trusting wifi." He held up two handfuls of cords as evidence.

"Has Olivia finished with the inhibitor?" I asked.

"Not yet," Juarez answered from under the desk. "Soon, though."

Miranda crossed behind me and sunk down in one of the chairs banked against the far wall. Her face had turned sort of pale grey.

"So, how's this going to go?" I asked Cedars while keeping an eye on Miranda.

"First, we'll subdue her using the inhibitor. Then we'll start the questioning."

"I want to know how she could willingly inject zombie nanos into her body," Miranda complained.

"What do you mean zombie nanos?" Reynolds asked.

"They're not zombies," I said quickly. "The nanobots as they exist currently do not die when the host does. That's something that really needs to change as soon as possible. Juarez, can you handle that?"

He scooted out from under the desk and pulled the chair towards him. "To die after the host does?" He repeated as he sat down.

"Or if outside the host for any reason," I nodded. "About a ten minute window?"

"Shouldn't be an issue," he grunted while reaching under the counter for more cords. "Convincing all the operatives to get it done? That may be an issue. Whew," he breathed as he sat up. "I forgot what a bother this was."

"Says the man not holding all the cords." Reynolds wiggled the tips of fingers not hidden by the jumble of wires.

Smiling at them, I said to Cedars, "We'll know if she's lying." I waved at the conglomeration of cables. "Obviously. But how are you going to ensure that she'll tell us anything valuable?"

"One of the protocols," he began, intentionally pitching his voice low after glancing at Miranda, "is a program that stimulates the pain center of the brain every time a lie is told."

"You mean torture?" I balked in surprise.

He looked as though he meant to defend it, but then said, "It is. It becomes more specific with each lie told, to the point that even a slight attempt to mislead or misdirect will trigger it. I don't think we have any other option. This could be just about Adam and you, some misguided attempt at revenge. But I don't think so."

"I don't think so either. Someone has been in contact with Millsap. The reporter too. I think it was probably her."

He nodded. "We'll find out one way or the other."

"Could it kill her?"

His silence was answer enough.

"We're all set here," Juarez said. "As soon as Olivia's ready, it's go time."

Cedars slid his phone from his waist. "I'll check," he said.

Leaving Cedars to his update, I sat down next to Miranda. "You okay?" I asked quietly.

"I should have let you handle Langston on your own."

"They're not zombies, Miranda."

"I know. But that whole scene was beyond creepy. It would make a really good opening to a movie."

Mimicking her, I laid my head on the back of my chair and stared at the ceiling. "Do we win in the end?"

"Only after we chop off all of the zombie's heads."

"With our nonexistent swords?"

"We find a collection in zomberina's room," she said dismissively.

"You mean Langston was a secret ninja?"

"Now you're catching on."

"She wasn't a very good ninja if she was the first one to get all zombiefied," I muttered.

"She was betrayed," Miranda protested.

"By who?"

"Her traitorous boyfriend."

"The one I kill?"

"Quite spectacularly, I might add."

"Wow, this is a good movie," I agreed.

"That's what I said," Miranda sighed, sinking deeper into her chair.

I turned my face towards her. "You know most of that stuff came from actual events in our lives."

She nodded knowingly. "We're the stuff of legends."

CHAPTER 15

EVERYTHING WAS READY FOR THE interrogation to begin. Olivia had tweaked and re-tweaked the inhibitor as necessary. No need to repeat what embarrassing moment had precipitated that, but I'll never look at Juarez the same. Wrangle was the one tapped to administer the inhibitor. He was a dang good shot, if I did say so myself. How he'd managed to develop that skill within the confines of the Colony boggled my mind. It was obvious Kenny's escapades had been about more than having a little delinquent fun. I should probably look deeper into that, now that I'd become a rogue myself. You never knew when a secret army would come in handy.

But regardless of what brought us to this moment, Lindsey was now subdued and wired for lie detection. When Juarez gave the go ahead, Cedars cleared the room, leaving only himself, Olivia and me. This was the first time I'd ever seen Lindsey up close. She had shoulder length brown hair and brown eyes that were cold. It was hard for me to picture her ever being someone important to Adam.

"Ready?" Cedars asked, pulling the mike into position when we nodded.

Olivia stationed herself under a large air filter on Cedars' left, and I stood on his right. He began the questioning with those required for calibration. They were the benign, what's your name, where do you live, and so on. When Cedars headed to the meatier questions, she readily answered. She even answered questions that were not asked. And some of her answers, they didn't trigger the lie detector, but they were not what I expected.

"Something's not right," I frowned. One look at their faces told me that I wasn't the only one who thought so.

"She's being very cooperative," Olivia said disapprovingly.

Cedars reached up and muted the mike. "What do you get from her?" he asked Olivia, though he'd asked twice already.

"Still the same. Malice, hate."

"You could just look at her eyes and see that," I said. "She's sitting on something."

"Waiting for the right time to spring it?" Cedars suggested.

"When she thinks it will hurt the most," Olivia added.

"She's waiting for me," I sighed.

Cedars slid the mike off and handed it to me.

"Hello, Lindsey," I said.

A slow smile spread across her face. "Macy Greer," she drawled as her eyes greedily searched the mirror. "We meet at last."

Strange that she should know me by the sound of my voice. "Been looking forward to it, have you?" I responded flippantly.

"Macy," Olivia hissed in warning.

Lindsey chuckled tolerantly. "There's that endearing sense of humor. You're going to need it in the days to come."

"Oh, really?" I droned. "Why is that?"

"At least try to be polite," Olivia muttered angrily.

"Come now, Macy," Lindsey continued. "I think we are beyond pretending ignorance."

"Why don't you just tell me the little tidbit your hiding," I said impatiently. Olivia could huff all she wanted, but polite and Lindsey didn't mix for me.

"Macy Greer," Lindsey continued as though I hadn't spoken. "So smart, so talented. So stupid," she snarled contemptuously.

"She really hates you," Olivia whispered, as if she were just now figuring that out.

Rolling my eyes at Olivia for stating the obvious, I asked Lindsey, "And why am I so stupid?"

"Because you, the hope for the future, haven't figured it out yet." She laid back in her chair, more at ease now that she felt in control of the conversation. "I've heard about you for so long.

How you were going to be exactly what the Organization needed. The key!" she shouted, using her finger to punctuate the air.

Olivia came and stood on my right side. "Try conciliatory," she said quietly.

I made a disgusted face at Olivia.

"Just try," she urged.

Fine. "I'm sorry," I said without a trace of regret, "that you were made to endure such nonsense about me." The look on Olivia's face at my less than authentic apology suddenly made the apology worth it. "I'm sure Adam—"

"Not Adam, you idiot," Lindsey snapped, jerking forward in her chair.

O-kay, not Adam. So who was talking to her about me? "Julia," I breathed. She had been the only one who knew of my genetic makeup.

"Oh, yes," she laughed softly. "You were her dream come to life. How she lived to see you join the Organization. Or did live."

Julia wasn't dead. I'd seen her, what…a day or so ago. A window did exist, but given the fact that Julia could just whisk herself away, it was a small one. Unless they injured her first.

Pulling the mike aside, I asked, "Was Julia's time travelling common knowledge?"

Cedars stared blankly at me.

"Julia can time travel?" Olivia asked.

"Um…yeah. I'm gathering that no one knew about it?"

"I don't think so," Cedars answered.

"Well, then I'd guess Julia's not dead. But there's no need to tell her that." Readjusting the mike, I focused on Lindsey again. "So, you betrayed the Organization because you resented Julia for recruiting me?"

"Oh no, you were always destined to come here." She spun the chair slowly around, winding the cords around her ankles. "One way or another."

She was talking out of both sides of her mouth. One minute she didn't want me here, and the next, she was fine with it. I looked at Olivia for help, but she shrugged her shoulders uncertainly.

Sifting through the conversation with Lindsey, I settled on the fact that she thought Julia was dead.

"Why do you believe Julia is dead?" I asked her.

She finished rewinding her chair, stopping when she faced the mirror. The smile she displayed was more melancholy than pleased. "That's what usually happens to turncoats. They get caught in their own crossfire. It's a shame really. All that genius snuffed out. I wonder if they'll even give her credit for it?"

"Credit for what?" Olivia and I asked together.

She tilted her head, the dreamlike state broken. "Don't you know?"

"She can't be talking about hybrids," Olivia said quietly.

I nodded in agreement. The whole world knew she was responsible for that.

Lindsey brought her hands up, steepling her fingers underneath her chin. "Is it possible that the very one sheltering the new era of humanity has no inkling what she holds inside? I'm starting to get the impression that you don't know the true mission of the Organization?"

"True mission," I mouthed silently to Olivia, but she looked just as surprised as me.

"Let me help you, just a little bit," she said, leaning forward and using her thumb and forefinger as a ruler. "What flows and never runs out of time?" She opened her arms as though she was presenting me with a gift. "A genius like you shouldn't have any trouble figuring that out."

I hated riddles. They weren't like puzzles where each piece had a defined meaning. In riddles, the meaning was hidden, intentionally. I glanced at Cedars and Olivia. Their faces were as clueless as mine.

Rolling my shoulders to ease the tension, I began to study Lindsey again. Maybe I'd been going about this the wrong way. I had to consider the fact that Lindsey wasn't dumb. Nobody at the Organization was dumb. I had been presuming that she was acting out of her hatred for me. That in turn had meant that every move she made was calculated to injure me in some way, to produce a desired reaction. But what if that wasn't what was motivating her?

Her response earlier when I had mentioned Adam…it was disdainful, as if Adam wasn't a factor. Olivia had already confirmed as much too. Her anger towards me seemed to be linked to Julia. But she had labeled Julia as a traitor. Since Lindsey considered bringing me here as fulfilling part of Julia's dream, I didn't think she meant Julia was a traitor to the Organization. No, it had something to do with the supposed true mission.

Lindsey's smile widened as the silence stretched on between us. She laid back in her chair, as if she had all the time in the world, like she was in total control. It was an illusion, not the recently acquired projecting kind, but an illusion just the same. I needed to rattle her, crack that calm exterior. I thought I knew how.

"What was it that made Adam dump you?" I asked suddenly.

Her eyes narrowed at my question, just the response I was hoping for.

"Was it the drab look you have? I do think he prefers blondes. Or was it your over the top dramatics?"

Outwardly, she bristled at my attack. The muscles on the side of her jaw stood out as she used them to clamp her mouth shut.

Olivia grabbed my arm. "What are you doing," she whispered furiously.

Not wanting to give Lindsey time to collect herself, I momentarily ignored Olivia and plowed on with Lindsey. "Or, maybe it was the way you constantly threw yourself at him."

"I did not throw myself at him," she snarled as her control slipped.

Covering the mike with my hand, I whispered to Olivia, "Fishing." Then I waggled my eyebrows at her.

"Be careful what you catch," she warned softly. "You won't be able to throw it back."

Wasn't planning on it. "You think Adam didn't talk to me about you?" I continued, making sure my voice expressed my astonishment.

"He wouldn't," she breathed through clenched teeth.

"Wouldn't what? Betray you? Did you think that after all of this was said and done that he was coming back to you?"

The look she gave me was murderous. Oh, that was exactly what she had been expecting. That's why Olivia couldn't detect anything, because she still believed Adam was hers. What possible motivation could Adam have for wanting to return to her?

As I watched her, she lifted her hands and smoothed back her hair. Her eyes revealed the calculations taking place in her brain. "Don't you want to know where Adam is?" she asked calmly.

"I already know," I said indifferently.

Her eyes darted around the mirror in a vain attempt to find mine. "That is impossible," she hissed.

I chuckled into the mike. "You're giving away your secrets, Lindsey." She obviously didn't know about the bond I shared with Adam.

She crossed her arms over her chest, her forehead creased in concentration. "If you knew where Adam was, you wouldn't be talking to me right now. You wouldn't be able to stop yourself from rescuing him or at least attempting a rescue." She paused, nodding to herself over the veracity of her argument. "No," she jeered. "You'll not be rescuing him any time soon. At least, not soon enough. You see, I've made sure that you'll never see Adam again."

"Wrong," I shot back without thinking. "I already have, and this is a waste of my time." She wasn't going to tell us anything useful. Reaching up, I started to undo the mike, but Cedars stayed my hand.

"You're lying," she screamed, a little bit on the hysterical side. "He'll never be your Adam again. I made sure he'll never hold you again."

I understood what she meant then. He would never be in human form again. Refusing the fear that rose within me, I turned to anger instead. "I think you forget one of my core traits," I said calmly, belying the depth of anger I felt. "I never lie."

Her eyes widened, and then she gave up all pretense of cooperating. "That's impossible!" she cried. Straining against the straps holding her in place, she broke one after another. When she was free, she assaulted the window between us. "You're lying!" she screamed as she pounded the glass with her fists.

The desperation that poured from her was truly vomit worthy. Tossing the mike to Cedars, I yanked the door open and exited the room. Lindsey's tirade followed me, echoing until the door closed. Turning my back to the wall, I leaned over and planted my hands on my knees. What she said...it couldn't be true. But I'd seen it already, hadn't I?

The door opened and closed. Olivia positioned herself against the wall next to me. "You okay?" she asked.

"Just give me a minute," I said through controlled breaths. "You understood what she meant?"

"That Adam is somehow confined to his leopard form? Yeah, I got that."

"Do you believe her?"

"I believe that we will get Adam back, and we will deal with whatever we have to in order to get our Adam back."

She had answered without hesitation, an indication of how much she believed her words. I closed my eyes, trying to absorb some of her confidence. She had to be right. Even if Adam was stuck in leopard form, we were an organization of geniuses. We would figure it out. We had to. Just the thought of Adam being confined to that form was almost more than I could bear.

"Macy!" Miranda shouted, rounding the corner and skidding to a stop in front of me. She grasped me by the shoulders and yanked me upright. "Don't you believe her, not for one second. You hear me? We will get Adam back, and he will be Adam. You have to believe that."

I nodded, breathing in the hope her words represented.

"She's right," Olivia said, gripping my forearm tightly, as if to communicate the strength of her belief. "We will get him back."

"We will get him back," I repeated.

"That's right," Miranda said, giving my shoulders a squeeze.

"All of him," I added.

"All of him," Olivia agreed.

The moment of fear passed, and I relaxed into the faith that replaced it. My breathing was returning to normal when Cedars stepped into the hallway. He came right to us and put his big arms around all three of us.

"We will get Adam back," he said, reiterating the end of our exchange.

I smiled and nodded at him. Smiled because I felt secure, supported. For once, Olivia had chosen not to argue with me and instead had my back. Just like family. You could argue and fight, but when it counted, when it mattered the most, it was all hands on deck.

"We're going to get him back," Cedars continued, "because you cannot expect me to handle all of you crazy women on my own."

"You forgot about Juarez," I reminded him.

"Please," he said, letting go of us and starting down the hallway. "He can barely handle Olivia."

Olivia made a face at Cedars' retreating form, but she didn't argue. How could she? What Cedars said was true. She was a minefield.

Miranda leaned against the wall next to me and watched Cedars go. It was still strange, seeing her so devoted to one guy. But there was no mistaking the look on her face.

"So, what's next on the list?" she asked when he disappeared from view.

"I wish I knew. Half the stuff on it appears to be written in invisible ink by someone other than me." I took a deep breath and exhaled it loudly. "Do you have any idea what she meant by all the hope for the future talk?" I asked Olivia.

She shook her head. "It sounded like she was insinuating that, whatever it was, it was inside you."

"Something other than the smart genes."

"That's the way I understood it," Olivia nodded. "I haven't finished sweeping Julia's office yet. There might be something there."

"I could help with that," Miranda offered.

"I could use it," Olivia agreed. "We could also turn Juarez loose on her computer files."

"In his spare time?" I asked skeptically.

She chuckled dryly. "I don't think so. I got the feeling that what she was talking about was big."

"Shouldn't that be smelled like it was big," Miranda joked.

Olivia and I stared blank faced at Miranda, who rolled her eyes at our lack of amusement.

"Anyway, we could start an analysis of my DNA. See what we can find," I suggested.

"That would take even longer," Olivia sighed. "But I'll start on it in my spare time."

"And the riddle?" I asked them.

"I wrote it down," Miranda said sheepishly.

Olivia shook her head. "The only thing flowing with no end in sight is my frustration at this whole mess."

I heard that. "This didn't go the way I was expecting. I thought she'd tell us who she was working with. Lay it all out for us."

"Yeah," Olivia nodded. "I did not expect her to tell us that she wasn't Millsap's contact." Frowning, she shook her head in visible frustration. "We didn't ask the right questions."

"Hard to do when you're missing information," I said ruefully.

"Maybe Langston was Millsap's source," Miranda suggested.

"Maybe," I agreed. "But she definitely knows what's happening to Adam."

"Which means she's working with whoever has him," Olivia concluded.

"She didn't know Biogen," Miranda said. "That doesn't necessarily disqualify Mallet. If he's associated like we think, he could be keeping it from her."

Reaching up, I pushed my hair behind my ears and tried to picture Mallet working with Lindsey. I didn't think it was a likely scenario. He wasn't interested in playing around with the shift. He wanted hybrids dead and gone.

"I don't think it's Julia," Olivia said thoughtfully. "Lindsey expected her to be history."

"But she labeled Julia a traitor," I objected. "And, I know that Julia knows where Adam is. Julia is involved somehow."

"Cedars told me that you said Julia was trying to help," Olivia argued.

That's what Julia had said. I hadn't verified if it was true or not yet. Pushing off the wall, I started down the hallway, headed back to the suite.

"So who was Lindsey reporting to?" Miranda called after me.

"I don't know yet," I answered without turning around. "But I'm going to," I muttered to myself.

CHAPTER 16

MIRANDA CAUGHT UP AND WALKED with me back to Adam's quarters. After everything that had transpired today, I felt like a wet noodle. The way we were splayed on the couch sort of confirmed it. Miranda wasn't even fully on the couch, sort of half on and half off with her butt suspended in the space between the couch and ottoman.

"Is that comfortable?" I asked doubtfully.

"You'll be amazed at the positions you find comfortable when you're pregnant."

"Doesn't look comfortable," I muttered.

She pulled herself onto the couch, propping her legs up on one end. "Better?"

"Much," I nodded.

"It seems like rescuing Adam is going to be the easiest part of all of this," she sighed.

"Yep. As long as they can nullify the stasis field."

"They'll do it," she said confidently.

"And, if I can repeat the performance."

"You'll do that too," she yawned.

Quiet descended for the next few minutes. So much so, that I thought Miranda had fallen asleep. Her question caught me totally by surprise.

"Macy, you believe in God, right?"

I popped an eye open and squinted at her. "Right," I said hesitantly.

"Well, I've been thinking a lot lately. About things you've said in the past, and my life in the past...and now."

We were seated directly opposite each other on the large sectional. I could clearly see her face as she struggled with the words. "Miranda, we've known each other for ten years. We're officially sisters. You can tell me anything."

"Do you believe in angels?"

I pushed myself to an upright position, mostly to stall for time. "You've seen an angel?" I asked carefully.

"No," she said quickly. "I've just been thinking about cosmic realities." She brought her hand up to gently caress her stomach.

Cosmic realities was it? Because dealing with the weird reality we now found ourselves in wasn't complicated enough.

"Now with the baby...Macy, I don't know what it will be like, what it will look like." She pressed her lips together, ashamed that she'd given voice to the thought.

Heaving a sigh of relief at the true nature of her concern, I leaned back into the couch. I mean, sure I believed in angels, good and bad, but I didn't know if I was qualified to advise her on the subject. Motherhood? Still not qualified, but at least it didn't involve the supernatural.

"Miranda, it will be your baby. It will be a combination of you and Cedars. You're going to love him or her no matter what."

"And nanobots and animal DNA," she added, bringing her other hand protectively to her stomach. "What if it's some kind of freakish looking thing?" she whispered.

"I don't think so," I disagreed. "The nanobots are already biochemically adapted to the baby via you and Cedars. The second generation Colony hybrids were okay. I had nanobots while just a zygote. So did you. I don't think the nanobots interfere with development so much as read the cellular programming and act as an aid."

"You really think so?" she asked all teary eyed.

"I haven't actually studied the nanobot technology, but from what Juarez said and my powers of observation, I do think so, yes. And anyway, every baby is a hybrid of mom and dad. If it does arrive as some kind of little beast, we'll say it takes after Cedars." I had mere seconds to protect myself from the pillow she hurled at me. "I've heard of throw blankets—"

"Watch it," she growled in warning.

I wasn't trying to be insensitive, but I chuckled despite myself.

She let out a long sigh. "I guess you're right. Even Jesus was a hybrid, albeit a supernatural one."

Pulling the pillow below my chin, I stared at her in confusion, but she wasn't looking at me.

"Or maybe he was a vampire with the drink my blood thing." She even had the nerve to say it using the Dracula voice. "You know that a recent study has shown that injecting old mice with the blood of younger mice actually stopped the aging process. Drinking the blood of an immortal being has to do better than that."

Startled by the turn in the conversation, a confused, "What?" came out of my mouth.

"You know, communion. This is my blood, drink my blood, eat my body. Oh, wait. I guess the eat my body part would mean sort of an animal type of thing. Werewolf, like me maybe?" She waggled her eyebrows at me.

I tossed the pillow aside. "Miranda—"

"Ooh," she said, snapping her fingers. "I guess coming back from the dead technically makes him a zombie. And a vampire. A double vampire," she said excitedly.

"Miranda!" I yelled. "Jesus is not a vampire!" Picking up the pillow again, I clutched it to my stomach. "Or a werewolf. Or a zombie," I said more calmly.

She let her hand drop to her lap and very dramatically rolled her eyes to me. "Well, he is a supernatural hybrid." Seeing the look on my face, she challenged, "Was his father an otherworldly being or not?"

I pressed my lips together as I considered the question. Assuming that God was from the planet Heaven would certainly make him otherworldly. Human mother...

Losing patience with me, she blurted out, "You can't play

stupid with me. A human mother plus a supernatural entity father equals supernatural human hybrid, and you know it."

"You've seen too many episodes of Ancient Aliens," I grumbled.

She smiled smugly as she crossed her arms over her chest. "And he did rise from the dead, like a vampire. And, also a zombie. If you believe the Bible?"

I stared at her face, the raised eyebrow and slight tilt of her head. Did I still believe in the Bible? Of course, I did. Didn't I? Hybridizing the human genome didn't take away the spirit and soul. I still had them. Did that mean animals had souls, too? I grimaced as I tried to recall the story of creation in Genesis, which I hadn't read in a very long while. Great. Another thing to add to the list of what I felt guilty about.

"I'm not even factoring in the whole Holy Ghost thing, either," she said, adding air quotes around Holy Ghost.

Vampires, werewolves and now ghosts? Oh. My. "And I suppose that his second coming will be definitive proof of extraterrestrial life?" I asked while frowning at her.

"Absolutely," she grinned.

Collapsing back on the couch, I propped my feet on the ottoman. "When did you become such an expert on the Bible anyway?" I complained.

"You've been away a lot," she snickered. "You know what happens when I'm left to my own devices."

That usually meant some ill-conceived paint color or being subjected to the latest diet trend. One time, I arrived back home to find kiwi all over the kitchen. Apparently, she had watched an infomercial on how good kiwi was for you. We had kiwi jelly, which she had made and was disgustingly sweet, kiwi smoothies, kiwi butter. Who the heck eats kiwi butter? But, I tolerated it until I had my first bite of salsa. She had thrown away the stuff that was supposed to be in the jar and replaced it with her own kiwi inspired concoction. It had barely touched my tongue when I spit it out, well before she had a chance to move out of the splash zone. Let's just say I drew the line there, and she has never crossed it since. You just didn't mess with a person's salsa.

But this…It was like some sort of Halloween countdown based on scripture. Never thought I'd view the Bible through that prism.

"And, anyway, I'm not an expert. More like an interested party. Especially now with Jamie and the baby. The baby is not going to be strictly human. We are not strictly human anymore. What kind of world are we constructing?"

I thought the better question was why were we constructing it at all? Who put us in charge? I was not qualified to lead this. Look at the mess we were in now.

"What if someone mixes vampire bat DNA or mosquito or another blood sucking specimen with human? What's not to say that doesn't trigger the creation of vampires? What if everything we've seen in the movies becomes reality?"

She had been doing some thinking. Thinking that I was way too tired to counter. But she might be on to something. The public, particularly young adult females, had an obsessive fascination with all creatures supernatural. Could we create the very thing that we, as a culture, had been imagining? It was a scary line of thought.

"I don't know, Miranda," I finally admitted. "But, I don't think Jesus is a vampire, werewolf or zombie. Regardless of the technical definitions. Hybrid, I'll give you."

"I didn't mean to rattle your faith," she apologized.

"You didn't rattle my faith. It's just a lot more difficult. Not to believe in God, but the bigness of it all. With this leap we just made with the nanobots and the one we are about to make medically…this is change the world type of stuff. If we unleash nanobots on the world that essentially wipe out disease, repair what used to be life threatening injuries…what does that mean for humanity?"

"You mean as far as immortality goes?" she asked

"Yeah. I mean, you could still be killed, but it changes things."

"That it does," she sighed.

"I feel like we've been here before."

"On the precipice of disaster?"

"The very edge."

"This time, I guess I can't say we're too young to decide the fate of the world."

"You think God felt this way when he was creating all this?" I asked.

"Nah. He obviously had some type of super computer that ran the necessary algorithms. He knew exactly what he was going to end up with."

"Where do we get one of those?"

"They don't exist on Earth."

"Dang it."

"Indeed."

The door chime sounded, effectively ending our conversation.

"It's Jamie," Miranda said.

I got up and opened the door. Cedars stood there with Margaret behind him. Behind her was the beloved food cart.

"Get out of the way, I mean, come in," I urged Cedars, stepping aside so he could pass. Greedily I rubbed my hands together in anticipation. "What you got for us?" I asked Margaret.

"Italian wedding soup, crusty bread and bread pudding."

Crusty bread and bread pudding?

"You're looking a little thin," she said, eyeing me up and down as she pushed the cart in.

"I don't think I've ever actually had Italian wedding soup," I said as I trailed her.

"You haven't?" she exclaimed. "Well, I hope you like it." She collected a bowl from a lower shelf on the cart and ladled soup into it. Reaching for a spoon, she handed them both to me.

I brought the bowl to my nose and sniffed. Normally, I wasn't much of a soup person, gumbo notwithstanding, but if it tasted as good as it smelled, liking it wasn't going to be an issue.

"I'd like to go over the plan," Cedars said as he handed Miranda a bowl of soup.

"Let's hear it," I agreed, reclaiming my former seat across from Miranda.

"We think we've figured out a way to nullify the stasis field." He rounded the couch carrying a bowl in one hand and a loaf of bread in the other and sat down next to Miranda. "Juarez is constructing the device now, but you'll have to be the one to engage it."

"What does that entail?" I asked while reaching for one of the ice teas on the tray that Margaret had placed on the ottoman.

"From what I understand, pushing a few buttons." He shoveled another spoonful into his mouth and followed with a hunk of bread. "Doable?" he asked around the mouthful.

I thought about it a minute. "I think I can do that. As long as there's not a time table I have to stick to."

"Not for starting the device. How long it will last?" He raised his shoulders as if to shrug, but held them there. "I don't know if they have any security measures to counteract what we're attempting. Or how Adam will respond." His shoulders dropped, and he looked straight at me. "Best to work quickly once the device is enacted."

"Work quick. Got it."

"If you guys don't need anything else, I'm needed elsewhere," Margaret cut in before the conversation resumed.

"I think we're good. I'm good," I said, looking to Cedars and Miranda.

"All good here," Miranda nodded.

"Refills are self-serve, as is dessert. I trust you know your way around a refill?" she asked, eyeing me in particular.

"What?" I said defensively.

"Don't worry," Miranda intervened. "We're experts."

"I thought so," she chuckled. "But someone needs reminding."

Oh, whatever. It wasn't like I was trying not to eat.

"Getting back to Adam," Cedars said when Margaret had cleared out. "Olivia thinks it would be better not to engage in any kind of attempt to switch forms until we have a better idea of what's going on. That being said, bringing Adam back as a leopard without knowing his mental state is dangerous. We'll need to bring him directly to a cell we're preparing now."

"Exchanging one cell for another? How is that better?" I demanded. Setting the bowl down on the ottoman, I stood and stalked away from them. Before I made it across the room, I knew he was right. The way Adam had growled at me when I inadvertently teleported to him hadn't been a friendly greeting. "Don't bother explaining," I said dejectedly while massaging my forehead. "I understand and agree."

"Good," Cedars said. "Because there really is no other way."

Miranda reached over and patted Cedars knee, causing him to smile gratefully at her. I took it to mean he didn't like what he was saying. About as much as I liked hearing it, I reckoned.

"When we're done here," Cedars continued. "I need you to become a teleporting expert, including being able to take someone with you."

"Sure," I agreed, despite all the objections screaming at me. No problem. I'd become a guru. Sleep was for sissies anyway. I picked up the bowl of soup I'd abandoned and started working on it again. "What happens after we get Adam back?"

"Then we concentrate on getting Adam back," Cedars said.

"Of course. I mean, what about finding out who Lindsey is connecting with. And Millsap, or the Julia factor. There's a lot of stuff we don't know."

"Macy, we have got to get our house in order first before we start conducting any more operations."

"I understand that, but—"

"Macy," Cedars said, absently pointing a hunk of bread at me. "This is a rescue operation only. You are not equipped for anything else."

I swiped the bread out of his hand and aimed it at him. "You do realize that is the same excuse Adam used. It didn't work for him, and it doesn't work for you. And, you sound a little bit like Olivia right now."

Miranda, who had remained quiet until now, cleared her throat. "Little bit," she nodded at Cedars' questioning look.

"I'm not trying to sound like anyone," he cried in frustration. "I just don't want to get Adam back only to have him kill me because something happened to you." Reaching over, he tore off another chunk of bread to replace the one I'd taken.

I could almost see the anger rising from him as he began tearing off smaller pieces of bread and plopping them into his mouth. Couldn't help but feel sorry for him. True, getting Adam back was his number one objective, but aside from wanting to rescue a friend, he wanted out of the role of leadership that had been forced upon him. Not sure he recognized what was motivating his anger, but I could totally identify with him. The freedom of being the boss was great. The responsibility that came with it was the problem.

The rest of the meal was finished in silence. While Cedars used the time to cool to a simmer, I focused my thoughts on how I was going to use this new teleporting ability to gather information. As I'd said, his opinion that I wasn't equipped for it didn't work for me, and if he didn't want to involve the Organization to find out what was going on, I'd do it on my own.

"Do you want any company?" Miranda asked as I exchanged my empty bowl of soup for a serving of bread pudding.

"For my Jedi training?"

"I don't remember Yoda ever teleporting."

"He should have. Then he could have gotten off of that swamp planet."

"Dagobah?"

"Dago don't go there. It's sweaty and stinky." I shuddered at the thought of the murky, slime filled water.

Miranda folded her arms and glared at me. "I repeat. Do you want any company?"

Deciphering the "I hope not" in her tone, I relented. "No. The less people the better."

"Then I'm taking a nap," she said through a yawn.

"Take another one for me," I kidded.

"Two naps. I like it," she said, punching the air with her fist as she walked past me on her way to the door. "Practice real hard now, ya hear?"

"As if there's any other way," I scoffed.

She gave a backwards wave of her hand as she walked out the door.

Wow. She really was tired. No dessert and no smoochie smoochie with Cedars. "Hey Cedars, how is impending parenthood treating you?"

"You want the whole week or just today?" he asked grumpily.

I chuckled to myself. Whether it was two months or nine, it was going to be a long pregnancy. "Tell me again how I get to the practice gym."

He rolled his eyes as he stood up. "I'll draw you a map." Bending over Adam's desk, he quickly sketched out the route.

"Easy enough," I said after looking it over. Leaving the map on the desk, I set the empty dessert plate in the tub meant for dirty dishes. "I'm now off for my afternoon dose of humiliation," I announced glumly.

"Whatever it takes to keep that head of yours from exploding," Cedars responded dryly.

Scowling at him, I snatched up the map and headed for the door. "Don't forget to clean up," I called over my shoulder. The growl of frustration he uttered made me smile.

The map he'd created worked like a charm, directing me to the gym without a single wrong turn. Olivia and Scout were already waiting for me when I arrived. They wasted no time in putting me through the paces, nor were they shy with the criticism. But I did learn. Well enough to satisfy even Olivia, though I now despised the saying, practice makes perfect.

With Olivia's seal of approval, the mission was a go. As soon as I was suited up—sadly, not in the previously outlined uniform that Miranda and I had designed—I would leave to rescue Adam. If everything went according to plan, the whole thing should only take a few minutes.

"You ready for this?" Miranda asked as she watched Juarez strap the stasis nullifier to my chest.

"Me? Born ready," I joked.

"What if there are people there?" she asked worriedly. "People with weapons?"

I waited until Juarez had walked off, then I pulled her further aside, positioning her directly in front of me. "Don't freak out. Watch quietly," I whispered. Then I disappeared.

During my practice session, teleporting was not the only thing I had mastered. Remembering what Juarez had said at the very beginning of this about me moving through time at different rates, I figured that if I moved faster than everyone else, even just a little, it would put me out of phase with their time, and they wouldn't be able to see me. Somehow, I was able to communicate this to my nanobots, and voila, I was the invisible woman.

"I don't get it. Where'd you go?" she said when I reappeared in front of her.

"Nowhere."

"But you weren't here."

"I was. You just couldn't see me."

Her eyebrows shot up.

"Yes," I answered quickly before she could say anything. "Want to try?"

Her face melted into a devious smile. I took that as a yes.

Taking hold of her arm, we disappeared. A few people glanced curiously at where we'd been, but most didn't care. Except for Kenny. Always Kenny. His eyes were narrowed, staring at the spot where we had been.

"Can they hear us?" Miranda asked.

"Kenny!" I yelled. "Guess not," I said after he didn't react.

Miranda turned sharply to face me. "You're not going to stick to the plan, are you?" she demanded.

"Yes I am," I argued. "I just have some additional—"

"Macy," Miranda groaned, covering her face with her hands.

"It'll be fine, Miranda. Everything else will be as planned."

"When has that ever happened?" she snapped and pulled free of my grasp.

She immediately reappeared in the room. I was only a split second behind her, but it didn't escape Kenny's notice. He quickly found his way to my side, looking back and forth between us with raised eyebrows.

"Can I help you?" I said gruffly.

"I wondered when you'd learn to do that. Keeping it secret?" he taunted, pitching his voice for only us to hear.

"Yes, as well as her other plans," Miranda snarled unhappily.

"Miranda," I warned, but it was too late. Kenny was already eyeing me with new found suspicion.

"What plans?" he asked.

"She plans to find out what's going on for herself," Miranda accused.

"What's going on?" Cedars said from behind me.

I prayed to God that Miranda could shield this from Cedars.

"We are discussing Macy taking me with her," Kenny spoke up, diverting Cedars attention from Miranda.

"You're reconsidering?" Cedars asked hopefully.

I wasn't, I thought angrily.

"I know you haven't been too keen on the idea, but I'd feel better if you didn't go alone. And having two of you doubles our chances of nullifying the stasis field."

Staring at me with those big hope filled eyes of his, how could I say no? "Sure."

"Thanks, Kenny," he said, clapping him on the back. "I think it's for the best." Then he wrapped his arm around Miranda and pulled her away.

"Thanks, Kenny," I mocked, earning me a glimpse of his cocky grin.

This was not what I had planned. Not that I intended to trash the original plan. I just had a few amendments. Getting Adam back hadn't changed. That was still my number one priority. But the other item on my agenda, the one that Miranda had nailed me for, was hunting. There were a couple of people I needed to talk to.

"It's time," I heard Cedars say.

Miranda approached me once more. Shaking her head in reluctant surrender, she wrapped me in a hug. "Take this," she said, pressing something into my stomach. "I had a feeling you'd put your own spin on the plan."

"Thanks, Mir," I murmured into her shoulder as I wrapped

my fingers around the mini tranq gun. Tucking it into my jacket pocket, I stepped away from her and offered my elbow to Kenny. "All aboard."

"You're not the only one who wants answers," he leaned in and whispered as he locked elbows with me.

Maybe not, and now, I wasn't the only one putting their life on the line to find them. "Ready?" I asked him.

"Ready."

"Brace yourself," I warned.

The next moment, we materialized in the back corner of the cell, a spot I'd never seen Adam in. I tensed, waiting for the energy sucking cold to hit, but there wasn't any. And Adam was nowhere in sight. Kenny and I exchanged worried looks as I let go of the deep breath I'd taken right before the leap. Moving to the edge of the cell, Kenny swung the door open and we exited.

"Do you smell him?" he asked.

"I did in the cell. It's fainter out here. But I'm not sure how good my tracking is in general."

"If you want to find Adam, you're going to have to do better than that."

"Well, you're coming, aren't you?" I said testily. His hesitation rang all kinds of bells. "Kenny, you are coming?" I asked again, but was met with his tight lipped face. Forcing him to a stop, I swung around to face him. "Why did you come?" I demanded.

"Langston," he sighed. "I saw her at the Colony before."

His confession surprised me so much that I nearly let go of him. "When?" I asked as I realigned our arms.

"Right before Crystal. When she was…"

"You think Crystal's death might have been a projection?"

"I'm hoping," he nodded.

"I won't be able to track Crystal at all. I don't know what she smells like."

He pulled a ribbon from his pocket. It was the one she always wore whenever she had a ponytail. He placed the ribbon beneath his nose and inhaled. Then he handed it to me.

After breathing it in, I pulled away in surprise. "It smells like ironed sheets," I laughed.

He smiled. "Crisp linen is what I call it."

Handing the ribbon back to Kenny, I gripped his shoulder with my free hand. "Let's find them both."

"It might help if you shift," he suggested. "With the tracking, I mean."

It did. Now, I had no problem tracking Adam across the lab and to the door.

"The door randomly opening is going to look suspicious to anyone who happens to be watching," Kenny said.

"True, but I'm not hanging around and waiting for someone to open it for me."

He pushed the door open. "After you," he said.

Taking the lead, I started down the hallway in the direction Adam's scent led us. "I don't like that they've moved him," I said nervously. "It indicates that either something's changed, or they've reached some milestone in their plan." My mind wouldn't let me forget what Lindsey had insinuated. I had to find him before any change became permanent.

"We're going to find him," Kenny said reassuringly.

We needed to find him faster. Before Garrison or Julia did something I'd make them regret. There was no saving Mallet. He was done as far as I was concerned. I wished I'd had more of a chance to identify Garrison's scent at the meeting. But without shifting, the number of men in the room had confused the scents. At least, for me.

"Were you able to identify Garrison's scent?" I asked Kenny.

"Never forget it."

"Well?" I demanded when he didn't elaborate.

"He smells creepy."

"Creepy? Could you be a little more specific?"

"No, really," he laughed when I elbowed him in the ribs. "You'll recognize it when you smell it. But make no mistake about it. That guy is dangerous."

Yeah, I knew he was, which was why it was so important to nail down whose side he was on.

"Wait," Kenny said, pulling on my elbow. "Do you hear that?"

Tilting my head sideways, I strained to pick up what Kenny was hearing. "The tapping?"

"It's walking," he said, craning his head around in search of the sound. "A woman."

"You can tell it's a woman?" I asked incredulously.

"I can tell it's a *woman*," he drawled, "by the sound of her walk. The gait is too light and short to be a man's. Unless she's like you. You walk like you're mad."

"I do not—" My words faltered as Kenny pulled us down behind a cart in the hallway. "I do not walk like I'm mad," I hissed in irritation.

"Clunker," he said dismissively, then shushed me.

Hey, that was my job. I was the shusher. And I didn't clunk. I walked with confidence. This little pitter patter sounded like someone entirely lacking confidence. Wait a minute. It was entirely too loud to belong to anyone other than a hybrid doing the same thing that we were. Not the hiding part, but the winking in between time thing. Suddenly, our hiding place did not feel so secure.

"Think this will work?" I whispered as I peered around the cart.

Kenny looked sideways at me and sighed.

Yeah, me neither. Then I spotted her, and all intentions of staying hidden vanished. I stood up or tried to, but Kenny yanked me back down.

"That's Julia," I whispered angrily.

"Who?"

"The one who started this whole hybrid mess," I whispered through clenched teeth.

Kenny didn't try to stop me when I stood this time.

Her attention was focused on the file she was reading, so she didn't immediately see me when I stepped into the center of the hallway, directly in her path.

"Interesting reading?"

She paused and looked up. "Macy," she said, her voice echoing the surprise on her face.

"Hello, Julia. You're looking remarkably well."

She barked a laugh as she closed the file and tucked it under her arm. "I was wondering if you would show up."

"Now you know," I said sarcastically.

Her eyes swept me up and down, lingering on the hybrid traits visible on my face. "I see Adam's had a hand in your conversion."

"Where have you taken Adam?"

"Taken?" Her eyes narrowed. "That would imply that you knew where he was."

She was a sharp old broad. I smiled tightly at her, but didn't confirm her conclusion.

"Who's your friend?" She shifted her gaze to Kenny, who I had dragged into the hallway with me. "He's not one of mine."

"None of your business. Where's Adam?" I growled low, unconsciously taking a step towards her.

"I wouldn't," she warned softly.

I caught myself before I responded instinctually. Threatening her was a worthless endeavor. She could disappear before I reached her, and I hadn't learned the magical trick of tailing someone through time. Not yet, anyway.

"I am going to get Adam out of here and fix whatever you've done to him."

"What I've done to him?" she repeated. "I think you're going to find that things are quite different than you suppose. As far as you finding him, I have no doubt that you are."

What was her game? She seemed unconcerned about Adam's status. It didn't jive with the woman I'd witnessed talking to Adam when she thought no one was watching. "Are you going to try and stop me?" I asked her.

"Oh no, my dear. I know that you are quite unstoppable." She reached inside her jacket and pulled out a small device. She spun it uncertainly in her hands a few times before tossing it to me. "You're going to need this sooner or later. You'd better hurry if you want to save Adam." Then she turned and started walking back down the hallway. "I'm rooting for you, Macy," she called without turning around.

Remembering the threat on her life, I called out to her. "Hey Julia, someone's planning on killing you."

She stopped abruptly and pivoted, fixing her stern gaze on me. "I'm curious to know, if you would be for or against that particular objective."

Returning her stare was easy. Answering the question was not. I shrugged my shoulders indifferently. "Haven't been convinced one way or the other."

She smiled sadly. "There's hope then." Turning on her heel, she resumed walking away from us.

"I do not understand that woman," I hissed after she'd turned the corner. "Why didn't she just tell me where Adam was?" Opening my clenched fist, I stared at the device she'd given me. "And what the heck is this thing?"

"Looks like a transmitter," Kenny said. Frowning in concentration, his eyes became unfocused. "It's not transmitting anything."

"What? You've got some kind of sonar going on? High def ultraviolet imaging? Ultra red—"

"Ultra red is not a thing," he said flatly. "Maybe it's a remote. On and off."

That would correlate with the one button it had. "She gave me the key to something?"

"Maybe you need it to rescue Adam."

"She said sooner or later. Recuing Adam is now."

"She wants you to see something for yourself, with your own eyes?" he guessed.

"Is that good or bad?"

"It could just mean you wouldn't believe it otherwise."

"That's what I thought, bad." I tucked the remote away in my pocket.

"Have you tried contacting Adam?" Kenny asked.

I hadn't. In fact, I hadn't even thought of it since we'd been here. The disappointment linked to our non linkage was too great, so I'd stopped trying days ago. Maybe it would be different now that I was so close to him.

Closing my eyes, I reached out to Adam. At first there was nothing, and then the roar started. Growling and snapping filled my mind, blinding me with the sound until I was sinking to the ground with my head grasped between my hands. This was not the Adam I knew.

Stinging suddenly erupted across my right cheek, and I blinked into Kenny's face. "You hit me!" I yelled at him while cradling my cheek in my hand.

"You were screaming," he shrugged.

Staggering to my feet, I pulled Kenny up with me. "Something's wrong," I choked out. "We have to find him now."

Kenny being better at tracking, I made him take the lead. I couldn't believe the number of doors this place had, most of which were locked. I moved us through the ones I could see on the other side of, but solid doors we had to wait for someone else to open. The last door we went through opened into a room with no other exits, except into the focal point which was a viewing area sort of like a baby nursery. Only, babies were not the displayed subject.

"That's a lot of leopards," Kenny whistled. "Can you tell which one is Adam?"

There had to be at least fifteen cats in there, all of them big and angry. I'd only seen Adam as a leopard in my dreams and once during my brief appearance in his prior cell. But these cats all looked alike to me.

"I have no clue which one is Adam," I admitted.

We stepped back out of reflex when one of the cats lunged at the window. It left a trail of saliva where its jaws had connected with the glass.

"I don't think it's a good idea to go in there," Kenny said.

Adam, I tried. *You have to let me know which one you are.*

"You're bruising my arm," Kenny said.

"Sorry," I whispered and loosened my grip. "I was trying to contact Adam. I guess I was bracing myself."

"Here's an idea. Let me hold you while you try." He repositioned us, standing behind me and wrapping his arms around my waist.

"Watch for any sign, okay?"

"I think they're the ones watching us."

"I noticed," I said, looking warily at the leopards. "And then there's the drool," I added, grimacing at the long streak still sliding down the glass.

"Let's hope no one else notices them watching," he said under his breath.

Right. Closing my eyes, I reached out to Adam again. *Adam?* The weight of the sound crashed against my mind. I felt Kenny's arms tighten around my waist as it overpowered me again. *Adam!* I yelled, determined to press through the noise. I opened my eyes just in time to watch the cat nearest the window fly at the glass.

"Is that him?" Kenny squeaked, dragging me backwards as the cat continued its assault.

"Let me go," I complained as I struggled to reach the glass.

He loosened his hold enough to let me approach the window. Placing both hands on the glass, I stared directly into the eyes of the aggressive leopard. *Adam?*

The cat stilled and returned my stare. *Go away.*

The anger and loathing behind his words sent a jolt through me. "It's him," I gasped as the connection broke.

"He does not seem in favor of us being here," Kenny said. "I know you're quick with the teleporting, but I don't think we are going to be able to do this without someone losing some blood."

I dug through my pocket for the tranquilizer gun Miranda had given me. Looking at it now, it didn't look big enough. Hopefully it packed a strong enough wallop to subdue Adam.

Holding the gun up for Kenny to see, I said, "I'll use this."

"This seems familiar," he replied coldly.

"I know," I sighed, freely acknowledging the scorn in his voice. He had a right to feel this way. He'd been on the receiving end more times than I could recall. "I didn't like it then either." One day, I was going to not have to shoot the people I cared about with tranquilizer guns.

"This isn't like before," he admitted grudgingly. Nudging my shoulder as I continued to stare at the gun in my hands, he said, "Using it gives us the best chance."

I knew the circumstances were different than before, just as much as I knew this was probably the only safe way to get Adam back to headquarters. But that didn't mean I liked it any better.

"I'll need you to be responsible for maintaining contact between us again."

"You'll only get one shot at this," Kenny said. "Make it count."

One shot? That's all I had anyway. Strengthening my grip on the gun, I knelt in front of the glass, bringing us level with Adam. "Kenny, Adam's not the same. He told me to go away."

"Yeah, I got that," he snorted. "Exhibit A." He pointed at the multiple saliva trails on the glass. Gripping me around the waist again, he rested his chin on my shoulder. "Once we go, Doc, it's all or nothing. You sure you want to do this?"

"Have you ever known me to be a quitter?" I scoffed at his remark.

"Can I get a, hell no," Kenny said, heartily mimicking a preacher's tone.

"That's disrespectful," I said, even as I laughed at him.

"You want respect?" he said. "Get us all back to headquarters safely. I'll give you all the respect you can handle."

I was so going to make him eat those words.

"Alrighty, let's do it then." Everything was going to be okay, I told myself. Funny how the meaning of okay kept migrating to ever looser definitions. Pretty soon, just alive would mean okay.

I relocated us directly behind Adam's backside and immediately hit him with the tranquilizer. His body bent in half as he whipped his head around. Kenny's sudden tug backwards was the only thing that allowed me to avoid Adam's snapping jaws.

"How is he seeing us?" Kenny snapped while quickly rolling us out of the way as Adam lunged.

"It's a bond thing, I guess."

Adam's front legs buckled, and he did a little dance in an effort to stay on his feet. The other cats, leery of his behavior, scattered to the corners of the room.

"The drugs are starting to work," Kenny said, his voice strained by the effort of avoiding Adam's attacks. "You ready?"

Blinking dazedly, I brought my hand up to wipe at the blood beginning to drip down my forehead. Kenny's last maneuver had slammed my head against the glass. "I don't know," I stuttered.

The smell of my blood enraged Adam. Gathering his feet underneath him, he leapt at us. Our backs were already against the wall. We had nowhere to go and no time to get there. I stared in disbelief as Adam's teeth filled my entire vision. Just when I thought it was over, that there would be no escape, Adam's head listed to one side. The weight of Adam's limp body crashing into me nearly knocked the wind out of me, but I had enough presence of mind to forcibly hold Adam's jaws shut. The tranquilizer, though strong enough to knock him off his feet, wasn't enough to stop him from trying to attack. Nor did it stop him from yelling, *Get out!* at me over and over again.

Hugging his head to me, I transported us all to the cell at headquarters. Reentry wasn't smooth this time. I accidentally placed us about a foot off the floor. The impact from our drop left us rolling in three different directions, which wasn't an entirely bad thing.

"Kenny," I yelled and reached out to him. He took my hand, and I moved us outside the cell, but once again, we appeared about a foot off the floor. I heard Kenny yelp when he hit.

"You have got to stop doing that," Kenny moaned, rubbing his newly bruised hip.

"Sorry," I said absently as I watched Adam struggle inside the cell. "I think it has to do with not being upright when I moved us. Something off in my aspect ratio."

"Something's off in my aspect," Kenny groaned, still rubbing his backside. "You okay?"

I wiped my sleeve across my forehead. The man I…*loved?*…just tried to kill me. Make this one more downgrade in the definition of okay. "Never better," I grumbled.

"He's not himself," Kenny said softly. "You know he would never—"

"Doesn't matter," I cut him off. Adam was safe for the time being. That's what mattered.

"Macy—"

"Kenny, don't." Right now was not the time to start focusing on how I felt. There were still things that needed doing. Thinking about how Adam wanted to take my face off wasn't going to get any of them done. "You ready to go back?"

Kenny massaged the back of his neck with one hand as he stood. Slowly, he let that hand drop to his side. "I think you'd have a better chance of saving Crystal if Scout went with you. With all the handholding," he shrugged. "I'm slowing you down."

The difficulty of the decision he was making was evident in the stiffness of his shoulder and the pain in his voice. He was right, of course. But I wasn't going to exclude him from searching for Crystal, not until he recognized the need for it.

"Scout knows her scent?"

"He does," he nodded strongly. "He's on his way."

Gathering my legs underneath me, I pushed to a stand. "You have a bond?" I asked.

"It was a stupid blood brother type thing we did a couple of years ago." He laughed dryly. "We didn't realize what we were doing."

Join the club. Closing the distance between us, I placed a hand on his shoulder and pulled him into a hug. "If she's there, we'll bring her back," I promised.

"You'd better," he whispered as he hugged me tightly.

I pulled away as Scout rounded the corner. He clapped Kenny on the back in a show of support and then reached for me. "We gotta move. They're suspicious."

"See ya soon," I nodded at Kenny.

CHAPTER 17

Leaving Kenny behind was both hard and a relief. I hadn't realized how much of a drain transporting him had been, not until I was doing it solo again. Unsure where to start, I brought Scout back to the room that had previously held Adam. It was now filled with naked and confused people rather than leopards. By the way the workers were searching through the crowd, the reason was obvious.

"They're looking for someone," Scout observed. "Adam?"

"That'd be my guess."

"It didn't take them long to miss him."

"A leopard suddenly disappearing might have been a small clue," I offered.

"Little one," he agreed with a smile. "I don't see Crystal."

"I don't see any teenagers at all." That didn't make them any less important, but I couldn't randomly transport people back that I didn't know. What if they were bad guys? "You know, as little as two weeks ago, me standing in front of a room watching people in their birthday suits would have seem farfetched."

Scout barked out a sympathetic laugh. Placing his hands on his hips, he said, "Where would you keep a bunch of shifty, hating you teenagers, if you were a stodgy government worker?"

My eyebrows rose in surprise. "I'm a little shocked to hear you classify your buddies as shifty. I'm not disagreeing, mind you, but I didn't expect to hear you say it." Especially since I was pretty sure he had been in on the shiftiness.

"We had a lot of time on our hands to learn. Trust me, they're shifty."

No trust necessary. I had witnessed it first hand, and Miranda had the pictures to prove it.

"As to your other question, clearly, I would tuck them somewhere out of the way, buried so deep they couldn't get on my stodgy nerves."

The answer hit us both at the same time. "Basement," we said in unison.

Scout turned and jogged to his end of the hallway. "Any idea what floor we're on?" he called.

"No," I answered as I left for the opposite end.

"I got more hallway and doors," he called out.

"I got stairs," I yelled after spotting the exit sign above the door. One nanosecond later, I gasped as Scout appeared at my elbow. One blink after that, and I was looking at him standing underneath the exit sign. "Show off," I mumbled.

He pushed the door open and leaned over the stairwell. "There should be an elevator nearby."

"No elevators," I said firmly.

"Why no elevators?" Scout asked as I appeared next to him.

The memory of my last elevator ride inside the mountain made me cringe. "Not really a fan of elevators. I'm actually considering abstaining from all forms of shafts and tunnels."

"There's a story there. I just know it," Scout said jokingly.

Boy was there ever. Mimicking Scout, I leaned over the rail and looked down. "That is a long way down."

"Let's ping pong it."

Pulling back, I stared at him in confusion. "Ping pong it?"

"Just watch." He leaned over the stairwell. Then he disappeared and reappeared about three floors down. "Very good, padawan," he teased when I appeared next to him.

Scout's method led us to the bottom of the stairs in a relatively short amount of time. The problem now was the blank cement walls facing us.

"Why is there no door?" Scout said as he turned in circles again. "There has to be a way out. Or in."

"There haven't been any doors for the last few floors," I commented. "You can't see through walls, can you?" I asked him.

"Nope. Well, I've never tried, but I'm assuming no."

I tried. "It's a no for me too."

"I can't see through them, but I can see them. Does this wall look funny to you?" Scout asked, his voice rising in alarm.

The wall he was pointing to had small ripples rolling across its surface. The movement became faster and faster until the whole wall was shimmering like the ocean at sunset. Backing up, I stepped onto the bottom stair.

"You do see that?" Scout asked again.

"I see it. Maybe you should come over here," I suggested.

The wall was completely transparent now, like a glass window. On the other side of the wall, the room extended downward, revealing an auditorium with a raised dais in the center.

"Sounds good to me," he agreed when another wall started rippling.

We watched silently as that wall went through the same process as the previous wall.

"Is that the president?" I asked.

"With secret service in tow," Scout nodded.

President O'Conner stepped through the newly transparent wall flanked by several men in black suits. They walked right in front of us and through the other transformed wall into the auditorium. With a quick look at each other, we rushed to step through after the president's men.

"So glad we didn't try to flash through to this side," I whispered while staring at the steel catwalk we were standing on. It had been completely invisible from the other side.

"That could have been really bad," Scout agreed. "A few inches in either direction and we would have been kissing the seats below."

There was a kiss I could do without. "Come on," I said, tugging Scout forward.

The president and his men had made it to the central dais when we stepped onto the platform. It was clear the president was waiting for someone, and by how uncomfortable he looked, I guessed he wasn't looking forward to the meeting. Or maybe he hated waiting. Nothing wrong with that.

As the minutes stretched on, I found myself fidgeting uncomfortably. Wait a minute. What was I waiting for? I could talk to the president right now. Sticking one little finger out, I touched his arm. "Mr. President," I said to his startled expression.

He looked quickly behind him, observing his men spinning wildly as they searched for him. Then he quirked an eyebrow at me. "A bit dramatic, don't you think?" he said without emotion.

"Oh, I don't know. Every girl has her moments."

He glanced at Scout, giving him the once over before returning his gaze to me. "Hybrid suits you," he said thoughtfully.

"Who are you waiting for?" I asked.

"Am I to understand that if I step back, free of your touch, I will return or reappear to them?" he asked, jerking his head to indicate his frantic agents.

"You would," I nodded.

"And you wouldn't try to stop me?"

"No."

He stared at me a moment longer, then took a breath and let it out slowly. "I'm waiting for General Garrison. He is going to present to me the latest test results on the hybrid inhibitor we've been working on."

"You're devising a way to block hybridization?"

"We are. As in the Organization and Garrison. You didn't know?"

No, I didn't know, I wanted to yell at him. But I'd save the yelling for Olivia. Olivia, who'd been working with Garrison all along, who'd repeatedly lied to me.

"Mr. President," I said calmly, trying to at least fake some sense of control. "Are you aware of Mallet and the DTP?"

He frowned, his eyebrows pulling low on his face. "It was my hope that you would become aware of Mallet."

"If you mean his mission to destroy hybrids, then I'm aware."

The door on the far side of the auditorium opened, admitting

Garrison. As he ascended the stairs to the platform, the president looked straight at me. The frown never left his face when he said, "Keep digging."

Abruptly, he stepped away from me and reappeared on the dais, motioning to his agents to be quiet and leaving me to wonder what he meant. Mallet was after more than just the death of hybrids? And why didn't he want Garrison to know that I was here?

"What's wrong?" Scout asked as I led us to the opposite side of the platform.

"I'm tired of all the lying and secrecy," I snapped at him.

"Who lied to you?"

"Olivia. She's been working with Garrison. She knew he wasn't dead."

"She probably believes she has a good reason for not telling you," he said placatingly.

Turning on Scout, I glowered at him for defending her.

"Look, she's a little nuts about the rules, but she's not inherently evil."

I wasn't convinced of that yet. There were times when she seemed okay, but then there were times like this.

"Let's find cover," I said, dismissing the subject for now.

"Gladly," he said. "I feel like a sitting duck."

We retraced our steps and settled on one of the mini platforms suspended from the steel framework. We were still close enough to hear the conversation, but far enough away to feel secure.

"Good morning," Garrison said, smiling broadly at the president.

"I hope that smile on your face means what I hope it means," the president said, grasping Garrison's extended hand.

"Indeed it does." He approached the computer bank, and several screens began to activate under his direction. "We've been able to completely nullify the hybrid DNA in one subject, and even better, we've successfully inoculated all the candidates."

"Scout, can you smell anything?"

He inhaled. "The president and his guys."

"What about Garrison?"

His eyes narrowed as he worked at obtaining the scent. "No," he said. "Not sure how that's possible."

Me either. Everyone had a scent, but somehow, he was masking his.

President O'Conner joined Garrison at the display screens. "They've shown no signs of hybridization?"

"None. The fetuses appear to be following a normal human development."

Fetuses?

Scout stiffened beside me. "Is he working with Millsap?" he whispered angrily.

I shrugged in response. "Maybe he took them like he took Adam."

"Are we ready to bring the Organization into this? Officially?" the president asked.

"Olivia is perfecting the dispersal method now. I don't know if the Organization is in any shape to handle this officially. I'll leave that up to her."

The core of anger solidified inside me. Olivia was making an end run around the Organization. Maybe she was doing it because she didn't trust me. Fine. But leaving out Cedars? And did Juarez know?

"I wouldn't count Dr. Greer out just yet," the president said.

Garrison took a few moments to laugh. "Julia told me that she's on the premises."

"How do you think that's going to end?" the president asked.

"With Greer? There is absolutely no way to tell."

The president looked around the room, like he was looking for me. "Well, I hope she realizes that we are doing this for the good of the country," he said.

"I'm not sure she'd see it that way," Garrison responded as he manipulated the screens to show warehouses filled with sedated hybrids. "As to the other matter, these are ready for the inhibitors right now. Mallet's waiting on you to give the word."

I had to use all my strength to physically hold Scout down

when the screen nearest us displayed the Colony hybrids strapped to gurneys. "They know we're here," I whispered furiously. "He's fishing, Scout."

"What if it was Adam?" he snarled at me.

"It was Adam," I snapped back, shaking him a little as I said it.

The strength left him as he collapsed onto the floor. "That," he said, indicating the monitor, "might not even be them. How can we trust anything we see?"

Lessening my grip on him, I looked at the screen again. "Does projection work on us when we are invisible?"

"I don't know. I never knew about projection until dealing with it at the Organization."

The scene displayed on the monitor didn't look fake. It looked very real, and we weren't going to save them by staying here.

"C'mon, let's get out of here." Taking Scout's hand, I pulled him along behind me. We followed the steel framework down and dropped the last few feet to the floor. From there, we wound our way through the seats and headed for the nearest door hidden from the view of the platform.

As soon as we exited, the unending white halls were back.

"We should make sure Juarez gives this place ears," Scout said.

Relief flooded through me at the normal tone in his voice. He had me worried there for a moment. Pointing to the giant B painted above the door opposite us, I said, "Hey look. We're in the basement."

Scout cut his eyes to me, but he didn't smile. The only thing that would help him now was finding them.

"Do you think they really have a catchall hybrid inhibitor?" he asked as we walked.

"I don't know. Olivia sure whipped up one for Lindsey pretty fast." Something had felt off about that, but I'd been too absorbed with everything else to pursue it.

"Would you do it? Go back to being human?"

Being strictly human again would mean losing the connection I had with Adam. That might be gone already anyway. But there were other benefits to being a hybrid. Substantial ones.

"I don't know," I said. "I'm kind of getting used to the whole hybrid thing." Pausing in the hallway, I asked, "Do you hear that?"

"Yeah. Sounds like the buzz of a crowd."

The set of double doors in front of us suddenly burst open. Multiple workers rushed out, right through us. Closing my eyes, I gritted my teeth until they were gone.

"I am never going to get used to that," I said in a rush, shaking my hands to get rid of the feeling.

"You will," Scout disagreed. He pointed to the door caught in the open position.

"By all means," I nodded.

"It's a control room," he said after he assessed the interior.

"Scout, look." I pointed to the monitor just below the ceiling. On screen was the room that held the Colony hybrids.

"Where is that?" he asked, moving closer to the screen.

I glanced down at the computer terminals where several workers were seated, but each one was focused on a different hybrid. Crystal. My breath hitched as I recognized her.

"They're not alone," Scout said, causing me to snap my eyes back to the big screen.

The man entering the room had his back to us. But his stride was wrong, cocky, not like a scientist. Anger spiked through me when Mallet turned to face the camera. He smiled and waved, like he knew he was being watched. But he didn't know we were here. Julia, nor the president would have told him. Sweeping my eyes over the technicians, not one of them was focused on the screen showing him.

Scout backed away from the monitors, growling low in his throat. "Who's he waving to?" he breathed, his voice a guttural mixture of growl and English.

I didn't know, but we needed to find out.

We watched in silence as Mallet approached the gurney where Crystal lay. My hands were fisted so hard at my side that my nails were digging into my palms.

"We have to do something," Scout growled in frustration as Crystal struggled against the restraints.

"It'll be over soon," Mallet told her. "Then you'll just be a normal run of the mill human. Just like the rest of us. If it was up to me, you know I'd kill all of you. But the president...well, he has certain sensibilities. I'm on thin ice as it is, so I'm humoring him. I have to make it look good though." He stood up from where he'd perched himself on her gurney. "You should count yourself lucky. The others will die a painful death in a day or so. Something went wrong, you see." He chuckled to himself. "Aerosol dispersals are always so tricky." Leaning over, he began to stroke Crystal's hair. "You, however, will have immediate relief."

Now. I had to do something now. Grabbing the next tech that walked by, I pulled her in front of the screen. It happened so fast she didn't even have a chance to scream. "Where is that?" I demanded.

"Who are you?" she stammered.

I took her chin in my hand, forcing her to look at the screen. "Where is that?" I repeated soft and low, letting the anger I was feeling creep into the demand.

"Test lab six. But you can't go there," she said to empty air.

"You got it?" I asked Scout as I hurried to join him studying the map.

"Here," he said. "According to this, it's all the way across the complex from here. We'll be too late if we walk."

"So, we'll teleport there."

He turned back to the monitor. "Teleporting to a place you haven't actually been is risky."

"But it can be done, right?" I stressed.

He looked steadily at me. "If one detail is off... I got lost for a week one time."

The implication being that I could become lost. Or worst case scenario, both of us. But whatever Mallet had planned was happening now. "I don't think we have a choice. Not if we want to save them."

He glanced back at the screen, then back at me. "I'm willing if you are," he said.

Seeing Crystal lying there helpless, trapped on the gurney, I nodded. "I'm willing."

"It's going to look strange when people start disappearing," he said.

"Yeah, well, I get strange looks all the time."

He snorted, breaking the tension that had developed. "There is a reason for that, you know?"

I knew.

Back to business again, he asked, "Do we wait until Mallet leaves?"

I started to nod, when I had a thought. "Why don't we just take him and dump him somewhere where he won't be in the way."

"That would be kidnapping," Scout said neutrally.

Having been hijacked twice already, I was familiar with the concept. "He's tried to kill me. More than once. He owes me."

I didn't wait for further comment. Focusing on the screen, I appeared behind Mallet. The sound he made when I wrapped my arms tightly around his midsection was insanely satisfying. Almost as much as the thought of the abandoned ammunitions plant in the middle of Nowheresville he was headed to.

We arrived in the room where President O'Conner had conducted the meeting, and I released him before he got a look at me. The meltdown that proceeded upon his realizing where he was left me grinning from ear to ear. When he reached inside his pocket and pulled out his phone, I only had a moment to react. Touching the tip of my finger to his phone, I caught it as it dropped.

"What!" he roared, turning in circles as he looked for his now missing phone. Another deeply satisfying moment.

Not wanting to delay any longer than I already had, I deposited the phone in a barrel of oil that was standing in the room. I stayed just long enough to make sure it didn't resurface, and then I rejoined Scout in the control room. Only, he wasn't there.

Checking the screen, I saw that he was already moving people out. Mallet's people were moving them too, out the door and down the hallway. It was now a race against time.

Concentrating on the screen and Scout leaning over the gurney, I made the leap. It took longer than I thought it should. I was starting to think I had gotten myself lost, when we materialized.

"What are we doing here?" I asked, startled by the Organization people surrounding me.

Scout raised an eyebrow at me. "Where did you come from?"

"Same place you did."

"How did you do that?"

"Make it here?" I asked. "I do not know. I was trying to join you in the lab." Grabbing the gurney to steady myself as the room spun, I took a deep breath.

"You need to let go, Mace," Miranda said, uncurling the fingers of one hand and pressing a cup into them.

As soon as I let go, the gurney was whisked away. I wasn't even sure who it was that we'd rescued. "They're moving them," I told Scout as I brought the other hand to the cup.

"I know. I barely got out before they flooded the room with aerosol." He leaned over pressing his hands into his thighs as he worked at returning his breathing to normal. "I thought I was toast. I've never held my breath so long."

"By my count, there were still four heading down the hallway." Lifting the cup to my lips, I drained the very bitter coffee from the mug. "Where to now?"

"No where!" Olivia yelled as she exploded into the room. "You are unbelievable! And you!" she yelled at Scout.

Miranda took the empty mug and pressed another cup into my hand. It was chicken noodle soup this time. "Drink it and ignore her," she smiled encouragingly.

"Done and done." Lifting the cup to my lips, I took a long swig, slurping the noodles just for the fun of it. Besides, it helped me not to deck Olivia.

"I got a look at the hallway," Scout said, ignoring Olivia as much as I was.

"Good enough." I handed the cup back to Miranda and reached for Scout.

"No you don't," I heard Olivia say, and then we three were standing in the hallway.

"Welcome to the team," I said without enthusiasm.

"This way," Scout said. Taking the lead, he led us down the hallway, presumably in pursuit of a scent he was familiar with.

"Wait," I called, stumbling as we crossed paths with the musty smell of blood and something else…danger? Garrison, I thought in sudden recognition. Spinning around, I asked, "Do you smell that?"

"I can't scent the way you can," Olivia said tightly.

There was no way she was missing this smell, I thought as I narrowed my eyes at her. It was more like it would mess up her plans for me to know that she was working with Garrison.

"We don't have time for this," Scout warned.

"I know," I growled in irritation. Going after Garrison or Olivia would have to wait. "Let's go," I nodded.

Scout picked up the pace, and we were soon standing outside the new holding cell.

"Don't go in!" I shouted, grabbing Scout's elbow. "Look at them." Through the small window on the outside, we viewed the four hybrids, no longer strapped to gurneys, but unmoving just the same.

"Stasis field?" Olivia guessed.

Like she didn't know. "Good thing we have a destasisfyer thingamajig," I said, lightly tapping my chest where it was strapped. I'd just about forgotten it was there. "So, here's the plan. I go in, activate it, and then you guys—Hey!"

Olivia ripped the device from my straps. "Why do you get to have all the fun?" she said angrily.

"Do you even know how to work it?" I snapped at her.

"Yes, I know," she said, even more angry than before. Then she disappeared, reappearing inside.

"Dang it," I growled softly while watching her struggle to activate the device. I'd have to confront her soon. Otherwise, it might be all over but the fighting.

"Think she needs help?" Scout asked when she still hadn't managed to activate the device.

I waited a moment longer, almost consenting, when she sat up. "Whew," I breathed in relief. "You know, Adam's cell was much smaller. The device might not work on such a large area." Tapping loudly on the glass, I called to Olivia. "Move it closer to you." I pointed at the device and then mimed hugging it to my chest.

A flash of understanding passed over her face, and she took the device with her as she maneuvered herself between two hybrids. Setting the device on the floor, she was gone in the next instant, reappearing almost instantaneously in the same exact spot.

"She's fast," Scout said in awe.

That she was. She had all four Colony hybrids safely within Organization headquarters in no time at all. Literally, no time. When she reappeared next, it was outside of the room next to me and Scout.

With her hands on her hips, she stared at me. It reminded me of the glare she used to give me when the Organization first kidnapped me.

"What?" I said mockingly to the look on her face.

"You're going after Garrison."

"Are the Colony hybrids secure?"

She nodded. "Miranda's handling them."

"And Adam?"

Her hands slipped from her hips. "That's where I was before you showed back up at headquarters. From the brief look I got at him…" She sighed. "It's going to be a long road, I think."

Yeah, that's what I thought, but in the meantime, I needed answers. Answers that might somehow help speed up his recovery and slow you down.

"Macy," Scout said, gently touching my arm. "I'm going back. I have friends back there that need my help."

"Absolutely," I nodded, turning to hug him. "Thanks for the help. Tell Kenny to take care of things."

He chuckled. "Kenny never needs telling." Then he was gone, leaving only Olivia to deal with.

"What do you want?" I asked rudely.

Her eyes narrowed in anger. "Not to join you," she retorted. "I only wanted to tell you a few things before you go charging in with guns all ablazing." She did an impression of what I guess she thought resembled a two gun wielding cowboy.

"Olivia, I haven't even got any guns with me." Something she should probably be grateful for right about now.

"You know what I mean," she snarled.

Whatever. I didn't have time to get into this with her right now, but later…later was a done deal. "Well, this has been fun," I said dismissively and made to brush past her.

"Julia's my mother," she blurted out.

That stopped me.

"And, I think Garrison is my father."

Oh, I nodded to myself in understanding as the pieces clicked. It was Julia on the phone with Garrison that night, and Garrison was who she had turned to for comfort. Slowly, I turned to face her.

"I think he may also be the donor for the base male DNA that was part of your creation," she said hesitantly.

My eyes widened a little at that bit of information.

"I still have a few more tests to run for confirmation…but it's looking that way."

"But that would mean…"

"Yeah," she smiled bitterly. "Half sisters. At least. I haven't done a mitochondrial study yet."

Left unsaid was that Julia might be mom? The hallway seemed to spin. Family was springing up at me from all directions, like at a shooting gallery. I cradled my hands in my face. Wait until Miranda heard this.

"I just wanted to make sure you knew before you confronted him and did something…rash."

"I'm not planning on killing anybody," I snapped.

"Unless circumstances, etc.," she challenged with raised eyebrows.

Circumstances. Man was I tired of being subjected to them.

"You know what? I'm done with circumstances. From now on," I said as I marched past Olivia, "things are going to go the way I want them to."

"I don't think it works like that," I heard her whisper softly as I left.

Yes it did, for no other reason than I said so. I was going to locate Garrison. I was going to get answers, and by God, I was going to figure this thing out. Well, either that, or I was going to create one heck of a mess trying. Who was I kidding, the mess was a given either way. Good thing I had boots on.

CHAPTER 18

WHAT WAS WITH ALL THIS "potential" family coming out of nowhere? I had all the family I needed already. Adding more crazy to the family tree was completely unnecessary.

Abruptly stopping my forward march, I placed my hands on either hip and forced myself to breathe. Why was I so upset? I squeezed my eyes shut, trying to manufacture a focus that I did not feel. The reality of a real blood linked family lurking around was terrifying. It was too much too fast.

I hadn't had a real family for so long, not since I was a kid and they fuzzily disappeared. That must have happened during a hibernation period. Garrison probably told them I died. Whatever the case, left on my own, my family had been my choice. There were no permanent ties, nothing I couldn't sever. It had just been Miranda and me. Then the Colony hybrids had wriggled their way in. Adam plowed his way in. Cedars just plain snuck in. And how could I exclude the cadets? Now this? Talk about family overload. And we hadn't even had our first holiday together yet.

Taking yet another deep breath, I allowed all the angst I was feeling to fade to the background. All these...*relationships*...could be ferreted out at some, hopefully far away, moment in time. Right now, I had to find my master manipulator father—man if that didn't chafe—and figure out what the heck he was up to.

Having somewhat dealt with the sour emotions churning in my gut, I turned my attention to the hunt. As always, the scents came alive, each one presenting a story. I liked this about the leopard DNA. A lot of things would be easier as humans if we all had this ability. For one thing, being lied to was just about impossible. Lies had a smell all their own, and it wasn't a good one.

Jogging through the complex in search of his trail, I slowed when I picked up his scent again. This time, I was able to digest the smell more slowly. It was a strange mixture of things, blood chief among them, but overriding everything was the scent of danger. Though I had ribbed Kenny for his description, it had been right on the money. Garrison's scent was creepy.

I wondered if creating fear in others was his talent. That would be a useful skill to have, prompting others to turn away in their pursuit of you. Lucky for me, I was too stubborn to listen. Or too stupid, as Olivia might say. I pulled up short, frowning at the thought. Nah, I shook my head to dispel the image. I had verifiable proof that I was smart.

The next corner I turned placed me in a hallway hosting a lunchroom. Cafeteria food never smelled so good. I looked woefully at the tray one man carried as he exited and walked past me. Spaghetti and meatballs. A little messy for eating at your desk in my estimation, but it wasn't my tie that would be dotted with tomato sauce.

My stomach grumbled loudly in protest as I turned from the café and continued down the hall. It wasn't too happy either with the multiple times I had to backtrack because I lost Garrison's scent among the hail of food assaulting my senses. It just wasn't possible to concentrate on both Garrison and hoagies or frito pies, or that delicious looking piece of chocolate cake that woman was carrying past me. What was wrong with these people? Didn't anyone actually eat in the cafeteria?

Grimacing as the pain in my stomach roared to life again, I stopped walking until it passed. All this smelling of food and not consuming any was working a number on me. I was shaking, and having visions of tackling the lady with the cake.

Pull it together, Greer, I ordered, promising my stomach that I'd eat later, right after I did what I came to do. I could have sworn it replied that it didn't eat words. Shaking my head in an effort to clear it, I started over again. This time with a laser like focus on his scent. I knew for certain I was on the right track when I realized I was gritting my teeth against the feeling of impending doom. With a sigh of relief, I moved quickly to put distance between the cafeteria and myself.

Sprinting after Garrison led me to a conjunction of hallways. I stepped into the small rotunda that connected them. Six hallways branched from it, just like spokes in a wheel. Just like my notes, but this one had two more arms.

The sound of heels clicking loudly on the floor behind me intruded on my inspection. They were much too loud, and I'd heard that particular staccato before. Squaring my shoulders, I turned around to face Julia.

Her approach slowed as she neared. "Macy," she nodded, like she expected to meet me here. "I see you've got Adam back where he belongs."

I didn't confirm it, just held her gaze as she studied me. She had the answers I needed. I was going to get them this time. "You were at the Colony the night Adam was taken."

Her face froze. She didn't think anyone knew about her presence there. "I intervened."

An explanation rather than an answer. That was good, but I didn't see how her intervention had helped Adam. "You're responsible for bringing him here?"

"What Millsap had planned was far worse," she said, slowly bringing her hand to her forehead. It shook as she massaged her temple.

"What is Millsap's part in all this?"

Her face went slack, as though she had been expecting the question but dreading it all the same. "He's my son," she said weakly.

I had not expected that answer. "Renard is Millsap's father?" I asked uncertainly.

She nodded. "I'm sorry for what he did to you. He was never quite...right."

"Lady, he is so far from right that there isn't a category for him." I sighed in disgust. Did she know it was one of my goals to kill him? Miranda, I thought suddenly. Did Millsap's condition apply to all hybrid children? "Hybrid children..." I left the thought unfinished.

"Not all hybrid children turn out like him," she said sadly. "You turned out quite well. And Olivia."

Yeah, no thanks to you. And Olivia's status had not yet been determined. "Pike?" I said as another piece fell into place. "He was Millsap's son?"

She nodded. "They didn't know, of course. Millsap was in no way capable of being a father." She shrugged defensively. "I did the best I could."

"Why were they so screwed up?" I asked, my voice tight with emotion.

She clasped her hands in front of her protectively. "I believe that mine and Renard's nanobots were too dissimilar. Back then, I didn't realize all the ramifications."

"That's why you had built in birth control added to the nanobots."

Her eyes widened. "Exactly."

Okay, not a controlled breeding thing like they were trying to do at the Colony.

"The manufacturing process was also changed, along with other material changes. I presume the problems have been surpassed, but testing that theory wasn't a priority."

After what she dealt with in Millsap, I could see why. But that meant Miranda's baby would be test subject number one. I could not describe the weight of sadness that settled on my heart. There was no way I was going to tell my best friend in the whole world that her baby might be anything less than perfect.

This was what the death of a hero felt like. Standing there, looking at this giant of a woman in the world of science and growing angrier by the second, it was hard to believe that I'd ever looked up to her. All I wanted to do in this moment was attack her, and she unequivocally deserved it. Oh, I know she said that Renard was to blame for a large part of it, but that didn't excuse her. She was there. She could have done something, anything. All of this could have been done so differently. The effect on the world could have been amazing. But after her handling, it was one bonafide pile of crap. That I now had to clean up. By order of the president!

"This wasn't how I planned everything," she said defensively. "I'm not reading your thoughts," she added quickly. "But I know what I would think if our roles were reversed. It's a mess. I know."

Breathing in, I exhaled slowly. If there was anything these last couple of weeks had taught me, it was how life had a way of doing the opposite of what you had planned or hadn't even imagined. "How did everything get this messed up?" I asked.

"I trusted people I shouldn't have." She shrugged. "Loved people I shouldn't have. The choices I've made were the best that I could make at the time. I can't account for what I didn't know."

Scrubbing my hands across my face couldn't erase the fact that she sounded like me. Or rather, if what Olivia had intimated turned out to be true, I sounded like her. One big messed up family.

"What do you know about Mallet?"

The features on her face sharpened, filling her eyes with anger. "He is a traitor," she spat, then gasped in pain as she stumbled forward a few paces. "I'm alright," she said, putting her hands up to ward me off.

What was wrong with her? I stepped back in confusion while she collected herself. "You told Adam that you were trying to help. You asked him to help clear your name."

She looked at me blankly.

"I was there."

"I see," she drawled.

Suddenly, I was reduced to a specimen. I smiled at her tolerantly. It was, after all, how I used to look at the Colony hybrids.

"There have been some marvelous advances in nano to nano technology," she said to herself. "Not all of my...*associates* have anticipated such progress."

"But you did," I said, suspicious of the sudden gleam in her eyes.

"Yes," she smiled. "I am absolutely counting on it. As I am you."

"Yeah, about that. Is there an alternate mission for the Organization? Something about the future of mankind?"

"The Organization has only ever had one mission," she stated firmly, but hope danced in her eyes in opposition to the contradiction her words implied.

"The advancement of genetic engineering?"

She nodded, her stare bearing an intensity that made me believe there was more to it.

"Lindsey asked me a question. What always flows and never runs out of time?"

Puckering her lips, she considered it. "That is an accurate representation. Here's another. What has time as its source?"

Seriously?

"Macy, I can't tell you everything," she said in frustration. "I mean I literally cannot tell you, but I've done my best to give you the skills you need to figure it out."

Couldn't tell me? "Why can't you tell me?"

"I literally cannot tell you," she said again.

I repeated her words silently. "You are prevented from telling me," I said slowly.

"Yes," she answered.

"Physically prevented?"

Unable to speak, she nodded.

The control chip, like Langston. "So, who's doing all this microchipping?" I asked.

She smiled at me.

Right. A super-secret group I knew nothing about. "What you gave me earlier? It looks like a remote."

She frowned at me as she tried to speak several times but couldn't get the words out. Shrugging helplessly, she dropped her hands to her side. "Follow your instincts, Macy. That's all you need to do. It's all you've ever needed to do. But, be careful. It is true what they say about power and responsibility. I've learned that the really hard way." Then she disappeared.

Follow my instincts. Great. That's how I got dragged into this mess to begin with.

Reaching inside my pocket, I pulled out the device and stared at it. Did I trust Julia? I replayed the monologue Julia had delivered to Adam. There had been no mistaking her sincerity at the time. I didn't doubt it now either. She was trying to help. I guess having a control device implanted in your brain would limit the amount or kind of help you could give. Perhaps my hero hadn't died after all, just been knocked down a peg or two to mere human, or in our case, hybrid.

I rolled the device over in my hand. "Are you help?" I asked it. Help didn't usually come with a warning, did it? And the ever important question, did I trust myself enough to keep following my instincts? Well, I was still alive and more super than ever. Snorting at myself, I tucked the device back into the pocket. Even if that wasn't perfectly true, I was going to keep moving anyway. Starting with finding Garrison.

As I resumed the search for Garrison, I examined what little I knew about him. He was the one responsible for introducing me to this new world of hybrids. And the explosion at the agency? That had been the Consortium's attempt to eliminate him. Then he popped up at the meeting with the president, and bingo, I'm fingered for the big reveal. And again, working with the president…on hybrids and fetuses…to what end? If he was saving them, great. If not, then we had a problem.

It took me a second to realize I recognized an image on a wall I'd just passed. Slowing to a halt, I backpedaled to stand in front of it. It was a replica of the symbol engraved into the floor of Organization headquarters. That couldn't be coincidence.

The panel it was attached to looked like any other section of the wall. There were no visible points of entry. No handles or keypads. Pushing against it didn't accomplish anything either. Remembering the remote that Julia had given me, I pulled it from my pocket and aimed it at the emblem.

"All aboard the crazy train," I mumbled and pushed the button with one eye closed.

The design began folding in on itself, winding away until there was an opening big enough to enter. With a sigh and shake of my head, I stepped through, not bothering to turn around when it closed behind me.

The room I now stood in was huge, as tall as it was wide. Row by row, lights turned on, but they were soft, dark even. Immediately, my eyes were drawn to the far wall. Glowing a soft blue, it was the only area with any color, and I really hoped it wasn't what it looked like from this distance.

Racing toward the wall, I weaved around the grid like lab tables until I stood in front of it. My mind could scarcely take it in. To my horror, my initial sight had been correct. It was an aquarium of fetuses. Simulated wombs floated loosely in fluid filled enclosures. It looked like the fish section of a pet store.

Leaning away from the glass, I roughly counted the enclosures. There were at least a hundred here. Even if I could by some miracle get them all back to headquarters, I knew nothing about how they were being sustained, and we certainly weren't equipped to raise a hundred children at once. Not even Margaret was that good.

Gently, I reached out and touched the glass in front of me. How could they have done this? All these babies created for what? Some sick goal of achieving world dominance?

The feeling of dread crept up my spine a second before I turned around.

"Startling, when you see it for the first time, isn't it?" Garrison said as he walked into the room. "The miracle of creation. To be able to grow a human being outside of the womb? More miraculous still."

"I was thinking more like unnatural," I said as I reversed the shift. Didn't seem right to talk about being unnatural when I looked like a hybrid.

He smiled at me. "Did you know that all human babies develop exactly the same until twenty weeks of gestation?"

"Of course, I know that," I answered tightly.

He stopped when he reached me, taking a minute to let his gaze steal across the assembled fetuses. Using a knuckle, he tapped the glass in front of him. The baby nearest him jumped in response.

"These don't," he said proudly. "What would you estimate as the approximate gestation time?" He turned and looked at me. "Three weeks," he supplied, not waiting for my answer.

Narrowing my eyes, I looked at the enclosures again. As far as developmental markers went, they looked to be about sixteen weeks. I guess Pike had been telling the truth about the maturation rates.

"And," Garrison continued, "the rate of growth is increasing."

"It would have to."

"What do you mean?" He turned his back to the glass and leaned against it.

"The trials that Millsap conducted with maturation rates?"

He dipped his head and laughed. "Millsap never conducted any trials. Julia fed him that information to keep him distracted."

"And whose idea was it to let him go after me?"

The smile left his face. "That was unfortunate. He should never have been allowed to remain unsupervised. To tell you the truth, I expected him to be dead by now."

"He wouldn't be alive if he didn't have someone at the Organization feeding him information." I turned to look at him. "Any idea who that is?"

"My knowledge of the Organization exists in only the broadest sense. I'm not familiar with the day to day operations."

"Excluding working with Olivia, of course."

"Of course," he allowed. "She's been a big help with these children."

"What do you mean?"

"The creation of these children flows in the same vein you were created with. But the Consortium made a few minor adjustments. They included animal DNA from the start."

"These are the Consortium's creation?" I couldn't deny that I was relieved their creation hadn't been his doing.

He nodded. "As a matter of national security, I didn't feel it was safe to leave them with the Consortium. So, I brought them here, and since Julia spearheaded the original project, I've brought her in to oversee this one."

If he brought Julia in, then he meant to keep the genius aspect. "And you used the inhibitor you developed with Olivia to neutralize the animal DNA."

He looked at me, not necessarily with respect, but it was approval. "We did," he nodded again. "The workmanship was poor. Not surprising, given the source. We left the rest of the DNA alone. It has been tested, after all."

Great, so we were looking at a roomful of geniuses to be. "If the maturation trials were a farce, then why the exponential growth rate?"

"I never said they didn't happen."

I shook my head in disbelief. "You conducted the trials? Why?"

"To gain an understanding of humanity's bounds, Dr. Greer. The wonder of our genetic capabilities. Do you not reach for that yourself?"

"This is not the same as an adult consenting to experimentation."

"True." He folded his arms over his chest and looked at the ceiling. "Would you rather I had let the embryos perish? That's where they were headed. The hospital furnace. At least this way, they get a shot at life."

There was something so wrong about all of this. Let them die or give them an unorthodox, highly experimental chance at life? What kind of choices were those?

"That's a finely drawn ethical line you're walking," I grumbled.

"It is," he acknowledged. "I've never said the decisions I've made were easy."

Hearing his acknowledgement felt wrong too. For some reason, I didn't want to picture him as someone facing moral dilemmas. Or someone with any feelings at all.

"How many are there?"

He straightened from the wall and faced me. "This is only one of the rooms. We've got hundreds."

The count was staggering. A nation with thousands of geniuses at its disposal? What did the future hold?

"Have you marked them?"

"Can we tell them apart from other humans? Yes." He walked to one of the lab tables and pulled out a chair, indicating for me to sit. "Macy, tell me what you know of the Consortium."

I'd already paid my admission, might as well go along for the ride. Taking the seat he specified, I waited until he was seated to ask, "Are they the ones controlling Julia?"

He stared at me a moment, caught off guard by the question. "Not exactly."

"Are you the one controlling Julia?"

"No," he said, his frown deepening.

"Are you a good guy or bad guy?"

"Those are relative terms," he said, quickly growing frustrated by the turn in the conversation.

"No, they're not. There is good and there is evil. Which are you?"

"It's not as black and white as you would like to make it," he said angrily.

"Let me put it this way," I growled, leaning forward and gripping the table with both hands. "If you are going to save those babies...good guy. If you are going to enslave those babies for the *good* of the country...bad guy. Which. Are. You?"

"I am not a monster," he said, his voice shaking with anger. "I have just as much invested in the lives of those children as any other human being."

Not the short answer I was looking for, but an answer nonetheless. "What's with the feeling of doom surrounding you?" I complained, rolling my shoulders to try and dissipate the feeling.

The anger slowly left his eyes, and the corner of his mouth lifted in a half smile. "It's actually a cologne of sorts. A secretion of hormones that trigger the fight or flight response."

That was just cruel. Genius, but cruel. "You have the ability to control your scent?"

"And influence others reactions," he smiled.

That was nothing to smile about.

"It doesn't work on the individual who possesses a strong sense of self control. You wouldn't believe how rare that is."

Slight correction on my earlier assessment. Evil genius.

"What's to stop the Consortium from creating a new army? They've already tried it once." I waved my arm at the wall of babies.

"We are going to stop them. Since you haven't volunteered what you know," he said, pointedly looking me straight in the eye, "I'll tell you. The Consortium is not a group of people. It's a collection of nations that know that we never stopped the hybrid program. They have been intent on capturing the technology any way they can. Steal it, create it, it doesn't matter to them. The only thing that matters is getting there first."

"And the control chip?"

"As with any other group, there are splinters, factions more radical than the whole."

"They're after what Julia created in me?"

He nodded.

"Do you know what that is?"

This time he shook his head no. "Riddles, that's all I get."

"You've been with Julia for how many years, and she never mentioned the hope for mankind that resides in me?"

He grimaced in annoyance. "My relationship with Julia is complicated. In any case, we are not together, as you say."

I stopped drumming my fingers on the table when he looked angrily at them. "What are you going to do with them?"

"The children?"

I nodded.

"The United States has an obligation to see that they develop into productive citizens of this nation."

"They are not robots."

"No, but they are moldable, aren't they?" He arched an eyebrow at me in challenge.

I knew he was directly referencing my upbringing. He had

probably engineered the whole dang thing himself. But there was one thing he couldn't account for.

"I think that you have overlooked one very important thing. Life is unpredictable. All the programming and inhibitors in the world cannot account for free will and the brain's capacity to adjust."

The smugness left his face, and it wasn't with the same confidence that he said, "Well, we are going to do our best." He shrugged his shoulders and set back in his chair. "We don't have a choice. We have real enemies out there. Some of them wouldn't think twice about starting world war three if they thought they'd come out on top. Their desire isn't limited to the ability to create hybrids. They want to prevent us from achieving a dominant position with the technology we already have. They have great fear regarding a United States military equipped with hybrid abilities. Their fears are not unfounded, of course. It is agreed by all that transforming our military is necessary to retain our supremacy."

He leaned forward, his posture imploring me to understand. "The world's changing, Macy. You know that there are elements in this world that cannot be trusted with this technology."

Yeah, I knew it. Just wasn't sure if he was one of those. "What about Mallet and the DTP?"

He grimaced. "I am aware of Mallet and his operation, but it's not a top concern."

"Not a top concern?" I said accusingly. "He almost killed me. He is killing other hybrids. Look what he did to Adam. How is this not a top concern for you?"

"Despite your opinion of me, I am only one man, and the time I have to devote to avoiding certain calamites is limited," He barked, causing the feeling of dread to sweep over me.

"Cool it with the woo woo juice," I growled as the assault on my senses caused the shift to race through me.

His eyes widened, and he pressed his lips together as he sat back in his chair again.

My stomach rumbled angrily in protest of my attempt to

reverse the shift. In the end, I didn't have the reserves necessary for the task and gave up trying.

"I knew that you would retrieve Adam," he offered as an apology. "Did you ever doubt that?"

I lifted my eyes to him.

"No," he laughed. "I didn't think so. I also knew that you would find the others. And that you would ferret out Mallet. That's why I had you at the meeting."

I had figured as much, but man, he was placing an awful lot of trust in me. "I've given the information about DTP to Cedars with orders to put a stop to it."

He considered this a moment and then nodded. "You're in the better position to know if the Organization can handle it."

"Great, now if there's nothing further, I need to get back to Adam." I stood and started walking towards the door.

"Macy, I'm sorry, but there is more."

Pausing my exit, I hung my head and closed my eyes. "I cannot put anything else on my plate."

"Buy a bigger plate," he said harshly as he rounded the table to face me. "When I said we were going to stop the Consortium, I meant it. An opportunity has arisen, and I need you and whatever hybrids you choose to represent the US delegation in Geneva at a world conference on genetic advancement."

"Geneva, Switzerland?" Like I had time to go there.

"Key members of the Consortium's talent bank are going to be there."

"Why can't you go or have the president pick someone else?"

"I am not a one man show, Macy."

"Neither am I!" I yelled, venting my frustration on him.

"The president trusts you," he said quietly.

"Because you're making him," I objected.

"Because I trust you."

"Why?" I pleaded.

"I think you know why," he said barely above a whisper.

My shoulders sagged even further. Was he seriously trying

to play some parental card right now? "When did I become the national resource for all things hybrid?" I griped.

He smiled patiently at me.

Fine. "Talent that you want me to neutralize?"

"That is the plan, yes." He turned and started towards the nataquarium, as if the discussion was over.

"I'm not making any guarantees," I said to his back.

He stopped and folded his arms, his head moving side to side as he stared at the developing infants. "I'll get in touch with you about the details."

Great. Just freaking great. I needed a buffet table as my plate.

CHAPTER 19

TELEPORTED DIRECTLY TO THE KITCHEN of Organization headquarters, marched to the fridge, and yanked the door open. A can of soda was my medication of choice. Popping the top, I guzzled it, relishing the familiar burn as it ran down the back of my throat.

"You look like you could use something stronger."

Olivia stood with arms folded, one hip cocked to the side, and a sour look on her face. Eyeing her over the rim, I took another swig. Later had just arrived.

After burping disgustingly—hey guzzling equaled burping. It was a law of digestion—I consented to acknowledge her. "Oh, the traitorous half-sister or would full sister be more accurate?" Maybe acknowledge was too nice a word.

"I am no more a traitor than you are," she sniped.

After slamming the can of soda down on the countertop, I walked until my nose nearly touched hers. "If you ever use that inhibitor as a weapon on anyone I care about, I will hurt you. And I won't need any hybrid skills to do it."

She stepped back, stunned by the depth of my anger. "Yes, I worked with Garrison in the development of the inhibitor. But if you know that, then you know why."

"You should have been honest about it. Did you even tell Cedars? Juarez?"

She looked away guiltily. "Adam, I would have told. But Cedars is hamstringed by Miranda. You know how I feel about the state of leadership around here."

"So you decided to appoint yourself as leader?"

"How's it feel!" she yelled.

"This is about payback? Are you kidding me!"

"What else was I supposed to do!" she demanded. "Tell me, Macy, what?"

"You tell me something," I growled. "Did you know Adam was there?"

Her eyes became like saucers. "No!" she cried. Then her face crumpled. "How could you even ask me that?" she sputtered with tears spilling onto her cheeks.

"Oh, I don't know. How about because he was in the same facility that you've been sneaking around in!"

Cedars paused uncertainly in the doorway. "What's going on here?" he asked.

"Do you want to tell him?" I offered angrily.

"I'm sure you will do a fine job of that," she snapped as she turned on her heel and sped out of the kitchen.

Cedars stepped aside to let her leave, and then fixed his gaze on me. "Care to explain?"

Swiping my soda from the counter, I finished the can before answering. "She's been working with Garrison all along. Garrison, who intercepted thousands of embryos the Consortium created and then handed them over to Julia to manage. Using the inhibitor developed by none other than our own Olivia, Julia neutralized the animal DNA but left the genius DNA intact, which seems to be her trademark."

Cedars stared blankly at me. Taking a deep breath, he melted into one of the stools at the island. "Garrison's alive?"

"I tell you that one of our team members has been double dealing, and that's all you've got to say?"

He snorted quietly. "I knew she was up to something."

"I'm beginning to think she is never not up to something." I huffed down in the stool next to him. "Do you trust her? I mean really trust her."

He drummed his fingers on the counter as the seconds ticked by. "I used to. I know Miranda doesn't."

"All along," I started, crushing the empty can in my hand.

"She's been where Adam was all along." Uncurling my fingers, I released the can and pushed it away from me. "She says she didn't know he was there. It didn't smell like she was lying, but I just learned that Garrison, aka her father, can control his scent."

Cedars inhaled and exhaled slowly. "I suppose that's where her talent originated from."

"Did she tell Miranda that she is the latest new member of the family because Garrison was also the male DNA donation for us?"

His calm demeanor disintegrated into a stream of muttered obscenities.

Guess not.

"About this inhibitor," he said, after he'd calmed down a bit. "I am assuming it is like the one she constructed for Lindsey?"

"How should I know?" I exclaimed. "I'm well behind the curve on this one."

"I wondered how it came together so quickly. Olivia's done some amazing stuff." He shook his head, shifting his eyes to the counter. "I guess I just hoped that whatever she was up to wasn't to our detriment."

"She probably did help the babies," I admitted grudgingly. "Garrison didn't approve of the Consortium's workmanship."

"But she kept it from us. From me."

The hurt in his voice was undeniable. I propped my elbows on the counter and dropped my chin into my hands. "Yeah," I whispered sullenly.

"How long have you known that Garrison was alive?"

I lifted my chin from my hands. "Did I forget to tell you?" I cringed. "Uugh. I'm sorry, Cedars." Catching my head as it fell forward, I ran my fingers through my hair and tucked it behind my ears. "It wasn't intentional. Really," I added as he skewered me with his amber eyes.

"What else are you not remembering to tell me?" he asked skeptically.

"I'll let you know when I remember," I sneered, rolling my eyes at his attitude. It wasn't like I had deliberately excluded him from knowing. Miranda knew. I figured he would too.

In the interim silence that developed between us, Cedars got up and went to the pantry. He pulled out a bag of potato chips and began eating them in rapid succession. Crumbs flew everywhere. I would have laughed out loud if not for the look of concentration on his face.

"The inhibitor we used on Lindsey had to be injected. Do you know the dispersal method for the one Garrison talked about?"

I shook my head. "Aerosol, injection? I don't know. Where are the Colony hybrids?"

"I believe they're with Adam or somewhere close by."

Adam, another issue I needed to deal with. "Do you need anything?"

"Humph," he snorted, causing crumbs to cascade down his shirt and onto the floor.

Right. Nothing I can provide. Leaving Cedars to his moping, I teleported myself outside of Adam's cell. The gang must have been nearby because they weren't here. Adam was curled up against the far wall. He looked so peaceful and not like the angry cat I'd witnessed earlier. I walked forward and pressed my hands to the glass.

"Adam." There was no response from him. *Adam*, I tried again.

He hissed without opening his eyes, curling his lip to give me a clear view of his teeth.

I am not your enemy, I said angrily.

He opened both eyes and glared at me.

You think I'm your enemy? I stammered as the realization dawned on me. *Adam, I'm not. Don't you remember me? You made me—*"

Get out of my head! he screamed.

His command roared through my mind, causing me to grip my head with both hands. My heart pounded while I stood there helplessly staring at him. They had somehow made him think that I was his enemy. He would actually kill me if given the chance.

Gritting my teeth against the pain, I fired back at him. *I am not your enemy. You made me a hybrid. You rescued me from Millsap.* Nothing I was saying was registering with him. *Granny!*

I cried, grasping at anything I thought might trigger his memory. *Remember Granny?* I felt his mental stumble at the suggestion. *Think back, Adam,* I urged him. *What is the last thing you remember? Do you remember your mom and sisters? Before the Organization?* I had him until I mentioned the Organization. Anger flooded back in, obliterating the progress I had made. Deflated, I said, *Try to remember Granny, Adam. Just try.*

"They've overwritten his memories," Olivia said softly as she approached. "At least, I think that's what they've done. Either that or they have disrupted the connection between his memories and the conscious mind. Maybe both."

"Can you fix it?" I asked, still so shell shocked by Adam's response to me that I forgot how angry I was with her.

The pause before her answer said everything she didn't. "I'll tell you what you always tell me. I'll do my best."

"How did that feel?"

"Like poop on a stick."

I barked a laugh at her unexpected comment. I couldn't help it. It was so unlike her.

"Macy, about the inhibitor and Garrison...you are right. I should have told you. At the very least, I should have told Cedars. It's just that everything here is in such a state of chaos. And then figuring out who my parents are... I also might have been overreacting a little because of my recent experience." She wrapped her arms around herself protectively. "I'm sorry, Macy."

I wasn't. I meant what I said.

"And I really didn't know that Adam was there. I don't know how to feel about the fact that both Garrison and Julia knew, but didn't tell me. I could have brought him back just as easily. And sooner, before this." She gestured to Adam still motionless on the floor. "For some reason, they wanted you to do it."

Anger pooled in my gut as I focused on the new thought. Why hadn't they gotten him out immediately? "Maybe they wanted to use it to get me to perfect the time shifting?" I said halfheartedly.

"But risking Adam?"

"Garrison didn't seem to think it was much of a risk. He told

me flat out that he knew I'd find Adam." Julia on the other hand…
nope, she seemed pretty confident too.

Olivia shook her head. "That's not good enough. Not for me."

Me either. Neither was the way things currently stood with
us. "Olivia, we really can't afford any more secrets between us.
I've extended all the mercy I'm going to regarding your deceit."
Forcing myself to stop staring at Adam, I turned towards her and
waited until she met my eyes. "I'm not kidding."

"And I'm not a liar."

In an unmistakable show of doubt, both my eyebrows shot
skyward.

"I didn't lie," she asserted again. "I just didn't tell you what I
knew."

My face cratered as I shook my head. "Withholding, omission,
or outright lie, it's all the same to me." Having studied me so
much, she should have known that already. Maybe she thought
it was all an act. It wasn't. "If you expect any semblance of a
relationship to exist between us, it has to stop. I won't work with
people I can't trust."

She reached up and pinched the bridge of her nose. "You're
the new one around here," she griped. "How did I become the
untrustworthy one?"

"You want me to draw you a diagram?" I offered sarcastically.

"No," she hissed. Dropping her hand, she lifted her eyes to
me again. "I understand what you're saying. But you haven't been
entirely truthful either."

"What are you talking about?"

"The reporter? Going off on your own to find Garrison?"

"That wasn't done in an attempt to deceive anyone. I just
didn't want to deal with the crap I'd get from you about it. Miranda
knew. Kenny and Reynolds knew. So did Scout. You see, I work
with people I trust."

"Fine," she huffed. "I get it."

I really hoped she did because she was out of wiggle room with
me. On the lying and the jockeying for leadership. There had to

be some way to work together cohesively without all this turmoil and general anarchy.

"Don't you think between you, me, and Miranda, we ought to be able to stop the chaos around here?" I asked.

"You would think so," she replied dully. "I guess I just have to accept that things are changing—have changed." Linking her arms together, she turned her face to me. "I don't suppose you've got any plans of abandoning ship?"

I stared at her like she was wasting my time.

"I thought as much," she sighed and lowered her eyes to the floor. "As already demonstrated, things won't be the same as before, but I guess different doesn't necessarily mean it's a bad thing."

Hallelujah. Progress.

"Aah!" I gasped, my heart rate surging at the unexpected slap of Adam's paw against the glass.

"I wish he'd stop doing that," Olivia complained while massaging the back of her neck. "You wouldn't believe how much hate is oozing from him right now."

I bet I would. I could feel it like a stake in my heart.

For a moment, we watched quietly as Adam angrily stalked back and forth in front of the glass, giving one of us the stink eye the entire time. How that was even possible for a leopard to pull off was anyone's guess, but he managed it quite effectively. Clearly, he didn't care for all our talk about the Organization.

"Hmm," I hummed as something struck home. "He seems to hate anything related to the Organization."

"No seems about it. Just look at his eyes."

I didn't have to look at his eyes. The anger piercing my heart was more than enough evidence. It was tied to the primal nature of the leopard, instinctual almost. He couldn't reason against it while still a leopard, which they were forcing him to remain as. Because they controlled his ability to shift? They had control of his nanobots, I thought in sudden horrified understanding.

"Olivia, how did they gain access to his nanobots?"

The hand kneading her neck stilled.

"Please tell me that not just anyone can broadcast new programming to our nanobots."

"I'm not sure," she stammered. "Juarez is the code genius."

"Oh my God," I moaned. Swinging away from her, I pressed the heels of my palms into my eyes as I meandered in circles.

"Hold on," she said, brandishing a single finger at me.

Lowering my hands to my hips, I listened while she relayed the question to Juarez. The look of fear that rolled across her face telegraphed the answer.

"Dad gum it!" I belted at the new complication. Now we were sitting ducks in the deadly game of reprogram the nanos? When did the problems end with this bunch? And why hadn't Julia seen this coming? Probably because she had initially assumed that the Organization would be the only one who could do the programming. Whatever, it was my problem now.

"We need to call a meeting and get this handled immediately," I ordered. "Before someone else gets reprogrammed. Better yet, let's take care of that and start eliminating some of the chaos by getting everyone on the same page."

"There's a book?"

As long as you had your super spy decoder glasses handy. "Kitchen in ten?"

She hesitated, then shrugged off her objections. "It's as good a place as any."

Before my next heartbeat, she was gone. Skills. The woman had skills.

Stepping closer to the glass, I met Adam's predatory stare again. *I know you don't believe this right now, but I'm not your enemy. Olivia thinks that the connection to your memories has been disrupted somehow. I think it's because they have control of your nanobots. It may take us a while, but we'll figure it out. Just please try not to kill anyone in the meantime, okay?*

He engaged a new tactic. Turning from me, he paced to the center of the cell and laid down with his backside to me. It worked, if his goal was trying to tick me off.

Real mature, Adam.

Fisting my hands at my sides to keep from pounding uselessly on the glass, I turned and stomped down the hallway in search of the others. "Kenny! Reynolds! Anyone!" I yelled angrily. I wasn't angry at them, but it was either yell or start crying like a baby. Since I hated crying, yelling it was.

The door on my left popped open. "Looking for us?" Wrangle asked.

"I am. There's a meeting in the kitchen. Now."

"My favorite kind. Everyone's invited?"

"Everyone."

He paused in the doorway. "You okay?"

The look I gave him caused him to raise his eyebrows in fear which in turn washed away my anger. "Sorry, Wrangle. Just tell everybody, okay?"

"Will do," he saluted and disappeared quickly behind the door.

His quick retreat spared him from seeing the tears of frustration tracking down my cheeks. I'd said it was one or the other. Swiping at the offending tears, I thought, Great, that took care of the guest list. Now all I had to do was craft an agenda that didn't end in blows. On second thought, it might be easier if we just tied Miranda to a chair.

Choosing not to teleport to the kitchen until I had regained some measure of composure, I wandered aimlessly through the halls. Getting Adam back hadn't alleviated any of the stress. He was physically safe, which was a relief, but the new problems he came with weren't. The growing feeling that things were coming to a head, globally speaking, was only adding to the pressure I felt, like screws being tightened all around with a torque wrench.

All these people were depending on me, looking to me to do all these different things. How the heck did I end up in this position? Failure had never been such a costly proposition. I could really lose everything I loved. It was really worse than that. If I failed, the world could pay a price, not just me. Recalling Garrison's warning, images of nations torn by war and mutant hybrids running amuck filled my vision. It played like some futuristic science fiction movie. That's where we could end up. If I failed.

If, such a little word to hold the fate of the world in the balance. Placing a shaky hand on the wall, my steps slowed until I was standing still. Failure couldn't be an option. Not this time. For my family, for my friends. I could not allow the world to descend into an amorphic state of chaos.

"Failure is not an option," I repeated aloud to myself.

I would do everything in my power, to the best of my ability, until everything that needed doing was done. And if the world blew apart anyway, it wouldn't be my fault.

"Not an option," I said one last time and then teleported myself to the kitchen.

CHAPTER 20

"WHOA," I MOUTHED SILENTLY AT the sight of Margaret. Her version of chopping onions would make a ninja jealous. And not to be critical of the woman expertly wielding the foot long knife, but she was in serious need of some onion goggles. Regardless of how ridiculous they made one look, they would have been better than all those tears pooling under her chin into one continuous drip.

"You know, if your knife was sharper, you wouldn't be dealing with all the waterworks," I teased as I stepped free of the alcove where I had appeared.

"It's cathartic," she answered without missing a beat.

Noting the pile of peppers yet to be touched, I grabbed a cutting board from the rack. "How do you want the peppers?"

"Diced," she hiccupped, indicating the knife block with a wave of her blade.

"Seeds or no seeds?"

"The boys…like it…hot," she stammered.

"Viva la seeds," I proclaimed, brandishing the newly procured knife. Margaret didn't respond, and now that I was closer, I didn't like what I was seeing on her face. Between all the snuffling and the blotchiness, there was too much evidence to point to anything other than a full on sob fest not caused by the lack of a sharp knife. "Something bothering you?" I ventured carefully as I laid the cutting board on the counter.

She paused briefly in acknowledgment of the question, then resumed cutting with a vengeance. Poor onions.

"Adam doesn't know me," she finally managed to sputter.

Blinking away the tears of sympathy that sprang to my eyes, I finished dicing the pepper I was on and reached for another. "Me, neither."

"How could he not know me?" she demanded abruptly.

I wasn't sure she had heard my comment. Or cared, for that matter.

"Me!" she shouted.

Startled by her outburst, I froze. Her eyes were wild and angry, kind of like the reckless carving of the air she was doing with the knife. My eyebrows rose when she aimed the steel squarely at me.

"You," she hissed. "You, I could understand. But me?" She flipped the knife back towards her, inadvertently pricking her chest with the tip.

Apparently, she did hear me. I couldn't decide which was worse, her off the chain behavior or the fact that she thought Adam forgetting me was understandable. Was I that forgettable? Poof, just gone, and that was okay? Oh, I winced in sudden comprehension. I'd lost maybe a week at the most. She'd lost decades.

Finally realizing the existence of her self-imposed injury, she sighed in disgust as she tossed the knife into the sink and yanked a new one from the stand. Most of her anger now spent, the onions were spared having to bear the brunt of it. My ego, however, still stung from her slicing.

Forcing myself, I took a breath and let it out slowly. I supposed that due to her highly emotional state, which obviously came from her pain, and the fact that she had the ability to wield large knives as sabers, I was going to let the previous comment slide. Anyway, I would have been surprised if she actually meant to trivialize me. It was her pain talking. Maybe I could help with that.

"It's not a choice he made, Margaret," I said as I resumed cutting. "He didn't choose to forget you. He's had the connection to his memories snapped. Didn't Olivia tell you?"

"Oh, she mentioned some gobblety gook about neurons and such. But I don't understand how anyone could just not remember."

"It happens all the time. That's what amnesia is. But with

Adam, there was a deliberate interruption in the connection that allows him access to his past memory." Her prolonged silence prompted me to pause and look up at her. Doubt was written all over her face. "It's like a train track," I said in an attempt to explain further. "There are switches that allow a train to move from one set of tracks to another, right?"

She nodded slowly.

"If the switch was broken, the train would not be allowed onto the other track."

"It would have to keep going on the same track?"

"Right," I nodded. "Adam's memory is being kept on one track right now."

"Let me guess. Hating all things Organization?"

"Yeah," I sighed as I drug another pepper towards me.

"But Adam's still in there?" she asked hopefully.

"Somewhere." He had to be, otherwise…Well, I didn't want to think about otherwise.

"Macy," she whispered softly. "I'm sorry. I didn't mean to imply anything. It's just that you think a person would remember twenty something years."

"You'd think," I agreed. "Don't worry about it. There are probably a lot of people that would like to forget I existed."

She laughed dryly at my jab.

"What are we making?"

"Chili," she sniffed. "A big, steaming pot of chili. It's Adam's favorite."

Was Adam's favorite. I wondered if losing his memory affected what he liked for dinner. No way was I going to mention that possibility to her. She'd start crying all over again.

"I heard there's a meeting."

I looked up to see Kenny standing in the doorway. When the rest of the gang filtered in around him, the kitchen shrank before my eyes. "Uh, Margaret. I think we might need to relocate the meeting to a larger space."

"Use the dining room," she mumbled from behind the towel she was using to tidy her face.

"Dining room?"

"Not everyone has to be within three feet of their food at all times," Kenny heckled from the crowd.

"Yeah. Some of us like having our taste buds in their original form."

"Unseared?" Kenny asked, turning to Wrangle for confirmation.

"Completely sear free zone," he nodded. Sticking his tongue out, he wiggled it as proof. "Most civilized people prefer it."

"Do you see what I have to put up with?" I complained to Margaret.

"What you have to put up with?" Kenny muttered under his breath.

"It's over there," Margaret giggled while hefting the board piled high with chopped onions.

Over there. That was a bit vague. This kitchen was huge. There was a lot of over there. Seeing my hesitation, a path opened through the boys, revealing a set of doors that I never should have missed. Especially since they were huge and looked like they belonged in a castle. Weaving my way through, I gently pushed on one of the doors. "Wow," I breathed when it easily swung open. Like the door, the interior was fit for a king. I guess in our case a motley crew of hybrids would have to do.

"It used to be reserved for only the higher ups," Reynolds said as he appeared at my elbow, a stack of bowls pressed between his hands. "I guess they had to lower their standards once you showed up."

"Ha, ha," I scowled at him. Or more accurately, his back since he had already moved past me into the room. I had to sidestep Charlie and the container of flatware he carried, and he wasn't the only one carrying stuff in. Seemed to me like it would have been easier just to stock the buffets to begin with. Buffets, plural. Reynolds might have deemed my presence as a downgrade for the Organization, but it was a definite upgrade for me.

Just when I thought I couldn't be more impressed, the large curtain covering the opposite end of the room began to withdraw, revealing the majestic view of the surrounding mountains. Did I say upgrade? Leaving the buffets behind, I crossed the room to stand in front of the expanse. Why had I ever thought that Montana was flat? Did that mean there were volcanoes in Montana?

"Penny for your thoughts," Miranda whispered, gently nudging me with her shoulder.

"Not a chance, they are way more expensive than that."

She snorted quietly in response. "It's beautiful, isn't it?"

"I was just wondering if there were any volcanoes nearby."

"Have a hankering to blow something up? Ginormous pyroclastic eruption?" Using her hands and mouth, she simulated an explosion.

"Not presently, but the day's not over with yet. What do you think about crossbows?"

"God help me," she groaned, dropping her forehead to massage her temples.

"What? You don't like crossbows?"

"You just got claws. Can you not be happy with them for a while before we increase your arms?"

"Those are for close quarter fighting. I need something long range."

"Do you? Do you really?" she challenged while eyeing me sternly.

"Well, I might."

"Where is this coming from?"

"The room inspired me," I shrugged.

She crossed her arms and turned to stare out the window. "For today, let's say you don't need one and leave it at that."

"Fine," I muttered unhappily and mimicked her stance. Somebody was in a mood. But one day I was going to get a crossbow. And that leather uniform.

"Jamie told me about the Olivian half sisterhood. Is it really true?"

That explains the mood. Pulling my mouth to one side, I grunted softly. "I don't know. That's what she says, but I haven't seen or run any DNA on it."

"You can bet your bottom I'm going to. I'll work with Charlie on it. You would not believe how much he knows about this place after having been here such a short time."

"Oh, I believe it. Those kids are pretty amazing. When they're not being smart…rear ends."

"Just can't bring yourself to say it."

"Like," I continued, completely ignoring her dig. "How does Charlie know anything about testing DNA? Or how did Wrangle become a sharpshooter."

The smug look left her face. "You're right. They know things that I know they didn't learn at the Colony."

"So where did they learn them?"

"Makes you wonder, doesn't it?"

"They told me that Adam trained them. This may not even be the first time they've been here. How did that happen under the noses of the HCF?"

"I don't know," she shook her head.

"There are a lot of things we don't know. I didn't even know this room was here. Did you?"

"Yeah. Jamie used it to woo me, I think."

"Right," I moaned in total understanding. "Did you see all the buffets?"

"I did," she nodded, smiling sweetly at the memory she was reliving. "Wait until you see the cafeteria."

"There's a cafeteria?" I baulked in surprise.

"You think Margaret cooks for all three hundred something of us?"

I hadn't thought about it at all. "Who works there?"

"Let's just say it takes KP duty to a whole new level," she smirked. "Here." She indicated for me to take the piece of paper she held. "I've taken the liberty of drafting a list of things that need to be addressed."

Still frowning over the potential kitchen duty in my future, I took the paper and scanned it. "You are the best partner ever," I whispered and wrapped her in a grateful hug.

"No need to get all emotional about it. It's just a suggested agenda," she protested.

"I know. I'm just so grateful it's not another to do list."

Laughing, she wriggled out of my grasp and made her way to the table where Cedars, Juarez and Olivia were already seated. Watching them interact, it seemed like things had settled between them. Maybe this was one growing pain we could finally put behind us. Hopefully, it wasn't the calm before the storm. It would be nice to start working on a new chapter in the history of the Organization.

With that in mind, I read over the list again. Miranda had been pretty thorough, but she didn't know about the conversation with Garrison yet. Or the potential powder keg that existed with the unprotected nanobots. Speaking of powder kegs, I pressed a hand to my stomach that rumbled loudly at the first hints of chili wafting in. Probably shouldn't delay any longer. Once the food got here, I might lose them for a while.

Eager eyes met mine from every direction when I approached the table. The sight almost took my breath away. How could I fail with all of these smart, capable people working with me? Nope, if I had to save the world, this was the group to do it with.

"Hello, everyone," I said as they quieted. "Good to see all of you alive and without anything poking out of you."

A few of them chuckled in response. Kenny wasn't one of them.

"This has been a crazy last few days. I'm really not sure who knows what. So, I'm going to use the agenda that Miranda generously created for me as a guide. But I've been known to go off script."

More enthusiastic laughs sounded this time.

"As you all know, we have Adam back. Sort of. Adam's ability to access his memory has been impaired. By controlling his nanobots, his captors were able to direct what he thinks, his ability to shift. Almost succeeded in making it permanent. But we're not here to figure out Adam's problems. Not specifically anyway." Shifting my gaze to Juarez, I asked, "Any luck with finding a lock?"

He shook his head. "I've been looking since Olivia asked,

but I haven't found one yet. My thinking is to stop looking and construct my own."

"You're talking about locking down access to the nanobot programming?" Miranda asked. "That wasn't part of the original design?"

"Apparently not," I shook my head.

"You mean that we are all susceptible to what happened to Adam?" Reynolds concluded.

"Without a firewall? I think that's a good bet," I nodded.

"At any time, anyone can control us?" Reynolds persisted, his tone more angry now than surprised.

"Not anyone," Charlie corrected. "A, they'd have to know about the existence of nanobots and hybrids, and B, they'd have to know how to program them. That's a rare combination."

"Maybe, but someone obviously has it," Reynolds countered.

Despite Charlie's attempt at reassurance, the room stirred uneasily at Reynolds' assertion.

"Easy troops," I crooned. "That's why we're here. Juarez, how long do you think it will take to get a firewall up and running?"

His eyes glazed over as he concentrated on the calculations. "Time," he said softly, then jerked his head side to side and repeated, "Time," more loudly. "I don't mean to be cryptic, but it's not an easy task. I have to make sure every line of code is subjected to it for each hybrid core program. Initially, they'll be errors that have to be corrected, variations to account for…Time," he shrugged helplessly.

"I can help," Flash offered.

"Me, too," Charlie added.

"That works for me," Juarez nodded.

"Me too," I agreed. "The sooner the better."

"Can we make access individualized? Like a pin number?" Miranda suggested.

"Anything to make it more difficult to broadcast one signal that would catch all of us," I nodded approvingly.

"I can hide the access key in the code," Juarez said thoughtfully.

"But, it's going to take even more time to make each change individually."

"But worth it in the long run," Miranda stressed.

They both looked at me for a final decision.

"The process I observed with Adam involved injections of something. I'm not sure they were able to have a completely wireless transaction."

"We don't know that for sure," Cedars objected.

No. But if we had time, I wanted to use it to get this right. "Olivia?"

She took a minute, her forehead creasing as she deliberated. "I think it is safe to assume that they have not made that jump yet, at least not without a lot of prep work. If they had, they would never have needed to take him. Which would mean that anyone out of their reach wouldn't be in immediate danger."

Our eyes met as my thoughts slipped to the other three hundred or so members yet to return. We were going to have to scan them before they touched anything here. Actually, we should all be scanned.

"I know this will probably take even longer, but while we are adding the lock, we should also do a sweep to make sure we are not infected with homing beacons, control chips, etc."

"I'll see what I can do," Juarez nodded.

He'd get it done. Juarez was good like that. "Getting back to Adam…For now, you are to assume that he hates you and will kill you if given the chance. Please do not give him that chance. If you want to talk to him, stay outside the cell."

"Who'd be dumb enough to go in?" Wrangle wondered aloud.

"I do not want to find out," I said firmly. "So consider it an order."

"Ooh, an order," Van whistled.

"Van," I huffed as I squeezed my eyes shut tight. "If any of you disobey and end up dead, so help me, I will personally visit the underworld and drag your sorry butt back to the land of the living just so I can send you there myself. Is that clear?" Opening my eyes, I fixed them on him.

"Yes, ma'am," he gulped, somewhat cowed by my anger.

I was sorry for that, but I was not making a trip to Hades or Heaven or wherever he ended up. I simply did not have the time.

"Moving on," I said, punctuating each word as a sentence. "If you didn't know, Miranda and I are sisters, and it appears now that Olivia is another sister." I stopped and looked at Charlie. "Still nothing?"

"Not yet. Trust me, I'll let you know when I find something."

"Thanks," I nodded. "And I do trust you." Returning to the list, I found the point where I'd left off. "Also, President O'Conner is a hybrid."

"The President of the United States is a hybrid?" Margaret blurted from the doorway.

"He is. Also, Garrison is alive and well."

"Who's Garrison?" Wrangle asked.

"The Creeper," Kenny supplied, causing the Colony hybrids to moan in understanding.

The Creeper? I liked it. Couldn't wait to use it myself. "The Creeper." I paused to smile. "Is working for the president." I paused again. At least, that's what he wanted the president to think, but as far as I knew, the president could have been Garrison's pawn. Now that I was actually thinking about it, that seemed the more likely scenario.

"Macy?" Miranda prompted.

"Right. Working with the president and with Olivia and Julia. Together, they have developed an inhibitor similar to the one used on Lindsey, but in this case, it doesn't just block an ability, it reverses hybridization."

"Reverses?" Kenny asked. The suspicion and alarm riding his voice made me think before answering.

"That is my understanding," I nodded. "Olivia, do you have anything to add?"

"The inhibitor works to nullify the animal DNA developed by the Consortium," she said directly to Kenny. "Like an internal kill switch."

My eyes shot to Margaret, who gently shook her head. Okay,

maybe Olivia didn't know about Margaret's natural ability, but it was a very unusual coincidence nonetheless.

"Hold on a minute," Reynolds said. "The Consortium did not have Adam." He lifted his eyebrows, prompting me for a response.

"That is unclear. The Consortium is not Millsap. He was sort of like a subcontractor for them."

"So let me get this straight," he said with increasing hostility. "There's potentially another group or groups that have the ability to change us at will?"

"Not for long," I said while gritting my teeth and holding his eyes in spite of the anger raging in them. "We'll lock down access to the programming, and everything will be fine."

Taking the cue, he leaned away from the table and pressed his lips together until they formed a white slash across his face. He didn't like being patronized, but I didn't want the group riled up.

"That brings us to Julia," I said, dragging my eyes from Reynolds. "Contrary to what Lindsey said, she is alive and not a traitor. Maybe."

"Maybe she's alive, or maybe she's not a traitor?" Miranda asked.

"She's got a control chip in her brain."

Olivia's sudden intake of breath drew my attention.

"How do you know?" she all but whispered.

"She couldn't tell me outright, but she did tell me."

"Who is controlling her?" Miranda asked.

"Some splinter group of the Consortium." Yes, another group, I thought as I ignored Reynolds' growl of frustration. "Also, Millsap is Julia and Renard's son."

"What?" Cedars bellowed.

"From her own mouth," I affirmed. "She said that he is so... *unstable* because the nanobots were too dissimilar."

"What about my baby?" Miranda cried in alarm.

All heads whipped her direction. "Your baby?" several of the others asked in unison.

"Surprise," I hummed, bringing my hands up slowly and

awkwardly imitating jazz fingers. "Miranda and Cedars are expecting a little one."

Miranda's face caved in at the realization of what she'd done.

"A baby!" Margaret cheered, launching herself across the room so fast that I half wondered if she'd teleported. "This is so exciting," she chattered as she hugged Miranda.

Following Margaret's lead, everyone else was quick to offer their congratulations.

"You and Cedars have the same nanobots," I said after finding Miranda's eyes in the swarm. "Your baby will be fine."

It wasn't a lie. Julia had said as much. Since she was the expert, I was choosing to defer to her. Would Miranda see it that way if something went wrong? I didn't think so, but I couldn't tell her that this was going to be the first attempt at a normal hybrid baby and have her unknowingly communicate her fear about another Millsap to the nanobots. If they interpreted that fear as a desire, things could go really bad. Maybe she'd understand that. Maybe she'd be able to quash her fear, but I wasn't willing to take that risk. So for now, it was all on me.

"To prevent another accidental Millsap was the reason why Julia incorporated birth control into the nanobot programming," I said to the room as the melee settled. "Not as some sort of overreaching need for control."

"We are sterile!" Reynolds howled in disbelief.

Oh boy. Reynolds was just about over his limit for bad news today.

"It's completely reversible," I promised and pointed to Cedars as an example. "And, you're not sterile, just ah…"

"Lacking in ammunition?" Wrangle suggested with a wry smile.

"Something like that," I nodded. "The point is, to let you know it's there, and it wasn't done maliciously."

"You want to reverse something? Reverse this," Kenny growled.

"I'm not the one who's been reversing anything," I snapped.

"You don't think we should reverse this immediately?" Reynolds bawled, just about coming unglued by the mere insinuation.

"I didn't say that! We'll put it on the list, okay," I barked at him. Seriously. It wasn't my fault they were incapacitated. Why did they even care anyway? They were too young right now, and the last thing we needed was a sudden crop of babies running around.

"What about Olivia?" Margaret asked quietly.

I guess Olivia had told her who she suspected was her mother. And though Margaret didn't spell it out, the implication was clear, and understandable when reviewing Olivia's erratic behavior over the last week or so.

"Renard is not her father." I looked at Olivia who nodded at me. "Garrison is."

"Julia's her mother?" Flash guessed as he followed the conversation.

"If the mitochondrial analysis is correct," Olivia confirmed. Looking pointedly at Miranda, she added, "And not just mine."

Miranda's face looked like she'd just eaten a lemon. I had to turn away to keep from laughing. It wasn't funny, really it wasn't. And yet, it was hilarious.

"I can see it," Wrangle said. "Come on," he groaned to the many disbelieving faces aimed his way. "Olivia looks just like Macy, and they all act alike."

"We do not," we said in unison.

He threw his hands up in the air. "I rest my case," he proclaimed.

"Weak," I coughed into my hand, but not before Miranda threw a spoon at him. Uh oh. Somebody get the rope. "Anyway," I said, officially closing the subject for comment. "Julia said that Renard went bonkers. That when he learned the hybrids would one day be able to shift completely, he rejected hybridization altogether as something unnatural."

"We are going to be able to shift completely?" Charlie asked.

"That is the general thinking," I nodded.

"That is...that is...wow," he breathed.

Behind his clearly fascinated eyes, I could see the questions building. Charlie, like me, had an insatiable curiosity, one that

I could not spend time satisfying right now. So before he could start, I moved on.

"The Department of the President. A few of you may recognize their initials."

"DTP," Reynolds said. "And Gene Mallet?"

"Yep. This group is led by none other than Gene Mallet. Their mission is to destroy all hybrids everywhere. Our mission is to stop them. Cedars is heading up the counter operation." I turned to look at Cedars. "Not that it really matters, but Garrison agreed with my decision to have you eliminate them."

Cedars nodded, but his expression said he couldn't have cared less.

"As I was saying earlier, the Consortium is not Millsap. It is actually a group of nations that know the United States never stopped the hybrid program. They are hell bent on learning everything we know while, at the same time, stopping us from using it. Apparently, they'll latch on to any hope of getting ahead in respect to hybrid technology, even something as farfetched as Millsap's plan. Which actually…has turned out not to be so farfetched. You know about the plan Millsap had of using my DNA to make an army of hybrids and the super growth serum." I paused and frowned, primarily because I hadn't actually verified that my DNA wasn't used. I had just assumed it wasn't mine. Surely Garrison would have told me if my DNA was involved. No, I thought as my stomach sank. He wouldn't have.

"What Macy was going to say was that Garrison has secured thousands of fetuses created by the Consortium," Olivia supplied on my behalf.

"Thousands of fetuses?" Miranda asked.

"Yep," I smiled sadly at her.

"How is that possible?" she argued, incredulous at the very idea.

"He's got this weird nataquarium thing."

"Simulated wombs," Olivia interjected. "It took quite a bit more work to get it right than I would have thought. We lost some in the process."

Miranda's head turned in slow motion as she targeted Olivia. On her face, I could see that she had just now pieced together Olivia's back room dealings.

"The Consortium added animal DNA to the mix," I said, trying to draw Miranda's attention from Olivia. "It was a bad combination. Julia used the inhibitor Olivia developed to neutralize the animal DNA. To give them a fighting chance."

Miranda stared blankly at me. I knew she didn't want to believe what I was saying. With the difficulty I'd had swallowing it, I could relate. But now that I'd had more time to digest it, I didn't know if I'd have done any different than Olivia, except not to keep it a secret.

"So they're human?" Reynolds asked, breaking the connection between me and Miranda.

"They are," I nodded.

"What about geniuses?" Kenny asked.

"That too."

"Did they use your DNA?" Miranda asked.

I looked at Olivia who shrugged. "I don't know," I said. "Either way, they exist. I'm not really sure what the president intends on doing with them. Just know that they are out there."

"The hybrid population seems to be expanding by the minute," Wrangle said wistfully. "How do you know he got all of the embryos that were created?"

"I suppose I don't," I allowed.

"Then I guess it's a good thing that you're going to introduce hybrids to the world," Charlie said. "Because it seems impossible that this is going to remain a secret for much longer."

Yep. A good thing. Yay, me.

"About the Consortium," Cedars said, "it's a league of nations?"

"I don't know the exact structure, or the specific nations involved, but Garrison does. For obvious reasons, he is intent on destroying their talent pool, as he called it. There is a meeting in Geneva that he wants me, and whoever I choose, to attend and carry out that mission."

"You mean like assassins?" Miranda scowled.

"I am not an assassin," I stated firmly. "Garrison wants to use the inhibitor to neutralize them."

Tapping the table, my eyes drifted downward as I considered what to say next. I did not want to go to Geneva. And I didn't want to do this again, to spend my time shooting at people for whatever reason. I didn't even know the technology I'd be working with. Looking up, I locked eyes with Kenny. That was all the motivation I needed to decide there was no way I was going to go through this again. I might not be familiar with the tech, but Olivia was. President O'Conner had chosen me to handle this because he trusted me. We were about to see how far.

"Olivia, I'd like you to handle this whole operation. Pick your team, go to Geneva, do what needs doing. Are you up for that?"

She looked surprised that I'd chosen her. With our trust issues, that was not unexpected. But we had to start somewhere.

"I can do that," she answered slowly.

"Good."

Margaret appeared in the doorway. "Chili's ready. Want me to bring it in."

"I'll help," Wrangle answered for me.

How about that, I marveled upon seeing the red splotches peppering Wrangle's cheeks. Looked like Wrangle had himself a little crush. Totally understandable. The way Margaret kept plying me with food, I almost loved her myself.

While they brought the chili in, I pulled out the chair in front of me and sat down. Cedars' behavior worried me. He'd been unusually quiet during the meeting, and the little communication he did have had been disagreeable. It wasn't that he was mad. He just seemed distracted, like his thoughts were elsewhere. Maybe he was still smarting over the whole Olivia debacle.

"Hey, Cedars."

He finished his conversation with Juarez and turned to me.

"I think we should bring everyone back. Get the Organization back up to full strength."

"You mean start functioning again," he snorted.

"I do," I nodded.

"Are you ready to assume the bill for that?" he asked, eyebrows raised in challenge.

"Isn't that your job?" I asked uncertainly.

He added a smile to his challenge. "Adam's."

"Okay, look," I sighed. "Obviously, I'm not going to be heading up the day to day operations."

"Yeah," Miranda agreed. "Her job title should rest somewhere between Badass Project Director and Janitorial Services. You know, for all the crap—"

"Why don't we all take a stab at creating an organizational chart," I proposed, intentionally cutting her off.

"What about Adam?" Olivia asked.

What about Adam? "You'll work with him. I'll work with him." Raising my shoulders, I let them drop with a huff. "Beyond that, I don't know. But we can't keep standing still, or we're going to get run over." Heck, we might still get run over, but at least this way we'd be a harder target to hit. "I'm sure when he recovers he'll insert himself wherever he wants to." Noting that Wrangle and Margaret were finished, I said, "The rest will hold, let's eat."

As one by one they rose to fill their bowls, I remained seated. It just felt like I was leaving a lot of things out. The reporter, the medical advances I was supposed to be revealing. The big reveal itself. I hadn't addressed those at all. Then there were the riddles about something lurking inside of me. I needed a clearer picture of who was doing what.

After Margaret was kind enough to bring me a pen, I flipped Miranda's list over and began blocking it out. Starting with Juarez, I listed four items. He was to create a lock for the programming, a sweep for embedded devices, restoration of virility, and I remembered to add a shelf life for the nanobots. I also made a note to enlist Charlie and Flash and tore off the strip of paper.

For Olivia, I listed the Geneva trip and to get with Garrison for the details. Then added the sweep of Julia and Renard's offices. The only other thing on her list was Adam. No further description was needed there. I tore off her strip and slid both of theirs over to them.

Charlie's list was even shorter. Help Juarez and signal acquisition were all that was on it. The list I made for Cedars had the same amount of items, but was a great deal more complicated. Restore the Organization to operational capacity and destroy DTP were short titles that encompassed a great deal of work.

"What about me?" Miranda asked, setting her bowl down as she slid into the seat next to me.

"You're with me. We have to fix Adam, draft a speech to the nation about hybrids and medical advances, actually come up with afore mentioned medical advances, decide what to tell the reporter and make sure everybody else's lists get done."

"Perfect. We'll sleep in a month or two."

"You think we can get it all done that quick?" I asked jokingly.

"End of the year at the latest," she smiled. "But you forgot to add the most important thing."

Looking down at my list, I reread it. "Oh, and verify Julia as Mom," I said as I wrote.

"That's not it."

Frowning, I looked at the list again. "What am I missing?" I asked while pushing away from the table to join the chili line.

She took the time to swallow and then looked up at me. "You have to learn how to deliver a baby."

The world froze. Did she say deliver a baby? Did I agree to that? I don't remember agreeing to that. I tried to take a deep breath, but the oxygen had been sucked out of the room. "Could somebody turn the air down?" I said weakly as the room swam in and out of focus. Gripping the chair in front of me, I brought one hand to my now sweating forehead. She couldn't be serious. What in the world did I know about delivering babies?

"Kenny, catch her!" I heard, and then the world went sideways.

CHAPTER 21

I CAME TO STRETCHED OUT ON the dining room floor. A slight breeze whispered across my face from the napkin that Miranda absently twirled above me. Most of her attention was focused on the thick piece of cornbread she held in the other hand and the butter that slowly drizzled down her fingers because of it. I didn't know there was cornbread, I thought groggily. Then the reason I was prostrate surfaced, and my eyelids drifted south as the world threatened to go dark once more.

"Miranda," I exhaled. "I cannot be responsible for delivering your baby."

"Oh good, you're up."

"That's debatable," I objected. Opening one eye, I watched as she plopped the remainder of the cornbread into her mouth, then took the time to lick the butter from her fingers. All this, and I hadn't even had one bite yet. "Miranda—"

"It's childbirth, Macy," she sniped, whipping the napkin away to employ on her hands. "You're acting like it's some lifesaving surgery."

"It could be," I said hoarsely. "What if there are complications?"

"What am I going to do, Mace? Go to the hospital? How would I explain that?"

Her frustration was palpable. Oh, God, she was serious. Rolling onto my side, I levered myself into a sitting position. "Miranda, you know I love you—"

Olivia materialized next to me, cutting off what I was about to say. "Waxy gray is not your color," she whistled. Pulling out the nearest chair, she ordered me to sit. "Can somebody bring her some food?"

Yeah, food. We came here to eat, right? Wrong, I frowned at myself. We came here for the meeting, nothing but a blurred memory now. Using the table, I hauled myself into the chair and laid my pounding head on my hands.

"Did I unilaterally solve all the world's problems during the meeting?" I mumbled through my hands. Olivia's immediate peel of laughter quickly dashed any such hope. Dang it. Lifting my head slowly, I scanned the virtually empty dining room. "Where is everybody?"

"Starting on their respective lists," Olivia answered. "There's a lot to do."

You didn't have to tell me. I was on record as having complained about the size of the list since day one. "Hey, wait a minute," I said, abruptly puncturing my own thoughts. "Everybody already ate?" I'd seen these guys eat. The odds of leftovers were not in my favor.

"Relax, there's plenty," Miranda grumbled as she slid into the chair next to me. "Honestly, like you don't have more important things to worry about."

"Tell that to my stomach," I muttered. Now that I was thinking about eating, hunger pains gripped me without mercy. I couldn't remember the last time I had eaten. Oh from what heights had I fallen. Once upon a time, I used to eat regularly, with abandon even. Now it was disgusting nutrition bars—had I assigned that redesign to anyone?—and irregular intervals, and then puking up what I had managed to eat. My pants were hanging off my hips as it was. They might be down around my ankles if I missed any more meals, and wouldn't Miranda have a hay day with that. She'd probably be mad that she wasn't the only one naked from the waist down.

"Don't we have any doctors around here?" I complained as a result of the reminder. "Real doctors, not the PHD kind?"

Before anyone could answer, I closed my eyes and inhaled sharply.

"We've lost her," Miranda announced solemnly. "You won't get another sensible word out of her until she eats."

"Is that what it takes?" Olivia retorted.

Whatever. The only thing that mattered now was the chili headed my way, though at this point, I was so hungry that I would have eaten green peas if they put them in front of me.

"Yes!" I shouted and slapped the table with both hands as Olivia set the bowl in front of me. "Saved from green peas."

"And here I thought green peas were good for you," she chuckled.

I found her amusement mildly insulting. This saving the world stuff on a regular basis was seriously hunger inducing. Well…in spates. Sometimes it took away the urge to eat anything at all. But it always came painfully roaring back. I'd have to remember that in the future, to eat even when I didn't feel like it.

"Oh, the quagmire that is your mind," Miranda teased.

Quagmire? That about summed it up, though it was a little more settled now that I'd actually set people to work on the various tasks composing the quagmire.

"In answer to your question," Olivia started, "we've never needed that kind of doctor before. The nanobots pretty much take care of what we need medically. Therefore, there are none within the Organization's ranks."

It figured they wouldn't have any baby doctors on call. Couldn't the Organization just kidnap someone and force them to do it? My whole posture froze with the question I'd just asked myself. Since when did I think it was okay to kidnap someone and force them to do what I needed?

"Macy?" Miranda chirped.

Okay, maybe I couldn't outright kidnap someone, but wasn't there someone, anyone we could convince or bribe?

"Hello. Earth to Macy," Miranda sang.

I cut my eyes to her when she began snapping her fingers at me. She did know that I was not a baby doctor, right? "Miranda, I don't know squat about birthing no babies."

Her breath caught, and then she belted a laugh right in my

face. "You sounded just like Gone with the Wind. Should I slap you now? And duh, that's why I said you needed to learn how to do it."

Rolling my eyes at her total disregard for my sincerity, I focused my attention on eating…and murmuring in my head. There was a reason I wasn't an OB doc. All the blood and bodily fluids, and little naked people coming out of other naked people. Whoops, almost threw up in my mouth. Clenching my jaw, I forced myself to swallow. If she thought that I was going to suddenly morph into an obstetrician, she was out of her mind. The only tongs I wanted to use were for salad or turning things on the grill.

The smug look on her face told me that she thought she'd won the argument. But it wasn't over until she went into labor. I still had time. Though maybe not as much as I would have thought. How could she be showing already? Wasn't that sort of impossible?

"Now that that's settled," Olivia said wryly. "Macy, I would like to take Scout with me, if that's okay with you? Naturally, we won't leave until Juarez can install the firewall. And, I feel like he's already proven himself with the whole illegal rescue operation."

I see how it was. Me she viewed as a traitor for taking part in the "illegal" rescue operation while Scout was a hero. Talk about a double standard. But she was right about Scout's competence. And it was my intention to fold the Colony hybrids into the Organization anyway. The distance made me a little nervous, but that was a poor excuse to hold him back.

"Ask him," I finally said. "I'm okay with it if he is."

"Already did. He said I had to clear it with you first."

They were growing up, I thought as I nodded to myself. "Who else are you taking?"

"Camo. I think between the three of us, we can get the job done without too much effort."

"Camo's back?"

"Not yet, but I called him. He's game."

Camouflage and teleportation. The Consortium would never know what hit'em. No wonder General Hurser was so eager to have an army of hybrids at his disposal. Hmm. I'd have to keep an eye on him. That kind of power had a way of changing people.

"The targets that Garrison has singled out, are they naturally smart or artificially intelligent like us?" I asked.

"I don't think that's the right classification," she frowned. "We're not robots. Genetically enhanced, maybe? Anyway, that's the way the inhibitor works. It inhibits DNA that wasn't part of the original genome."

Swiveling to face her, I said, "It hasn't been with them since birth?"

"No."

Miranda and I exchanged confused looks.

"You mean, one day you could be dumb as a doorknob and smart the next?" Miranda scoffed.

"Not exactly. But the added DNA does allow your brain to make connections not previously attempted. Given time, overall intelligence increases."

Was she kidding me? "How could you possibly know which DNA to inhibit?"

"We know the sequences to look for," she shrugged.

We. Meaning Julia, of course. That woman was obsessed with intelligence.

"I'm really hoping the genius genes were hijacked from Julia and not a direct result of her work," Miranda said.

"That was the impression I got," Olivia answered.

"Do you believe her?"

"I have no reason to doubt her. She seemed pretty peeved by the whole situation."

"No reason but a control chip," I reminded her.

"Right."

"It seems to me," Miranda said, "that trying to block DNA that an individual has had access to, for however long, would do more than just inhibit them. That drastic of a change would be detrimental because essentially, you're causing a brain injury."

"I agree," I nodded. "It might be that black and white for

non-human DNA because it was never supposed to be there, but human?"

Olivia looked at me, then at Miranda before averting her eyes. "I don't know," she said reluctantly. "I understand how it works to stop animal DNA from being utilized, but I'm not sure about the brain. Brain chemistry is tricky."

"Will the effect be immediate?" Miranda persisted, jamming her spoon into her cobbler as she spoke.

There was cobbler?

"Don't know that either," Olivia sighed. "The brain is huge, reactionally speaking. For the animal DNA, the hybrid would go to access the shift, like they always had, and that in itself would activate the permanent lock down. But basing it on cognitive functions? How many thought paths could you take and arrive at the same conclusion? I am guessing it will be a slow downgrade, but that's all it is, a guess."

"Garrison sees it as an immediate measure," I said. "Does he know something you don't?"

"Doesn't he always," she scowled. "Julia and I were the main engineers for the inhibitor, but he had a hand in it too."

"So, it could do something more than slowly wear the mind down?" Miranda concluded. "Which, by the way, would be awful enough."

Olivia leaned all the way back in her chair and fixed her eyes on the ceiling. "The conference is in a day and a half. That doesn't give me much time to go through the code, searching for something I don't recognize."

The predicament facing us hung heavily in the air. I didn't think Garrison was above permanently getting rid of anyone that he felt needed to go. Where was the line between murder and self-defense?

"Don't do anything you're not comfortable with," I cautioned. "We both know that Garrison is working a hundred different angles."

"I know," she nodded absently.

"I wouldn't do anything unless I knew for sure what I was

doing," Miranda spat. "This time," she added quickly upon seeing my disbelieving stare. "People's lives are at stake. And I, for one, do not want to become one of Garrison's angels."

Olivia smiled as she continued to stare at the ceiling. "I've been around longer than either of you, and I knew that Millsap was not the whole of the Consortium. I also know that there has never been one good thing to come from them. Every bit of tech they have is stolen in one way or another and cobbled together to form some grizzly patchwork."

"Like the Furries?" I said.

"Like the Furries," she repeated. "Do you know how long they live? Six months tops," she answered without waiting for a response. "The last three months, they aren't able to shift back to human at all. That's when they're the most dangerous."

"Why would anyone volunteer for that?" Miranda asked.

Olivia turned her face to Miranda. "Who said they did?" She let her words sink in as she returned to staring at the ceiling. "The Consortium's goals aren't noble. They have no interest in furthering science, protecting mankind or anything resembling being honorable."

"They just want to rule the world by force," Miranda guessed.

"No. They want to rule the world by any means possible. Left unchecked, they've got the money and the power to do just that."

"That makes them a very dangerous enemy," I said, frowning as my view of the Consortium broadened.

She nodded silently in response. "Well." She leaned heavily on the table as she stood. "If you ladies have nothing further, I have some code to study."

Miranda waited until Olivia cleared out before whispering, "What are the chances she'll actually find something?"

"I don't know. She was able to whip out the Lindsey inhibitor fairly quick."

"I guess we'll hope for the best," Miranda said, then smacked her lips together like she'd eaten something unpleasant. "I'm really beginning to despise the word best. What it really means is I can't do what you want."

"I'm done with maybe."

"I thought you liked living in the gray."

"It's overrated. Sometimes you just want a clear yes or no."

"Now you're just talking crazy."

"It's my native tongue."

"You are crazy," she laughed, causing me to join in.

"The Consortium created thousands of children to use as weapons in their war," I said after we'd quieted. "That right there lets you know what kind of people we're dealing with. Whether Olivia finds something or not, I'm good with taking them out."

Miranda caressed her stomach as she processed what I said. "I'm finding it difficult to muster any sympathy for someone who would engineer children for the express purpose of stocking an army. What kind of mind games, or torture to ensure compliance was lying in wait for their futures?" She shook her head as the smell of anger coalesced around her. "I'm good with it too. Does that make me a murderer?"

"I think it makes you someone with a heart to protect the innocent."

She was quiet as she considered my answer. Then nodding slowly to herself, she asked, "Want some cobbler?"

"You have to ask?"

"Forgive me," she apologized. "I momentarily forgot who I was talking to."

Her return to the table supplied me with the cobbler dish and serving spoon. "Were there no more bowls? Or smaller utensils?" I asked warily, though not refusing either.

"I'm sure you won't let it stop you."

I looked at the giant spoon in my hand and shrugged. She knew me well.

"Yum," I moaned, wiping at the accidental overage on my face. "Do you remember when you were so excited about us coming here and being coeds together?"

"Seems like only last week," she said dreamily.

"It was. And, I got a say, this is way more work than I bargained for."

"Saving the world isn't easy," she agreed.

"Didn't we just do this last week?" I griped. "Shouldn't it be someone else's turn?"

"Quit complaining. You're living in a huge, beautiful lodge—"

"Which I can't find my way around in."

"Surrounded by majestic mountains—"

"I ain't got time for no mountains."

"Then there's Margaret."

Okay, that was a plus. "Do you think I still have my job at the university?"

"I don't see why not."

"I miss the house in New Orleans, and the life we had there. I thought my life was complicated then. But this…This is complicated." On impulse, I turned to Miranda and grasped her hand. "If anything ever goes wrong, look for me at our old house."

"Okay," she said, drawing the word out. "You want to have a secret handshake too? Maybe a code word?"

"Very funny," I droned and released her hand.

"What do you think our neighbors would think about us now?"

I laughed at the thought. On our block, we were the normal ones. Our neighbors were a wild hodgepodge of free spirits. Free as in believed in all kinds of weird stuff. When we were in town, we used to meet at Mr. Autin's house on Wednesday nights to watch the show, Ancient Aliens. Miranda was hooked immediately. Granted, I wasn't a big television watcher, but this show had enough oomph to keep me engaged. I didn't know if everything on the show was based on empirical fact, but they did present a bunch of legitimate questions. At least in my mind. To Hazel, it was biblical canon. Man, the rows that took place over crawfish etouffee or boudain balls with Ms. Mary's homemade buttermilk ranch dressing.

"I miss boudain balls," I said mournfully.

"I miss the fresh baguettes with the butter that Mr. Autin made from the cow he kept hidden in his backyard."

Cobbler dribbled out of the corners of my mouth as I laughed around the giant spoon before I could pull it out. "It's a wonder we never died from some parasitic infection."

"Nothing short of miraculous," she agreed while tossing me a napkin.

"I think that our neighbors would say that we'd been abducted by aliens and subjected to experimentation that left us this way."

"I'm betting Hazel would say that I was the love child of an alien and a human."

"Seems reasonable," I joked. Pausing with the tip of the spoon in my mouth, I watched in horrified fascination as her warm ups lost the battle and began a slow roll down her stomach. "Here's something else entirely reasonable. I think it's time for you to consider getting some new clothes." Using the spoon as an extension of my arm, I aimed it at her stomach now on full display.

She looked down and sighed. "Not what I used to dress like, is it?" Grasping the t-shirt, which I was guessing belonged to Cedars, she adjusted it to cover the bulge. "But you're right. It's time."

I could do with ordering some clothes myself. But first, a shower and then everything else on the list, including the items yet to appear. Because I knew they were coming.

"Ouch."

"Bite your tongue?" Miranda guessed.

"No. Ow," I moaned, nearly flipping the spoon out of my hand as the jolt of pain lancing through my head repeated.

"Oh my God," Miranda exclaimed, clutching a hand to her chest as Scout burst into the room. "You guys are going to have to come up with some designated landing pads or something."

"We got a problem, Doc."

Ah, the newest item. "What's wrong?" I asked, squinting up at him from under my hand gripping my forehead.

"Adam, he's...Just come see for yourself. Meet us at his cell." Then he disappeared.

Dropping the spoon into the dish, I pushed the chair back quickly, and then hesitated when I remembered Miranda.

"Go," she said upon seeing me pause. "I'll meet you there."

Standing in front of Adam's cell, I didn't know what to think. He was caught between various stages of shifting, unable to fully return to one form or the other. As quickly as the shift started in one direction, it reversed itself. There was no doubt he was in agony. Brief pulses of it shot through our bond, causing me to wince periodically. The roars of anger and pain coming from him tore at my heart.

"He's fighting the programming, trying to override it," Olivia said quietly.

I could see that. Pulling my eyes from him, I scanned the group gathered in front of his cell. Adam didn't need everyone watching him like this. "Hey, don't you have things to be doing?"

Kenny leaned back, finding me around the crowd.

"Now," I mouthed to him.

"Everybody out," Kenny barked as he began maneuvering the gang away from Adam's cell.

Miranda came in as they were exiting. She stopped when she reached me and joined in quietly watching Adam's struggle. For all of one minute.

"What did you do?" she accused.

"Nothing."

"I'm pretty sure it's not nothing."

"I told him to remember Granny," I shrugged.

"I've heard about Granny. I can't wait to meet her."

She might just get her wish. If this didn't work, I fully intended to bring Granny here.

"I thought his memories of Granny might go far enough back to circumvent the false memory loop they have him on."

"Looks like it's working," Olivia said.

If you called that working. With each second that passed, I could feel his strength waning.

"It's slowing down," Miranda observed.

"He's running out of juice?" Olivia whispered to me.

My nod of affirmation brought tears to her eyes.

In the end, the programming won out, forcing his return to leopard form. For all his fight, Adam laid exhausted on the floor.

"Macy, if there was anything I could do right now, without possibly making it worse, I would. But they've done the opposite of the inhibitor. I don't know what's involved. Not what they injected him with, not the code." Hugging herself, she groaned in frustration.

"I know, Olivia."

"We could tranquilize him again," she suggested. "Prevent this from happening."

"No," I shook my head. "I think he has the best chance of fixing this himself."

Reaching over, she squeezed my arm. "I'll check in later."

"Wow, one moment there, then gone the next," Miranda whispered. "It's crazy, this new world we live in. Or great, depending on how you look at it."

Yeah, it was great. We were all great. If we could just put everything back together again.

"I brought you something,"' Miranda said.

I watched her pull a book out from under her shirt and extend it to me. "A Field Guide to Midwifery," I read aloud. This day just kept getting better.

"I'm going to help Jamie for a while. See you later?"

Without looking at her, I nodded my understanding. When her footsteps faded, I tucked the book under my arm and leaned into the glass. *I'm sorry, Adam. I didn't know it would hurt you like this.* I had to stop as a sob took me by surprise. Wrapping a hand around my mouth, I tilted my forehead to rest against the glass. *I'm so sorry this happened to you,* I said in a strangled whisper.

Macy?

My breath hitched as I snapped my head up to look at him. *I'm here, Adam.*

Me, too.

That was all I got before the hate forced me out again, but that small glimmer of hope was enough.

"Macy?" said a tentative voice.

Rapidly scrubbing my hands across my eyes to dislodge the tears, I looked up to see Crystal standing uncertainly in the doorway. It was the first time I had seen her since she was rescued. She looked so vulnerable in the hospital gown.

"Come here," I panted, my voice tight with emotion.

She only hesitated a second before hurrying towards me. I didn't give her a chance to refuse the hug as I wrapped my arms around her. It felt so good to have her here, alive and safe.

"How are you?" I asked, holding her at arm's length in order to get a good look at her.

"Okay, I guess," she sputtered. "Way better than before. That man...he was crazy."

"Crazy dangerous. I am so glad you are not dead."

"Me, too," she smiled.

"What do you think of your new home?"

She grimaced slightly. "I haven't really seen much of it." Pulling the sides of the gown away from her, she said, "But I can tell you that it needs an upgrade in the clothing department."

"I don't know," I teased. "It's roomy." Reaching out, I grasped the fabric between my fingers. "Made of soft cotton. And it has those nice little flowers."

She jerked the gown out of my hand. "It's a peep show if one string comes untied," she snapped angrily.

"I guess we can't have that," I chuckled. "Is Kenny being overprotective?" I figured he was the reason she hadn't gotten around much.

The anger left her face as she shrugged without commenting.

Apparently, Kenny was a touchy subject.

"Why are we here?" she asked abruptly.

Sighing at the none too subtle subject change, I crossed my arms and turned to face Adam again. I'd been wondering when they'd get around to asking. "Here is the safest place I know of. The Colony is not an option right now. Too many bad guys know where and what it is. Also, the world is about to find out about hybrids."

"It's boring," she said flatly.

"Boring, huh?" I could do something about that.

"Kenny said the rest of the Organization people are coming back, and they're way smarter than us."

Remind me not to say anything to Crystal that I didn't want repeated. "There's all kinds of smart, Crystal."

She digested that a moment, then turned her attention to the cell where Adam lay. "I'm sorry about Adam. You two were real close?"

"We're something," I said obliquely.

"Whatcha got there?" She nodded to the book tucked under my arm.

"Just a little light reading," I said, holding it up for her to read.

"Who's having a baby?"

"Miranda."

"Really?" she asked with wide eyes.

"Really, really. Kenny didn't tell you?"

"Kenny doesn't tell me anything," she said dejectedly. "But that's just...wow."

"Yep."

We quieted as Adam rolled over. We should probably leave. Let him recover.

"Thanks for coming back for me," Crystal said in a small voice. "No one's ever cared that much about me. Except for Mama. But she's gone now."

Turning my head, I met her eyes. "Kenny does. He's the real reason we found you."

Unable to speak any longer, she simply nodded.

This was crap. Tossing the book on the floor, I wrapped an arm around her shoulder and squeezed. "Crystal, listen. I know that your whole life has basically changed. But you're not alone. Kenny...that boy loves you. Both he and Scout risked their lives looking for you. The rest of the gang is here too. And, I'm here."

She leaned her head into my shoulder, a worried sigh rattling through her small frame.

"You're going to be okay, Crystal. You all are."

Through the small window in the door at the end of the hall, I caught Kenny watching us. I smiled reassuringly at him, but his expression didn't change. I couldn't' tell what he was thinking, but I knew he was worried, and I knew he was listening.

"Thanks, Doc," Crystal breathed, sloughing off tears as she pulled away. "I'll let you get back to Adam." Turning, she started down the hallway towards Kenny. "You should eat," she called, almost as an afterthought. "Your bones are pokey."

Reaching up, I traced my collar bone, then lightly fingered my ribs with the other hand. My bones weren't pokey. Well defined maybe. I looked back up in time to watch Kenny fold Crystal into his arms. The sight of those two clinging to each other pinched my heart.

"There's two of the reasons I'm still here," I said to myself. Leaving them to their prolonged reunion, I swung my head back to Adam. "And here lies reason number one."

CHAPTER 22

FTER I'D SHOWERED AND PILED into Adam's bed, I half expected that I wouldn't be able to sleep. I was wrong, as evidenced by Miranda shaking me awake.

"Why are you always waking me up?" I demanded sullenly.

The bed shifted as Miranda dropped heavily onto it. "You know," she sighed. "I think our roles have completely reversed. You used to be the one waking me up, remember?"

"Great, then you handle everything and let me sleep," I muttered from under the pillow where I'd stuffed my head.

"No such luck, Oh Great One. There are speeches to craft, interviews to frame and well, you know, stuff. Oh, and the president's on the line."

Moaning bitterly, I reluctantly shoved the pillow aside. The book Miranda had given me slid off the bed and thumped loudly as it hit the floor. Rising up on one elbow, I pointed an accusing finger at it. "Have you seen what's in that book?"

"You act like you've never heard of childbirth before. Seriously, Macy."

"I just don't think—"

"I need you to do this," she interrupted. "Through thick and thin, remember?"

Growling softly, I let myself collapse back onto the pillows. I remembered. Dang it, but I remembered.

A few years after we'd become friends, her stepfather found her. It was bad. Really bad. Miranda almost gave up on life then. It was only the promise that I'd be there that had stopped her from ending everything. After the months it took her to recover physically, and as much as she could mentally, we'd created a pledge of sorts. That's what she was referring to now. The words were somewhat silly, but they were heartfelt, and I meant them with every ounce of my being. Then and now.

"Through high and low," I recited the obligatory line.

"Be it well travelled."

"Backwoods or off road." That was my special contribution to the lyric.

"Together we go," we repeated in unison.

Looked like I was really doing this. Dr. Macy Greer, deliverer of little naked bundles of joy that may or may not be sporting fangs and claws. "You're lucky I'm such a loyal friend."

"I am," she smiled.

Sighing heavily, I leaned over and scooped up the book. At the rate she was expanding, I bet half this stuff in here didn't even apply. And what if she was carrying multiples? Maybe that's why she was showing already, a whole brood of minis in there. Oh, man. This was about to get so off road.

"Do I at least get to wear scrubs?"

"As long as you wear clothes, I'm good."

"Ha! Look who's talking. You're going to be the one all spread eagled on the bed."

"That's crude, Macy. It's the miracle of birth."

"Let's reevaluate that after the fact."

The knock on the bedroom door startled both of us.

"One word," Miranda gulped. "Landing. Zones."

"That's two words," I corrected.

"Shut up," she snapped.

"Also, two words," I said, struggling to restrain my smile.

"Macy, you have a phone call," Olivia announced, not at all amused by our exchange.

"I've heard," I grumbled. Flinging the covers aside, I made a beeline for my duffle. "Are you in contact with Garrison?" I asked Olivia.

"Constantly. He's sort of a control freak."

Like I hadn't seen that coming. Locating one of the disposable phones I'd purchased, I tossed it to her. "Could you add his phone number and yours?"

"Sure," she said as she caught the phone. "We have phones we could give you."

"This will do for now." I was not about to be drawn into any conversation involving Organization wiretapping and tracking. If Walmart wanted to listen in, well, maybe they'd send me some coupons or something. "Add Juarez and Cedars too, if you would." I'd have to remember to get Reynolds' number, and I didn't even know if Kenny had a phone. I didn't remember him getting one, but that didn't mean he didn't have one. And what about Miranda? Catching her attention, I waved a spare phone at her questioningly, tossing it to her when she held her hand out.

"You two have got to get over your trust issues," Olivia muttered without taking her eyes off the phone in her hand.

True. But not today. "Did you confirm if Julia was all of our mothers?" I asked in a deliberate attempt to change the subject.

Olivia looked up from the phone. "I did and she is."

"But we're still missing one?"

"As it currently stands," she nodded.

"Doesn't it seem strange that we all ended up together," Miranda said.

"Considering who's manipulating the whole thing?" Olivia scoffed. "No." Finished entering the numbers, she tossed the phone back to me.

"Does he know that you're going to Geneva and not me?"

"He does. I think he was pleased by it. Not sure how to interpret that."

Well, this was it. The last remaining pair of jeans I had in my possession. It was with trepidation that I dragged them out of the duffle and held them up to my hips.

"Last pair?" Miranda guessed.

"Very last," I answered. "Do you know how long it takes me to break in a pair of jeans?"

"I do," she sympathized. "I'll order you some when I place my order later today. Not sure what size you are anymore," she said, tilting her head and squinting at me. "I can see your ribs."

"Yeah, well, I can't see yours."

"Oh, that's classy. Make fun of the pregnant lady."

"As interesting as this conversation is," Olivia interrupted. "Macy, you do have a rather important phone call to attend to."

Right. I slipped the jeans on, added a t-shirt and followed Olivia out the door.

"Line one," she said, pointing to the desk.

"Mr. President."

"Dr. Greer. So glad you could scrounge up the time to talk to me."

He was angry about the wait. Oh, well. "Is there something I can help you with? You know, other than the impossible tasks you've already assigned me."

Olivia's eyes widened at my comment. Miranda, who'd joined Olivia in front of the desk, just rolled her eyes heavenward.

"I understand that Olivia is going to Geneva and not you."

"That's correct."

"You also managed to retrieve Adam and the rest of the Colony hybrids."

"Yep."

"I further understand that you do not approve of the course we are charting for the...*children*."

"I'd say you've got a good understanding of things."

"Macy," Olivia hissed under her breath.

"I am trusting you not to interfere," the president warned.

I almost busted out laughing. He must not have gotten the memo that I'd turned over a new leaf where I did whatever the heck I wanted. "Well, Mr. President," I said, purposely ignoring the threat his words implied. "I won't make you any promises, but I will tell you that one baby is too much for me to handle right now let alone the amount that you have there." In the future, should that somehow change, all bets were off.

"Garrison keeps telling me that you are worth the trouble," he sighed. "I hope he is not mistaken."

Worth the trouble? Did he seriously just insinuate that I was more trouble than I was worth?

"What progress have you made towards the medical advances?" he asked, before I could tell him what I thought of his comment.

Aw, crud. "None," I grunted. The word tasted like leather in my mouth.

"None?" His voice was incredulous. "What have you been doing?"

My anger flared to life in one giant rush. It wasn't like I'd been sitting around doing nothing, taking advantage of everything that headquarters had to offer. "It's on my list," I snarled angrily.

"On your list? It had better be more than on your list. Time is running out, Dr. Greer."

Olivia snatched the phone from my hand and disappeared before I could muster a response.

"Can you believe that guy?" I demanded of Miranda, breathing heavily despite the lack of any physical exertion.

"He has a lot on his plate, too. State of the world and all. If this all goes south, who do you think the world is going to hold accountable?"

"Aah! I hate this!" I yelled, hitting the desk with both fists. "I need more time."

"Don't look at me," Miranda protested. "That is not my department." Then she made pointing motions at the ceiling.

I looked up and then back at her. "We have a time machine in the attic?"

"No, you idiot! Try praying. You know, what you used to do when you got into trouble." She raised both eyebrows in challenge as she backed towards the door, only pausing long enough to roll her eyes and shake her head despairingly before ducking out.

If she was going to keep rolling her eyes at me and flat out abandoning me, I was going to have to put in for a replacement assistant, I thought angrily. Sliding down in the chair until my head rested on the back, I stared at the ceiling as I mulled over her suggestion. Prayer. I did use to pray, back when the problems didn't seem bigger than God. What was that, like two weeks ago?

When the world wasn't upside down crazy. Where did I even start now?

Letting my gaze wander, it settled on a photograph that I'd never noticed before. Hoisting myself from the chair, I crossed the floor to stand in front of it. Adam, looking just like he did now, was pictured with a little girl who had her arms wrapped around his neck.

"This must be Margaret," I whispered, lightly fingering the picture. "I want Margaret to be happy." She did so much for everyone else. And Adam...I wanted him to wear this smile again, not the tortured expression he currently wore. In truth, I wanted all of us to be happy. For that to happen, I needed a string of small miracles. It didn't seem like a few simple prayers would be enough, but standing in front of that picture, I said them anyway.

In the hours that followed, I arranged for all the Colony hybrids to begin taking a series of aptitude tests. Finding out where their talents lay both academically and otherwise was the first step to integrating them into the Organization. I was pretty sure that Kenny wasn't going to like it, but he'd understand the necessity for it.

I also started an outline of medical advances I thought would most wow the public and get them quickly on board with the plan. It included things I'd already seen in myself and other hybrids, so I was relatively certain we could replicate it in others. The logistics of making that happen was currently outside of my league, but then, that's what the rest of the team was for.

The reporter presented a different problem. She was after information about the hybrids and not the medical advances. I wanted to time the interview where it would be overshadowed by the big press conference that I was not going to tell her about until it happened. She wouldn't appreciate being left out of the loop regarding the medical stuff, but I didn't appreciate having to give the interview. Call us even. Trying to anticipate her questions, I roughly sketched the interview in my mind.

I had just finished inputting Ms. Redding's number into the

contact list on my phone when the door chimed. It was Olivia who stood in the doorway.

"Heading out?" I asked her.

"Just about. Are you going to be okay holding down the fort while I'm gone?"

"Who me? Are you kidding? It'll be great."

She crossed her arms and leaned against the door frame. "It's not as easy as you think," she warned softly.

"Olivia," I sighed. "I've never thought it was easy."

"I'm sort of hoping that someone goes rogue, just so you'll know how it feels."

"Well, if you disobey orders and drop off the map, I'll assume you're the rogue and write you off. How about that?"

"Freedom? Might be nice." Straightening from the wall, she shook her head as she said, "Nah, I've got too much to come home to, too much work waiting for me."

"Maybe I'll go rogue again," I offered. "That worked so well before."

"Listen," she said, rubbing her neck distractedly. "In all seriousness, I'd like a home to come back to. Please don't take any unnecessary risks."

"I won't."

"Don't blow it up."

"I'm not—"

"Burn it to the ground."

"Olivia—"

"Vaporize it, teleport it to another dimension, flood it."

Flood it? How was that even possible? "Are you finished?"

"Yeah," she said despondently.

"I'm not going to destroy anything."

She lifted her eyes to mine. "I guess we'll see, won't we?"

"Yes, you will," I agreed and pushed her out the door. "Now go. And kick some Consortium butt or brain."

Allowing me to steer her into the hallway, she turned and flashed a brief smile. "See you later tonight," she waved and then vanished.

Miranda was right. All this sudden vanishing and abrupt reappearances was kind of creepy. What if two of us tried to reappear in the same spot or a space that someone else already occupied? I shuddered at the thought.

Withdrawing into the room, I let the door slide shut. Olivia was really worried that the trust she was placing in me would fail her. What if she was right? Lord knew nothing had gone according to plan so far. Now I was worried over her worry. How stupid was that? Fortunately, the phone ringing rescued me from an imagination that could have constructed countless scenarios of how this could go wrong.

After glancing at the caller ID, I picked up the phone. "Hey there."

"Jamie has most everyone returning by tomorrow morning."

"Tomorrow," I blurted.

"You said you wanted them back," she reminded me. "It turns out, since the majority never left the vicinity, they don't have far to travel."

"That's not much of a vacation," I muttered.

"Have you seen Montana?"

"Oh yeah. I forgot."

"He wants to schedule an assembly for late tomorrow. After dinner or something. Do you feel up to addressing them?"

"Me?" I recoiled. "I thought we decided this was Cedars' arena."

"Macy, you are kind of running the show. You need to at least introduce yourself. It would help if you could make a case for your appointment."

"Miranda, I—"

"I know you just want to work and otherwise be left alone," she talked over me. "But your time in the shadows is coming to an end. Tomorrow evening to be exact."

"You know I don't react well to being cornered," I snapped at her.

"It's a bunch of science geeks like us. You've addressed these types lots of times."

"But never when everyone in the room most likely knew more about the subject than I did."

"That's true," she agreed. "But you're not talking shop as much as you are giving an administrative run down."

"Now I'm the bureaucrat? This is a lousy pep talk," I sighed. "Let me see Adam again before I give a definite answer."

"Okeydokey. I'll tell Jamie he owes me a back rub. Because I knew you would stall, I made a bet with him. Did you catch the part where I said I knew you would stall?"

This was the downside of having a best friend that knew you too well. "I'm not stalling," I insisted. "I'm going to verify that Adam is not up for the job. That's all."

"Mmm hmm," she hummed doubtfully. "On a side note, the kids are not too thrilled with the *job* you've arranged for them."

"You mean the tests? I figured they wouldn't like it."

"Crystal swears she's never confiding in you again."

"If that were only true," I said wistfully, then laughed. "We have to have a starting point. I'll talk to them about it when I get a chance. By the way, have we ever verified that the other Colony hybrids we rescued arrived safely?"

"No, we never verified. I did. Why did Adam choose to send them to Tennessee instead of here?"

"I don't know. They had a facility readily available?"

"That's what Jamie said. And something about the state being populated by people who mainly kept to themselves."

Like Granny. I wondered if she was involved in this somehow. She would make a spectacular drill sergeant.

"But that answer doesn't really fly. This place is plenty big enough, and if Adam planned on bringing you here, then he would have made the assumption that you would be okay with the separation. Do you think he would have come to that conclusion? Also, why was Adam training them?"

I frowned at her round of questioning. The way she was talking, it was like she was implying that Adam had some ulterior motive. I'd had these thoughts myself, but I'd never taken the time to examine them beyond the surface, and I definitely hadn't given voice to them.

"You think Adam was planning something."

"I think he was going to break from the Organization, maybe start something in Tennessee. I've searched, but whatever he's cooked up, I don't think he left a trail here. I'm not telling you to mistrust Adam," she added quickly. "We know he had issues with Julia, for reasons we now understand."

"I bet Kenny knows something."

"Will he spill, though?"

"Not likely. It might not matter anymore given what's happened with the Organization."

"Maybe not," she allowed. "But it's good to cover all our bases."

A sports analogy. And she used it correctly. "I'm impressed," I said. It took her a second to read the sarcasm in the comment.

"Are you ready for all this, Macy? Are you really prepared for what's about to happen?"

"Excuse me, has my track record informed you that I am one who makes preparations?"

"That's what I thought," she huffed. "We're about to go through another crap storm. There ought to be some kind of hazard pay when people sign up to work with you. Find me after you've seen Adam."

Rude, I thought as the line went dead. Slowly, I placed the receiver back in its cradle. I wasn't looking forward to another confrontation with Adam. I wished I could be sure I was evoking the reaction that he needed to recover. My gut told me it was, but it was hard to trust it in the face of Adam's anger. And now that Cedars was waiting on me for an answer about the assembly, I didn't really have a valid excuse for delaying any longer. Exhaling sharply, I made the jump to his cell before I could talk myself out of it.

Reynolds was there, and he looked rough, like he hadn't slept in a while. Lightly tapping him on the shoulder, I said, "Reynolds, you doing alright?"

"You can call me ER, you know? Everyone else does. I actually prefer it."

"O-kay," I stuttered. "Have you been here all night?"

"Most of it. He had more of those shifting sessions. They're lasting longer, like he's gaining more control."

That was good, I guess, but, as he was still a leopard, not good enough. "I'm here now...uh...ER. You can get some rest. I'll stay with him."

"I don't like how spread out everything is," he said abruptly.

"How spread out everything is?" I repeated back to him.

"Everyone's off doing separate things—"

"I need them doing those things," I objected.

"What I mean," he growled softly in anger, "is that no one is covering the whole. Things are bound to fall through the cracks." He turned towards me. His face was hard, and his eyes held an intensity I'd seen only fleetingly before. "It's too much for any one person to handle."

Breaking eye contact, I focused on the glass in front of me. This serious side of Reynolds—ER was creeping me out. I'd had brief glimpses of it before, of the man he was becoming. Like when he'd shot the guy that shot him and on the plane. Maybe it had always been there, and I just hadn't wanted to see it. Whatever the case may be, I had better figure out what this serious Reynolds was trying to tell me. A lot of things were not being addressed currently, I knew that. We all knew that. But we could only do so much. Everyone was working...Oh.

Lifting my eyes from the floor where they'd drifted, I corrected myself. Not everyone was working. "Do you have a job title in mind?" I asked him.

The corner of his mouth lifted in a smile. "Adam's back, but he is not functional. I could resume being your shadow."

"I don't really need a shadow."

"Yeah, I guess you're not the helpless girl we started with."

"Helpless girl?" I sneered. "I was never helpless. Requiring help every now and then does not make one helpless."

His smile grew with every word I spoke until finally, I shut my mouth. Fuming, I swung back to face Adam and tried to picture what he would do with Reynolds. You know, after he'd punched him for that arrogant smile he wore. Remembering Adam that way made me smile. His style of leadership truly was more feudal than mine. He'd probably make him a squire or something. Hey, that wasn't half bad. I needed someone in the helping me department.

"How would you like to be my squire?"

One eyebrow darted sharply skyward as the smile left his face. "Like a knight's squire? Who does everything the knight tells him to do? You being the knight of course."

My smile was broader than the one he'd brandished. "Think you can handle it?"

He shrugged his shoulders. "That was pretty much what I was doing anyway. Picking you up when you fall. Gluing you back together. Putting you out when you're on fire. Need I go on?"

"I was never on fire," I spat at him. The nerve of some people, really. "Do you want the job or not?"

"I prefer the title of assistant," he laughed. "But yeah, I'll take it."

"Great. Now go away. I want to talk to Adam."

"And so it begins," he said mournfully while backing down the hall.

"Hey, get an update from Juarez," I yelled after him.

"Certainly, Oh Great Knight of the Hybrid Realm."

"Get moving," I barked at him.

He chuckled all the way down the hall, a grand improvement from the face he wore only moments before.

Taking a deep breath, I repeated the phrase in my head. *Get moving. Remember that Adam? How you used to love to tell me to get moving?*

He had given no outward sign that he was awake, but I felt him watching us and now me.

I heard you had a rough night. Uugh, I groaned inwardly. This was so wrong. It felt like I was a complete stranger to him.

You are.

The unexpectedness of his response startled me. I hadn't

realized the connection had been restored. Consequently, I hadn't been guarding anything I thought or felt. There was no way of knowing what he'd picked up from me already. The good thing was he would know that I was telling the truth.

You've got it backwards. You told me that you'd been watching me for years. I didn't know you until a little over a week ago. You're a stranger to me, not the other way around.

And yet, we are supposed to be madly in love?

My breath escaped in a rush. *I never said that we were in love.*

He rose and stretched languidly before sauntering slowly towards the glass. *Oh, not you. Every other little pion you shuffle in front of this glass.*

I haven't sent anyone here, I snapped. *Whoever came did so of their own volition. And, whatever they said…well, I'm sure they were just trying to help. To get you to remember.*

It's not true? he asked while reaching deep within me to find out the truth for himself.

I don't know, I managed to stammer as I gasped at the suddenness of his invasion. Gritting my teeth, I resisted the urge to force him out. If I did that now, he might never trust me. *We…I mean you…* Why couldn't I put the words together?

Adam put his front paws on the glass, intentionally bringing his gaze level with mine. Staring into those eyes that were his and yet so different, all thoughts of speaking fled. I could see into him as clearly as he could see into me, and I understood that his actions weren't meant to harm me. This Adam, the hard, seemingly cruel version, was only after the truth. The fear generated by the ferocity of his intrusion disappeared as I relaxed. With no guard in place, I was completely stunned when he shattered.

A roar of agony tore from his throat, splintering him as different aspects of the shift began to race through his body. His claws began to pierce the glass under the strain of the assault. I knew he was trying to shield me from the pain. I knew, because when he no longer could, the pain hit me like a punch to the gut. Stumbling forward under its weight, I watched helplessly as he fell.

"Adam!" I yelled, pressing against the glass nearest to him. The speed at which the transformations whipped from one extreme to the other were causing him to writhe uncontrollably on the floor. He looked positively inhuman. I caught myself involuntarily backing away from the glass and stopped. *Adam?* I whimpered.

In response to my plea, the bond flew wide open, allowing the true extent of his pain to plow into me like a tidal wave. It burrowed inside until it obliterated my ability to see. I crumpled to the floor with my arms wrapped around my head in a futile attempt to protect myself from the all-consuming light that had replaced my vision.

"Macy!" Reynolds yelled. His footfalls were fast and heavy as he sprinted towards me. We spun wildly as he scooped me into his arms.

Adam, I whimpered, but there was no response. Funny it should be so dark when everything was only light. Panting in rhythm to the pain as it pulsed through my body, I heard Reynolds call for help. I even felt the gentle strokes he made smoothing my hair back. But it was as if it was happening to someone else.

There had to be some way I could help Adam, some way to end this monstrous merry-go-round. I just couldn't see it from my perspective. Locating the thread connecting us, I followed it until it led me to Adam. I knew the throbbing mass of light was him, and I knew what I was about to do would hurt. Still, I delved into Adam without a second thought. The sudden intensification of pain was almost enough to drive me out, but I held on until I could breathe again. There was no threat of Adam forcing me out. He was so deeply engrossed in his struggle that he couldn't spare the energy to resist my presence.

Squinting at the fireworks happening inside of him, I watched the light dance across luminous pathways in some predetermined pattern. The choreography wasn't hard to follow. After a moment's observation, I identified the brightest burst of light as correlating with the beginning of the reversal back to leopard.

"Dad gum it," I exclaimed as I understood the problem.

Whoever had worked on him had connected the shift back to

human with the pain center of his brain. His body wasn't physically capable of handling the pain and the shift at the same time. That's why he could only take it so far before the shift reversed itself. I saw them clearly now, the pair of neon arches that flared each time Adam reached his limit. Even as I watched, the waves of pain searing across the pathways were becoming stronger. If he didn't stop, it would kill him.

Consumed by panic, I grasped the arches and willed my nanobots to help Adam, to be the surrogate for his pain so that he could complete the transformation. In no way was I prepared for the new onset when it hit. I screamed as the light blazed through me, scorching every fiber of my being. But no amount of screaming could assuage the conduit that I had become.

"I got you, Macy," Reynolds said, gripping me tighter as I thrashed wildly about.

Others were racing towards me now. I could sense them, though I couldn't see them. It felt like my nanobots had turned against me, crushing my cells from the inside out. "Don't you do that," I gasped angrily at them.

"I have to hold you, Macy," Reynolds said guiltily.

He didn't know I wasn't talking to him. But my nanobots recognized my voice. There was an immediate release of pressure as they stopped following the dictates attached to the pain they were siphoning into me.

"What happened?" I heard Miranda demand as she ran.

I wanted to tell her, but I could no longer form words. All of my energy was focused on finding a way to dispense of the pain without sending it back into Adam and without it killing me.

"She's burning up," Reynolds said. He sounded scared.

"Macy," Miranda whispered.

Her voice was close, like she was kneeling over me. A tear splashed onto my cheek. For the second that it existed, it created a little pool of relief from the pain. I could almost see the photons arc towards the moisture before it evaporated against my hot skin.

Realizing I was on the verge of losing consciousness, I forced myself to form the words. "Water," I rasped.

A bottle was put to my mouth, but I wrenched it free and poured it onto the floor.

"Macy!" Reynolds protested, trying to get me to drink again.

"Reynolds stop!" Miranda ordered. "Look. She's working on something."

When Reynolds' grip loosened, I slid to the floor and moved until my right hand found the puddle created by the spilled contents of the bottle. Curling in on myself, I brought my left hand over to join the right and pressed it palm down into the water. With the bridge now in place, I quit fighting against the circuit of pain coursing through me and pictured it flowing out of my hands and into the water. I could only hope the nanobots would understand and do what was necessary to make it happen.

My hands began to tingle, but that was quickly overshadowed by the heat. With everything in me, I had to fight the urge to yank them away from the water.

"Is the water glowing?" I heard Crystal ask.

No one answered her question.

"Give me another water bottle," Miranda commanded.

I sighed in relief as she added its contents to the quickly evaporating puddle. When the pain began to lesson, I ventured another look inside Adam. Pulses no longer travelled across the arches. They were even starting to dim. "Adam?" I whispered.

There was a pause in the commotion around me. "He's Adam. Human Adam," Miranda answered.

Battling the fatigue that threatened to drag me under, I used the last remaining strength I had to focus on the arches once more. I couldn't leave them in place. Not when there was a chance of them providing a pathway again. Waiting until the light had completely faded, I ripped them apart. Then working my way backwards, I pried each end from Adam's brain. I now had two fistfuls of the channels that had caused us so much pain. Sparks showered from my hands as I crushed the remains between my fingers. No one was ever going to use these to hurt him again.

Adam? I thought as I felt him stir.

The feeling of shame washed over me, then abruptly, I was on the outside. Tentatively, I reached for him, but the wall was back in place. This time however, there was no doubt it was his doing. No longer possessing the strength to deny the darkness, I let it take me. As the present faded, I knew two things. Adam was back, and after what I'd just been through, I could find a way through any wall he created between us.

CHAPTER 23

THEY SAY THAT LEGENDS ARE the stuff of dreams. Or something like that. But in my dream, we weren't legends. We were, for lack of a better term, family. We were big and undeniably messy, a little crazy for sure, but above all, family. Adam was there with me. Cedars and Miranda too with a little blonde haired boy about four years old. Where did the blonde come from?

Olivia, Juarez, all the Organization people I knew were there. It was Christmas. Kenny was under the mistletoe with Crystal, who was pregnant. Then as dreams go, I looked down. I was pregnant, too.

I awoke with a gasp, tearing at the blankets to obtain an unobstructed view of my stomach.

"What's wrong?" Olivia asked, rushing quickly to my side.

Relaxing back against the pillows, I took a deep breath. "It was just a dream."

"A bad one?" she guessed.

"No," I whispered softly. It was good. And it felt so real.

"How are you feeling?" she asked. The worry creasing her forehead made me worry.

"Like I've been whooped up one side and down the other. Where's Miranda?"

She leaned away from me, the wrinkles in her brow relaxing just a little. "I believe she's still sleeping. She was here the first two nights. I made her go get some rest."

The first two nights? My brain felt thick as I struggled to

recall why I should be asleep for so long. "How long have I been asleep?"

"About three days."

"Three days!" I exclaimed, struggling to push myself to an upright position.

"Calm down," Olivia said soothingly. "That's an order." One eyebrow darted upward when I opened my mouth to spit another question at her.

Whatever. I didn't have the strength to argue with her anyway. Closing my eyes, I tried again to remember what had landed me in this bed. The last thing I remembered was hiring Reynolds. Then I started talking to Adam. Adam! My eyes flew open as the memory of what happened suddenly rushed back in.

"Adam?" I asked sharply, my eyes boring into hers.

She rolled her shoulders back, unconsciously betraying her unease. "He seems fine."

"Seems?" I frowned at her.

Arching both eyebrows in a show of frustration, "He won't let anyone near him," she huffed.

Gently, I reached through the bond, probing for him. It was still walled up tight. If I wasn't so unsure of what state he was in mentally, or my state physically, I would try to force my way in. But as it stood now, I'd have to do it in person. Tossing the covers aside, I threw my legs over the edge of the bed.

"Where do you think you're going," Olivia said with a hand on my arm.

"I'm pretty sure you already know the answer to that," I said sarcastically.

"Macy—"

"Has he talked?" I asked, altogether ignoring her objection.

"Not to me."

Shaking free of her hand, I stood up. The room swayed only slightly. Taking a step away from the bed, I asked, "To anyone?"

"Not that I know of. Macy," she said, her voice laced with concern as she followed me. "I don't think it's the best idea for you to see him right now."

"I'm fine," I assured her. I was almost to the duffle when I froze. What was I going to do for clothes? And what happened to the ones I was wearing?

Seeing my obvious dilemma, Olivia picked up a bag from a nearby chair and handed it to me. "I did not pick these out," she stated emphatically.

I turned the bag upside down and dumped the contents on the bed. Nope. These clothes definitely had Miranda written all over them. I picked up the white t-shirt and held it up. "Watch me," I read the inscription aloud. White? What was she thinking?

Tossing it back down, I studied the pair of jeans next to it. They had intentional rips in the legs and rhinestones studding the back pockets. Blingy. But I didn't have the luxury of being picky. Her choice of underwear made me smile. The bottoms sported cookie monster with the words smart cookie written across the rear. The last was a pair of shoes that looked like an ankle boot mixed with a trail running sneaker. I turned them over in my hands, looking at them from all angles. "I've never seen anything quite like these before," I mused.

Olivia took the shoes from me and tossed them on the bed. "Macy, you don't understand. I'm not just worried about you. There is guilt and shame rolling off of Adam at levels I've never smelled before. Seeing you will only make it worse."

I couldn't imagine what Adam had to feel guilty about. "You don't know that," I scoffed. "If I could just talk to him—"

Grasping me by the elbows, Olivia spun me around to face the mirror. The image staring back at me left me speechless. My face was swollen, dappled by an array of mottled bruises. Leaning forward, I peered intently at my eyes. The whites were completely covered with tiny red dots.

"What happened?" I breathed.

She shook her head in response, gesturing to me with one hand. "Whatever you did with Adam did this."

Numbly, I sat down on the edge of the bed. "Does he look like this?"

"No. He looks fine."

I closed my eyes and swallowed. Olivia was right. If Adam saw me like this, it would only add to whatever guilt he was feeling. Reaching behind me, I collected the clothing. "I'm going to take a shower and get dressed," I said robotically. "I'll meet everyone in the kitchen in twenty."

It was her cue to exit. I could tell by her expression that she wasn't sold on the subtle "get out", but I wasn't opening the floor for discussion. Rising from the bed, I headed for the shower. Hopefully the hot water would clear away the remaining cobwebs.

Without the option of meeting with Adam, I was left to play the episode over and over again in my head. I couldn't explain the communication taking place between the nanobots and myself, but it solidified the theory I'd been harboring regarding them. It was like we were a team, partners in the fight. I was the brain and they were the muscle. I didn't think I could view them as simply mindless robots anymore, and God knows I needed partners. Not that I didn't have any, I did. In fact, we were starting to gel pretty well, now that they had given up and let me be the boss.

Sighing at my own thoughts, I reached into the shower and turned on the water. Things weren't that bad at the moment. Adam was back, physically at least. I was assuming everyone else was currently accounted for, a miracle in itself. Some of them were even better than before. Though I'd only had the briefest of contact with Kenny since Crystal had returned, I had noticed how his whole countenance seemed lighter.

The thought stuck in my head. Something about being lighter...looking better. And Mallet. I didn't know what the connection was, but something was there. Shutting the water off, I turned from the shower and made my way to the desk. After completing the riddle rigmarole, I typed Gene Mallet into the search field. Too many items popped up. Narrowing the search, I added hybrid to the keywords and pressed enter. After scrolling through the results, I identified one report that looked promising. It was a NSA classified report detailing the government's handling of the original hybrid reveal. But the report was longer than I had hoped. There was no way I had time to look over it right now.

Knowing that it would have to wait until after the meeting, I scooted away from the desk. Get an update from everyone first, then I'd research this nagging feeling in my brain. In that order. Glancing at the clock revealed three minutes of the original twenty left. Would three days' worth of grunge come off in three minutes? Where was NOLA when you needed her?

With no time to mess with my appearance, it was with dripping hair and sans makeup that I walked into the kitchen. Wary eyes watched my entrance. It was like they were afraid I was going to fall apart at any moment. Given the way I'd been passing out lately, it wasn't totally undeserved. But it was annoying.

"You're somewhat of a freak show," Miranda whispered to me as I claimed the stool next to her at the island.

"I've noticed," I whispered back. "I look like a zombie or something."

"You're entitled. After what you've been through, you should look like death warmed over."

"As always, you are my solitary ray of sunshine in my otherwise dismal day."

"It's what I do," she said dismissively.

I chuckled at her, and then took a deep breath. "Have you been to see Adam?"

"Yes, I have," she answered while absently plucking a grape from the fruit bowl.

"And?" I prodded her impatiently.

"And...It's sad, Macy. He's human, but well, for the longest time he just sat there with his back to the wall. Wouldn't talk to anyone. Wouldn't even get dressed, just buck naked on the floor. By the way, you've got something to look forward to there, let me tell you—"

"Miranda!" I said sharply.

"I'm just saying. He's got clothes on now," she added sheepishly. "But he's so angry, Mace. I tried to talk to him. Tell him what you would say if you were there. But the only thing he would say to me was, 'I hurt her.'"

I pulled my knees to my chest, balancing my toes on the edge of the stool. Aw, crud. I forgot my shoes. Anyway... "Olivia said he was ashamed. She didn't think I should show up looking like this."

"She's probably right, but you might not have a choice. You might be the only one who can reach him."

"Has he talked to anyone else?"

"Juarez. But Juarez won't say what they've talked about."

Knowing what he'd been through with Olivia, it wasn't hard to guess. "Olivia said I was out for three days."

"Something like that," she nodded. "We weren't sure you were coming back." Her voice broke on the last word, and she looked away quickly. "Stupid hormones," she muttered under her breath.

Frowning at the worry lines collecting around her eyes, I said, "I couldn't leave you to fend for yourself? You know you're not good at fending."

"Better than you," she sniffed.

"May I remind you who taught who how to cook?"

"Nowadays, anybody can learn to cook from a computer, which you still don't use properly."

"I do too," I objected.

"Really? And how many new devices have you had to buy due to damage incurred in the line of Macy's ire? Your learning curve was incredibly expensive."

"Touché," I smiled as the lines on her face eased. Stretching one leg out, I nudged her stomach with my big toe. "You're having a boy."

"Oh? Is physic ability one of your new talents?" she asked doubtfully. Using the napkin holder, she pushed my foot away. "Please refrain from touching me with your piggies."

Miranda had a phobia about feet. That's precisely why I did it.

"You know that feeling of deja vu you get that you've been there and done that before?" I asked.

"Yes," she said slowly.

"I feel that way right now." Letting my feet slide to the floor, I started for the dining room where everyone else was gathering.

"How am I supposed to interpret that?" she yelled after me.

Heck if I knew.

Reynolds met me at the door as I was entering. He looked me up and down, his face a complete mask. "Can't say the sleep looks like it did you any good," he frowned. Squinting, his eyes lingered on the bruises tattooing my cheeks. "Swelling may have gone down a little." Then he had the audacity to lean in and sniff me.

I reared away from him in disgust. "That's why I like you, Reynolds. I can always count on you to be honest."

Leaving my cheeks, his eyes traveled to meet mine, narrowing when he worked out the sarcasm. "Seems like we have that in common," he quipped before leaving me to stand in the doorway.

If I thought about it much, I might wonder why I had all these cocky, arrogant, male beings in my life. And that was putting it politely.

"You should cut him a little slack," Miranda said from where she still sat at the island. "He carried you to your suite and stayed with you until Olivia made us both leave. He was really worried about you."

"He just told me I looked like poop," I countered as I whirled to face her.

"So did I," she dismissed. "Only people who truly cared about you could offer such an honest appraisal." She tried to maintain the stern look she aimed at me, but the smile in her eyes gave her away. "Okay, maybe anyone who caught even the tiniest of peeks at you could say the same," she laughed. "But the outfit is marvelous. You must tell me who your stylist is?"

"You're hilarious," I drolled. "You should do stand up." Turning from her, I completed my entry into the dining room. As soon as I crossed over the threshold, silence engulfed the room. My steps faltered in the unexpected spotlight.

"You always did know how to capture a room," Miranda taunted as she walked past me to take her seat at the table.

They were probably just stunned by my outfit. My bright blue bra with chocolate chip cookies strategically placed was clearly visible through my white t-shirt. And if that wasn't plain enough they could just follow the instructions to watch me written across my chest. Seriously. As if my facial appearance wasn't sufficiently startling. Thank you so much, stylist.

Taking a deep breath, I started forward again, not stopping until I'd reached the head of the table.

"I'd like to start this meeting by saying that contrary to my appearance, I am not auditioning for a role on The Walking Dead." A few spatters of laughter dotted the room. "This is just… well, I don't know what this is," I said, gingerly stroking the side of my face. "It's a side effect of helping Adam."

"To shift to human again?" Wrangle asked.

I nodded at him, then, for the first time, noticed the platters of food scattered down the length of the table and no one making a move for them. "Please, don't wait on me," I said, urging them with my hands to eat. After three days without eating, I knew I should be starving, but this was one of those times my appetite had deserted me. The very thought of eating right now was nauseating, and if I wasn't going to keep it down, what was the point.

As I waited for them to fill their plates, I recognized that the number of participants had grown since the last time we were assembled. Camo had returned, and there were a couple of other faces I recognized from when they rescued me from Millsap. I didn't recall ever knowing their names. The Colony hybrids had grown too. Crystal had joined us as well as Bethany, Charlie's girlfriend. For the first time in how many days, Charlie wore an easy smile. I hadn't realized they were so close. Back at the Colony, Charlie had always kept everything low key. But there was nothing low key about the way he was relating to her now.

When I finished counting the Colony hybrids, I recounted them. We were short one. Scout was not currently among us. My eyes flashed to Olivia and Camo. Neither one of them acted like anything was wrong. If something bad had happened to Scout during the trip to Geneva, surely she would have told me already. If not her, Miranda definitely would have.

Sighing as I pulled out my chair, I noted that Scout wasn't the only one missing. I wished Adam was in here with us, instead of in that cell. Reaching through the bond, I did the equivalent of knocking on his closed door, but he ignored my call. He was going to have to get over this guilt nonsense and rejoin the rest of us messed up hybrids trying to save the world. Right after this meeting, I was going to tell him as much, face to face.

"I have some news," Olivia announced.

My stomach clenched involuntarily at her words.

"Only one of the Consortium assets that Garrison identified showed up. We administered the inhibitor easily enough. The effect was not immediate, but it was catastrophic."

"Like we suspected," Miranda said quietly.

"I am recommending we shelve it," Olivia said.

"I recommend we don't trust Garrison," Miranda countered.

"I second that," I agreed. Father or not, he acted a little too freely with regard to life, be it human or hybrid. "Garrison has the specs for the inhibitor?"

Olivia grimaced and nodded. "Once we incorporate the lock for our programming, it won't work on us, but any other hybrid would be susceptible."

"Let's make sure the programming for the lock stays under Organization control," I said, looking straight at Juarez.

"Copy that," he nodded. "I've already designed the code to be virtually invisible. The only three people in the world that know what to look for are here. After this initial update, it won't even be a thing anymore. It'll be standard protocol for any new hybrids created."

"That works," I nodded. "Olivia, where's Scout?"

She looked up, squaring her shoulders to face me. "After we witnessed what happened with the target, he told me to tell you not to worry. Then he disappeared."

I hadn't anticipated Scout being the one to go rogue. The temptation to look at Kenny was strong, but I didn't think anyone else knew about the bond he had with the other Colony hybrids. I'd have to grill him about Scout later, along with all the other things I needed him to answer for.

"I guess we'll have to trust him for now," I said. "Juarez, are we ready to start the upgrade?"

"That's it?" Olivia said in disbelief. "Scout takes off, and you're fine with it?"

"Um, yeah?" Did I like that he'd taken off without me knowing all the details? No. But sometimes life had detours.

She crossed her arms over her chest, scowling for all to see.

"He said not to worry," I said placatingly. "He's obviously working on something, and he'll let us know what it is when we need to."

"It's called trust, Olivia," Miranda sneered. "You should try it sometime."

The scowl on Olivia's face deepened further, causing me to smile. I didn't know why it worked this way between us, but it did.

"Anyway," Juarez intervened. "We've got the core programming done. All that's left is inserting the code containing each individual's pin. We'll start that process after the meeting."

"The sooner the better," I nodded. "Cedars, where do we stand with the DTP's pending operations?"

"I've been able to narrow down the next set of targets, but not pin point it exactly. My research into Gene Mallet...something's off."

"Yeah," I said distantly. Something was off. I didn't have any evidence to back it up currently, but I felt it like a weight in my gut. Blinking back to alertness, I said, "I plan on doing some research later. I'll let you know what I find."

He nodded. "I delayed having the majority of our people return until we could incorporate the upgrade as part of reentry. When that is complete, I'll start assigning teams to deal with DTP's operations. Also, now that Adam is really back, I think he should be the one to address the assembly." Raising his eyebrows, he looked at me for approval.

"I would prefer to let Adam handle this," I agreed, avoiding Miranda's eyes as she snorted. Hey, my stay as CEO was only ever supposed to be temporary. I always anticipated handing it over to Adam. How soon that was depended on him. "It might be a while before Adam is up for it."

Cedars' brows tilted downward, creating a large crease between his eyes.

"Regardless of the delay, I think we should wait for Adam to address the assembly," Olivia chimed in. "The smoother the transition in leadership, the better the Organization will handle it."

"Then we wait," I concluded.

Reynolds cleared his throat. "Is the virility issue part of the upgrade?" he asked.

"Virility?" Crystal repeated, confused by Reynolds' question.

Kenny's eyes widened in embarrassment. It was a look not seen often on his face. I watched in amusement as he reached over and grasped her hand in attempt to quiet her.

"Next on the list," Juarez answered, not even attempting to hide his smile. "In a totally nonrelated note, we're conducting a sweep of the facility for tracking devices."

"How's that going?" I asked.

"Slow," Flash answered. "A lot of this complex is shielded by the mountain that surrounds it. We're having to physically sweep each location."

"Don't forget ventilation shafts," I said knowingly. "You'd be surprised how much stuff you could hide in there."

"We're not leaving any area unsearched," Juarez confirmed.

"Good." Turning to Charlie, I said, "Have you found another rogue sister yet?"

"It could be a brother," Miranda said before he could answer.

"Or brother?" I corrected.

"Just you three so far," Charlie said.

Right. We sisters three. With any luck, we wouldn't beat the crap out of each other before it was all over. "Alright, baby report." I looked at Miranda expectantly.

"Uh," Miranda stuttered. "Everything's on track?"

"Are you not monitoring yourself?" I mean, come on. If we were going to do this, let's at least do it right.

"Yeah, in the two days I've had in between picking your butt up off the floor," she snapped angrily. "Who's the pregnant one anyway?"

"I'll handle it," Olivia offered.

"Thank you," I told her, ignoring Miranda's death glare. I was going to be there for the birth. That would have to be enough.

"Am I forgetting anything?" I asked the group.

"Yeah, us," Kenny drawled. His disapproval of the testing was manifested in the grim expression he wore.

"You know the testing is necessary," I said flatly.

"You do not get to assign us without consultation with us," he said, jabbing his thumb into his chest on the last us.

"There is always consultation," Cedars said. "This is not a dictatorship."

Kenny looked at Cedars, but he waited for my response.

"Agreed," I nodded. "I wouldn't do that."

"The old Macy would," Wrangle said quietly.

Taking a breath to respond, I held it. He was right. The old Macy would have followed orders even if she didn't like it or agree with it. But those days were over.

"That's true," I conceded. "But that Macy is irrevocably gone. This Macy doesn't do things she doesn't feel good about."

"I think I like this Macy better," Crystal whispered to Kenny.

She wasn't the only one.

Margaret appeared in the doorway. Seeing her made me think of food. Nutrition bars!

"Margaret!" I shouted, startling her from the doorway. "I have a very important mission for you."

"You do?" she asked, puzzled by my claim.

"Yes. I need you to work on a new and way—I'm talking so far away that it's in another continent way—improved source of nutrition to replace the gruesome bars that now fill that niche."

She kind of chuckled like she didn't believe I was serious.

"I'm not kidding, Margaret."

"A new nutrition bar?"

"I don't care what form it takes, just make it taste better. Please."

"You would be doing all of us a huge favor," Reynolds added. "You have not been around her when she gets really hungry."

"All sorts of cranky," Kenny nodded.

"This isn't just for me," I protested. "You can't tell me that any of you like that bar." Looking at the impassive faces around the table, I demanded, "Well?"

"Little like peat gravel," Cedars admitted.

"It reminds me of accidently crunching down on the shell of a sunflower seed," Olivia said, then shivered in revulsion. "But with less flavor."

"Flavorless shells and peat gravel? Say no more, I'm convinced," Margaret declared. "But I'm not a biochemist or bio anything. Don't get your hopes up just yet."

"Use whatever resources the Organization has to offer," I yelled after her as she left the dining room. God knew she'd need it to rework those things.

"What about the riddles? Have you come up with anything?" Olivia asked.

"No," I shook my head. "Not even in my dreams."

"What riddle?" Camo asked.

"What flows and never runs out of time?" Reynolds stated for the table.

Camo looked at Reynolds then at me. "Why are we solving riddles?" he asked.

"Lindsey insinuated that the Organization's original purpose was something different from what it is now," Olivia supplied as she leaned forward and addressed him. "She gave Macy the riddle. Julia confirmed it."

"Julia also gave me another one," I added. "What has time as its source?"

The room grew quiet as we each digested the new addition. The only thing I could think of regarding time was a clock, and I didn't know of any clock that used time as an energy source. Time by itself was never an energy source. That I knew of, anyway.

"I would think that time referred to a clock of some sort," Reynolds said.

"But a clock's time runs out every twelve hours. It's not endless," Olivia commented.

"Don't forget we're looking for something that flows. Something fluid," I said.

"Like a river or something?" Crystal asked.

Olivia leaned back in her chair, her face a mask of concentration. "A river with time as its source," she thought aloud.

"It could be time, like the seasons," Cedars said. "As the seasons or time marches on, the snow on the mountains melts, feeding all the other rivers and streams."

"Too literal," Olivia said, shaking her head in disagreement. "I don't think we are talking about an actual river."

"A metaphorical river with time as its source," Miranda said. "The river of life? Like in the Bible?"

I shook my head. "I think that's too...religious. We can't forget the biological component. It's tied to me, remember?"

"What's more biological than living forever?" Miranda countered.

"I'm pretty sure I don't have a river running through me," I said flatly.

"Maybe not," Olivia said, leaning into the table and looking at me intently. "What if Julia found a way to create cells that regenerate perpetually?"

"It wouldn't be cells," Miranda corrected. "She was a geneticist, not a cellular biologist."

"DNA that doesn't degrade over time," I said, amending Olivia's thought.

"Maybe she discovered an alternate process of DNA replication," Cedars said. "RNA creation was her forte."

If Julia created RNA with the ability to prevent DNA degradation...That would be as close to immortality as you could get. This side of heaven anyway.

"But I thought the nanobots gave us that with their constant repair functions," I said.

Olivia cocked her head to the side. "In some ways that's true. But from what I've been able to determine, at some, at this moment incalculable, time in the future, the amount of cells needing repair will exceed the nanobots' capabilities."

"So as long as we keep our need for repair below that threshold, we live on indefinitely," I thought aloud.

"Sounds good to me," Juarez chuckled.

Olivia, Miranda and I exchanged glances. I knew they were thinking the same thing I was. Miranda was the one who voiced it. "A perpetual fountain of youth," she said.

Olivia and I nodded in agreement.

"Maybe we need to analyze your DNA sooner than we planned," Olivia said.

Yeah. Maybe I did have a river of life running through me.

CHAPTER 24

THE MEETING DISSOLVED ON A somber note. It wasn't every day that you might have made the biggest medical discovery of all time. If we had answered the riddle correctly, and if it was true. Either way, it didn't change things much for us. Due to the nanobots, we were already going to live on for however long. So unless they could suddenly make us impenetrable like Superman, we were still susceptible to death in all manner of gruesome ways. There was a pleasant thought. I was basically guaranteed the only way I could die was through some ghastly, brutal act. Closed casket ceremony, anyone?

Shaking my head at my own morbidness, I pinched the bridge of my nose. Did Adam know about any of this, I wondered. It wouldn't surprise me, not with the way he kept secrets. Releasing the skin squeezed between my fingers, I turned my thoughts to the impending confrontation with him. I was in no hurry to reach his cell as visions of our first fight danced in my head. I didn't know for sure that was what awaited me, but I really didn't see it going any other way. He wanted a pass on life, and I wasn't going to give him one. At the very least, there was bound to be some yelling.

The hallway in front of Adam's cell was empty when I arrived. I couldn't tell by his lack of response if he knew I was there or not. He sat with his back against the wall, his long legs stretched out in front of him, and his eyes firmly fixed on the floor. The black athletic pants and fitted tee he wore did nothing to dispel the parlor of dejection that surrounded him. And the bare feet only added to the overall depiction of gloom. It made him seem vulnerable, which made me mad. Of all the things I knew Adam to be, vulnerable was not one of them.

Forgetting everything I had previously rehearsed, I raised a fist and pounded on the glass. "Hey! You done feeling sorry for yourself?" I shouted angrily.

Not one muscle moved, except for his eyes, which slowly lifted to mine.

"Yeah, I look like a freak show," I barked in response to the almost imperceptible lift of his brow at my appearance. "Hey!" I hit the glass again when he made to resume staring at the floor. "You do not get to do this!" Unable to stop the anger that boiled out of me, I continued to pound the glass as I yelled at him. "You do not get to sit on your ass while the rest of us scramble around like idiots." It was working. I could feel his anger rising. "You've been through some stuff, boohoo. We all have."

"You didn't all hurt...one of your teammates," he said coldly.

Was he talking about me? I was now downgraded to the status of teammate? "Are you kidding me?" I jeered. "Weren't you the one that gave me the spiel about being part of a team and accepting the risks that go with it?"

Adam exploded off the floor, the abject misery supplanted by an anger that pulsed through his movements as he paced within the confines of the cell. I wasn't sure this was any better, but it was more in line with the Adam I knew.

On a whim, I tried the door, pausing when it slid open freely. Not. Even. Locked. "Why are you still in here?" I demanded in clipped tones.

Because you are in my room, the thought raced at me.

My grip on the door tightened. "I need your computer," I said hoarsely, trying to conceal the hurt his thoughts had caused.

He looked at me in confusion, then regret as he realized I'd heard his response. "I hadn't meant for you to hear that," he said gruffly.

"Whatever," I mumbled, dismissing the slight. "Sorry about cramping your style, but you'll just have to tolerate it for now."

Adam's face was a complete blank.

"Alrighty then," I smiled tightly. "The Organization needs you, and you can't do very much from inside this cell." Not waiting for his approval, I took the few steps necessary to grab his arm, and then transported both of us to his suite. "I've got mad skills, I know," I deadpanned in response to his look of surprise.

He jerked his arm from me like he'd been burned and warily moved a few paces away.

Deep cleansing breath, I intoned silently as I squeezed my eyes shut and counted to ten before opening them again.

"You've made yourself at home," he observed, nostrils flaring while he swiveled his head in an effort to catalog my prior movements in his suite.

I cringed at the judgment in his voice. Talk about feeling unwanted. Turning from him, I stomped to the desk and plopped down in front of the computer. The sooner I got what I needed, the sooner I could get the heck out of here. When the process for gaining access to the computer started, I could barely get the words out. Not with him staring me down. Try ignoring the two hundred pound leopard that had you in his sights. I felt like a baby gazelle. It got even worse when he positioned himself directly behind my chair where I could feel him, but no longer see him.

"Who is Gene Mallet?" he asked after reading the name in the search field.

"The head of the Department of the President, a covert group with the goal of eliminating hybrids. He is also currently an advisor to the president, who is also a hybrid."

"Ironic," he said without emotion.

"He also likes to stamp his initials on his bullets," I added, but immediately regretted my words when I felt him stiffen.

"You know this how?" he said in a slow growl.

The hairs on the back of my neck stood out in response to the menace in his voice. My instincts were to defend myself against the threat, but I didn't want to fight Adam. I wasn't even sure it was Adam talking.

"He's tried to kill me on more than one occasion now," I

answered. "As a general rule, I like to identify the people trying to take me out."

"He's still alive?" It was more an expression of outrage than a question.

"Cedars is working on it," I tried to explain, but he was already moving. Racing from the desk, I swerved to cut him off. "Where do you think you're going?" I asked, placing both hands flat against his chest and leaning into him.

"Move," he ordered, his voice taut with anger.

"No," I shook my head. "You are not going after Cedars."

His eyes narrowed at my refusal, filling with a rage that was foreign to human eyes. If I didn't know any better, I wouldn't have believed I was staring into Adam's eyes.

"You're not even trying," I accused.

Without warning, the bond flew open, rocking me backwards with the force of the conflicting emotions rolling through him. Adam was in human form, true, but he was still warring with the leopard for control.

"Don't," he warned when I reached out to him. "I am trying."

"Try harder," I choked out, angry at the tears that were forming. I hated how much I wanted him back, how miserable I felt to have him right in front of me and still so far away.

Reaching one hand, he gently brushed my cheek. Then faster than I could follow, withdrew it and backed away from me. "It's not safe for me to be around you," he said, watching me through eyes that now glowed a soft green.

The emotion had faded from his voice again. I supposed it was easier to maintain control if he withdrew into himself, denied any emotions he might have. Become the leopard permanently? Wait a minute. These weren't my thoughts. They were his. My eyes widened at the sudden realization. I didn't even have words for how that made me feel.

"Macy, I'm sorry," he panted awkwardly.

Clenching my teeth, I closed my eyes against the feelings of betrayal that roiled through me. He wasn't the only one who could do emotionless. "You can't go back, Adam. You can't be the leopard," I said robotically. "The Organization needs you."

He couldn't understand why I would still want him here after what he'd done and wanted. I tried to figure out what he thought he'd done, but the thoughts circling through his head were now too fast and convoluted to keep up with, and there was no use in waiting for an explanation from him. Sighing deeply, I abandoned the conversation and returned to the desk. I didn't know how to help him right now, and I still had work to do.

Doing my best to ignore him, I located the NSA report I'd found earlier and began working my way through it. I exhaled in relief when the sound of the shower starting penetrated my thoughts. Was there a gulf between Adam and me, and were we miles away from where we were before he was taken? Yes on both counts. But he was out of the cell and taking a much needed shower. Things were looking up.

I wished I could say the same about this search. The entire text of the report wasn't telling me anything I didn't already know. The photographs featuring Julia or Renard along with the original hybrid creations were interesting, but not particularly helpful. I wondered if this was any of my hybrids' parents. It was hard to tell because here they still looked young and fresh, not what they were by the time I got to them.

My hand stilled on the mouse when I reached the last page of pictures. Standing in the background of one of the photos was a very irate Gene Mallet. Clearly, he was not happy to have been caught on camera. Zooming in on the picture, I isolated Mallet in the photo. "Hold up," I whispered as I leaned forward to more closely study his features. He didn't look much different than he did today. Just like Julia. There could be only one answer for that.

Crossing my arms over my chest, I frowned at the screen. Mallet was not a scientist. His resume had identified him as a military man through and through. And yet, here he was, with Julia and Renard at the hybrid launch party. The picture didn't make him look cozy with either of them, and Julia had claimed that Mallet had betrayed her. But this was too early for that. Besides, he would have needed them to adapt the nanobots' purpose from controlling the shift to bodily upkeep. After that was complete, that's when the betrayal would have occurred.

Did it involve theft of the nanobots? Or maybe Mallet had been the reason for Renard's change of heart regarding hybrids. Whatever the case, it didn't matter now. What was important was the fact that Mallet had used the information to his benefit. He had potentially been hogging medical technology to himself for the last forty years.

I shook my head at the waste. How could anyone be so selfish? At least Julia, even in her forced exile state, had started an organization meant to defend the world against crazies. And Mallet wasn't just selfish, he was ruthless. He had intentionally stifled research into this area because he already knew what he needed to. Dad gum it. Because he already had a team of researchers in place, an organization of his own. Not Biogen. That was under Garrison's thumb, and he had no use for Mallet.

So Mallet had gotten his hands on nanobot tech and ran with it. Surely he wasn't the only one benefitting from it. A man like Mallet would wield that kind of power very selectively, carefully building his base until he felt secure enough to step out. Mallet might be more dangerous than I'd given him credit for. But he had one fatal flaw, the help he needed to survive.

Leaning back in the chair, I clasped my hands behind my head. What would I need if I was trying to create eternal youth? The most obvious answer was ageless cells, which would imply ageless DNA. The same thing Julia might have created in me.

Telomeres, Adam thought.

I didn't know if he meant to communicate with me or was just thinking to himself, but I knew that he'd been following my assessment. His interest had piqued when I found the photo with Mallet.

"Telomeres," I repeated out loud. The string of junk DNA at the end of a chromosome. The latest theory was that the longer the telomeres were, the longer the life an individual had. That had to do with the fact that every time a DNA strand replicated, the tail end of it was chopped off. If it was junk DNA that was scrapped, it didn't matter. But when the cutting started eating into vital DNA, that was when trouble started. Once that process began, it was downhill from there until catastrophic failure, better known as death, occurred.

Circumventing that issue would require cellular machinery that would perpetually resupply the telomere. But that wouldn't correct any defective genes a person carried. That would require another set of cellular machinery that would clip out defective genes and replace them with corrected versions. Before that, you would have to locate the defective genes. Even with today's technology, the programming would have to be massive, not to mention the job of actually replacing the DNA in every affected cell. Then you still wouldn't be done. The programming would have to be updated as science advanced. Which meant Mallet would be going somewhere regularly to receive updates.

"Bingo." That was traceable. Unclasping my hands, I reached for the phone to dial Cedars. *No vigilante behavior,* I quickly warned Adam as I detected another, larger spike in interest.

He growled at me in response.

"Cedars here."

"I've got something," I told him.

"Me, too. You first."

"I found a picture of Mallet from forty years ago. He looks practically the same as he does now."

"He's a hybrid?" he asked doubtfully.

"No. I think he has been using the nanobots for medicinal purposes."

"Like what the president wants," he said thoughtfully.

"Exactly. We need eyes on Mallet. Everywhere he goes. If we have any past intel, that needs to be analyzed for places he visits that don't fall inside the normal pattern. He's going somewhere to update the programming."

"We've got some data on him, but we weren't looking for this. I'll get someone on it."

"Can we also start a search for any data on an engineered

RNA that would snip out defective genes and replace them? It would help tremendously if we already had something to go into production with when I do the big reveal."

"What big reveal?" Adam asked as he exited the bathroom.

I'll fill you in. Give me a minute.

"Was that Adam's voice?" Cedars asked.

"He's here with me," I confirmed.

"Good," he sighed.

I wasn't sure that Adam's presence equaled the emotion that Cedars expressed in that one word, but I was working on it.

"Your turn. What did you find?"

"The anomalies in Langston's tox screen kept bothering me. After further study, I have determined that she was primed with a liquid tracer."

"Like a tracking device?"

"Worse. Something to do with the viscosity of the fluid allowed her nanobots to communicate with all of ours. Olivia thinks that is how the projection trait works."

"It works by temporarily allowing her thoughts to reprogram ours," I concluded, horrified at the possible ramifications.

"Exactly. Only the tracer is tied into something at the other end, not isolated within her."

Meaning that if whoever had been controlling her managed to reestablish the link, we were all sitting ducks. "We need that update yesterday," I breathed, just managing to skirt the panic that rose. "The last thing we need is a bunch of hybrids running around acting like crazy people."

"I'm not sure how we'd tell the difference," he said flatly.

It took me a minute. "Did you just make a joke?" I asked in surprise.

"Today will have to do," he laughed. "We need you down here. Juarez is just about ready for you."

"Is Adam's ready?"

There was a pause. "We didn't think we would need it so soon."

It might not even be safe after what he'd been through, but we couldn't risk not doing it. Adam under the influence of anyone other than Adam was a danger to us all. "Get it done," I said quietly. "We're on our way."

In one motion, I hung up the phone and turned to face Adam. "I discovered that our nanobot programming was susceptible to basically anyone who knows how to do it. I've had Juarez and his team working on a lock. That's now being initiated, and it's our turn."

He tossed the towel he'd been using to dry his hair over the back of the couch. "And the big reveal?"

"The president has asked me to reveal the presence of hybrid technology couched in medical advancement."

He squinted one eye at me. "The President of the United States?"

"Hey, that was your idea, not mine. Also, Miranda, Olivia and myself are sisters."

He looked taken aback. "Come again."

I motioned for him to start walking. "There were actually four engineered embryos, mine being one of them. In Granny's bunker we, well, Charlie and Flash, were able to isolate the nanobot signature that I carried..." I trailed off when I caught a glimpse of his confused face.

"You were in Granny's bunker?"

Oh, crap. He didn't know about her house yet.

"What about her house?"

"Don't get mad," I said in a rush, then clamped my mouth shut. Probably shouldn't have started with that.

Stopping where he was, he put both hands on his hips and let his chin fall forward. "What have you done?" he asked reluctantly.

"It wasn't me."

With his chin nearly touching his chest, he twisted his head to stare at me.

"You told me to go to Granny's!" I yelled at his accusatory stare.

"What. Happened?" he repeated.

"I went to Granny's—like you said—and someone was already there. Somethings, actually. They were watching her house. They attacked. Granny's okay, but the house…it was destroyed." Under his glare, I felt about the height of an ant.

"Granny's house, my childhood home, is gone?"

"Yes," I confessed, unable to meet his eyes.

"Humph," he grunted and started forward again. "Maybe this time we rebuild, she'll let me do something other than a hunter's cabin."

My head whipped his direction. "This time?" I yelled at him.

"We've rebuilt it half a dozen times already," he admitted as I caught up with him. "Granny's not the gentlest of types."

"Rebuilt? That was mean," I charged. "I have enough stuff to feel guilty about without you adding to it." Before the words were even out of my mouth, I was kicking myself. "I didn't mean it like that," I assured him as I reached for his arm, but it was too late.

Shying away from my touch, he reinstated the wall between us.

Not wanting to do any more damage, I let my arm and the subject drop. How did you rebuild a relationship with a live wired leopard? One little bitty grounded nail at a time.

CHAPTER 25

ADAM WAS GIVEN A WIDE berth as we waited for Juarez to return. The tension the others felt at his presence rolled over my skin, leaving monster goose bumps in its wake. This was the most uncomfortable I'd been since…well, okay, nearly all the time spent with Adam so far had been uncomfortable, but this was almost unbearable. I wanted to yell or laugh, anything to get rid of this feeling. Not much chance of that happening with this stone-faced bunch. The only thing moving on them were their eyes which followed Adam's every move. Then Miranda crashed through the door.

"Adam!" she cried as she caught the door's rebound. "Didn't expect to see you here." Flinging the door wide again, she hurried over to him. "How you doing?" Each word was punctuated by the hand she used to slap Adam on the back.

Everyone in the room, including me, held their breath as they waited for Adam's response. The look he gave her could have melted paint off the wall.

"Fine," he exhaled through clenched teeth and stepped away from her hand still resting on his back.

"I tried to take care of her in your absence," she asserted, oblivious to his discomfort as she closed the distance between them again. "But it's gotten more difficult than it used to be." She winked one eye at me. "Always fainting and puking. I can't tell you how many times I've picked her butt up off the floor just this week."

She was doing her best to lighten the mood. It was lost on

Adam, but I appreciated the attempt, and it was loads better than the strained silence.

"It's a wonder she's still alive with the way she constantly leads us into ambushes," Kenny muttered.

"And plane crashes," Reynolds added. "And then slaps you when you have to glue her back together."

"Gets mad at you when you have to slap her because she's screaming uncontrollably in your face," Kenny countered, as if this were some kind of contest.

Rounding on them, I skewered both of them with my glare. "That is about enough," I warned.

"People do seem to be impaled around her quite often," Van noted.

"And shot," Reynolds nodded while rubbing the place on his chest where the wound had been. "I'm sure Scout would agree."

"Scout shot himself," I snarled in frustration. This runaway train had to stop before it ran me over.

"If I'm not mistaken, two houses associated with her have also been destroyed," Charlie said.

Et tu, Charlie, I thought as I whirled to face him. What was wrong with them? It was like I had suddenly become the outlet for all the unease they felt around Adam. "That was not my fault," I growled. "None of that was my fault."

"Even more disturbing," Wrangle drawled, "is how most of her outfits never make it through the day. You would think she liked showing everyone her underwear. Including the President of the United States."

Adam's eyes lifted to mine. Written in them was the question or more appropriately, the accusation.

"Miranda's pregnant," I blurted out, using my whole arm to point directly at her. It was a blatant attempt to shift the focus away from me. Guilty as charged. But I still hoped it worked.

He held my eyes a moment longer and then transferred his gaze to her stomach. His head tilted to the side as he concentrated on her. "You are," he said, his voice conveying his surprise.

"I am," Miranda said, patting her stomach and giving me

the stink eye at the same time. "Juarez should have you up and running soon. So, you know, no need to be careful until then."

"What?" He asked sharply.

"What Miranda should not be saying to you," I said through clenched teeth as I hurried over to intervene. "Is that well...you're not currently...you know..."

"You're shooting blanks, man," Charlie finished curtly.

Adam looked like he'd been punched.

"Julia had birth control inserted into the nanobot programming," I explained quickly. "Millsap is her son. It scared her away from any future natural births of hybrids."

He brought a hand to his forehead and massaged the temples on either side. "What are we waiting on?" he growled angrily.

The brief interlude of not peace, but something less tense than before, evaporated as his unease blanketed the room again. Thankfully, Juarez chose that moment to bustle through the door.

"Some of us are restricted to outdated modes of transportation like walking," he said testily, wielding the large mug of coffee he carried as a weapon to clear the way before him. He set the mug down near an isolation booth they had constructed for the reprogramming and began booting up the laptop sitting there.

"Is this where the magic happens?" I joked, lightly gripping the sides of the booth which looked more like a rickety shower stall than a secure isolation booth.

"I know it doesn't look like much," Juarez said without looking up from the computer. "But the inside of the enclosure is coated to ensure the only programming affected belongs to the one we're targeting." After a long draw of coffee, he leaned away from the computer, crossed his arms and looked pointedly at Adam. His face had perturbed written all over it. "Any time you're ready," he challenged.

Wincing at the direct provocation, I kept my eyes fastened on Adam. He was busy examining the booth and hadn't seen Juarez's behavior, but I was sure he could smell and hear the anger coming from him.

Sensing my angst, Reynolds stepped forward. "Let me seal you in," he offered to Adam while staring intently at me.

I held my breath as Adam turned to look at Reynolds. A good five inches shorter than Adam, the top of Reynolds' head ended at Adam's nose. But Reynolds never flinched as he continued to hold the tent flap of a door open. It felt like the whole room breathed a sigh of relief when Adam stepped inside. As if that little zipper Reynolds was making quick work of would somehow protect us from the man inside.

"Nice going, genius," Miranda whispered angrily to me as she took the opportunity to confront me.

"It worked, didn't it?"

"To draw attention away from you? Yeah. Brilliantly."

"I thought you loved being the center of attention."

"That was before. If you haven't noticed, I've changed."

"Oh, I noticed," I said, intentionally glancing at her stomach.

"It's not just the baby," she argued. "Cedars, too. You can't tell me that knowing Adam hasn't changed you."

That'd be a bunch of crock. Knowing Adam had literally forced me to change. Undeniably and irrevocably changed. "I know one thing, I've got a lot more bite than I used to have."

"No kidding," she laughed. "Hey, what is it with these men and their obsessive need to have the ability to procreate?"

I shrugged my shoulders. "Maybe it strikes a blow to their manliness."

"I don't feel it. Do you?"

"Wounded Manhood? No. I vacillate between anger and the need to pass out."

"Ha," she barked in total agreement with my statement. "I would appreciate a little less of the passing out."

"I'll get right on that."

She nudged my arm with her elbow. "He seems okay," she said low enough for only me to hear.

I didn't know what she was seeing. Standing there, still as a statue inside the booth, he might look okay. But he wasn't. The wall he had constructed was slipping. He was angry at everyone, even me. I hoped he could keep it together long enough to make it back to the suite.

Olivia poked her head in the doorway. "Macy, we've got another booth set up next door."

"Have fun," Miranda taunted, patting me on the back consolingly as I left to join Olivia.

The moment the door shut behind us, Olivia started talking. "He's angry," she said. "I almost choked when I opened the door. I'm worried, Macy."

Not wanting to give voice to my agreement, I nodded at her. "Hey, Flash," I waved as we entered.

"Good to see you in an upright position," he teased. "Stand here." He pointed to the newly constructed booth. It looked even less stable than the other one.

"Is this safe?" I asked skeptically.

"Perfectly," Flash answered with a smile. When I stood there staring at him, he nodded his head toward the booth in a signal for me to enter. "If you actually get inside."

"Fine," I mumbled as I stepped inside the stall. "What are you doing?" I asked Olivia who was sticking electrode looking thingies on my forehead. "I thought these things were wifi enabled."

"They are. This is just to monitor the transmission." She stuck the last one on, and bent down to begin zipping the door. "Do you know what you want your password to be?"

"What are the parameters?"

"Only that we can type it on the keypad."

What should my password be? Nothing that I've used before. It should be something symbolic, something representative of my life now. Hybrid was too easy. Hellacious could work, but I wasn't sure about the spelling.

"It's not rocket science, Macy. You don't have to put this much thought into it," Olivia complained.

"I'm working on something here," I said, which was better than the, shut up, I'm thinking, comment I almost said.

She rolled her eyes as if she had discerned the true meaning behind what I said. Pretty specific, this smelling ability she had. Take another whiff, why don't ya. Back the hell off.

"I think Adam's anger is bleeding into you," she remarked, then took a few steps back.

She was probably right. Now, where was I? Right, the state of my life. Over the last couple of weeks, my life had been transformed. Illuminated. The amount of knowledge I had gained was...was...a revelation. "I've got it."

She pointed to the keypad attached to the side of the stall. "When we tell you, type it in."

"That's it?" I asked when we were done. "Seems anticlimactic."

"I know you're used to all hell breaking loose around you, but really, that's it."

Scowling at her, I stepped free of the booth. "Is anyone keeping a master list of passwords?"

"Juarez will have a master list." She held a hand out for the electrodes, which I readily surrendered. "And we can store it somewhere so the rest of us can get to it if needed."

"How long until everyone is done?"

"Everyone here will be finished shortly. The rest of the three hundred and thirty two members will take longer. Their arrivals are going to be sporadic, but they've all been given orders to report directly to us. First wave starts tomorrow. It's going to be a long couple of days," she sighed heavily.

"We need to also do this with the other Colony hybrids," I said.

"We plan to," Flash said. "Charlie had already thought of it."

Good. I could count on Charlie to make it happen. "I'm in the clear?" I asked hopefully.

"Yep," Olivia nodded as she conferred with her tablet. "No trackers and no embedded control chips."

That was a relief. Though I somewhat suspected that I could get my nanos to remove any if I needed them to, it wasn't a theory I was in a hurry to test.

"Hey," Olivia called. "If you see Margaret, send her here."

Pausing in the doorway, I rotated to face her.

"I know she doesn't have nanobots," Olivia said before I could voice my objection. "But I still want to sweep her for trackers and any other hidden control mechanisms. Just in case."

"I'll let her know," I agreed.

I knew Margaret didn't want anyone else to know about the nanobots she'd had or her reaction to them, but at some point, we really needed to identify what had happened in her. Should the need ever arise to be able to resist nanobots, that information would be priceless. Gaining that information, yet another item to weigh down the list. Pretty soon, I was going to need a wheelbarrow just to haul it around.

When I opened the door to the adjacent room where I'd left Adam, a blast of tension tainted air hit my unprepared nostrils. In between the sneezes, I scanned the room for Adam and found nothing but a bunch of tightlipped faces.

"Where's Adam?"

"He left," Charlie said. "He got a phone call. I think he went to see Lindsey," he said uncertainly.

Dang it. How was that going to turn out well? "Did Juarez go with him?"

"I think he went to referee," Charlie nodded.

I was out of the room before he could finish his answer. Storming down the hall, I wrestled the phone out of my pocket and dialed Miranda. "Where are you?" I demanded when she picked up.

"Listen, Ms. Prissy Pants—"

"Adam's gone to see Lindsey."

"Oh. That can't be good."

"How do I get there?"

"Where are you now?"

I stopped walking. "Next to where we were."

"Okay. Go to Adam's cell. Old cell."

"Done."

"Walk down the hallway and turn right. Do you see the set of doors?"

"Yeah, there's a keypad."

"Hang on." Silence filled the seconds as I assumed she connected with Cedars. "Jamie's already headed that way."

"Thanks, Miranda."

"Not a problem. Please be careful. I'm at my quota of Macy collapses for the week."

"I'll try. He's here."

"Try hard," she said and hung up.

Cedars was moving at warp speed. "Is Adam strung as tight as I think he is?" he asked as he punched in the code.

Reporting on Adam felt like a betrayal of sorts, but Cedars needed to know what he might be walking into. "He's carrying a lot of anger around."

"If I have to restrain him, are you going to interfere?"

What immediately popped to mind was the thought that I didn't think restraining Adam was within Cedars' scope of capabilities, not by himself anyway. What I said was, "We might not have to."

"Do you believe that?" he asked doubtfully.

I didn't know what I believed. "How did he even know about Lindsey?" I demanded angrily.

"I said something on the phone. I'm sorry. I didn't realize what state he was in."

"It's not your fault," I grimaced. "I should have said something."

Stop.

The command came through so strong that I stopped automatically. *Adam?*

I don't want you here.

To witness what you're contemplating doing? I can see your thoughts, Adam.

Bristling at the loss of control, he dropped what little shield there was left. The full impact of his intentions caused me to bolt forward. Cedars was right behind me.

Do you remember telling me not to give in to the leopard? That it was difficult to find your way back to human after that. You cannot give in to the leopard anymore.

He wasn't listening to me. The leopard DNA had risen in

supremacy. I nearly fell when Cedars latched onto my arm and jerked me to a stop. Directly in front of us, Juarez stood unmoving outside the last door separating us from Adam.

"I can't go in," Juarez said. "He ordered me not to, and I literally can't go in." The alarm in his voice was disturbing.

"Your nanobots recognized him as alpha?" I guessed.

He shrugged angrily, turning to stare at the door again.

"I take it that's not normal."

"No, it isn't," Cedars said gruffly. He put his hand to the door.

"Let me try first," I pleaded, reaching a hand to stay him. "I'm the one he's least likely to hurt."

"If you need help—"

"I'll holler."

He nodded and opened the door for me.

Adam's disregard for my entrance indicated how little of a threat he considered me. Still, I moved slowly and maintained my distance from him. Standing along the side wall, I studied him as he studied his prey.

"You've disabled her," he said.

"We thought after her actions, she no longer needed to be a hybrid. So, yes, I ordered her disabled."

"You ordered?" He turned his face to me. His eyes were glowing brightly.

I shrugged and looked away from him. "You weren't here."

"I'm here now," he said low and threatening.

The animosity in his voice startled me. His leopard was looking for more than just dominance in Adam, it wanted total control. Correction, it was in control. Not enough to drown Adam out completely, but at this rate, it wouldn't be long.

Lifting my eyes to him as my heart sunk at the realization, I walked forward until I was within inches of him. "You once told me that I didn't have to give in to the leopard, told me not to. But you're giving in."

"The leopard was the only thing that got me through," he bit out tightly.

"But it's not the whole of who you are—"

"You don't know who I am," he growled threateningly as he swung to face me.

Nodding my head, I lowered my eyes. "Maybe I don't. But they do. Cedars, Olivia, Juarez…they do. They're counting on you to step back into leadership of the Organization."

"Make no mistake, Macy. I will be resuming leadership of the Organization."

The steel in his voice left no doubts about his return to power. I needed to give him some. Fixing my eyes firmly on him, I said, "You won't. Not like this."

His head tilted to the side. "Are you challenging me?" he asked, his eyes alight with an eagerness that I'd never seen before.

"Is that what you want?" I asked angrily. "Do you want to kill me? Because you're going to have to get rid of me and everyone else with the direction you're going. They are not going to trust you to lead them. Not when you're like this."

He raised a single eyebrow in disdain. It was the highlight of the look of contempt marring his face.

This could not be happening. I was not going to lose him to the leopard again. His callous disregard for my words unleashed something in me that I hadn't felt since I battled Pike. Anger surged through me, and I shoved Adam as hard as I could.

"Are you going to kill Cedars?" I demanded. Shoving him again, I yelled, "What about Miranda and her unborn baby? Are you going to kill them, too? How will that make you any different from the people who took you?"

Adam's façade cracked. His arms tightly crossed over his chest fell to his sides as he took a step back.

"What about all those cadets who believe in you so much? Who are trusting you to put everything back together again." The questions I hurled at him were like missiles. I could see the confusion on his face as his two natures warred with each other. "Do you remember the state in which we rescued Olivia and Juarez? Are you going to be the one to injure them this time?"

He caught my arms as I lashed out at him again, but I continued to pound him with my words.

"Are you going to be Pike now? That's what you're going to choose? You're going to let the leopard have its way because it's too hard for you?" Twisting and turning, I fought against Adam's hold until he spun me around, trapping me within his arms so that I could no longer move. "If you let the leopard DNA rule you, you will lose everything." Against my back, I could feel his breathing becoming labored as he struggled for control.

"They killed you. Over and over again," he said in a strangled whisper.

His words startled me enough to stop struggling. "What?"

"They tortured you right in front of me. I couldn't stop it. Sometimes, I was the one hurting you."

Images burst forth in my mind, painting the pictures he couldn't give voice to. Understanding flooded my being, and all the fight went out of me. They had used projection on him to make him see those things, believe those things had happened. Sinking so far into the leopard had been what saved him from going insane. Even now, he wasn't certain that what he was experiencing was real.

His hold no longer tight, I turned to face him. "None of that happened. It's not real, Adam. I didn't die, and you never hurt me. Never."

He opened his eyes. The glow was gone, but in its place was the specter of pain and uncertainty.

"You never hurt me. Don't," I said sternly when I felt him about to apologize. "You haven't done anything wrong."

Realizing his arms were still wrapped around me, he let me go and backed away.

"Adam, I understand why you did what you did now," I said as I followed him. "Allowing the leopard preeminence saved you. I get it." I stopped, unsure how to say what needed to be said without sounding totally insensitive. "I'm not trying to dismiss what happened to you, but it wasn't real. I'm right here. I'm not hurt—uugh,"

My words were cut off as Adam rushed at me. Sweeping me into his arms, he backed us up to the wall, his lips planted on mine with a hunger that frightened me. The bond roared back to life, and I could feel his desperation to know that I was okay. Just as palpable was his fear that this was just another projection and that I would be ripped away at any moment.

Did they replicate the bond?

His lips stilled against mine. *No.*

Then you know that I'm really here. It's me, not a false image.

Relief engulfed him like a tidal wave. Tucking his chin into my shoulder, he hugged me closer, molding my body to his.

It's okay, Adam. It's over. I whispered softly. *I was never hurt. It was all a lie. These people…they have to be stopped. We can't let them do this to anyone else. I can't stop them by myself. The Organization needs a leader who can be trusted. Who actually knows what they're doing. We need you, Adam.*

They need me or you need me?

There was no hiding from the truth anymore. *Both.*

Bringing his face level with mine, he stared into my eyes. The bond seemed to have taken on a whole new dimension for me. Cedars had pegged it correctly. It was like a digital cinema.

I need you, he whispered.

I'm right here.

The door opened and Cedars stepped inside. "Everything okay in here?"

What do you think? I asked Adam.

I'm far from okay, but I'm better.

"We're fine," I told Cedars.

He deliberately kept his distance from us as he ventured into the room. Standing in front of the glass, he quietly observed Lindsey. After a moment, he said, "Lindsey really is a liability," as though he wasn't aware of Adam's eyes on him.

"What are you saying?" I asked, leaning around Adam to see Cedars' face more clearly.

"Even without the nanobots, she still knows too much," he answered.

"We can't just kill her, can we?" I asked, looking back and forth between them.

"Her actions were treasonous. The president wants her tried and executed as a traitor to the United States. She's leaving this afternoon for a secret military tribunal. She'll be dead before the day is done."

"We have eyes to verify the kill?" Adam asked.

"We do. Scout."

That's where he went.

Deciding that it was safe enough, Cedars turned to face us. "I could really use your help, if you're not busy." He looked purposely at Adam's arms encircling me.

Turning his back to Cedars, Adam focused on me again. "Can you manage without me for a while?" he asked.

"Well, I guess that depends on the definition of manage," I said sarcastically, then laughing at the rueful narrowing of his eyes, I shoved him playfully. "Go. I'll be fine."

Somehow, his withdrawal from me didn't seem any less intimate, especially when, in his mind, he was showing me what he'd rather be doing. Cedars had to fight the smile my red cheeks caused as he exited.

After the door had shut, I sagged against the wall. "Whew," I breathed out heavily. Dealing with Adam's aggression—on multiple levels—left me feeling like I'd run a marathon.

With my legs still shaky, I approached the glass confining Lindsey. She was sprawled on her bunk, oblivious to the fact that her future held less than twelve hours. It was sad, but it was her own actions that had built this future for her, and I had no hankering to intervene. One less person trying to kill me was a good thing anyway I looked at it.

Leaving her to her fate, I left the room only to find Olivia waiting for me. The way she was leaning against the wall with that smug look on her face, I knew she had some point to make.

"What?" I snapped at her.

"My, how the tables have turned."

"What tables?"

"I remember not long ago, seems like only last week." She paused, amused by her own speech.

Cue the giant eye roll.

"Yes, only last week, I was giving you a speech about responsibility and joining the Organization."

Those tables. Then yep, I'd say they'd turned, flipped over and caught fire.

"Good thing you listen so well."

Right. Because appealing to Adam's better nature had been what brought him to his senses. "Did you actually hear any of the conversation?"

"A little. But I smelled enough to know one thing." She straightened from the wall and lifted her chin in preparation for a triumphant exit. "You are one of us now." Pronouncement made, she spun on her heel and started down the hallway.

"I never said that," I yelled at her retreating form.

"Didn't have to," she sang softly. "I read it in your heart."

I bit off my comeback when she disappeared. How could she know what was in my heart? I didn't even know what was in my heart half the time. The only thing I knew for certain was that *my heart* wouldn't let me leave the people I cared about. Keeping them safe was the most important thing to me. Whether that was within the context of the Organization or something else, it really didn't matter. That was the part of the conversation that had totally escaped Olivia. I didn't need the Organization like she did. I just needed my family. And if I had to use the Organization to ensure their wellbeing, then that's what I'd do.

CHAPTER 26

"I NEED A VACATION," MIRANDA YAWNED.

"Cedars working you too hard?"

"Him and you. Apparently, I have become human resources for all three hundred and thirty two Organization members. I'd like to know who gave my number to them. Do you know what it's like dealing with a bunch of know-it-alls constantly?"

"Aren't you a know-it-all?" I retorted as I plucked an apple from the fruit bowl.

"Well, yeah, but obviously, I actually do know it all."

My well placed bite went askew, leaving errant bits of apple and associated juice smeared along my chin. "Dad gum it, Miranda." Swiping a paper towel from the counter, I removed the applesauce caused by her serious but seriously doubtful comment. "What have I told you about making me laugh when I'm taking a bite?" I demanded.

"Not to," she chirped happily without looking up from her computer.

Clearly, she didn't understand the meaning of instructions that began with "Do not."

"Why are you working in the kitchen anyway?"

"When have I ever not worked in the kitchen?"

"But this place is huge. You could have a real office."

She stopped typing and looked up at me. "And have to ride the elevator from hell to get there? No, thank you."

Right. I forgot about the elevator situation. "There aren't any normal elevators?"

"That is a normal elevator for this place."

"Oh."

"Oh is right." Closing her laptop, she placed both elbows on it and dropped her chin into her hands. "Cedars told me that you and Adam had sort of a breakthrough."

Breakthrough might have been too strong a word, but I told her about what they did to Adam and some of the images he had shown me.

"That's awful," she stammered when I was done.

"Yep. He wasn't even sure that I was real."

"Poor, Adam," she blubbered, no longer able to contain the tears. "And he doesn't even get time to recover before he's plunged into what's going on here."

"A vacation would have been nice," I agreed as I watched her bury her face in a wad of hastily assembled paper towels.

"How am I supposed to deal with this?" she wailed from behind the mass.

Like a normal human being not disposed to over dramatize everything. Groaning inwardly, I reached a hand and began patting her on the shoulder. She needed a heavy dose of redirection. "Why don't you tell me about what you've been working on," I suggested.

She jerked the paper towels down like I'd slapped her. "Is that your answer to everything? Bury it in work?"

Geesh. These hormones. "I'm not burying anything, Miranda," I replied tersely. "There's nothing to bury. Those things didn't really happen, and I need to help Adam believe in that reality. Coddling him or making room for those emotions only enforces the belief that he has a reason to feel guilty. And he doesn't. He doesn't," I growled when she made to argue. "All the emotions associated with hurting me need to go away. They're based on lies."

"That's cold, Macy."

"Maybe, but I don't see any other way to help Adam." I wish I did. Doing something would be better than this doing nothing. But everything I thought of magnified the emotions, spotlighted them, and that was the opposite of what he needed.

"I don't think ignoring them is going to make them go away," she argued. "And you could try being a little more approachable."

"Approachable?" Where the heck did that come from? "Trust me. Adam has no problems approaching me. All kinds of approachable, right here." Just in case she wasn't sure where here was, I swept my hand down the length of my body.

"What are you talking about?"

"Cedars didn't tell you about yesterday's encounter. Didn't replay the footage for you? Well don't watch it now," I protested when her eyes glazed over.

"Shush," she muttered as she concentrated.

Great. Now I was an involuntary actress on demand. Closing my eyes, I waited for the critique I knew was coming.

"That was kind of scary," she said quietly.

I popped one eye open. "The part where he looked like he wanted to eat me, or the part that looked like he tried to eat me?"

"Both," she snorted and began wiping the remaining tears from her face. "He is the perfect man for you."

She was too busy dabbing her eyes to see the imitation stone face I gave her.

"I'm serious," she insisted when she finally looked at me. "He's the one, Mace. He makes you work, and you love to work."

"Yep. I'm a real workaholic. New topic, please."

"You're going to have to admit it sooner or later."

"Didn't I just do that?"

"You know what I'm talking about," she grumbled.

"I admit it, okay," I snapped in frustration. "I just don't particularly like it."

"You don't like being in love?" she asked softly, not the explosive reaction I expected.

"It hasn't exactly been all roses," I griped. "Unless you count the monster thorns, which there have been a lot of. And it's not the love that bothers me. It's the chain on my heart. And not just with Adam. Chains." I held my arms out wide in demonstration. "They're pulling at me from all directions."

Miranda's gaze turned thoughtful as she mulled over my

words. "You feel trapped," she said after a moment. "Because you equate loving someone with protecting them." Her fingers, which she'd begun to drum on the counter, stilled. "Macy, even with all your super powers, there is no way you can protect everyone all the time." She frowned as her eyes swiveled to mine. "No one is expecting that from you. No any one person could do that. We all have our parts to play. Some things you are going to have to trust to someone else."

Then I quit. That's what I wanted to say. What was the point of having all these abilities if I couldn't guarantee that the people I loved were going to be safe? Oh, I knew what she was saying, but it didn't do one thing to lessen the grip the chains had on my heart.

"Do me a favor, would you? Point me in the direction of this mysterious someone else. I have a few dozen things I'd like to trust to them."

"Right after I find him," she sighed.

"Hey," I objected. "I called dibs."

"So you do know his name."

Smiling at the lighthearted challenge, I retrieved a new apple to replace the one that had turned brown. "So, what's bugging you about the Organization?"

"Where do I start?" she mumbled. "From everything I've looked at, the Organization has been having problems for a while. I mean, logistically, financially, peoplely, you name it."

"Peoplely? Miranda, that is not a word."

"Whatever. This place is short staffed. And for the most part, the people we have are not assigned correctly. I'm surprised that Adam could even do his job with the limited resources they gave him." Closing one eye, she lined up her shot. "They are so lucky they found us."

"Lucky!" I gasped, nearly choking on the bite I was in the process of chewing. "That is hilarious. Don't let Olivia hear you say that."

"Say what?" Olivia asked, catching the ball of napkins that went wildly astray. "Were you actually aiming for a trash can?"

"Miranda thinks that the Organization should thank God for the day they found us," I supplied.

"I've got some words for the architects of that scheme, but I don't know if thanks is among them." Depositing the napkin in the trash, she moved to stand across the island from us. "Now to something truly important, or at least true. Cedars filled me in on Mallet. I'm about to start searching Renard's office. Any info you'd like to add?"

"No, just probably what he told you. Finding something on the microchip would be helpful. To Julia at least."

Placing both elbows on the island, she leaned into them as she looked at me. "And how do you know she's microchipped again?"

"She basically told me. Not in exact words, but I got the gist."

"I never saw any indication that she was under someone else's control. Not once."

"Maybe you didn't ask the right questions," I shrugged.

Her face pulled to one side in a frown. "It's true that I wasn't looking for it. But you don't even know her, and you spotted it right off." She shook her head in aggravation. "How?"

"The pain?" I guessed. "Some of the answers she gave were accompanied by actual physical pain. It let me know something wasn't right. And I already knew about the one in Langston."

"You connected the dots," she said flatly.

"Something like that."

Satisfied with my explanation, she pulled herself upright. "I've gotten a good look at the implant in Langston. I've never seen the Consortium do anything this advanced, which I guess supports your splinter group theory. It would definitely explain all the things we blamed on the Consortium that I personally never believed they were capable of. It's frustrating to think we've been fixated on the wrong target."

"With Julia under their control, it was pretty much unavoidable." I reached and grasped Olivia's arm. "It's not your fault."

She snorted disbelieving before uttering a reluctant, "I know."

"Do you think you could fix what went wrong when we tried to disable Langston's implant?"

"If anything went wrong," she countered. "Juarez doesn't generally make mistakes like that. Lindsey's poison was probably the actual trigger. But either way, I think I'd better figure it out."

The look of pure exhaustion that followed her assertion rang true with me. We all needed vacations filled with days of sleep.

"I'll let you know what I find in the search," she said, then disappeared.

"If I could do that, then I could get my own office," Miranda said wistfully.

"Miranda," I said, before she became engrossed in her work again. "I need to also disappear for a little bit."

She looked quizzically at me until it dawned on her. "The reporter?"

"It's time," I nodded.

She blew out a breath between her lips. "Couldn't we just remain in anonymity?"

"I'm afraid that's not an option. Out of the shadows, remember? And anyway, I gave my word." I slid from the stool and tossed the apple core into the trash. "It was always just a matter of time. At least this way, we get to determine what's being revealed."

"I never really thought this day would come," she said despondently. "Hybrid apocalypse. Ooh. That would be a good title for a book or movie."

Still smiling at her, I shifted to our house in New Orleans.

The first thing that struck me was how quiet and ordinary it was. It would have been so easy to delay, to curl up on the couch and take a nap, but I had work to do. The story of my life.

Ms. Redding didn't pick up, so I left a message, and then settled in to wait for her call. I cleared out the mailbox, which was stuffed, threw away the revolting stuff in the fridge and the moldy dishes that were in the sink. An hour had passed, and she still hadn't returned my call. I was debating whether or not to go back to headquarters when there was a knock on the door. The peephole revealed Ms. Redding on my doorstep.

"You've been watching the place," I surmised as I opened the door.

"Just trying to assure I get that promised interview," she said tightly. "You didn't say so in your message, but I assume you are ready."

"Sure am," I crowed and opened the door wide. "What about you? Where's your camera?"

She turned and waved at the white van parked across the street. The side door slid open and a young woman carrying a television camera stepped out. "That's Haley. She'll be assisting me today."

From the way she crossed the street, I could tell that I liked her. She had a smile on her face the entire time and an energy that felt peppy, without being obnoxious.

"Where do you want to set up?" she asked as she bounded up the stairs.

This deserted ammunitions plant sure was coming in handy. I closed the door, and then reached out and grasped both their arms. "I'll show you."

"Where are we?" Ms. Redding cried with eyes like saucers.

"Not important, Virginia. Can I call you Virginia?"

"I prefer we keep it professional," she bit out angrily. Clearly, she didn't appreciate the change in location.

"Red it is. Haley, you okay over there?"

Her startled face melted into a big grin. "That was beyond epic."

That was me. Beyond epic. Hey, a slogan for my next t-shirt.

"Red," Haley snorted softly to herself, having just registered my choice of name.

I knew I liked her. Collecting two of the chairs that were left over from the meeting with the president, I drug them to an empty space free of all identifying marks. "How about right here?"

Haley joined me and fiddled with the windows until she was satisfied with the lighting. "We'll have to do some things in editing, but it'll work."

Red, who hadn't moved since we'd arrived, walked stiffly to the chair closest to her and sat down. By the look on her face, I knew she was gearing up to hammer away at me. Good thing I could take a hit.

"Before we begin, I feel obligated to warn you that what you will learn here today could possibly put your lives in danger. In no way is this interview sanctioned, and well, I'm better suited to defend myself than you are."

"Don't worry about me, Dr. Greer," Red said flippantly.

"What about Haley?"

"I'm good," she piped up quickly.

Neither one of them realized what they were getting into, and being that I was still trying to figure out what we were into, I couldn't clarify it for them. "Don't say I didn't warn you."

Red eyeballed me for a moment, then turned her attention to the camera. Her opening monologue was ominous. Hearing it gave me goose bumps. When she was done, Haley slowly lowered the camera.

"Is this for real?" she asked hesitantly.

Red turned to me. "What about it, Dr. Greer. Is this for real?"

I smiled big enough to reveal the canines I'd let descend.

"Holy Crap," Haley hissed in surprise.

"Genuine, authentic hybrid, at your service," I joked as I retracted the fangs.

"Very funny," Red deadpanned. "When you're ready, Haley." A few seconds ticked by with no response from Haley. "Haley," Red said sharply.

"Oh, right," Haley breathed, her confidence shaken by the revelation. She began to lift the camera, and then stopped and looked straight at me. "You're not like...going to eat us or something when we're done?"

"Eww," I groaned in response. "I prefer beef or chicken or anything not human."

"Me too," she sighed in relief. "But just so we're clear, Red would taste better." Raising the camera, she signaled Red that she was ready.

The look on Red's face...it could have cut through solid

granite. It was all I could do not to laugh myself out of the chair, especially when I caught sight of Haley's grin behind the camera.

"Today I have with me renowned molecular geneticist, Dr. Macy Greer. You might recall Dr. Greer's work with cancer, but what you don't know, is the new direction Dr. Greer's career has taken. As indicated in the promo, it's going to change the way you view the world."

Now I was nervous. I didn't know if I could live up to her billing.

"Dr. Greer," she began as she turned to face me. "You are alleging that the government never ended the hybrid program. Would you explain to our viewers why you are making these charges?"

That was slick, acting like I'm some sort of whistleblower and not the victim of blackmail. How about some truth in reporting. Like that bit of tape would ever see the light of day. Just like they'd never see that smug smile she now wore.

"Roughly two years ago, I was approached to work on the hybrid project."

"You're knowledge of this begins two years ago?"

"That is correct."

She waited for me to continue, but I was no longer inclined to hand it to her on a silver platter. Her smile faded when she realized I wasn't going to play her game.

"This hybrid project that you worked on, what task were you given?"

"I was tasked with discovering the why and how behind the advanced abilities of the second generation of hybrids."

"Second generation?"

"Yes."

"The first generation of hybrids had abilities beyond that of a normal human. You said that the second generation was more advanced. How so?"

"It depends on the DNA that was added, but generally, they were faster, stronger—"

"The first generation abilities were already exponentially

greater. How much faster could they be before they looked like something out of a movie? Like a werewolf."

I smiled tolerantly at her. "There are wolf hybrids, but they are not subject to the many myths in folklore."

"But they are similar to what we see in the movies?" Her voice held the slightest twang of fear.

"Depends on the movie."

"Are there vampire hybrids?"

"Not that I've come across."

That seemed to reassure her some. Taking a moment, she collected her thoughts before beginning again. "What was the government's purpose in continuing the hybrid program?"

"Don't know."

"You don't know the government's purpose?" she asked skeptically.

"That's what I said. I wasn't around when they made that decision so I cannot tell you the why. I can tell you, that I believe someone in the government is now moving towards designer hybrids."

"Aren't all hybrids by design?"

"In a manner of speaking. But this is different. More sinister. I got the feeling that any new hybrids created would be for a specific purpose, whether the hybrid approved or not."

"Like slaves?"

"Like slaves," I agreed. "And since they were off the grid, they could do anything they wanted with the hybrids."

"Is that why you are coming forward now?"

"No. I planned to handle it on my own. Then I met you."

She held my stare briefly, before consulting her notes. "At the time of our meeting, you referred to a rogue hybrid. Are there others engaged in trying to stop the creation of these designer hybrids?"

"The rogue was not trying to stop anything. And I'm not sure that the one behind this new push is the United States Government. I have and am discovering that there are many players in this game."

She looked up from the notepad she held in her hands. "I don't think this is a game."

"But most of the players do. And they are after the prize."

"What would that be?"

"The world."

She laid her pen across the pad and motioned for Haley to turn off the camera. When Haley lowered the camera to the ground, she leaned towards me. "Are other governments involved?"

"Yes."

"Are you saying this has the potential to lead to war?"

"There are governments that would do anything to get their hands on hybrid technology."

"Like what happened in New Orleans?"

"Much worse."

Standing up, she paced slowly in tight circles as she worked it over in her mind. When she stopped, her shoulders sagged in defeat. "I hate this," she said quietly. "If I air this, reveal the existence of hybrids, I take away any impetus to remain in the shadows. I would essentially be freeing them to do whatever they like."

Offering a silent prayer of thanks for her reaching the conclusion that I'd bet on her reaching, I called her name. "Red." Well, my name for her. "There is a good side to this."

Her eyebrows lifted in doubt.

Originally, I hadn't planned on telling her this, but I needed allies. "We have discovered amazing medical applications for normal humans."

She walked over, picked up the notebook and pen she'd abandoned, and sat back down. "What kind of applications?"

"Just about anything you can imagine."

"Cures for disease?" she asked flatly. The lack of enthusiasm for which she voiced the question was telling of her disbelief.

"Yes."

"Cancer?"

"Yes."

"Heart disease?"

"Yes."

She looked up at me then.

"Paralysis?"

"Yes."

"Loss of sight, hearing, missing limbs, deadly wounds?" They were issued as a challenge.

"Yes, yes, yes and depends on how deadly and how fast we get to it."

"Are you serious?" she asked.

"Very. The president has asked me to hold a press conference and spearhead the implementation of all of this."

"How is this possible from animal DNA?"

Clever girl. "It's not from animal DNA?"

She tossed the notepad down in disgust. "Then what the hell are we talking about?"

"Nanobots."

"Nanobots," she repeated in a monotone voice. "Tiny little robots inside our bodies. Is that what you are telling me?"

"Yes."

"What do nanobots have to do with hybrids?"

"Initially, the nanobots were used to speed up the transformation. And to reverse it."

"Shifters."

"Essentially."

"We really are talking about Hollywood like creatures," she said to herself. "Think of all the money they could save in special effects, costuming." Shaking her head in disbelief, she asked, "How far can they take the shift?"

Not feeling comfortable relaying too much of the information about nanobots in hybrids, I tried to direct the conversation back to the medical. "Depends on the individual. But better than that, is the application we can use it for in normal humans."

It took her a moment, but she finally got it. "You want me to leave out the hybrids and focus on the medical aspect."

Smiling at her, I inclined my head.

"How soon is the press conference?"

I shrugged. "Any day now."

She nodded to herself and indicated for Haley to start rolling again. "Best get started then."

CHAPTER 27

THE SCENE THAT GREETED MY return to the kitchen was not the peaceful homecoming I had anticipated. Even without being shifted, my first inhale reeked of blood and anger. Jumping back quickly, I pressed snugly against the wall in order to avoid being clocked by the broom Margaret held as she rushed past. Everywhere I looked, things were broken or smashed, including the half of a peanut butter sandwich clinging to the wall next to me.

"What happened?" I cried, centering my focus on the island where Kenny, Wrangle and Linc had someone pinned down. The gap they created when they turned towards me offered glimpses of Miranda hunched over the individual stretched across its length.

"Get off!" Reynolds snarled, identifying himself as the injured party.

I took a step forward and froze at the roar that sounded from outside the kitchen. Dread began to build in my stomach. *Adam?* The roar sounded again, further away this time.

"The boys were playing a little too rough," Miranda joked, but the strain in her voice negated any effort to lessen the severity of the situation.

Glass crunched beneath my feet as I made my way to the island. Inserting myself between Linc and Wrangle, I leaned against the counter for a better look. Deeply gouged claw marks sliced from one end of Reynolds' chest to the other. My heart sank at the severity of the wound and the person likely responsible. Reaching forward, I laid my hand on Reynolds brow in a show of comfort.

The roar sounded again, inside me this time. Adam did not want me touching Reynolds.

"Jamie and many several others have Adam," Miranda said. "He's not hurt."

No, he was mad. And that was the only picture he would paint for me. "What happened?" I asked again.

Seeing the pained look in my eyes, Reynolds turned his face away. Kenny, however, didn't flinch at the request. "Adam and Reynolds got into it over you."

Me? Dumbfounded by Kenny's answer, I looked to Miranda for confirmation, but she was busy opening another suture kit.

"He shouldn't treat you the way he does," Reynolds hissed through his teeth as Miranda started sewing again.

Accepting the wet towel that Margaret extended to me, I began to clean the blood from the cuts on Reynolds' face. "And how is he treating me?" I asked quietly.

"Wrong," he spat. "Like something he owns, rather than a person he loves."

That would be the result of the two natures warring within him. Neither one of which I recognized very much. The Adam that I knew had only manifested in small doses, and even then he was different. And the other Adam, the one responsible for Reynolds laying here...I didn't know how to answer for that without admitting how scared I was of that version winning.

Folding the bloodied towel, I handed it to Margaret in exchange for another. "Reynolds—by the way, I just can't do ER. You're already Reynolds to me." The brief aside did nothing to lower the tension in the room. Sighing, I set to work on removing the blood coating his neck. "What Adam is working through... it's hard for him to separate the leopard from the man right now. Adam's leopard was possessive to begin with, more so now. You have to give him some time."

"And space," Kenny added. "Lots of space. From her." He pointed at me, then looked directly at Reynolds as he spoke. "When I first got Crystal back, I almost broke Wrangle's neck just for hugging her."

"It's true," Wrangle nodded when I looked at him.

Kenny shrugged and shook his head. "I couldn't bear the thought of her in someone else's arms. I knew it was nothing, but it didn't matter. My response was instinctual. It pretty much has been since the day I thought I lost her." His eyes swirled with color as he relived the memory, finally settling to a red so dark that it was almost black.

"And now?" I whispered.

He tilted his head, fastening his eyes on me. "I still have the urge to kill any man who touches her, but I'm not acting on it. Reynolds is fortunate. If Adam hadn't shown some restraint, he could have easily killed him." He blinked slowly, deliberately. "Especially considering that your scent is all over him."

Reynolds stiffened at the insinuation, as did I.

"There is nothing going on between me and Reynolds," I snapped. "Other than him catching me when I..." What word should I use? Faint, lose consciousness...double over like a ragdoll?

"Collapse," Miranda supplied.

"Right, collapse." I made a mental note to take longer showers and scrub harder.

"Does Adam know that?" Kenny challenged.

My frown deepened. Of course Adam knew that. Didn't he? *Adam?* There was no response. Dang it. I thought we were past the worst of it.

"For the time being, I think it would be best if all persons of the male persuasion remained at arm's length from Macy," Miranda said.

Reynolds' face looked like it had been carved in stone. "You're not being fired as my assistant—"

"Assistant?" Miranda barked in surprise. "I thought that was my job."

"You're busy," I told her. "I needed more help."

"Say no more," she pleaded. "I've thought you needed help for years."

I started to look away, then whipped my head back to her.

The tone in her voice made me question whether she meant that comment the way I initially thought she meant it.

Oblivious to my scrutiny, she leaned over Reynolds to study her handiwork. "The bleeding has stopped." Holding her hand out, "Let me see that towel," she said.

I handed her the towel I was holding and watched her blot the wound.

"I think that will hold you until you heal." Satisfied with her inspection, she handed the bloodied towel off to Margaret. "Try not to get into any more scuffles," she admonished Reynolds as she sat up.

Before Reynolds could move, Kenny tightened his grip. "Don't even think about going after him," he hissed when they locked eyes. "You won't win. And if you did, then what?" He jerked his head at me.

Go after Adam? Was he insane? "Reynolds, you had better not. That's an order."

Reynolds' eyes slid to me in slow motion.

"Reynolds, please," I moaned softly. "He's not fully himself right now. You have to know that."

Kenny backed away as Reynolds sat up and slid from the island. Grasping the remains of his shirt, Reynolds ripped it off and tossed it in the trash bag Margaret held open for him. Then he placed both hands on his hips and turned to face me.

"I am not an idiot," he said calmly. "I know that Adam is fighting for control. I just gave him something to fight for."

Understanding washed through me, followed by anger in the next beat. "You did what?"

"It could work," Kenny interjected. "It is for me."

I ignored Kenny's comment as I rounded the island and stalked angrily towards Reynolds. "Adam could have killed you," I accused. Balling up the finger I was about to jab into his wounded chest, I lowered it to my side. "He could have killed you," I repeated.

"After Wrangle's unintended challenge, I realized how much I'd been relying on my other side. I almost killed my best friend.

Over nothing. That's when I really started fighting, not to maintain balance, but to regain control. Still am."

Turning sideways, I let my gaze sweep Kenny. However encouraging he meant it to be, his honesty was disheartening. Just how many of us were one step away from total meltdown? I'd been on the edge once or twice, but not for any length of time and not long enough to have the leopard DNA assert dominance. Even then, it was hard for me to pull back. Adam's leopard was strong, stronger now for what he'd been through.

"Don't you ever do something so stupid again," I snarled at Reynolds. "I do not need or want you sacrificing yourself for me."

"Is that an order?"

"Yes. It is," I grated. "Along with stay out of his sight for a while. At least until I can talk to him."

"Yes, ma'am," he saluted and presented me with his back. Grabbing an orange from the displaced fruit bowl as he left, he began tossing it up and down, like he didn't have a care in the world. Stupid, hardheaded, idiot that I would wholeheartedly thank if it worked to bring my Adam back.

Reynolds' exit seemed to signal my body that the crisis was over. I thought if I closed my eyes, I might literally see the energy draining out of me.

"How about I get you some coffee?" Margaret suggested.

"Just what she needs, more stimulus," Miranda droned. After cinching the trash bag in her hands, she looked me up and down. "You okay?"

Shrugging, I slunk down into the nearest stool and cradled my chin in my hands. Margaret set a cup of coffee in front of me and patted me on the shoulder before returning to clean up duty. The way Wrangle followed her around, obeying every command she gave, it was sweet. Almost enough to make me forget the mess of a relationship that was mine and Adam's.

Sighing, I picked up the coffee mug as Kenny took the seat next to me.

"If this works, you're going to owe Reynolds big time," he said.

"Little hard to collect if you're dead," I grumbled.

Kenny frowned at me while I watched Margaret shower the island countertop with alcohol spray. As per her instructions, Wrangle followed behind her with paper towels and wiped the surface clean. I shook my head in bewilderment. They made it look so easy. I guess it would be easy if Adam did everything I told him to. Fat chance of that ever happening.

Miranda waited until Wrangle had passed her, then pulled up another stool. "How'd the interview go?"

"Great."

"You met with the reporter?" Wrangle asked.

"Yep."

"Did you give her the 411, the score, the down low? Or is that low down? Download? I'm never sure with slang what's actually being said," Miranda shrugged.

I lowered the cup, poised to respond, then thought the better of it. I didn't know which one it was either. "I told her what I could. Nothing about the Organization, although she knows different groups of people are involved, including governments. Fortunately, she caught on to the idea that presenting the hybrid side of it could end in disaster. It was either that, or she didn't want to be upstaged by the press conference which I promised to get her into. Oh, and the camera girl asked if I was going to eat them, then for good measure told me Red would taste better."

"Red?" Miranda repeated. "Red," she moaned in sudden understanding, then, "Red?" squeaked in alarm.

"I take it Red is significant," Wrangle said, amused by Miranda's alternative pronunciations.

"Breathe, Miranda," I chided as I smiled at Wrangle.

"Macy, she's tough."

"But she's fair. And, she credits me with saving her brother's life."

"Cancer?" she guessed.

"Yep."

"Still, you're betting an awful lot on her," she said worriedly.

"Just our lives," I dismissed. "And the existence of hybrids. The world, at the most."

"In that case," she muttered, rolling her eyes to display her irritation.

"Speaking of the world," Wrangle said. "Have you given any thought as to how you are going to implement the plan?"

That was a very good question. "I guess I need to start working on that."

Finished with his part of the cleanup, he straddled a stool across the island from me. "I think you should run it like a project where hospitals submit proposals. That way, we can use their knowledge to construct a workable plan."

"Considering I don't run hospitals, I think that would be best," I agreed.

"What about security with the nanobots?" Kenny asked.

"Juarez will cover that angle, I'm sure."

"I'm not talking about the design, but with transport and retrieval."

Retrieval?

"Getting ahead of yourself," Wrangle said to Kenny. "Manufacture comes first. And before that, the development of the nanobots for each medical application. You have narrowed that down, right?"

Both of them swiveled their heads to stare expectantly at me.

I didn't think my blinking at them over my coffee mug was the response they were hoping for. "Congratulations," I announced as I lowered the cup. "You two are now team leads for the medical application project." Pleased with my spur of the moment initiative, I waggled my eyebrows at them. "MAP for short. I'll expect a full report addressing the issues you mentioned, along with any others you can think of, and," I drawled, "possible solutions." Now it was their turn to stare blankly at me.

"Did she just hire us?" Wrangle finally asked.

"I believe she did," Kenny nodded.

"Now I'm confused," he huffed in mock frustration. "I haven't completed the aptitude tests yet. I might not be qualified for the job."

Kenny snorted as he scooted the stool back and stood. "We should get started. I heard the boss is a real wildcat."

"Oh, shut up," I said, throwing the abandoned roll of paper towels at him as he turned to leave the room. They ricocheted off of his back, hitting Wrangle in the head. Catching them on the rebound, Wrangle set the roll back on the counter, out of my reach.

"I figured the yelling and throwing of things wouldn't start until after we had presented our work. Seems I was wrong." Smiling, he stood and followed Kenny out of the room.

"That ought to keep them busy for a while," Miranda commented when they'd gone.

"Yeah. And maybe they'll bring back something I can use." Abruptly, I pulled my cup down and stared into the inky liquid. "Didn't I used to drink my coffee with cream and sugar?"

"Times have changed in the kingdom," Miranda said mournfully.

Sad. I hadn't even noticed until now. Shrugging, I took another swallow. Bitter.

Claiming the stool that Wrangle had vacated, Margaret asked, "What are you going to do about Adam?"

Do? What was there to do? I took another sip and grimaced. Times hadn't changed that much. Setting the mug on the counter, I looked at Margaret. "Talk to him. Try to reassure him. Not much else I can do."

"I've never seen him like this," she whispered. "He's different now."

There was no denying that. Was it permanent? That was what concerned me.

"He's in his suite. Calm for now," Miranda said. "I wasn't sure how much communicating you guys were doing," she said apologetically.

Yeah, that would be none. "Thanks. And thanks for being so busy."

"You're welcome," she smiled at me. "Thanks for hiring help."

"More like drafted."

"Did he get a signing bonus?"

"Did I say drafted? I meant impressed into service."

"You mean like slave labor?"

"I gave him the title of Squire."

"Poor, Reynolds," she tsked. "At least, I get paid for it." She set her mug down hard and looked at me. "I do get paid for it, right?"

"Honestly, Miranda. I don't really know anymore."

"Oh, I'm getting paid," she mumbled as she brought the cup to her lips again. "I'm…" The last bit was garbled, but her eyebrows dancing above the rim of her cup gave the gist of her thoughts. "And that's all there is to it," she declared, yanking her cup down abruptly like the exclamation point.

It was doubtful that she even knew where the budget for the Organization originated, but if I knew her, which I did, she'd get to the bottom of it. Who she had to go through and the fallout that would entail, that was going to be a fun one to watch.

"Oh, by the way," she said as she went for a refill. "Not that this has anything to do with anything, but Crystal has presented me with a list of demands. She is convinced she's getting wings."

"Wings? Do we have any winged hybrids?"

The coffee pot rang as she shoved it back into place. "Do I look like I have memorized the capabilities of all three hundred and something of us," she demanded.

"Uh," I stuttered. Maybe I wasn't the only one who should lay off the caffeine. "Another one for the list?"

Miranda's face crinkled in anger. "I'm really starting to despise that list," she hissed.

"It's the person with the pen that I have a problem with."

"Yeah, let's beat them up, and then break the pen in half. I'd like to take a dad gum nap! Or a shower. Preferably the shower first and then the nap…"

I only half heard Miranda's rant after that. My thoughts drifted to Adam and the DNA haunting him. There had to be a way to regulate the animal DNA's influence. Like a governor on a gas pedal. A way to ensure that the human DNA would always have preeminence.

"Macy," Miranda said firmly enough to catch my attention. "Go see him."

Smiling at her, I nodded. "I think I will."

Adam was stretched out on the golden couch with one arm thrown across his forehead, breathing steadily in sleep. He looked more peaceful than I'd seen him in days. He'd shaved too, leaving the sharp lines of his chin visible. I'd forgotten how handsome he was.

"If you keep thinking those kinds of thoughts about me, I'm going to have to do something about it," he growled softly.

Smiling at his challenge, I circled the couch to sit down beside him. "How are you?"

He opened his eyes to look at me. They were glowing slightly. "Still trying."

Ignoring the spike of fear inspired by the last time he looked at me with glowing eyes, I leaned forward and kissed him lightly on the lips then pressed my forehead to his. "Good." Before I could pull away he threaded one hand into the hair at the back of my neck and pulled me back into a kiss. Unlike the last time, he kept it gentle, but I couldn't shutter my fear.

"I didn't mean to frighten you," he said as he released me. "Before...in Lindsey's cell."

"I know," I said unconvincingly.

"Macy, I wouldn't hurt you. I wouldn't force you to do anything you're not ready for."

That was distinctly not what I felt before. No matter how much Adam regretted his prior actions, I didn't think his leopard cared about anything but dominating me as alpha, in whatever form that took. As long as the leopard was in charge, I couldn't trust Adam.

"Macy, I can feel your emotions churning. Talk to me," he said softly, pulling me into the circle of his arms as he sat up.

I didn't want to talk to him. Not about this. But I couldn't let what he'd done to Reynolds go uncontested. That wouldn't be fair to anyone. "You hurt Reynolds."

His arms tightened protectively around me. He wanted to say he didn't mean to, but we both knew that wasn't the truth. "He tried to make a claim on you," he said in clipped tones.

"He told me."

Adam's breath caught. "Does he have a claim to you?"

A claim as someone he could trust to have his back...as a friend. "Not in the way that you mean."

"Do I?"

I could feel Adam's heart rate increase and his breathing become shallow as he waited for my response. "You know we've only known each other for less than two weeks."

His frustration with my answer permeated the lengthy sigh he heaved.

"And," I stressed. "Part of that time, you have not been entirely yourself."

"Macy," he huffed, taking me with him as he leaned back into the couch. "I met you over five years ago, and I've loved you for just as long. A few days acting more like a leopard than a man does not overrule that."

My mouth suddenly went dry. "It's not five years for me."

"I know," he sighed again.

"And even if it had been, the way you have been...relating to me..."

"You're talking physically?"

"With me and now with Reynolds. You are not a beast, Adam. You are a man in possession of animal DNA. You possess it, not the other way around."

"You don't trust me," he suddenly realized.

"Do you trust you with me right now?"

I witnessed him replay the scene in front of Lindsey's cell. The anger and suspicion, the challenge and finally the hunger with which he had kissed me. Disgust filled him as he acknowledged that he'd only been a passenger and not in control.

"I won't let that happen again. I meant it when I said I wouldn't force anything on you."

"You can only do that if you're in control."

"You're right," he breathed.

Something in him shifted. Determination rose from his core and slowly rolled through him, settling over him like a cloak. For the first time since his return, I felt truly hopeful about his recovery. But hopeful or not, I wasn't about to ditch my principles.

"And I'm not…" I stopped when he began to laugh silently.

"May I repeat that I've been following you for five years. I am aware of your views on marriage and intimacy."

Squeezing my eyes shut, I asked, "And you're okay with that?"

He shifted uncomfortably behind me, alternately flexing and relaxing his biceps. I knew he was looking for a big way to say no without saying no.

"I wouldn't say I'm okay with it. A man has needs, wants…I want you."

My heart sank at his words.

"I am, however, determined to wait until you're ready."

"And if that is not until after marriage?"

Tightening his hold on me, he planted his chin on my shoulder. "Then I'll fiercely anticipate the honeymoon."

"I'll bet," I laughed.

"Any chance you want to get married now? I'm sure someone around here has credentials."

"Could I please have some time to adjust to the idea?" I pleaded.

"Just remember, I've been waiting for five years already."

"It doesn't count if I didn't know you were waiting," I retorted.

"It counts," he growled softly. "Of course, I could sway you to my way of thinking." As proof, he began trailing kisses along my shoulder, slowly working his way north.

I could see how that might work. Luckily for me, the door chimed.

"Down boy," I scolded when he growled in protest. Freeing myself from his arms, I began to make my way to the door. "I have—No." I paused and turned to look him in the eye. "We have work to do."

He extended his hand to me, and I returned to pull him from

the couch. I was pleased to see that the glow had faded from his eyes. For now, anyway.

"I'll get the door. You put a shirt on," I ordered.

"Does this bother you?" he asked in mock surprise, pushing his very well developed pecks forward.

Working to drag my gaze from his chest, "You're bad," I laughed.

The door chimed again, this time punctuated by rhythmic pounding. "Macy. What's the hold up?" Miranda yelled. "Are y'all decent in there?"

Adam took the opportunity to strike several poses. "What do you think? Am I decent?"

"Go put some clothes on," I moaned, completely flustered by his behavior.

There was an abrupt halt to the pounding on the door. "Did you just say put some clothes on?" Miranda bellowed.

"Hold your horses, I'm coming," I yelled at her.

"What's going on?" she asked as soon as the door opened.

"Nothing."

"That's not what it sounded like," she argued, her eyes darting rapidly about the room for any scrap of evidence.

Crossing my arms over my chest, I waited until she consented to look at me. "Did you come here for a specific reason? You know, other than to insult me."

Her face fell as her search ended in disappointment. "Yeah," she said dryly. "Can you teleport me to Renard's office. Olivia needs help."

"Sure." Turning at the sound of Adam reentering the room, I watched him put on his shoes. "Where are you going?" I asked sharply. The look he gave me was priceless. *Sorry,* I cringed. *I'm a little overprotective right now, I guess.*

He finished lacing up the boot he was working on, then stood and walked towards us. "Excuse me," he said to Miranda, who willingly stepped aside. Taking my face in his hands, he kissed me gently. "I'm going to meet with Cedars and Juarez. Find me when you're done?"

I nodded and watched him leave. I didn't like letting him go, but I knew he wouldn't tolerate any babysitting. Still, I didn't want another episode like earlier.

"Hey, tell Cedars to keep an eye on him. Let me know if he gets..."

"Homicidal?"

I frowned at her.

"Jamie's watching. So is Juarez. After today, I think they all are. But he seemed better. That was much better than how he has been treating you."

"It is," I nodded.

"What happened?"

"He asked me to marry him."

"What?" Miranda whipped her head around so fast she had to grab ahold of the doorframe to steady herself. "What did you say?"

"It wasn't a real proposal."

"If that man asked you to marry him, he wasn't kidding."

"Probably not, but I have to make sure, and he has to make sure, that it's Adam asking and not Adam the leopard asking."

"Does it matter?"

"It does," I nodded. "You ready?" I extended my hand to her.

Clasping my hand, she threw the question back at me. "Are you ready?"

"That's why I said no."

The next moment we were in the lobby outside of Renard's office. It felt strange being surrounded by this much rock. The living quarters had gargantuan windows everywhere. Here, it was a cave. Following Miranda, I stepped through the door into the office. Olivia was seated on the floor in front of a row of filing cabinets. She looked up at us as we entered.

"Wow, these people didn't care for keeping up with technology," Miranda said, gawking at the antiquated filing system.

"They kept up," Olivia said. "Look over there." She pointed to a shelf on the opposite wall. Fish bowls packed with flash drives lined the shelf.

"I'm not sure fish bowls acting as storage for flash drives constitutes keeping up," she argued.

"Looks more like a dumping ground," I agreed.

"No stone unturned," Olivia said, reminding us of what was at stake.

Miranda shrugged and stuck her hand up to her elbow into the nearest fish bowl.

"There has to be a better way to do this," I complained softly. "Please nanobots, if there is anything you can do to help us locate anything useful, do it now."

"Not you too," Miranda rebuffed. "You're acting like they're living sentient beings. They're just robots."

"That's better than making them zombies," I fired at her.

"Well, they were," she yelled back. "They were alive inside a dead body. How much closer to a zombie can you get?"

Her statement stopped me cold. I looked at Olivia, who had hit the pause button on her search and fixed her eyes on Miranda.

"You don't think they're still alive...working to rebuild Langston's body. Do you?" Miranda asked nervously.

Oh, crap. "Killing Langston's nanos wasn't on the list."

"Because that was too much for the person with the pen," Miranda howled in disgust. Flash drives went flying as she jerked her hand from the bowl. "If she's not there..." She pointed her finger at me reprovingly, like it would somehow be my fault if Langston was now reanimated. "Go," she commanded.

I went.

The hallway in front of the morgue was quiet. I could have jumped directly inside, but that was too much of a horror movie moment for me to entertain. My heart already felt like it was going to beat out of my chest from this side of the door. I took one steadying breath, then eased the door open. There were no signs of zombie activity, though I'm not sure what that would have been exactly. Something grisly, I was sure.

Stepping into the room, I let the door close behind me. There was something different. This smell hadn't been here before. With careful steps, I approached the drawer and wrapped my fingers around the handle. What were the chances a zombie was waiting to spring at me as soon as I opened it? Crap, I moaned inwardly and pulled the drawer out in a whoosh. There was nothing but a soiled sheet.

"Oh, thank God," I breathed heavily. "Wait, what am I saying? Dang it," I swore loudly and slammed the drawer closed.

"I cannot believe this," Olivia breathed from behind me.

Startled out of my ever loving mind, I whirled around and punched her in the face.

"What the hell, Macy?" She cried, holding her jaw with her hand.

"Sorry," I barked. "It was a reflex. You scared the crap out of me. You can't be sneaking up on people. For goodness sakes we've got zombies on the loose." I waved helplessly at the empty drawer that used to house Langston.

"Did you think I'd let you come here alone?" she snapped, still cradling her jaw in her hand. "I was behind you when you opened the door. I thought you knew I was here."

"Well, obviously, I didn't."

What's wrong? Adam asked sharply.

Did someone do something with Langston's body?

Langston's dead?

Just ask, please.

The seconds, measured by the increasing beat of my heart, stretched unbearably as I waited.

Cedars said she was slated for cremation. Why?

She's gone. As in, it might be possible that she got up and walked out, gone.

There was another delay while Adam relayed the information.

"Langston wasn't acting of her own accord when she attacked Adam," I said, thinking aloud.

Olivia lowered the hand rubbing her jaw. "The nanobots which are obviously still active are susceptible to programming."

"Lindsey," we said together.

In the next second, we stood outside of Lindsey's cell. Empty again, except for the faint smell of decay tinting the air.

"Just in case you can't see me, I'm right next to you," Olivia said flatly, to which I gave a big eye roll.

Did Lindsey ship out already? I asked Adam.

After checking, he said, *Cedars says no. What's going on?*

We've got trouble. Lindsey's gone with a possible zombie in tow. How it was even possible was mind boggling, but there it was.

There was a long pause while Adam collected his thoughts. Finally, he said, *I was only gone a few days…at the most.*

Yeah, well, I work fast.

CHAPTER 28

ADAM NEEDED CATCHING UP ON a whole host of issues. Unfortunately, Lindsey's escape took precedence, and he had to table all his justifiable questions in order to deal with the situation. The first thing he did was to order a lockdown of the complex which allowed Juarez to initiate an infrared, something about nanowave—and I stopped listening after that—sweep of the complex. Everyone got to choose their place of quarter while the sweep was conducted. I was hungry, so the kitchen it was. Adam chose not to join me. I had the feeling he was deliberately forcing himself to go through the motions of leadership in hopes that it would feel normal once again. He was trying at least, and I was grateful for that. Olivia as my dining companion? Not so much.

"Zombies. Who would have thought Miranda would be right about that?" Olivia lamented. Then she chomped into her sandwich like she was mad at it. You know, for someone so polar opposite me in manners and dress, she sure knew how to put a sandwich away.

"We don't have proof of that yet," I argued. "The only slightly zombie colored issue we know of for sure is that Lindsey has Langston's nanobots running through her very alive body." There was also the smell factor, but I needed more evidence than a slight rotted flesh aroma before definitively declaring the existence of a zombie.

"Nanobots which we supposedly turned off," she countered. "And a dead Langston walking around isn't zombie enough for you?"

"As to your first point, obviously the nanobots got together and figured something out. The ones inside of Langston's body were still active. They were probably communicating with their buddies inside of Lindsey all along. We just didn't think to put a stop to it." I opened the microwave when it beeped and retrieved the bowl of soup I'd heated up. Looked kind of paltry next to her loaded sandwich.

"And the zombie?" she prompted.

The zombie. I shut the microwave door and moved towards the island. "Aren't zombies supposed to be the result of a plague or virus?"

"Who cares how it starts!" she exclaimed. "You've got a dead person walking around."

"Maybe."

"Maybe?"

"Look, here's a question. Why didn't the kill order work on Langston's nanos?"

"It should have." She looked at me and frowned. "It had to."

"But it did not have to work on any still residing in Langston," I said thoughtfully. "Those inside of Langston revived their counterparts in Lindsey?"

"Who then in turn revived Lindsey's?" Olivia laid her sandwich on her plate as she worked her way through the logic. "Langston's nanos would then need to use Lindsey's brain as a surrogate. Through the newly formed nanobot bond?" The frown on her face deepened. "Langston's bots communicating with each other from different bodies was conceivable. But two different breeds of nanobots talking to each other? That's a big metaphysical leap. One that would require them to act beyond the scope of their programming."

That's what I had been theorizing about since I started working with them. It seemed obvious to me that the nanobots had pushed beyond the limits of their programming. Why no one else could see it, or wanted to acknowledge it, was a mystery to me.

Sliding into the stool across from her, I set my bowl on the counter. "If Lindsey is the one controlling all the nanobots, then Langston is not a zombie. In the purest sense of the word."

"Whatever," Olivia shrugged. "It's close enough for me."

I sort of believed that when I saw her, I'd feel that way too. "I still don't understand why the transfer worked in the first place. I thought the nanobots had to be biochemically aligned?"

"They do," she nodded, her frown melting into concentration.

"Are Langston and Lindsey related?"

"Not that I know of," she quickly dismissed. "Macy, are you suggesting that by exceeding the limits of their programming the nanobots are developing into some kind of sentient..." She raised her arms as she grappled for the right word.

"Being?" I suggested after her floundering started to annoy me. "I'm not sure what I'm suggesting yet, but something is happening."

She shoved her plate away and let her head collapse onto her forearms. I ate in silence while she mumbled quietly to herself. I figured she deserved a few minute's reprieve for putting into words what had been stewing in me for days.

Lifting her head, she looked squarely at me. "Microscopic, living, thinking robots inside of us?"

"Seems that way," I nodded. "How else can you account for two different strains of nanobots forming a bond? Lindsey needed help getting out of that cell. Langston's nanos knew where to find it. Somehow they communicated and bam, here we are. Lindsey probably didn't even know what was going on until Langston showed up."

She held up two fingers. "Two problems with that. How did the nanobots know anything? They are for acceleration in morphagenesis and maintenance and repair. And two—" She stopped abruptly and looked at me. "You think they are reading our minds, making things happen based on their interpretation of our desires."

She hadn't phrased it as a question, so I felt no compunction to answer her immediately.

"But how...they would have...it's not..." She stopped trying to talk and stared vacantly at her sandwich.

After a moment, I couldn't stand her dismayed look anymore.

Setting my spoon inside the bowl, I said, "One. Morphagenesis is the technical name for the shifting back and forth?" I waited for her nod. "Two. I'm almost certain that's what they're doing."

Her face still reflected her shock, but it gave way as her brain took over. "That could be a very dangerous and unpredictable development," she said quietly. "It explains what's happening with Juarez. And I'm guessing you've had similar experiences?"

I nodded at her.

"Nothing like this ever happened until you showed up."

She wasn't accusing me of anything, just noting the timing for the record.

"Maybe it has something to do with the riddle. The river has been unleashed," I proclaimed with arms lifted high in the air.

She didn't offer even the tiniest of smiles.

Dropping my hands, I asked, "What was your number two?"

"My number two? Oh, how do we know for sure that it was Langston who freed Lindsey?"

"The faint scent of rot in the air. You didn't smell it?"

"How many times do I have to tell you that my ability is limited to smells associated with hormones? Otherwise, normal human nose." She rapped her nose with her knuckle a few times in demonstration of her annoyance before tucking her hands out of sight. "So, if all of our assumptions are correct, Lindsey is now consciously controlling Langston. A..." She pressed her lips together, unable to bring herself to say it out loud.

"Reanimated corpse?" I finished for her again. "Yeah."

"But how would we not notice that?" she pleaded softly.

"We've been busy," I shrugged. "The complex has been practically empty until now, and I'm assuming that Lindsey knows this place as well as any of you."

"A zombie. I still can't believe it." She jerked as a shiver ran through her. "I can't imagine there would be much of Langston left. Not after what the control chip did to her brain." She crossed her arms on the counter and leaned forward on them. "Do you ever feel like we've started something we can't stop?" She looked at me with eyes that hoped I'd disagree, provide a credible argument against her supposition. She was looking at the wrong person.

"For the last two years, I have felt that things were building. Now, I feel like we are all about to topple over the edge together. Friend and foe alike." I used my spoon to model the downward plunge.

"Lovely," she drolled. "And our emergency exit?"

"Being able to teleport is a pretty good parachute, I think."

"It's something at least." She got up and threw away the remainder of her sandwich, then went to the sink to wash her hands. "About the new form of life that may or may not be emerging," she called over her shoulder. "I think it would be best if we not reveal anything until we are certain what's going on."

"Sure," I answered. I wasn't prepared to issue any kind of theory on the matter currently, and I absolutely wasn't prepared to deal with the meltdown Miranda might have. "It's just a spark of a theory right now."

"I think it has more merit than that," she said grudgingly. "And I think you're right about it being related to the riddle."

"Might be related. I'll have to think about it."

Gripping the dish towel, she turned and leaned against the sink. "You know, if whoever was controlling Langston still has access to her nanobot programming, then theoretically, they could be controlling Lindsey too."

"I bet that's one possible side effect she didn't anticipate." It'd be funny if it wasn't bad news for us.

"Wasn't Langston's goal to kill Adam?"

Squeezing my eyes shut tight, I filled Adam in on our suspicions. He wasn't worried. The part of him he was trying to master relished the opportunity to engage her. Part of me hoped he got the chance.

"Assuming that whoever was controlling Langston before is still trying, we should be able to trace the signal to its point of origin," Olivia said. "Get some clue as to who is doing this."

Popping the top on the soda can I'd snatched from the fridge, I sat down at the island again. "Assuming that we find Langston or

Lindsey," I added. "And assuming Juarez can isolate the signal. He didn't have very much success tracing the signal that crashed our plane. But that group may not be linked to this bunch."

She nodded, then her eyes widened in fear. "Take my hand," she ordered, extending hers as she stomped towards me. The moment we touched we entered the diluted world of what I had termed between.

"What's wrong?"

"Juarez says they're in here," she hissed.

"Juarez? Since when have you two been able to communicate over distance without using a phone?"

"It's new. He was able to finagle some security protocol something or another and now we can talk. Well, he can talk to me. I can't talk back."

That was hilarious. Where could I get some of those nanos? "Olivia, let go."

"What?"

I shook our hands which were still clasped. "I don't need you to hold my hand. Maybe you need me to hold—"

"Shut up," she ground, practically slinging my hand away from her.

Looks like someone had a zombie phobia and didn't want to admit it. Setting the soda on the counter, I briefly skimmed the room. "It looks like they haven't developed the time jumping ability, but the fact that we can't see them confirms that Lindsey's hybrid genes are reactivated. Or she's using projection again."

"We're locked now. Projection shouldn't work on us."

"What if—" I did a double take when I got a look at Olivia's wild eyes manically scanning the room. That wasn't creepy at all.

"Talk to Adam."

"What?"

"Juarez says Adam's freaking out about you breaking contact."

That was all I needed, to have Adam go ballistic again. *Adam? Why did you disconnect?* he growled, furiously latching onto the link.

I didn't. Well, I didn't mean to.

Where are you?

In the kitchen. Where are you? You sound like you're speaking through a long tube.

With Juarez and Cedars. You have to get out of there.

I'm safe, I assured him. *I'm in between. I didn't know it would cut contact with you.*

In between?

I don't know what else to call it. It's where I am when I don't want to be visible.

Like when you transferred me out of the cell?

No, that was teleporting. This is different. Juarez can explain it better than I can.

"Look at the wall," Olivia said, pointing just beyond the end of the cabinets. "The swirls in the texture are the wrong way."

The wall didn't look any different than it ever had to me, but then, studying the wall when I was in here hadn't been a priority.

As soon as Juarez can lift the perimeters, I'll be there, Adam said. *Try not to do anything stupid.*

Who me? I shot back at him, irritated by the rudeness of his suggestion. *I have never set out to do anything stupid in my whole life.* I mean, who undertook any task with the intent of doing something stupid. He should have given that sage bit of wisdom to Olivia. That pair of crazy eyes she was sporting was rating high on the potential stupid meter.

Sorry, he apologized. After stumbling over a few more equally bad pieces of advice, he finally chose to remain silent, the best decision he could have made.

"We need her alive," I warned Olivia as she started edging toward the suspect swirls.

"We tried that once already. And technically, we don't. As we well know now, Langston's nanobots will stay alive regardless of bodily death. Lindsey's too. Her programming wasn't updated. What was the point when she was going to be cremated in a few hours." She took a few more surprisingly catlike steps towards the backwards swirls, then pausing, fixed her gaze on me. "You have to tackle her."

"Why me?" I protested.

"Because I want to hit her too much. I mean really hit her." Grinding her fist into her hand, she ground her teeth together as she said, "Pound her face into mush. Hit. Her."

Alrighty then, scary, slightly demented Olivia. This was a side of her I'd never seen. Wait, mush? "What if it's Langston?" I moaned, involuntarily shuddering at the thought.

"Hopefully her nanobots are up to the task."

She didn't take it any further, but I knew what she meant. Even though the nanobots had managed to restore some measure of blood flow, at the very least, the tissues in the extremities would have suffered damage. I didn't know if we were talking full on zombie, but I did not want to find out. And I certainly didn't want to touch it.

Grimacing, I started forward again and then froze. "Olivia, it's Lindsey." I was certain of it. "It's not projection. Not exactly. It's some sort of projected camouflage, like a shield. She got the swirl pattern wrong. Her original nanobots wouldn't have made that mistake."

"Only Lindsey had the ability to camouflage," Olivia said, understanding the conclusion I'd drawn. "It's projection, but not projection."

"Their nanobots must have worked together to come up with this modified ability," I said warily. "And we are not protected against this one."

"Where exactly did they get the code for this, I'd like to know," Olivia growled in frustration.

"They're creating it as they need it, or think of it." Boy did that sound familiar. "Did the prime directive forbid that kind of thing?"

"I don't know," she whined. "This isn't Star Trek. I don't even know if there is a prime directive." Gripping the sides of her face between her hands, she stared intently at the supposed hiding spot. "This is a nightmare," she moaned softly.

"Yep. Complete with a real live zombie." Heck, I was just waiting for the fairies and elves to show up. Maybe sprinkle in a few trolls. Centaurs! I've always wanted to see one in person. I did not understand how they were anatomically correct.

"Macy!" Olivia hissed.

"What?" I asked, startled by the fervency in her voice.

"What are you doing?" she accused.

"Uh...nothing." No sense in getting her any more riled up than she already was.

"I can see that," she said through clenched teeth while stabbing me with those crazy fire and brimstone eyes. Pointing at the swirls, she repeatedly jabbed her finger at them. "Go!" she shouted, but before I could take one step, she hollered, "Wait! I don't like this setup."

"Make up your dang mind, woman," I snapped angrily. "Am I coming or going?" When she suddenly straightened from the stalking crouch she'd adopted, I braced for trouble.

"We need to see her." Darting to the cabinet where the canisters were located, she pointed to the word "flour" written on the side of one. "It works in the movies."

In that moment, she was so like Miranda.

"You'll need to move fast," I cautioned her. "Once she sees you, you'll be susceptible to the new projection."

She rolled her shoulders back and arched her eyebrows. "Have you seen me work?"

And that was so like me, except for the face. With the brows and the crazy eyes, she looked like that Bellatrix character from Harry Potter. "For the record, I would like to state that you are a bit of a nutcase right now."

"Says the woman about to join in my delusion."

She had me there. All aboard for Crazy Town. With hands stretched over the island posed to grab the platter holding the fruit, I waited for Olivia to make her move. When she did, I missed it, even though I was watching her the entire time. But I knew she'd done it by the flour suddenly billowing through the air and all the coughing and gagging that Lindsey was doing. Dumping the fruit from the platter, I turned towards her just as a very long butcher knife clattered to the floor. I waited until Olivia scooped up the knife, and then I nailed Lindsey. She collapsed at my feet, the swirls slowly fading until she was plain old Lindsey wearing a flour coat.

"I ain't gonna lie. That felt pretty good." Placing the flour dusted platter in the sink, I brushed my hands off. "Good thing it is made of pewter."

"One down," Olivia sighed in relief.

As I turned my back to the sink, everything in me began screaming something was wrong. Immediately I recalled that Juarez had said they were in here. Plural. Closing my eyes, I inhaled. The barest hint of decomposition now tinged the air.

"One to go," I corrected.

"Langston?" Olivia asked worriedly. "I don't smell anything."

The shift raced through me as I turned in circles, straining to determine where the threat was coming from. "Stop moving," I barked at Olivia, who was prancing around like a terrier. Her aura was a bright orange with different colors shooting through it like fireworks. It was making me dizzy just to look at it. Once she stilled, I inhaled again. There was a definite rottenness hanging in the air. The hunt led me back to the island and up.

"You don't smell that?" I gulped, jerking my nose down in revulsion.

Moving to stand next to me, she lifted her nose and sniffed. "A little. Is it coming from up there?" Her words were accentuated by the fearful raising of her eyes to stare at the air vent above the island.

"No, let me. I insist," I said dully. I knew from the stricken look on her face that she wasn't about to check it out. What happened to the crazy Olivia that wanted to hit things? She didn't even blink when I climbed onto the countertop.

"It's getting stronger."

"You ain't teasing," I choked. Bringing my hand to my face, I covered my nose while tears brimmed in my eyes. Really wishing I hadn't eaten that soup now.

"Shouldn't Langston have collapsed when Lindsey did," she said nervously. "Why is she still moving towards us? I mean, I assume that's what the increase in stench means. That she's getting closer."

"Hand me that stool." Using my free hand, I pointed to the one nearest her. "She's probably following the last directive Lindsey gave her."

"To come here," she squeaked and hugged the stool protectively to her chest. "This is some messed up necromancy."

Dropping my head in exasperation, I placed both hands on my hips. "Yes, Olivia. Lindsey the powerful necromancer has sent for the zombie to eat us. Now give me the dad gum stool."

Her eyes widened in fear right before they narrowed in anger. "Here," she spat, and roughly shoved the stool at me. "You don't have to be so calm about it. Zombies are something you should be afraid of."

"What would make me calm is to know if there's a zombie lurking on the other side of this vent."

"Why?" she whined.

"So I can kill it."

"But Adam and Cedars will be here any second."

The images I'd gathered from Adam had told me as much, but the smell was getting stronger. I didn't think Langston was going to give us the option of waiting. And really, I'd rather handle this than have Adam tear into her and risk the leopard taking over again.

Standing on top of the stool, I turned and gave Olivia a halfhearted smile. "How much trouble can one zombie be?" The smile left as soon as my back was to her. God almighty, but how did I reach a place in my life where I was going to learn the answer to that question?

"Wait!" Olivia yelled, nearly succeeding in startling me off the stool.

"What," I snarled as I snatched back the hand that was reaching for the vent.

"What if she's really there? I think we should wait for the guys."

Was she trying to tick me off? "As far as I can tell, *you* aren't doing anything." Turning from her, I reached up to undo the first of four clips securing the vent in place. "Wait for the guys," I mumbled under my breath. I didn't need to wait for the *guys*. I could do things for myself. Things like kill a zombie. It couldn't be that hard. She was already dead.

As soon as my hand made contact with the second clip, the cover exploded outward. I barely heard Olivia's shriek over my own, though, to be clear, mine was in surprise, not horror.

"Macy!" Olivia screamed. "She's right on top of you!"

"You think," I barked at her. The only thing separating me from Langston was the vent grate I held above my head. And the way the metal was starting to bend, I didn't know how much longer that would be. "A little help," I ground at Olivia who was cowering on the other side of the kitchen.

"Watch out!" she yelled right before Langston took a swipe at my face.

"Thanks," I muttered. "That's just the help I needed."

The sudden shift in weight created by me jerking away from Langston's hand presented too much of a counter balance. At the same moment the metal gave way and folded in half, the stool shot out from under me. I had a split second to hurl Langston in the opposite direction of my fall. From the sound of Olivia's howl, it wasn't a direction she appreciated. I would have laughed, but the air was ripped out of my lungs the moment my back made contact with the granite countertop.

"She's coming back," Olivia called in warning.

The next moment the counter shook with the impact of Langston's landing.

"Did she gain some weight or something?" I gasped awkwardly. And how was she moving so fast? I barely managed to grasp her wrists before her talons cut a path across my face. Talons? Seriously? Bad nanobots. I let her momentum carry her over me and added a shove to gain some clearance. Flipping onto my stomach, I had to duck Olivia, who finally decided to join the party. With a bar stool grasped firmly in her hands, she intercepted Langston's rebound, hitting her squarely in the upper torso. It was enough to bowl Langston over, but not stop her entirely. The island rattled again as Langston leapt back on.

"Watch out for the—" Too late. Olivia's foot planted directly on the banana. "And my...soda."

Have you ever seen an already slick surface like granite smeared with banana and soda? Neither had I. I was practically retching in laughter when Olivia's next swing of the stool saw her follow it into a direct collision with the zombie. There were no words to describe the horror contained in Olivia's scream.

Using the time and space Olivia gained for me by generously throwing herself on the zombie, I rolled off the island and onto the floor. On all fours, I focused on trying to restore my breathing. It was from this perspective that I saw Olivia rise. Now covered in the fruity soda concoction and a little bit of zombie, she struck at Langston with new vigor.

What was that in her hair? Orange peel, I noted when Olivia spun, and it flew from her and landed on the floor in front of me. "Oh, no," I breathed, my stomach beginning to convulse in laughter again. My flattened soda can was stuck to Olivia's butt. I laughed harder when the stream of paper towels rolled off the counter and hit me in the head.

"Macy!" Olivia said sharply. "Stop laughing and help."

Help? I was just trying to breathe, a feat made more difficult by her comedy act. Grasping the island with both hands, I hauled myself up in time to see Olivia's next swing careen wildly out of control. It sent her lunging down to one knee and my soup bowl flying. It missed my head by mere inches, but I didn't have the air to gasp.

"Any time you're ready," Olivia chafed.

I hoisted one leg on the counter just as Olivia slipped on my spoon and went down again. When Langston charged forward, Olivia planted both feet smack dab in Langston's stomach. As a result of forward momentum, Langston lifted off the ground, like they were playing airplane.

"Oh my god, you're killing me, Olivia," I wheezed as my leg

slipped off the counter. Laughter and having the air knocked out of you so did not mix.

"Get off me!" Olivia screeched, trying to dodge the bits of stuff falling off of Langston. Drawing her legs in, Olivia wound up and launched Langston backwards through the air. When she sat up, she had bits of orange and maybe smushed grapes all up and down her back.

"There's an easier way to make fruit salad," I panted. "Ones that don't involve zombies."

She turned to look at me, the aggravation of the situation molded into every line of her frown. "There is something wrong with her," she said. "All she wants to do is get to you. She doesn't even register that I'm here." Picking up the stool as Langston regained the island, she held it like a battering ram and drove it against Langston. "Something is definitely wrong with her," she grunted.

Yeah, that's what was wrong. Not the fact that she was dead.

Adam's footsteps signaled his arrival seconds before he entered the room. He paused at the scene presented to him, then hurried over to me. Hooking me under the arms, he pulled me away from the island to lean against his chest.

"I'm okay," I assured him, patting his arms wrapped around me.

"What is that?" he asked, staring straight at Langston.

Except for the color the rotting flesh added to her, she was pale. Black drool oozed from her mouth and ears. And her eyes... they were the creepiest of all. It looked like someone had scrambled them into some weird black and gray abstract.

"That is Langston. Or what used to be."

"Why doesn't she give up," Olivia cried, swinging the stool like a bat when Langston once again righted herself.

Adam let go of me and approached Olivia. "May I?" he asked, holding his hand out for the stool. When she gave it to him, he slammed it against the island and tore off one of the loosened legs. Using it as a stake, he drove it through Langston's chest all the way into the granite. Now pinned to the counter, Langston's movements were reduced to random twitching of her arms and legs. It reminded me of a cockroach on its back.

I was never eating on that counter again.

Turning from Langston, Adam rounded the island to stand in front of Lindsey's crumpled form. My breath caught at the intensity of the emotions rolling through him. I took an involuntary step towards him, but something in the rigidness of his shoulders stopped me.

Adam?

His response was to shut me out entirely. Before I could deal with that, Cedars slid through the doorway. Sensing the tension in the room, his gaze shifted warily between us as he took a minute to ascertain the situation. Finally, he settled on Langston.

"Take her to cremation," he ordered.

"Me?" Olivia said in horror when she realized Cedars was talking to her.

"And Macy. The two of you can handle it."

"What?" I protested. Why was I being punished?

"Do your magical transport thing and take care of it," he said sharply.

Adam growled in warning.

"Sorry," Cedars apologized. "The nanobots and the body have to be destroyed."

That didn't mean I had to go. Unless he was trying to get rid of me. One glance at Adam and I knew why. Fine, I moaned inwardly. "You'll have to move us," I said to Olivia. "I didn't even know we had a crematorium."

Cedars crossed the room to stand next to Adam. "You up for this?" he asked calmly.

For an answer, Adam reached down and gripped Lindsey by the back of the head and pulled her upright. "Send for Scout," he said. "Juarez is going to trace the origin of the signal, and then we are going to dispose of her as well."

"The president's not going to like it," Cedars advised him.

"Don't care," Adam answered. Tucking Lindsey under his arm like a football, he whirled around and came face to face with me.

"She has an adjusted camouflage slash projection ability," I said cautiously, trying to keep any judgment out of my voice.

"I saw."

"Through my eyes?"

He jerked his head forward in confirmation.

I so wanted to ask him if he was okay, or more importantly, who was in control right now. But if he'd wanted to communicate, he would have answered the many internal requests I'd aimed at him already.

"Macy, she's not getting any fresher over here," Olivia called in an effort to deflate the situation.

"Right." I stepped aside and let Adam pass. My shoes felt like they were packed with iron as I walked towards Langston.

"He'll be alright," Olivia whispered. "He's angry, but not like before. I don't think it was his leopard DNA motivating him this time. I know he's struggling for control," she admitted when I flicked my eyes to her. "But this had more of the flavor of a man protecting his woman from an imminent threat. Did you notice how he didn't order you to move when you confronted him? The leopard wouldn't have ignored that challenge."

That was probably true. Her words made me feel a little better about Adam's state of mind, but having to hear it from her didn't.

"If he's shutting you out right now, it's probably because he's having enough trouble regulating himself without having to filter through your thoughts as well."

"Yes, I know," I retorted. I wasn't trying to be rude to her, but I didn't want to hear this stuff from her.

"You ready?" she asked and nodded towards the island.

I glanced over at what was left of Langston and shook my head. "Someone should answer for this. She didn't deserve to end up this way."

"Someone will. We'll find the persons responsible. Adam will get what he needs out of Lindsey."

My face fell at the mention of that scenario. Surely, I could trust Cedars to do things properly. But could he handle an out of control Adam?

"Let's look at it this way," she said. "He'll either get what he needs or kill her trying. However it turns out, the end result works for me."

Regarding Lindsey, yeah. Her fate was already sealed. But I didn't want Adam to lose himself in the process, to have what happened last time he confronted her repeat itself. Heaving a sigh taut with worry, I shelved the topic for the time being. I'd find out the answer soon enough, and in the meantime, I had a zombie to eliminate.

"Who do we have to talk to around here to get this counter top replaced?" I griped as I placed both hands on the counter and hopped up.

"Margaret," she laughed. "I had already made a mental note to talk to her." She looked at the counter where Langston still jerked sporadically and shuddered. "I don't care if they soaked it in alcohol and lit it on fire. There was no way I was ever going to eat on that again."

"I second that motion," I agreed. "Come on. Let's get this over with."

Olivia positioned herself opposite me and placed a hand on Langston. "I'm thinking this whole slab needs to go," she said, leaning left and right to survey the top.

"You ever moved anything this heavy?"

"No," she shook her head. "I don't even know if it will burn, but any nanobots on it will." Having made her decision, she extended her hand to me.

"Are you sure you can move all of this?" I asked, eyeing her hand but not yet taking it.

"We'll find out," she smiled. "I'm sure it will be fine. It's not a direct correlation in weight. I believe I can do it, so I can. Isn't that the theory we're working under."

"Not exactly," I grimaced. "And if that's the case, what are these little buggers believing for?"

We both turned our heads to stare at Langston's quivering figure.

"Take my hand. Take it now before I lose my nerve," Olivia insisted.

"I like it much better when I'm the one trying new things," I grumbled and clasped her hand.

"Funny. I don't concur."

"By the way, thanks. For what you said about Adam."

"We're sisters," she shrugged. "That's what sisters do, right? Try to help one another."

"Sisters," I repeated. It still sounded strange to me. "I guess it's better than not helping."

"Don't let go," she said seriously. "The crematorium is a small place."

What? Like I could accidentally end up in the fire? Narrowing my eyes at her, I squeezed her hand tighter. Anything crispy around me better be dipped in chocolate and most importantly, not be me.

CHAPTER 29

DISPOSING OF LANGSTON DIDN'T TAKE long. When we were done, Olivia dropped me off in the lobby with instructions to confer with Miranda about the interview.

"Look at this," I said, gaping at the gargantuan room. Every direction I looked there were huge windows framing picturesque mountains. One of these days, I was going to take a proper tour of this place. Who knew what else I had been missing.

"Check out the fireplace," Miranda said.

It was monstrous. Three or four people could have easily fit inside. "Whoa," I mouthed, shaking my head to dispel the image that my recent experience with the crematorium had generated. I really needed to start having more uplifting life experiences. Ending my review of the space, I plopped down next to Miranda, who was sprawled on one of the many large sofas decorating the room.

"Here ya go," she said tiredly and tossed a message pad onto my lap.

Garrison had called. Someone from General Hurser's office had called. And the president. Twice.

"Don't these people have anything else to do besides pester me?" I griped.

"Well, when the world revolves around you..."

I cut my eyes to her in warning. "I've just dispatched a zombie. You might want to go easy with the sarcasm."

"Zombie, you say?"

I couldn't help but laugh at the fake look of surprise she

plastered on her face. "Olivia did most of the work. Actually, I just let it in."

"So you were that girl," she said knowingly. "Anyone get hurt?"

"Only if fruit are people. In that case, Olivia murdered a whole family of grapes and an orange cousin. Oh, and a banana. You should have seen it, Miranda. I almost died laughing."

"It was hilarious, I'm sure."

"I'm not exaggerating. All the air was literally sucked out of me."

"That was the granite," Olivia scoffed.

"Ah, the fruit killer," Miranda hummed. "Or should I call you…The Blender."

Ignoring Miranda's jab, Olivia reached down and picked up the message pad. "What did the president want?" she asked.

"It was more of a panini pressing action," I said, pushing my hands against one another in demonstration. "Is there such a thing as a fruit press?"

Miranda squinted her eyes in concentration. "There's a wine press. And olives are pressed. Some apple juices, too. I've got it," she said excitedly. "The Juicer."

"The president?" Olivia drawled.

"What do you think he wants?" Miranda sneered. "A press conference."

Crap.

"I found your notes on the desk and took them to Juarez. He's reviewing them. And no, I don't make random circuits of Adam's suite. I just knew you'd been working at his desk and figured you'd left something there. Additionally," she said, taking a moment to bite her lip. "A little birdie told me that the president wants the press conference to take place tomorrow morning."

This took crap to a whole new level. There was no way I was prepared to unveil this project tomorrow. MAP at this point was barely even on the map.

"I'll have Juarez forward me his notes and yours," Olivia said as she tapped out the message to him. "Then we'll practice."

"That is a great idea," Miranda agreed.

Practice. Wait until they saw how little I had actually gotten done. We had a lot more work in front of us before any practicing could happen.

After Olivia had taken a few minutes to read the notes, she looked up at me. "We're not ready," she said flatly.

"Not hardly," I breathed in agreement.

"Then let's get ready!" Miranda exclaimed unexpectedly. "The president is waiting—nay." She stood to her feet and raised both arms in the air. "The world is waiting. We have a deadline people!" For her finish, she clenched both fists and dropped her head back to look at the ceiling.

Crickets. That was the sound heard in the wake of her pronouncement. Even the fire seemed to have tamped down on its roaring.

Olivia's eyes flicked from Miranda to me. "Should I be worried, or does she always get like this?"

"This?" I shrugged indifferently. "Wait until she gets excited."

Pressing the heels of her hands into her eyes, Olivia folded into the couch. "Let's get this done," she sighed.

"I suppose I've already signed up," I grumbled. "How'd that happen again?"

"You took the president's call," Miranda quipped.

"I have got to stop doing that."

"Ladies," Olivia said, attempting to steer us back on course.

"Right," I sighed. "Let's get to it."

Little did I know what I was getting into when I uttered those words. After hours of just me, Miranda and Olivia working on the plan, which about half the time meant arguing about the plan, Juarez showed up. Between him and Olivia, we were able to nail down most of the auxiliary details about each proposed medical advance. The real meat of the project wouldn't happen until the actual design and manufacture started, but that wasn't information that was going to be divulged anyway.

Getting ready for the international press conference was an entirely different beast. It turns out, it takes a whole gang of hybrids toting snacks and lobbing comments like hand grenades to be ready for one of those. It was to no avail when I tried to convince them that reporters didn't behave in this fashion. Thank God, cause I would never be able to maintain my professional cool. But despite their rowdiness, we managed to cover every aspect of my opening statement. No question was off limits, no matter the rudeness with which it was asked. By the time we were done and most of the gang had left, I was feeling pretty good about the whole thing.

"What is she going to wear?" Reynolds asked, throwing a monkey wrench into my good feelings.

My eyes went straight to Olivia. A monkey wrench for a monkey suit. I could already see the scheming twinkle in her eyes.

Winking at me, she stood and stretched. "We'll find her something," she yawned. "For now, it's getting late, and I have to finalize the details with the president. If there's nothing further…"

"Olivia," I said to stop her exit. "I want the press conference held in the Pentagon."

"Don't want the bureaucrats getting their hands on it?" she teased.

"No, I don't. All kidding aside, this needs to be ran as a military operation. We cannot allow this technology to leave our control. The point that Kenny and Wrangle made about having patients stay under lock and key until the nanobots have accomplished their task and verifiably keeled over, we cannot compromise on that."

"That would require an unprecedented level of security at participating facilities," she said neutrally.

"Too much for a simple hospital," Miranda observed.

"It would provide a use for decommissioned military bases, subs and the like," Reynolds said. "Or, they could construct entirely new facilities."

I turned to stare at him. That didn't sound like some spur of the moment thought. "Reynolds, were you in the military?"

"Yes, ma'am. I was given an honorable discharge to come here."

"And, exactly who did you serve under?"

He smiled real big at me.

General Hurser. "I always did like a military man with a brain." How he had ridden the wave of craziness to have his man end up on the inside at just the right time was more than a little impressive.

Dipping his head in acknowledgment, Reynolds said, "He's rather fond of you too."

Fond? I was proposing increasing the size and power of the military. I was going to be his favorite person in the whole world.

"I'm not sure this is what the president was planning on," Olivia cautioned.

"Too bad he's not giving the press conference," I retorted. "Just secure the location and I'll do the rest."

She skewered me with her best look of disapproval.

"Pretty please," I whined, batting my eyelashes innocently.

Shaking her head helplessly, she pivoted and began walking away from us. "This is how you get yourself into trouble," she called over her shoulder.

"What you call trouble, I call opportunity," I yelled back, but she was already gone. Turning to Reynolds, I said, "I just want you to know that despite whatever machinations were used to get you here, you are mine now, and I expect complete loyalty. Furthermore, as my assistant, you are going to be right in the middle of it, as a certain general may have intended. But any decisions you make better be on the level. Is any of this going to be a problem for you?"

"Yours?" he sputtered flakily. "I'm touched." Lifting his arm, he pretended to mop his eyes with his sleeve.

"He's just like you," Miranda muttered at Reynolds' fooling around.

"I think this is more up your alley," I disagreed and turned my eyes back to Reynolds.

"I see no problems with the current arrangement," he said. "I'm not under anyone's command—"

"Excuse me?"

"Except for you, Sir Knight," he amended quickly.

"And Hurser's never mentioned any sort of plan to confiscate nanobot tech?" I asked doubtfully.

"Of course he did. It's the reason I came here. I think he's right about folding this into the military. So do you. And, you came to that conclusion all on your own."

Because it was the only choice that made any sense. With the degree of security needed, the only apparatus big enough to provide that was the military. Even if the Organization got its act together and we were able to send our own people for the procedures, we would still need additional manpower for protection. From what Adam had told me, the great majority of the people here were engaged in research and not trained for that.

"May I just clarify something," Miranda said. "When she says right in the middle of it, she's not exaggerating." She lifted her hand to just above her eyes. "Up to your eyeballs, covered in crap of her making, categorically, inescapably, in it. You," she pointed at Reynolds. "Ain't seen nothing yet."

Here I was, trying to figure out the nature of the relationship between General Hurser and Reynolds and if I should be worried about it, and she was pointing out what a bad boss I was. Typical.

"Sorry, Mace," she said without a shred of remorse when I trained my scornful gaze on her. "But the guy needs to know what he's getting into."

"I think I'll be alright," Reynolds chuckled. "The taste I've had already wasn't too bad." Catching the pillow I launched at him, he chunked it back at me. "I'll see you in the morning."

With his exit, only Miranda and I were left. "What do you think?" I asked her.

"About what? The press conference, the plan? Reynolds?"

"Any and all subjects are open for comment."

"After this rehearsal, the press conference should be a piece of cake. The plan is not too shabby. As long as the reporters are not too zealous in digging for details, we might pull this thing off. And Reynolds...I'm going to keep my eye on him. I can't figure out what his angle is."

"His angle?" I asked, tucking my legs underneath me as I swiveled to face her.

"I don't know," she frowned. "One minute it seems like he's into you, and then it seems it's just platonic. I don't know. It's weird."

So it wasn't just in my head.

"Do you know what I'm talking about?"

"Yeah," I nodded. "It's this strange protectiveness he has for me."

"Like when he sacrificed himself with Adam for you, and how he stayed by your bedside when you nearly died. Why would he do that?"

"I don't know."

"And now he's like this secret agent for General Hurser?"

"You did catch that."

"Duh. I'm trying to decide if I need to worry about it." Crossing her arms over her chest, she sighed loudly. "He doesn't seem like a traitor."

"They never do."

"Does your badometer tell you anything?"

I snickered at her labeling. "No. But next time it shows up, I'll train it on him."

"You can't control it yet?"

"I can't control half the crap I do," I blurted loudly.

"Finally, she admits it."

"Is it okay if we overlook this for now? I really don't want to expend the brain power to figure it out or push a confrontation with Reynolds. He hasn't given me any reason to doubt him, and something tells me that he's his own man."

"Sure," she yawned. "Hope it's not something we need to figure out now. Maybe I should google the signs of a serial killer."

"He's not a serial killer, Miranda. And anyway, I can take him."

"You can take him," she repeated dully.

"Yes, I can take him," I reasserted. "And didn't you agree to dropping this?"

"Dropping it now."

"Great."

"Wonderful. Deep cleansing breath."

We both inhaled and exhaled slowly.

"Are you coming tomorrow?"

"I don't know what help I would be, but I'll be there if you want me to."

"It'd be nice to have someone there that I know is definitely in my corner."

"The piece that's broken off from reality?"

My yawn morphed into a coughing fit as laughter tried to intrude mid stretch. "That'd be the one," I gasped, pounding on my chest in an attempt to relieve the coughing. After regaining my breath, I asked her what I'd been wanting to ask her for the last two hours. "Have you heard from Cedars?"

"He, along with Adam and Juarez, are pouring over the code, trying to isolate the control subroutine? Anyway, Jamie says Adam's wound tight, but he's holding it together."

Closing my eyes, I nodded in relief.

"You two aren't talking?" she ventured gently.

"We're not *not* talking. Just not communicating very well right now."

She reached over and patted my leg. "It will all work out," she said. "You and Adam. The press conference. Tomorrow, you are going to change the world for the better."

It was going to change alright. I was praying it was for the better.

"I know these words are probably wasted on you, but try to get some sleep," she said as she stood.

"Thanks, Mir."

"Thank me after we're a resounding success."

"You know the definition of resounding is a loud echoing noise."

"Yes, but I put success after it."

"So I'm to be loud and success will follow? I can do loud. Loud and me are like this." I crossed my fingers and held them up.

"Goodnight, Macy," she chuckled as she left.

It was night already? Time flew when you filled it with a fantasy script. Fighting zombies...teleporting team members. Now a plot to transform the destiny of mankind using robots? My life sounded like make believe.

Peeling myself from the leather cushions, I moved to stand in front of the fire. Tomorrow, I would be thrust into the spotlight again. Or bulls eye, depending on how I looked at it. My face would forever be associated with this. Just like Julia's on the first go round. What wasn't like before was the public awareness of genetics. The world knew Dr. Greer. As soon as they saw me, they would expect the press conference to be about another breakthrough.

Fortunately, the president's agenda was letting me avoid the whole hybrid thing by latching onto the medical aspect. He was betting the promise of immortality would outweigh any duplicity regarding hybrid research, if that bit of knowledge ever even saw the light of day. With the president using me like a laser to focus attention squarely on ending human suffering, I was beginning to think that even if it came out it wouldn't matter. He could claim ignorance of the fact until he became president, and then explain how he had turned the project to the benefit of all mankind. And if any rogue nations forsook the behind the scenes cloak and dagger stuff to pursue a more direct route to hybrid tech? He would look like a hero standing against them.

Shaking my head at the absurdity of it all, I turned my back to the fire. Humans with inhuman capabilities? A possible elixir for immortality? In contradiction to the hope their promise inspired, they could literally tear the fabric of our society apart. I hoped the medical applications we were about to reveal wouldn't create the same fervor as the first time. It shouldn't. Only those of us who knew about hybrids would link this to them. To everyone else, it would be newly developed medical technology. I had to remember that the rest of the world wasn't living in a hybrid dominated environment.

Returning to the couch, I reached down and retrieved the messages. I should probably let General Hurser know that all his dreams were about to come true. I'd let Olivia handle the president, and Garrison? The less he knew the better.

Glancing wistfully at the fire once more, I wished I could curl up on one of the couches and take a nap. But that would have to keep for some time in the future when the fate of the world didn't rest on the speech I would make the next day. Tomorrow was going to be the most important day of my twenty...sixty-seven—whatever—year life. For both me and every other person on the planet.

"I sure hope you know what you're doing," I whispered to God.

CHAPTER 30

N THE MIRROR, I SAW Adam enter the bathroom and lean against the far wall. As he didn't put in an appearance last night, it was the first time I had seen him since he'd hauled Lindsey off.

"Are you ready?" he asked quietly.

My reflection verified that the last of the bruising had faded and that my eyes were nearly free of the red pin pricks. The bloodshot look earned from the late into the night phone call with General Hurser and the resulting sleeplessness afterwards was clearly present. But that was nothing that a few dozen cups of coffee wouldn't cure. I shrugged my shoulders at him. What did it matter if I was ready? It was going to happen anyway.

"Did you find what you were looking for in Lindsey?"

He stiffened at my redirection. "We're still working on it," he answered gruffly. Taking measured steps, he stopped just behind me. "If you're uncertain, there's still time to call it off."

"We are well past that point now," I snorted in disagreement. Ducking my chin, I began buttoning the jacket Olivia had forced on me.

"Macy," he said, reaching for me but stopping short of contact. "I'm sorry I've been distant. Both physically and whatever..." He paused to signal back and forth with his hand in indication of our bond. "*This* is between us."

His apology and his openness were unexpected. I turned slowly to face him.

"It wasn't done in an attempt to hurt you. I just...I'm not..." His words faltered as he searched for an explanation.

Closing the distance between us, I wrapped my arms around his waist and pressed my head against his chest. "I know, Adam," I whispered.

He was slow to return the embrace, like he wasn't sure what his response should be.

"I'm not upset. Not really." I knew he needed time and space to learn to be Adam again.

"You look beautiful," he said as his arms closed around me.

"Enough to distract the reporters from what I'm about to tell them?" I mumbled into his chest.

"Enough to distract me."

Lifting my head, I stared into his green eyes. "Even in this get up?" I asked doubtfully.

He smiled as he plucked absently at the sleeve. "Olivia dressed you?"

"Who else? Apparently, I have to look dignified for the press." Sighing at the straight jacket feel the clothing evoked, I added, "But I'm seriously tempted to pop off somewhere and change into a pair of scrubs."

His smile morphed into a wicked grin as he leaned down and whispered in my ear. "You want to play doctor?"

"Knock it off," I laughed, lightly slapping his chest in mock rebuke.

Using both hands, he cupped the sides of my face and gently lifted my chin until our eyes met. "You're going to do great," he said.

The smile slowly faded from my lips. "I'm nervous," I whispered. There were so many things that could go wrong. My winging it on the fly kind of style didn't mesh very well with the level of planning required for this whole undertaking, a point driven home by General Hurser more than once during our phone call.

"I know." Very slowly, he lifted the barrier between us, allowing his emotions to reach me. "I am with you," he said and gently pressed his lips to mine.

The sudden influx of emotion from him soothed places in me

I didn't know were aching. I melted into his arms, absorbing all of his love that I could. Neither of us moved until the door chimed.

"That's probably Miranda," I said as I reluctantly pulled away.

"She's going with you?"

"She is."

"Morning, Adam," Miranda beamed when the door slid open. "How's our girl? Wait, don't answer." Lifting the briefcase she carried, she used it to shield her face. "Do I need to give you two a minute or thirty?"

"Are you being bashful?" I teased. "Impending motherhood sure does change a woman."

"Just hurry up, would you? I'm not used to seeing you like this. In fact, I will give you two a minute." Turning on her heel, she disappeared from view as the door whisked shut again.

There was a new one. Usually, I was the person rapidly exiting the room with my face flushed in embarrassment. Smiling at her sudden onset of prudery, I picked up the emergency backpack I'd managed to cobble together and swung it over my shoulder.

"What's that?" Adam asked as he pulled me to him again.

"Let's just say I've learned from my previous experiences that I need this."

"Okay," he drawled, still puzzled by the accessory. Then the tenderness faded from his eyes, leaving them guarded, hard. "Let me know when you're returning. I can't keep the bond open continuously, but I'll answer when you call." As soon as he'd finished speaking, he severed the connection between us.

His sudden and unexpected absence surprised me. I couldn't hide my disappointment.

"I'm not there yet, Macy. The leopard side of me sees everything you do as a challenge or an invitation." He kissed me lightly on the forehead and then stepped away. "Until I'm certain who's in control, I have to operate with extreme caution."

There were several ways I could react to this. Get mad, sad or deal with it like I had been, which basically equaled ignoring it. "Well, I guess I don't want to provoke the big bad putty tat," I said dryly. "See ya when I get back." With that, I turned and left the suite. Huh? Guess I'd chosen mad. Who knew how Adam felt about it. Not me.

"Are you okay?" Miranda asked, looking sidelong at me as I stomped past her.

"Peachy," I replied tightly.

"Really? Cause you look sort of red, as in mad as hell. Which, by the way, is completely opposite of the smoochy smooch body language I was involuntarily subjected to just a few moments ago."

"Could we just not talk about it please?"

"Sure," she sighed. "Got your notes?"

"Yes."

"I see you've got the outfit," she muttered, rolling her eyes at the stiff suit I was modeling.

The skin directly underneath my collar began itching in reaction to her comment. Reaching a hand, I tried to thread a finger through the rigid web. Clearly, the woman liked her starch.

"Would you perhaps like a different outfit? Like, I don't know, the one stowed away in my handy briefcase."

Halting my march, I scowled at her as she flipped the briefcase horizontal and popped it open. "Miranda, that's the only thing in the brief case."

"Right. What do I need anything for? I'm not speaking."

I took a deep breath and exhaled loudly, allowing the tension with Adam to drain away. Anything had to be better than what I was currently wearing. And picturing Olivia's face when she realized I had ditched her choice of attire? That was something to smile about. Looking back up at Miranda, I grinned in approval.

"We'll get you changed after we take off," she whispered conspiratorially. Snapping the case shut, she lowered it to her side and began strutting down the hall like a woman on a mission. Thank God it was a mission that might actually benefit me this time.

"Oh," I gulped, my steps slowing as I entered the hangar. The whole team had gathered for my send off. They were now staring at me while I stood frozen in the doorway.

Backtracking, Miranda hooked her arm through mine and

pulled me towards the plane. "Don't worry about the crowd," she hummed in my ear. "Everybody loves a show. And besides, this alleviates some of their boredom." Her smile widened as Olivia approached. "Olivia's going to have her hands full."

"You look wonderful," Olivia beamed as she swept me with her gaze. "The president's agreed to let you hold the press conference in the Pentagon Briefing Room." Then her face turned deadly serious. "I know I don't have to tell you how important this press conference is."

"No—"

"Or how devastating it would be if you were to lose your temper and act rashly."

"I'm not—"

"Because that would destroy everything I've worked for my entire life."

Next to me, I felt Miranda bristle, but I smiled sweetly at Olivia. Stepping forward, I hugged her tightly around the neck. "I'll keep my cool," I promised.

Drawing back from me, she eyed me suspiciously. "See that you do," she said uncertainly.

I was so changing into that other outfit.

Transferring my attention from her, I scoped out the rest of the group. They looked worried. "Guys, I'm coming back."

"With or without your clothes?" Kenny sneered.

"I've been wondering that myself," Miranda whispered in my ear. "Did you put extra underwear in the pack?"

Jerking free of her grasp, I glared at her. There was no way I was admitting that I had in fact stuffed several pairs inside.

"Fifty bucks says the clothes don't make it through the day," Van called.

"They better make it," Olivia growled in warning. "That suit cost close to a thousand dollars."

A thousand bucks for this? Now I knew she was off her rocker.

"In that case, I'll take before the press conference is finished," Wrangle said.

"Ha ha, very funny. But the status of my clothing, or in this case Olivia's, is not worth betting on." Especially since they would all lose. This suit was going to be safely tucked away in Miranda's briefcase before we ever reached the press conference. My bet was on how frazzled Olivia would look when we got back. Locking eyes with Kenny, I pointed my finger at him. "Behave."

His eyebrows rose in defiance before they were joined by a smile. I just knew I was going to return to find the whole place toilet papered. Oh, well. The teenagers were Olivia's problem for the next few hours. Let the frazzling begin.

"We should get going," Reynolds said from behind me.

My stomach leaped at the designation. "We?" I asked timidly.

"Yes, ma'am," he saluted and started up the ramp to the plane.

I couldn't bring myself to step onto the ramp. Did Adam know about this?

"He knows," Miranda said as she passed me. Turning around, she walked backwards up the ramp. "Cedars cleared it with him."

"He approved?" I asked in surprise.

"Someone might have explained Reynolds' prior actions," she said sheepishly.

Truly, she was the best friend a girl could have.

"Go get'em, Doc!" Crystal yelled enthusiastically, unleashing a torrent of comments from the bunch that ranged from wildly supportive to over the top chest bumping.

I waved my goodbye to them just as chest bumping migrated to backflips. Miranda was right. They were really bored.

"One more thing," Olivia said as she followed me inside the plane. "You might want to add this to your backpack." She handed me a medium sized black zipper pouch. "There for defense only," she added as I unzipped the pouch.

There were four preloaded mini guns, labeled tranquilizer and inhibitor, respectively. Four more devices looked like regular pens. "What are these?"

"Pneumatic injections of the same." She rolled the pens over to reveal their labels. "The guns are for longer distances."

Miranda looked over my shoulder at the contents. "At least

they're clearly marked. Wouldn't want to go tranqing someone when I really wanted to take away their powers entirely."

"They're just in case options. For defense," Olivia said, repeating her former assertion. "You should be perfectly safe inside the Pentagon. But...I've learned to think outside the box where you are concerned."

About dang time. "Thanks, Olivia." Closing the pouch, I added it to the backpack.

"No thanks necessary." She reached the door and paused. "Just return it to me when you get back."

Yeah, like that was happening, but I smiled at her just the same. "Olivia," I called, causing her to pause in the doorway. "A word of advice about my team...get them some physical activity pronto, and whatever you do, do not order them around like you're the boss."

"But I am the boss," she frowned at me.

"If you want to survive these next few hours, I suggest you take the advice," Miranda muttered.

"The kids don't take well to strangers ordering them around. Trust us on this one," I nodded at Olivia.

She looked as though she was considering it for a moment, but her next comment said she'd clearly discarded it. "They need to learn to follow orders. To operate within the confines of structure." Satisfied with her conclusion, she waved and stepped out of the plane.

"This is going to go well," Miranda deadpanned. "I better have Cedars keep an eye on them."

He might need more than an eye. Maybe some duct tape and an ocean to put between them. Feeling frustrated by the new source of worry trying to push its way into my brain, I left my seat and poked my head inside the cockpit. "Reynolds, let's make this trip boring."

"Oh?" he smiled. "Not interested in any side excursions this time?"

"Just there and back, please."

"I'll see what I can do."

Dropping back into my seat, I buckled in for takeoff. As soon as we were safely in the air, Miranda handed me the brief case and pointed to a door at the far end of the cabin.

"We have a bedroom?" I hollered when I opened the door.

"Don't get any ideas. The flight's not that long."

Like I could sleep now.

Tossing the briefcase on the bed, I proceeded to disrobe. It took longer getting out of the outfit I was in than it did to put the new one on. I cannot say I was sorry for the long rip sustained by the panty hose Olivia had insisted that I wear. Seriously. What century was she living in? Not the same one Miranda was in, I thought nervously as I eyed Miranda's choice of slacks. They sort of looked like the material athletic pants were made of except thicker. The outer seam bore two black leather stripes which ran the entire length of the pants. In between the stripes, blackened studs. I breathed easier once I viewed what she'd paired them with. A fitted white top, and a long black leather jacket. I half expected to see the familiar boots, but she'd chosen a cute little half boot instead.

"How do I look?" I asked, twirling for her inspection.

"More like you."

It certainly felt more like me. Taking the seat opposite her, I fished my notes out of the backpack. But since I already had them memorized, my perusal was only a halfhearted attempt to pass the time.

"I hate waiting," I complained.

"I know."

"How much longer?"

"Seriously? You're like a two year old."

Whatever. Still didn't answer my question.

"You know, once this is out, it can't be undone."

"Nope."

"They'll be no taking it back."

"I know."

"It's going to be full on implementation time. This is no little task we're undertaking."

Squinting, I studied her through narrowed eyes. "Are you angling for a raise? Cause I thought we had established that I have no idea how we are financing any of this."

"Doesn't the military have a budget to fund secret stuff?" she pouted.

"I'm sure they do. But it's not like General Hurser handed me a debit card. Do we even know how much we need? What it costs to manufacture one nanobot, let alone the scale we're talking about?"

She frowned at me. "I suppose I'll put that on my list."

"I like the way you're thinking," I winked at her.

"You know that the world is going to assign ownership to the military."

I nodded at her. "The Organization needs to maintain its anonymity so that it can fulfill its role in fighting the bad guys, research, etc."

"So we're going to be the MAP wing of the Organization," she said thoughtfully. "I like it. It's why I got into this field to begin with."

"You got into this field to employ microscopic robots in the fight against mortality?"

"Well...not that part...but to kick mortality's butt? Definitely."

Me too, but I never imagined this happening.

"I always believed that we'd find cures to diseases. Like the cancer switch. I knew it was just the beginning. But discovering all this stuff that borders on the supernatural...that was only in my fantasies." She smiled and waggled her eyes at me.

"Please," I groaned. "Let's not go there."

"Now, I am the fantasy," she smirked. "Every man's dream."

And she went there.

"Yes, Miranda," I said dully. "You are God's gift to men. Or at least Cedars."

Her smile deepened at the mention of his name. "It's true. I guess my roaming days are over."

Now that was an actual gift to the men of the world. "How is he doing?"

"Jamie? He's…worried. He doesn't say so, but I can feel him carrying a lot of concerns."

"About the Organization?"

"That," she nodded. "And Adam, and Julia, and the riddle… the baby. He's got a list too."

"Mm," I hummed in sympathy.

"Things are about to get a whole lot busier, aren't they?" she sighed.

"We'll delegate," I shrugged.

"Can I tell you something?"

"Of course."

"I can't wait to sink my teeth into it. Figuratively speaking. This place is a mess. Straightening it out will be such a relief."

Uh oh. I'd been through countless reorg projects with her. The phrase, "No stone unturned," originated when someone saw Miranda's work. It was always worth it in the end, but the middle? War zone.

"Some people might not appreciate it," I said casually.

"Olivia's on board."

"Since when?" I whined in surprise.

"Since I told her I was going to fix it whether she liked it or not. I think she was secretly glad that someone besides her was willing to take it on."

Trust me, she'd get over that feeling soon enough. "Hey, you know who would make a great assistant for you? Margaret."

"Margaret," she purred as she thought it over.

"She knows everything about the place. She's well organized and efficient. And helpful. I've never met anyone as helpful as her. It's like she knows what you need before you do."

"That's true," she nodded, still undecided on the matter.

"Unless, of course, you prefer Crystal to be your only assistant."

Miranda flicked her eyes back to me. A look of shock passed over her face. "She is, isn't she," she said upon realizing she'd been duped.

"Did she give you a written proposal of demands?" I put air quotes around demands.

"Yes," she moaned.

"Did this proposal include suggestions for fulfilling those demands?"

"Yes," she moaned louder.

"Has she been following up with you, and have you been assigning trivial tasks for her to accomplish?"

"I plead the fifth!"

"Assistant wannabe," I pronounced.

"Crap," she swore under her breath. "I never even saw it coming."

"Crystal's not so bad. She just needs a little fine tuning. Little polish here and there."

"She needs more than a little."

"She'll grow out of it," I suggested. "Especially with you training her."

"I didn't sign up for this," she said unhappily.

"Did you think I was going to be the only one stuck dealing with the teenagers? We're in this together, remember?"

"Coercion? That's low, Macy, even for you."

"Hey, I got to deliver a baby. You got to help wrangle the teenagers. Seems fair to me."

"Seems lopsided to me. Yours is a one shot deal."

Like I said, seemed fair to me.

"I'll talk to Margaret," she said, her frustration somewhat mollified by the prospect of a real assistant. "See how she feels about it."

She'd accept the role. Margaret had a hole in her life, a lack in purpose. This would satisfy that. And with what she was cooking up with Wrangle, no pun intended, I hoped it would be enough to make her stay.

"Regarding people's feelings, how do you think the media is really going to feel about the announcement today?" I asked.

She crossed her arms over her chest as she stared into the distance. "Excited at first, but confused. Then immensely frustrated. We don't have the answers to their favorite questions."

"Who, what, why, when, where, and how," I guessed.

"Bingo. Beyond the basics, we don't have much of anything we can share. They'll want to sink their teeth into the details."

"Which are virtually nonexistent for them at this point."

"That's what happens when you rush to a press conference before the roll out is ready."

Why was the president rushing this? We weren't on any sort of time table as far as I knew. Unless... "Someone else is about to break the hybrid story?"

"That'd be my guess."

Not Red. He didn't even know about her. "I guess I better make this good then."

"You better make it outstanding enough to soak up all the media attention."

Back to the original plan I had with Red, only now she wasn't the reporter I was trying to scoop.

"To summarize, I have to be so awesome, so engaging, so magnificent that the world can't take their eyes off of me to address the potential existence of hybrids?"

"Just an ordinary day at the office," Miranda quipped.

"Well," I said, fingering the studs on my pants leg. "This outfit is sort of awesome."

"Yeah it is," Miranda hollered.

"And my speech will be close to magnificent."

"Yeah it will. And if you'd said yes to Adam you'd probably be wearing a ring which would make you engaged."

The word I was after was engaging, but whatever.

"Adam asked you to marry him?" Reynolds asked. It was the first time he'd spoken during the flight.

"Miranda," I hissed. "It wasn't a serious proposal," I assured Reynolds.

"I don't know about that," he disagreed. "Everything Adam does with you is serious."

"That's what I said," Miranda exclaimed in agreement.

Did Adam want to marry me? I didn't think he cared one way or the other. He just wanted a license for the honeymoon. I wanted a husband. Whoa. That was the first time I had admitted that. And this was the first time I truly wondered what Adam wanted from me other than the bedroom. Did Adam want a wife? He said that he loved me, but what did that mean to Adam? Had he ever told Lindsey that he loved her?

"What's with all the worry?" Miranda asked.

I smiled at her to cover my growing uncertainty. Discussing this right now or in front of Reynolds was not something I was going to do. "What's to worry about?" I joked. "I'm about to knock everyone's socks off."

Her return smile didn't conceal the disbelief she held for my response. But she understood me enough not to pursue it. I understood her enough to know this was just a postponement. Here's to uncomfortable awkward conversations yet to come.

CHAPTER 31

AN AIDE FROM GENERAL HURSER greeted us upon arrival and escorted us into the bowels of the Pentagon. I felt slightly guilty for not being able to appreciate the honor being bestowed on us. I mean, not everyone got to see the insides of the country's military guts. But the somersaults my own gut was doing precluded me from being duly impressed with where we were.

The aide dropped us off in what I guessed was some sort of green room and assured us that General Hurser would join us soon. Miranda and Reynolds headed straight for the assortment of food trays they'd prepared for us. With the speech beating a constant rhythm in my brain, I couldn't even think about food.

Turning my back to the buffet, I began to pace the room. At some point the reporters would decide they'd heard enough and start firing questions at me. With that in mind, we'd essentially summed everything up in three paragraphs. Surely, I'd make it that far before all hell broke loose.

"Have you eaten anything at all?" Miranda asked while standing in the middle of my pacing route.

Plucking a grape from her plate, I popped it in my mouth. After I'd swallowed, I said, "Yes."

"It is really going to look suspect if you pass out during the announcement," she said wryly.

"I'm not going to pass out." Taking a cheddar cheese cube, I nibbled on it, just to make her happy.

Rolling her eyes, she took her plate and herself to a chair across the room.

Swinging around when the door opened, I watched an unidentified man survey the room, and then step back to hold the door as the president walked in. President O'Conner ignored the others in the room and made a beeline for me.

"I do not like being blackmailed," he said angrily.

My natural instinct was to strike back at him, but I quickly thought better of it. He was, after all, the president and a hybrid of some kind. Not to mention, I had no idea what he was talking about.

"I'm sorry, Mr. President. I have no clue what you're talking about."

Narrowing his eyes at me, he said, "Why did you want the press conference here?"

"For safety's sake, of course," General Hurser answered as he entered.

"General Hurser," the president nodded.

"Greer's got this right," Hurser said seriously while reaching for the president's hand.

Greer could speak for herself.

"Mr. President, due to the delicate nature of the manufacture and the potential for theft and perversion of the nanobot technology, it is necessary to maintain the highest level of security with regard to every aspect of this program."

"And keeping this under the jurisdiction of the Organization had nothing to do with it?" he asked doubtfully.

"It is the property of the Organization," I snapped back, becoming truly angry for the first time. "As such, I'm going to ensure that it is handled in a manner that benefits the most people in the safest way possible."

"Good," he glared at me. "I would hate to think that you would do anything less."

Great. We were on the same page. So why was he so mad? "Oh, were you hoping to take sole credit for this?" I popped off. "Tuck it away in one of your bureaucratic holds? Like anyone would really believe that you actually developed this."

"You didn't create it either," he grated.

"Why don't we all just take a step back," General Hurser said soothingly. "No need to get so riled up. There's enough credit to go around." He reached and gently grasped the president's arm.

The president scowled at Hurser and shook his arm loose, but he did begin to rein in his anger.

Glancing in Reynolds' direction, I noted that he'd ditched his plate and moved closer to me. He was now standing within arm's reach, intently watching the exchange. Miranda, on the other hand, was avoiding everyone's eyes while she continued to munch away.

"Look, Mr. President," I sighed. "I'm not looking to hog credit. Truth be told, I don't even want to be here. You're the one who wanted me to do this. And now that I am, I'm just trying to make sure we don't screw it up. And as far as that goes, you might want to maintain a peripheral role until we know how this is going to play out."

The aide that had accompanied us earlier poked his head in the door. "Mr. President, General Hurser. We're ready."

"Thank you," the president nodded to the aide and waited for him to retreat before continuing. "Are you ready?"

"I believe so."

He extended his hand and held it there until I accepted it. "I'm not so much interested in credit as I am in getting this right. I do not want a repeat of the first disaster."

"Neither do I," I agreed.

He continued holding my hand as he studied me. What he was looking for, I didn't know.

"Don't let me down, Greer," he finally said. Then leaning closer, he whispered, "And don't worry about me. I'm not afraid of a little heat. Actually, I'm well equipped for it." He straightened and smiled at me, showcasing a mouth full of teeth. It gave me the willies.

As the president let go, leaving me to wonder what the heck that meant, General Hurser took his place. "I've studied your track record in some depth, Dr. Greer," the general said. "I can't say that I'm not worried about your mouth running away with you."

"Didn't we already cover this last night?" I sighed in aggravation.

"Yes, and as we discussed last night, it is imperative that you not go off script on this one." He regarded me severely, as if waiting for a response.

"What? Do you want a guarantee? I can't give you that. All I can tell you is that not going off script is the plan."

The general's face was grim as he executed a crisp about face and strode from the room.

I didn't know what he was so worried about. I didn't go off script that much. How could I when I made it up as I went along?

"Not a happy camper," Miranda commented after the general's departure.

"Generals like plans, certainties," Reynolds replied.

"Just to be sure," Miranda said, abandoning her plate and stepping in front of me. "There is only the one script, right?"

"There's always Plan B." Smiling, I patted my backpack.

Pulling her face to one side, she frowned at me. "You are aware that we are in the hub of the United States military."

"I remember. Five sides, bland color. Lots of people in uniform."

"They're waiting," the aide reminded us patiently.

Waggling my eyebrows at Miranda, I walked around her to follow the aide. Miranda and Reynolds' footsteps echoed behind me as they joined the progression. And what a progression it was. The somberness of the group felt like a funeral march.

"I thought we were announcing good news."

"Exactly," I nodded to Admiral Murdock.

"You're late," the president said, slowing to clasp Murdock's hand.

"I apologize, Mr. President. I was detained in the pursuit of your answer."

"And?"

Murdock glanced down either side of the hall before stepping closer to the president. "It seems likely."

"But not definite?" General Hurser asked.

"Not at this time," the admiral shook his head.

"What's all that about?" Miranda whispered to me.

"I don't know, but at least we don't look like a funeral march now." Not that I ever did. My nerves had faded and I was...happy, giddy almost. I was about to be on my turf, that being molecular genetics and the wonderful advancements it created. Game. On.

"You're smiling like you're drunk," Miranda said. "What would Olivia say?" Freezing at her own utterance, she shook herself and leaned into me. "On second thought, keep it up."

The aide leading the way opened a door and stood aside.

"Greer?" the president questioned.

"Good to go," I nodded.

"Don't be good. Be great," General Hurser growled and stepped through the door.

"I agree," the president said, motioning for us to follow Admiral Murdock.

Wow. Such confidence. It was inspiring. Inspiring me to tell them to kiss my rear end goodbye.

"I'm a little underwhelmed," Miranda complained as we filed into the Pentagon Briefing Room.

"Give me a moment, I'm considering quitting."

Miranda whipped her head to me. "Macy, you wouldn't."

"No," I hissed, garnering a look from the general. "I'm just getting tired of the condescending treatment. Why bother to pick me if you don't believe I can do it?"

"They believe in you. They're just scared. Red's here."

"Red," I confirmed. She was three rows back, further than I thought she'd be. She smiled tightly at me when she noticed me staring.

"She doesn't look happy."

"She always looks like that," I dismissed. I couldn't remember her ever giving me a genuine smile. "None of the others look very happy either." Just what I needed, a room full of grumpy reporters.

"Here we go," Miranda hummed softly as the president approached the podium.

The hush that descended over the reporters did nothing to conceal the hunger in their eyes. Here we go indeed. To the brave new world of medicine, where no one had ever attempted what we were about to. Visions of Star Trek danced through my mind as the president's voice faded. We truly were on the cusp of something fantastic. As long as it didn't implode.

No implosions, I said to myself. Stick to the script. This launch had to be flawless. And since I was in charge, it would be. I was going to be all over this...like white on rice...like red beans and rice...chips and dip...man I was hungry. Uugh, Greer. Focus. In charge. I was in charge. God help me, I would be Chargezilla!

The fire in my belly fizzled when my eyes landed on Red again, and she raised a single eyebrow in challenge. Crud. I was in so much trouble. God help us all.

ACKNOWLEDGMENTS

Special thanks to Lesley Baker whose effervescent personality breathed hope into the achingly long creative process, and whose time and talents were coopted for the sanity of the author.

Ashley Richardson Boone...ready to promote at a moment's notice, your eagerness—nay, demand to see this volume completed helped spur me to the finish. Thanks for everything you've done.

Thanks to everyone who previewed the manuscript, and every fan that waited, patiently or not, for the publication. I sincerely hope you enjoy it. (And tell your friends about it.)

AUTHOR BIO

C. E. Glines lives in southeast Texas with her husband, three sons and a dog named Scruffy. Besides the writing, her life is filled with chasing after her boys and one home improvement project after another. She loves to eat and hates to clean. She always enjoys good times with her friends and family and reading a good book, especially when the house is quiet enough to actually read it. She holds a degree in manufacturing engineering and was pursuing a degree in biology when she wrote a book, adding author to her resume. She won't force her opinion on you, but if you ask, be warned. She also longs for the day when she herself can become a hybrid and eat as much as she wants to and still look good.